Welcome Home

AN ANTHOLOGY ON LOVE AND ADOPTION

First Edition
First Printing, 2017

Book design by Jake Nordby
Cover font by Tup Wanders

Flux, an imprint of North Star Editions, Inc.

This is a work of fiction. Names, characters, places, and incidents are either the product of the author's imagination or are used fictitiously, and any resemblance to actual persons living or dead, business establishments, events, or locales is entirely coincidental. Cover models used for illustrative purposes only and may not endorse or represent the book's subject.

Library of Congress Cataloging-in-Publication Data (Pending)

978-1-63583-004-0

Flux
North Star Editions, Inc.
2297 Waters Drive
Mendota Heights, MN 55120
www.fluxnow.com

Printed in the United States of America

For those who've been found
And for those out alone,
For those still searching
And for those who've come home.

CONTENTS

Introduction

"Did you know Superman is adopted?"

Sometimes it's Superman. Other times, someone will bring up Batman or Spider-Man. Whether it's Aquaman, Gambit, or the Teenage Mutant Ninja Turtles, superheroes have given us a way to quickly give adopted kids and foster children a place to potentially see themselves in the world's pop culture.

But there's a problem with that.

Not every kid feels super all the time.

Superman can fly away from most of his problems. Batman? As the affluent Bruce Wayne, he has enough money to *make* them go away. And Spider-Man, even though things are certainly rough for him as a super-powered teenager, for the most part always has Aunt May and Uncle Ben to turn to during times of emotional turmoil.

Welcome Home was inspired after talking with many authors and realizing there was a lot of room for other kinds of adoption stories.

Stories of kids struggling to connect with their new families (Dave Connis's "A Kingdom Bright and Burning"), former families (Erica M. Chapman's "The Sign"), and the idea of even having one in the first place (Mindy McGinnis's "Census Man"). And what of teenagers who find themselves *as* the person giving someone away, or as the person being taken away, not as a baby, but as a young adult? What's it like to wrestle with those feelings?

Enclosed in this collection are stories not just about family, but of friendship and first love, of finding strength in both solidarity and togetherness. Stories that remind us that not all reunions are happy—some are sad, scary, and downright dangerous. Sometimes these stories are told in familiar places, with two people in a coffee shop (Randy Ribay's "The Snow-Covered Sidewalk"), and other times they take you across space (Matthew Quinn Martin's "Lullaby") and time (Sangu Mandanna's "Upon the Horizon's Verge"). Some read like fables (Adi Alsaid's "Carlos and the Fifteen-Year-Old Heart") and others like updates from a friend's blog (Tameka Mullins's "Empty Lens").

It's my hope that no matter where these stories take place or whom they are about, you'll be able to see yourself in them. To know that there are people like you who have felt the same way, who have laughed and cried, felt angry and hopeless.

We can't all feel like Superman.

But that doesn't mean we can't all fly.

Welcome Home

AN ANTHOLOGY ON LOVE AND ADOPTION

edited by
Eric Smith

Mendota Heights, Minnesota

Carlos and the Fifteen-Year-Old Heart

by Adi Alsaid

Carlos Herald was born to a couple of strangers in a hospital in Mexico City. Not long afterward—a feeding, a medical checkup, a nurse's hurried coffee break—he was put in the arms of Janice and Cody Herald, two longtime Iowa residents who'd relocated to the Mexican metropolis a few months earlier, and who, for unknown reasons, were stuck in the year 1985.

They hardly noticed anymore, except for the earthquake, and Carlos wouldn't either until the age of six. His first-grade classroom: colorful construction paper posters, an animal-alphabet decal on the wall, an inexperienced teacher standing in front of the whiteboard. Carlos loved her flower print dresses, the softness of her voice. But she liked to give lectures and, one day, unaware that the subject matter of genetics was far too ambitious for her audience, she let slip an innocent comment about Carlos's parents being unlike everyone else's.

Twenty-five sets of eyes looked in his direction, and six-year-old Carlos slouched in his seat. He didn't understand what Ms. Nancy had meant, but he did not like how it made him feel. Ms. Nancy went on, oblivious: Carlos was not inheriting certain things from his parents, unlike most people. Someone in the back snickered. Carlos slouched further, a terrible hollow in the pit of his stomach.

This incident led to confusion, curiosity, and the eventual question posed to his dad a few nights later during story time. Cody was leaning near the soft orange night-light, reading in his mellifluous voice when Carlos interrupted the Roald Dahl tale. "What makes our family different from everyone else?" he asked, the hurt still clinging to his voice.

His dad slipped a finger into the book and closed it gently, immediately understanding. He called Janice over, and when she entered the room he gave her a look. "Already?" she asked. He nodded, and she sighed, then came to sit at the foot of Carlos's bed. Carlos loved the weight of her on the mattress, loved how close they were to him, even if the quiet moment that followed was a little scary.

"Yes," Cody admitted finally, "we are different than others. Your mom's blue eyes have nothing to do with your brown eyes. My red hair has nothing to do with your brown hair. These colors will never mix, because they are part of different palettes." Cody brushed hair out of Carlos's eyes, and Janice laid her hand on his foot, which was poking out from beneath his Looney Tunes covers.

"And yes," Cody went on, "you live in a future world that we will probably never know or understand."

"But we love you," Janice cut in. "And our relationship is no different than anyone else's, no matter what decade we inhabit or whose genes you've inherited." Some of the words were hard to understand, but they sank in anyway, absorbed through his heart, not his head.

After that there were a couple of years more of confusion—not necessarily about his relationship with his parents, but from navigating the effects of a decade he'd never lived in. Then the hell of middle school, the awkwardness of well-meaning friends who didn't understand, the meanness of those who did not mean well though they thought they understood. Every year, the earthquake. It was always forgotten by his parents by the time January came around and 1985 reset, and Carlos did not know how to warn them.

Until Carlos turned fifteen, when the only thing that seemed to matter to him was a girl.

That Carlos loved a girl at fifteen would not have been of any interest to anyone. Everyone loves someone at fifteen, usually recklessly. Fifteen is more or less when love begins, whether you have loved your family for your entire life or whether you won't admit to loving anyone for another ten years.

The fifteen-year-old heart does two things well: it fears, and it loves.

Lianne Lucy moved to town the summer before sophomore year, arriving in a flurry of moving trucks and little, bespectacled siblings. From across the street, Carlos watched her carry in box after box overflowing with books, not trusting the movers to treat them with enough reverence. Carlos tried to resist falling inexplicably in love too quickly, because he never believed the love stories that unfolded in fast-forward. But his heart resisted the criticisms and gave itself up so quickly that he didn't even have time to eat breakfast before the organ forced him to cross the street and say hello.

His friends would later tell him that first encounters with love interests should always be electronic, and that he had made a mistake. Maybe Carlos's upbringing in a 1985 household disagreed, or maybe the attraction was too strong to adhere to current first-hello norms. When he walked onto her lawn, Lianne eyed him as if she knew his heart had thrown itself across the street and Carlos was just following behind. She put her hands in the pockets of her dress and waited for him to speak.

Carlos wasn't particularly talkative, nor particularly prepared, since he believed speaking before breakfast should always be avoided. The only thing that he could think to say was "hi." Lianne lobbed the word back at him like an expert conversationalist, which put Carlos right back in the position he was in at the start of this paragraph. It was hot outside, and he could feel his t-shirt clinging to his lower back, his least favorite feeling in the world.

"My parents are stuck in 1985," he said, not sure why.

Lianne did not seem impressed, but she didn't turn away. Her warm brown eyes blinked once, and then she smiled. "Cool. Tell me more."

He couldn't shut up the whole day, telling her every single thing about his parents that he knew. How they didn't have cell phones, and so they didn't constantly check in like some parents do. Unlike his friends, who always had to scroll through *Documentaries about Depressing Things* or *Old, Vaguely Misogynistic Romances,* Carlos's Netflix account remained solely his, the suggestions perfectly suited for his tastes.

He told Lianne about New Year's Eve, and how every year at the massive neighborhood party his aunt and uncle throw, Janice and Cody Herald arrive with party hats that wish everyone a happy 1985. He did not tell her about the earthquake. Lianne kept her hands in her dress pockets most of the time, and she laughed as if no one ever told her to be wary of boys who cross the street to say hi before they even have their breakfast.

When he got back home, he was so giddy that he did all his chores for the week in one frenzied hour before bed. His mom raised an eyebrow at his dad at the sparkling kitchen floors, the dusted blinds, the garbage out at the curb, and an empty bag tucked perfectly into the bin.

"Weird," Cody said, folding his newspaper, wondering if maybe this was some unique form of teenage rebellion. But Janice, who had been peeking through the blinds intermittently throughout the day, had a better guess.

"My baby's in love," she whispered.

With the free time their son had provided for them by

tidying up, Janice and Cody popped in a VHS of *The Karate Kid*. They held each other close, thinking not so much of Mr. Miyagi, but rather of Carlos and how fast he was growing up.

It was a logical expectation that Lianne would attend Carlos's school in the fall, but it was a convenient twist of fate that put her in three of his eight classes. And who knows what wonderful thing was to blame for the seating arrangement placing them side-by-side. At first, he could only smile at her, say hi, maybe bring up another strange eighties thing about his parents. But Carlos eventually got better at saying things that made sense and could lead to conversation, and by the second week of school, they became close friends.

He kept his love to himself, not yet sure what to do with it or if Lianne would welcome it. At home, his parents smirked whenever he mentioned her name, which he did many, many times. He never quite caught what they meant by these smirks. Instead, he'd take advantage of the fact that his parents seemed to be okay with him talking about Lianne. Talking about Lianne was one of his favorite things now.

Some of his friends liked to mess with his parents whenever they came over. They'd do this by bringing up current events and modern technology, amused by the way the Heralds' eyes would glaze over at the mention of Wi-Fi, delighted by how the Heralds would laugh hysterically whenever someone mentioned that Michael Jackson was white and dead.

Lianne, though, was fascinated by them, fascinated by 1985 and how it felt to still be there. The first time she came over to do homework with Carlos, she was polite and nonchalant about their eightiesness.

Cody and Janice were nervous that day, probably more so than Carlos and Lianne. They paced in the living room, unable to sit still on their chintz couch, worried that Lianne would flee at the ugly pastel carpet that constantly needed cleaning, the neon wallpaper, the ubiquitous rubber-necked lamps. They were worried that Lianne might not understand, and that Carlos would blame them for it.

They heard the jingle of keys in the front door, and both of them leaped into positions of imagined casualness. When Carlos pushed open the door and saw them standing the way they were, he hesitated for a terrible second in which it seemed as if he might be regretting everything. Then he stepped inside, casting a smile backward at Lianne, who waltzed in confidently behind him. She looked straight at Cody and Janice, eyes warm with kindness. She ignored Cody's perm and Janice's shoulder pads. She said nothing of the furniture. Instead she waved and smiled, then cleaned her smudged glasses with the hem of her skirt as Carlos introduced everyone.

"We've heard so much about you," Janice said. "You're just as lovely as . . ."

"Mom!" Carlos interrupted.

Janice blushed, and Cody put a comforting hand on his wife's back. The room tensed for just a second, fears approaching reality. Then Lianne slipped her glasses back on and said, "It's really nice to meet you guys."

That night, textbooks splayed on Carlos's bed between them, Lianne surprised herself by cutting the distance between them in one literal fell swoop and kissing Carlos for the first time. He felt as if he was traveling through dimensions, even though every ounce of his being remained exactly where it was. More than that, his entire consciousness became focused on the spot where their lips met, not forgetting himself, but exactly the opposite, realizing where he was entirely. The kiss was imperfect (he kept his mouth open when Lianne kept hers closed), sloppy (a streak of saliva on Carlos's chin), yet transporting all the same.

They kissed again, a little better this time: less slobbery, fewer teeth. Then they turned their attention back to their homework for a second, although any attempt to focus led them right back toward each other. Downstairs, Janice and Cody cleaned the dishes that had piled up during dinner, listening to Prince on the radio. Cody would swear several 1985s later that the glass he broke that night was the result of a surge of joy that shot down his spine the very moment Carlos was kissing Lianne. Janice, a committed eye-roller of all things New Age, would never admit that she felt the same surge of joy.

Four weeks later, Carlos and Lianne got to spend a full night together for the first time when his parents celebrated their anniversary at a nearby bed-and-breakfast. They weren't quite sure which anniversary it was, because their condition made math tricky, but they felt as if they were about due for an important one.

Carlos and Lianne used the occasion to feel a little more grown-up. They ordered pizza and watched movies in bed, less clothed than they normally would be if his parents were still around. They tried to be simultaneously cool and appreciative about this, which resulted in a fair amount of giggling, touching, blushing, and one pizza slice dropped face down on the carpet when Lianne could no longer hold onto it through her laughter. Mostly chaste, they fell asleep in each other's arms (and legs, and more).

At 7:19 a.m. Carlos woke up in a panic, suddenly recalling the date.

On September 19, 1985, at 7:19 a.m. Mexico City was struck by an 8.0-magnitude earthquake that completely crumbled more than four hundred buildings. And every September, Carlos's adoptive parents from Iowa relived it, gripped in the terror of shaking, especially when you've never known shaking quite like this before.

Carlos tried to remember to mark it down each year, so that his parents wouldn't be taken by surprise, the fear and destruction of it all. But somehow he always managed to forget. By the time January hit and 1985 reset, it felt as if his family did, too.

Carlos grabbed his phone and looked up the bed-and-breakfast his parents were staying in, then dialed the listed number. He asked the tired-sounding receptionist to connect him to the Heralds' room.

He hoped he wasn't late. The phone connected to his parents' room and rang. He hoped the building had withstood 1985. The phone rang. Carlos looked at Lianne lying on her stomach, unperturbed, bathed in the soft gray morning light and the blue glow of the television they'd left on. The phone rang. Carlos hung up and stared at his cell screen as if it was to blame for everything.

Carlos climbed out of bed and quickly dressed, then leaned over his bed and kissed Lianne's cheek, placing a hand on her back to gently wake her. When she opened her eyes, he told her he had to go. Worry immediately filled her eyes, so he kissed her again and told her it was okay, that she could stay, sleep in, snoop around, run around naked, order more pizza, do their homework, never leave, whatever.

He had barely taken a driving lesson before, but he grabbed the keys hanging near the front door, got in his mom's maroon Oldsmobile Ciera, and turned the ignition as if he'd done it hundreds of times before.

Sunday morning, and the city was calm. The usually hellish traffic gave way to empty roads, the few cars around driving at a glacial pace, as if the drivers had never meant to get behind the wheel. Most people on the road respected red lights for only a second, then rolled through, even though, unlike Carlos, they were clearly in no hurry, had no pressing need to move on. Carlos kept his eye on the dashboard clock, thinking the shaking had been over for three minutes now. Five. Ten. He sped past cop cars with their lights on for no reason. Nervously slapping at the steering wheel, Carlos cursed the existence of distance, distance that had to be traversed. There was an unavoidable bond pulling him to his parents, a magnetic yank that felt more immediate the closer he got to them. It was not exactly magnetism, unless magnetism is the reason why people need each other (Who really knows how these things work?), in which case that's exactly what it was.

He pulled up in front of the bed-and-breakfast, turning on his hazard lights, the Mexican symbol for doing whatever you want with your car. Running right past the still-tired receptionist, Carlos made his way to their room and knocked, only then hearing the whimpering from inside. His parents could be stuck beneath rubble. The building could have collapsed in 1985; it could have burned. He did not understand enough about his parents' world to know if they were safe, and so he pounded on the door. What could have been a cry or could have been nothing escaped from the room. He called out for them, panic creeping into his voice.

That he could have a night with Lianne like the one he'd just had followed by this awful morning made absolutely no sense to him, even if he understood more than most that nonsense very much fit into this world.

Carlos sprinted back downstairs. He thought of Lianne, and if she'd be safe if an earthquake struck right now. Would she sleep through it, mouth slightly open, hair streaked across her face? Would she stir, look around, think it all a dream? Would she calmly take cover and simply wait for it to pass?

He wondered if this was what parenthood was like, never knowing if the people you cared about most were safe. The receptionist was flipping through a magazine, and calmly set it down when Carlos begged him to come upstairs with his master keys.

Three minutes later, the shaking had been over for nearly thirty minutes, or thirty years, depending on your point of view. The receptionist jingled the set of keys as if he was auditioning for a role in a horror movie. Carlos had to keep himself from snatching them away and pushing the door open himself.

When they entered the room, Carlos saw that his parents were huddled beneath a desk, the room perfectly intact except for the unmade bed. They saw Carlos and their tears changed from fearful to joyous. Carlos sprinted to his parents, not sure why he was crying. It was his fifteen-year-old heart that was to blame, loving and fearing all at once. The receptionist raised his eyebrows and walked away, a little jealous about the exchanged tears.

They embraced, arms and legs and more. They wiped at their tears. Carlos assured them he was okay, and they were okay. He didn't tell them they'd survived before and would survive again, didn't tell them the city had built itself back up long ago. They told him they'd tried to call but the landlines had been down. They didn't tell him they had a strange sense of déjà vu throughout the shaking, didn't tell him that the room they were in was still a heap of rubble and broken things.

They got up and brushed themselves off. Carlos had not had breakfast yet, and so all he could think to say was "hi." The three of them just kind of smiled awkwardly and cried at each other for a few moments. In addition to inhabiting different years, they were also different ages, and sometimes the gap between ages is even greater than the gap between years. Carlos was fifteen, his parents were both forty-seven, and that three-decade span hung around them like an elephant in the room that also had not had its breakfast.

"Is everyone okay?" they asked each other. Yes. "Have a good time before the earthquake?" Absolutely. "How is Lianne?" Carlos blushed and looked away.

Downstairs, the receptionist sent an email to his parents for the first time in months. Below the crust of the earth, the tectonic plates were done shifting around, having comfortably settled into themselves almost an hour ago.

Then Carlos decided he should go, since everyone was safe

and he was kind of interrupting their anniversary weekend. He was also interrupting his own planned cuddle session with Lianne. The receptionist felt all these plans in the air and sighed, wishing for more. More breakfasts, more cuddles, more anything.

Janice and Cody Herald stood at the doorway, watching their son move down the hall. They were still shaken, no pun intended. More than anything they marveled at the person Carlos had become. They felt that they were good parents, but his marvelousness was not something they could take credit for. Somehow, in fifteen short 1985s, this kid they had raised revealed himself to be an astounding person, kind and caring, brave, fearless, and taller than they'd expected.

Carlos returned to the car still parked in the middle of the street, unperturbed. He found a station that played eighties music and headed back home, hoping Lianne had fallen back asleep, just for the pleasure of slipping back into bed with her. Cars still drove at their Sunday speed, rushing through red lights and then slowing until they reached the next one. Sunlight streamed into the car, causing Carlos to marvel at the strangeness of the world, how fear could give way to calm, and vice versa.

He wanted to make a note in his phone for next year, to suggest his parents leave the city during the earthquake. But then "Video Killed the Radio Star" started playing, which was his favorite song (though he'd never admit that to his parents), causing the thought to flitter away, swept out by the wind coming in through the open window.

Back in the bed-and-breakfast, his parents felt their son's thoughts shift from them to Lianne, with equal parts sadness and joy. Then they went downstairs to find a restaurant that was still intact, and ordered themselves some breakfast.

Carlos failed to spot the significance of the relieved yet eager drive back home, his parents in the rearview mirror, Lianne waiting for him in bed. It would have been perfect for him to turn on his hazard lights and stop the car exactly halfway between them and her, and consider the shift about to take place. Except Carlos was too wrapped up in thoughts of Lianne to recognize what was happening. The spot on the back of her neck that, when kissed, would instantly send goose bumps down her arms. The faces she made when bored in class, trying to make him laugh. The graze of her fingers on his, the way it felt to have love in his life. He sped right past the midpoint, the way most of us would.

Adi Alsaid was born and raised in Mexico City, where he now lives, writes, coaches basketball, and drowns food in hot sauce. He's the author of the YA novels *Let's Get Lost, Never Always Sometimes,* and *North of Happy.*

"Sometimes, the obvious divide in a relationship ends up being not much of a divide at all. That's what I was going for in this story. I wanted the matter of adoption, the apparent chasm between parents and child, to be second or third fiddle. To age, earthquakes, but mostly to love."

Strong Enough

by Karen Akins

The light over the kitchen table turns green. It blinks on and off like a dying lightning bug. Everyone stops eating and stares at me.

This is it.

I gulp down a last bite of cinnamon oatmeal.

I've always wondered why the emergency-signal designers went with green and not red. I mean, red would make more sense. Red means *stop*. Stop crime. Stop the bad guys. Stop the runaway train. But then Dad pointed out one time that green means *go*. Go fight it.

I tap the end of my spoon against my chin, and it accidentally bends in half. But I straighten it out before Mom has the chance to cluck about it. All the times I've pictured this moment, I've jumped up, run out the door in a rush. But right now, all I can think is *stall*.

"Is it bad?" I ask.

Mom leans over to read the info screen, squinting. "Define bad."

"Bad. Like, a crashing school bus full of children bad. Off a bridge. Into a whirlpool of piranhas."

"That's *exactly* what it is, Gracie."

"Really?" I sit up straight and drop my spoon entirely.

"No." She tosses me a towel to clean up the oatmeal that spilled. "It's a car broken down on Sycamore and Third. You've got this."

"But it's blocking a lane of traffic," I say, swinging the screen around to face me. "And people are using the turning lane to get around it. That's dangerous. Kind of."

I pick up my spoon and shovel in a few more bites of oatmeal. "Maybe they should send someone else."

"You've already declined two test missions. And you're the closest super." Mom gives me a pointed look. The *with-great-power-comes-great-blah-blah-blah* look.

"Super in *training*," I say.

"Super." She kisses me on top of the head. "I'm not sure why you're so nervous. You could lift a passenger vehicle in your sleep. In fact, I think you might have done that once. When you were seven and going through a sleepwalking phase. Oh, man—and I thought the newborn phase was hard . . ." Mom might be sitting across from me at the kitchen table, but I can tell from her vacant expression that she's far away in Memoryland. "Do you want a ride?"

"Nah, I'll take my bike." It would give me a little more avoidance time. Plus, it's only a few blocks, right on the way to school, and a warm day for April. I try to switch my demeanor to calm, cool, collected—hoping my innards will follow, but they stay a twisting mass of nerves. My most recent simulations didn't go great. Okay, they went awful. The last one, I forgot to move the bystanders back and knocked down a tree by accident. I have only my Test Mission left before I move on to an apprenticeship. But if I flub it, they'll make me start over in the basics seminar.

Needs to harness her strength. That's what the eval had said.

"Wear a sweater," says Mom.

"Yes, smother."

"A smother with a daughter who's warm enough!" she calls over her shoulder.

We lock eyes in a stubborn-off, but a laugh quivers at the edge of her mouth. I win.

I still grab a hoodie.

She can't make me wear spandex, though.

As soon as my parents realized they had adopted a super (even they had to admit my tendency to heft my crib above my head was a bit . . . much), they read books and went to workshops—anything and everything they could get their hands on—to help them figure out the whole trans-powered family thing. Which, it turns out, is about as easy and as difficult as figuring out the whole any-powered family thing. But they did appreciate the tips on handling tantrums when your toddler can punch a hole through a wall. A brick wall.

Our garage is a shrine to my destructive wake. Broken toys, broken furniture, a whole pile of broken doorknobs, broken appliances. But Dad can't blame last year's grill disaster on me. I pull my hoodie on tighter and shiver against the morning chill that hasn't lifted as I open the garage door. Oh, to have fireball breath like my friend Emma.

Traffic has backed up to the next intersection, blocking the flow on two side streets. *Crap*. I pedal faster.

The super assigned to oversee the test hasn't arrived yet. A guy in a Volvo waves happily to me. I wave back, hoping for a few "friendliness" bonus points. Yeah, you smile, Mr. Broken Volvo, even though we both know the only reason you're so happy is that a trainee superhero is a heck of a lot cheaper than a real one. Or even a tow truck.

But then he points toward another vehicle, about five yards ahead. The Volvo isn't the vehicle that's stuck. The thirty-ton concrete mixer truck is.

"*Craaaaaap*," I whisper.

"Finally!" The driver of the truck sticks her head out the window. "I've been waiting almost half an hour."

"Sorry," I say. "I'm, umm, still in training."

"What? You're not even a real one? Great." She says the last word just loud enough that I know she meant me to hear it.

"We can start as soon as my supervisor shows up."

"Like *that* one?" The lady points toward the sky.

Sure enough, a rep from the Enhanced Abilities Council hovers above a maple tree, its fuchsia buds on the verge of unfurling. I can't remember what work name he goes by. Blaze, maybe? It's something fast like that.

His lips purse together in a taut line. He gives a little wave with his tablet. I'm not sure if it means "Hello" or "Proceed" or "This is too early in the morning to oversee a teenager tackling a traffic jam."

Blast. I snap my fingers. His name is Blast.

I rest my hands on top of the Volvo's roof and take a long, steadying breath like they teach us in training.

Creak . . . groan . . . creeeak.

"Umm, Miss?" says Mr. Volvo.

"Hmm?"

"I think you're hurting my shocks." Mr. Volvo taps my elbow. Sure enough, I'm pressing his car nearly to the ground. I let go so fast it bounces a good foot off the pavement.

"Sorry." I hear the *tap-tap-tap* of Blast's tablet above me. Points being docked before I've even started.

Okay. Back to the calming breath.

Honnnnnnnk. The concrete truck lady leans on her horn. "Come on!"

I look up. Blast makes a move-it-along motion.

Creeeeeeak.

I'm pressing down on the car again.

"Sorry." I let up easy this time, barely a jostle, and take two steps back.

I'm too strong. The thought bubbles up unbidden, and the images of all the broken things in our garage follow closely behind. But then I look over at the concrete truck. I've never lifted anything that heavy. Ever. I'm not strong enough.

"Take your time," says Blast, but I'm sure to him everyone is a snail. The truck lady huffs and throws her hands up in the air, and even Mr. Volvo lets out an impatient sigh.

I suck in another breath. Okay. I can do this.

I walk up to the truck and find a good, solid grip point on the frame. I begin to lift.

Tap-tap-tap.

Toot.

"Could you step out of your cab, please?" I ask the truck lady. She heads over to join the group of bystanders.

I start to lift the vehicle again. *Tap-tap-tap.* Double toot.

Check that the ignition is off, brakes are on. I look up to get the go-ahead from Blast. He gives me a bored thumbs-up.

I recenter myself. Begin to lift. My arms strain. It's an odd sensation for me, to feel resistance, a challenge for my muscles.

Nothing.

I step back and stare at the truck. Thirty tons of impossible.

I bite my lip. Maybe I could scoot the truck out of the way. I'll still have to figure out a way to lift it over the median into the parking lot.

Tap-tap-tap.

I look up at Blast. I can't tell if he's grading me at this point or checking his email.

While I stand there debating, the driver whips out her phone.

"I'm calling a tow," she announces, and the crowd bursts into a cheer.

My whole body droops. I look over at the parking lot. It's twenty feet, but it might as well be twenty miles. But then I see a familiar minivan, with its dented hood where I leaned too hard and an "I <3 My Super" bumper sticker.

Mom.

She must have driven the long route here to get around the traffic.

The tow truck rounds the corner, lights flashing. If he gets involved, I can smooch this test goodbye. Mom opens her car door, probably to tell me to hop in, to let the professionals take over. But she walks ten steps forward and points at an empty spot.

"It will fit here, I think," she says. "What do you think, Gracie?"

We lock eyes in a stubborn-off. My lip curls up. She won.

I've got this.

I take a final deep breath. The oxygen rushes through my veins and fuels every cell, down to my toes and deep into my core.

I don't hesitate. I grab the undercarriage of the truck and hoist it up, not pausing until it's over my head. I grit my teeth in concentration. Every step is a strain. I totter at the curb. The crowd gasps, but I regain my footing and place the vehicle down as gently as an egg crate.

The crowd claps, then dies down and moves on. Truck lady doesn't bother to thank me. Blast enters a final *tap-tap-tap* and flies away.

But I did it.

A chunk of the curb is smashed to dust. The sod in the median looks as if a pair of moles did the cha-cha underneath. I won't find out for a week if I passed.

But I did it.

Mom walks over and hands me a hot cocoa. We lean against the front bumper of the car. I'm careful to avoid caving it in.

"I almost wasn't strong enough," I say. Not for this situation. Probably not for a lot of situations. I trace my finger along the dent that reminds me that next time, the opposite might be the problem. "Sometimes, I worry that—"

"Gracie," Mom says, following her finger behind mine and taking my hand, "you're the perfect amount of strong."

Karen Akins writes humorous, light sci-fi for young adults and the young in spirit. When not writing or reading, she loves lightsaber dueling with her two sons and forcing her husband to watch BBC shows with her. Her YA time travel novels *Loop* and *Twist* are available now from St. Martin's Press.

"When I finished my graduate degree in counseling, I had no idea what I wanted to do with it. But I did know that I had a heart to bring hope and encouragement to hurting people. I ended up in a position as a regional director of a nonprofit adoption agency.

Over the next few years, I had the privilege of counseling birth parents who faced some of the most difficult decisions they'd ever make, of preparing and educating adoptive parents, and welcoming children to their forever families. I never could have predicted the beautiful and bittersweet journey it would be.

And on a completely selfish level, I also never could have predicted the joy and completeness that my precious nephew brought to my life when he joined our family through adoption. I love you, Noah!"

The Sign

by Erica M. Chapman

On my way to school I pass a sign that's in front of nothing. The painted letters have faded away, and all that remains are an A and an F. The withered wood has even warped toward the vacant emptiness behind it as if it's trying to run away from reality. Like we all are in some way. I've always wondered what used to be in that spot behind the nameless sign. Was it a restaurant or a school? What happened to the building? Did it close down? Did it burn?

Does anyone else care that it's gone?

My mom would. She cares about everything. She even names inanimate objects and talks to them as if they have hearts and cells. One time she hit a baby bunny with her car, and I swear she didn't stop crying for two days.

She doesn't know I'm here standing in front of my past that's dressed up in a white house with blue shutters and a welcome mat that says "Hi, I'm Mat."

My birth father is on the other side of that ugly blue door, and I have no idea what that means to me. If I'm going to fill that space behind my own abandoned sign or if he's going to take one look at me and decide to build somewhere else.

I reach in my jacket pocket for the letter he sent. The corners are bent, and I'm not sure if it's from me reading it so many times or maybe because he crunched it in his hand after he wrote it, contemplating whether or not to send it. I glance down at his handwriting. It's loopy but firm. Is he going to be the same way? The letter's short, only a few sentences about how he wants to meet me, and how he had no idea his daughter lived so close.

I wonder if we look alike. I have dimples in my chin and my cheeks—could that be from him? Does he have dark hair like mine that's always half-curly and half-straight when I do nothing to it? Does he have blue eyes that have flecks of brown like mine?

My breath sounds like a windstorm, and my palms are clammier than when I had a fever last month. Maybe I'm getting sick? No, that's not it.

I can do this. I can do this. I can do this.

I knock on the door, once, twice.

It flies open like he was waiting for me. Instead of my birth father, though, I'm greeted by two men. One has longish black locks, and the other is shorter, with pale, almost-yellow skin and hair to match. They are the perfect contrast to each other. My . . . dads?

"Is that her?" the long-haired guy asks the other.

The blond looks at him as if he's nuts, and then turns back to me. "Caden?"

I nod and lick my lips a few times because I can tell they're getting chapped. Confusion sweeps through my brain. Too much is happening at once. I don't know where to focus my eyes—if I should be glancing at the blond guy or the long-haired one. Will one of them be hurt if I don't look at him? Maybe they're nervous, too.

The long-haired guy leans over and lifts me up in a huge hug. I let out an audible "oof," as he says, "We're so glad you're here."

Partner, definitely his partner.

I pat him on the back a few times to see if he will release me. No such luck. A hundred minutes later he finally sets me down. I take a deep breath in.

The blond takes a similar breath in, too. Yoga breath, I recognize, in the nose and out the nose. I've been doing the same thing since he opened the door, trying not to pass out.

"I'm Sam," the blond says, "your . . . uh . . ." He pauses to look at his partner for help, maybe?

"Your father," his partner finishes for him, with a friendly nudge in the side.

Sam gives me a nervous smile. "Yeah, dad . . . or, yeah." He takes another yoga breath. "This is Mason, my husband."

"It's nice to meet you," I say, a little breathless, my voice sounding like I have rocks tumbling in my vocal chords. I clear my throat.

Mason opens the door wider and grabs my arm gently. "Come in, come in. We made lasagna, but it's not just regular lasagna; it's made with gluten-free noodles and eggplant and chocolate sauce," he says in an excited tone.

Did I hear him right? "I'm sorry, chocolate sauce?"

Sam starts laughing. "He's kidding."

"No, I'm not. It's a mole sauce," he says seriously, like *how dare we doubt him!*

Sam's smile disappears, and he and I shoot confused glances at each other. We both turn away quickly as if looking at each other breaks some sort of first-meeting law. I have no idea how to act around him. Should I have hugged him too? Should I call him Dad instead of Sam? Should I leave and never look back?

"Is Julie coming?" I ask, passing the stainless-steel-everything kitchen. The room smells like garlic and pasta and all the best restaurants.

"She's at a friend's. I thought we should . . . um, eat alone tonight, anyway." I try to conceal the sigh of relief, but Sam must notice because he gives me his first sincere smile. "Are you as nervous as I am?" he whispers so Mason can't hear him.

The posture I'd been holding up finally collapses, and I breathe a real breath for the first time since entering the house. "Oh, thank god it's not just me," I say as I sit at the table.

His posture quickly follows mine. "This is kind of awkward, and I'm the adult, so I'm supposed to be making this all work, right?"

I laugh. "I don't think there's a handbook."

He laughs, too, and I realize we have a similar chuckle, kind of scratchy. Instantly I want to run out of that room and go home. I don't belong here with him and our shared laugh. I have parents. Parents who love me and a brother who is mostly annoying but who I think in his own special way loves me too. I shift in my seat.

Before I have a chance to bolt out of there, Mason serves the lasagna. It smells amazing, but the idea of chocolate and lasagna together is like mixing pickles and peanut butter to me. "You're going to love this. It's my mom's recipe. I'm usually a horrible cook—just ask Sam." Sam nods vigorously in agreement, and Mason smacks his head without looking. "I know you're agreeing. I don't have to see you to know that."

I smile again without meaning to. Am I smiling too much? Should I be smiling? This is a man who gave me up. Shouldn't I be mad instead?

We eat dinner and it's actually pretty good. Not my favorite, but not bad. I could barely eat anyway. I mostly munched on bread like a bird picking at a worm.

After dinner, Mason directs us to the living room. It's white with blue accents, and photos of them and Julie are all over. It's obvious they've built a good home.

"I know you're probably wondering why I contacted you after all these years," Sam says.

I nod, my chest tightening with every second that ticks by on the ancient-looking clock that they probably got from IKEA instead of an antique shop.

Mason looks at the floor and starts fidgeting. Before Sam can say anything else, Mason pops off the couch and runs out of the room.

I'm so shocked I just sit there and look around like I'm being filmed for a reality show.

Sam closes his eyes briefly, his expression tired, concerned, annoyed. Like he's had to deal with Mason's outbursts before. "I'll be right back," he says, getting up slowly. He doesn't move very fast, as if he has arthritis or something.

A few minutes later, Sam returns but Mason doesn't. I don't hide my worry. "What's wrong with him? Is he okay?" Sam slowly sits back down on the couch. I didn't notice how he sat down at dinner. I must have been paying attention to something else. The room starts to shrink and the family photos start to creep in toward me. Something's wrong with him. Why am I here?

"He's worried about me. About you. He's a worrier."

"Why is he worried about you?" I manage to squeak out. My eyesight blurs, and all I want to do is run away, far away from everyone and everything.

"I'm sick, Caden. I've tried dialysis, medication . . . even a new kidney, but I'm not sure it's working like it should, so I'm . . ." He runs a hand through his hair and glances at the photo on the white wall. They're all in matching coral shirts, and the smiles couldn't be bigger. Disney's castle looms high in the background.

"I . . ." I expect sadness to be my first emotion. Where is the sadness? The fear of losing him? But that's not what's here. It's red and burning and regret, and I'm pissed off. "How could you do this to me?" I whisper, trying to find my voice. A rage I've rarely experienced starts in my toes and travels up to my mouth, and my voice comes back. "You find me just to tell me you're dying? Tell me, 'hey, here I am,'" I yell with my arms wide. "'Sorry I'm late, but I'd like to get to know you for the five minutes I have left!'" I stand up from the chair and realize tears are coming out of my eyes. No. He doesn't get my tears, dammit. "You don't get to know me." I know I'm irrational. I can see his face and how sorry he really is and how there's so much more he wants to say, but I can't. I can't do it. "I'm sorry. I have to go."

"Caden, wait," he says, and I know he tries to get up to chase me and I know he's slower because he's sick and I'm an awful person.

I run until I can't feel my legs, until the sun bleeds into the horizon. I lean over to breathe into my knees. Huffing and heaving and no matter how far I run I can't get rid of this insane combination of feelings that I've never had at once. Fear and anger and regret and sadness and pain and so many nameless other emotions. This is so unfair. All of it. Sam dying. Having to find out this way. Finding out at all, really. I could have just lived my good life with my parents and my brother and never known and then I would be blissfully unaware that my father isn't going to be here long enough for me to get everything I should from him. For me to show him everything I have and want and dream of. I never even let him explain why he and my birth mom gave me up. She's dead, so she can't, but he can. He can answer all my questions, but at this price it's not worth it. I can't say goodbye to someone I don't even know.

◇◇◇◇

When I wake up the next morning, I tell myself what happened yesterday was a horrible nightmare. But it wasn't. My sign has crumbled into a million pieces and its only use is kindling. Sam is dying, and I yelled at him. How long has he been sick? Is that why Mason ran out of the living room? How much time is left?

He could be dead now for all I know.

I get ready in zombie mode and head to school, passing that damn sign, wishing that someone would just build something behind it already so I can stop wondering why. I arrive at school early because I didn't look at the clock when I got ready and I got up an hour before I normally do. When I get to my locker, Julie is buzzing around it like a helicopter looking for a criminal. Her gaze meets mine. She knows. She knows everything.

My sister.

"Caden," she says with a sorrowful look on her face. It seems a little fake, but I'm not trusting anything anymore. Emotions are shifty little buggers.

"Julie." She purses her lips and I don't know how to react to her, how I'm supposed to treat her knowing that she's my sister, that the damaged blood flowing through our father's veins is the same. He's dying. She's known him this whole time, her whole life. "I'm sorry," I say without knowing if I really am, then want to take it back instantly.

Why am I apologizing?

I shouldn't be the one who apologizes here. My whole life changed in one night and here I am saying sorry to the girl who got to live *my* life. The girl who called me a toad in third grade because a frog jumped on my lap at recess, the girl who stole Jacob Taylor from me in seventh grade and kissed him in front of everyone. What if all that was supposed to be mine? What if it was supposed to be me kissing Jacob Taylor?

Wait. This is ridiculous.

No, I liked my life. I like it now. If I let them in, would my mom be mad at me? Would our relationship change? I would have another dad—a Sam. My dad's not perfect. He plays video games all the time and yells at the TV, and he always looks bored when I'm talking about Snapchat or what book I've read, but he's been there. He's here now. And Sam wasn't.

I'm sorry. I'm sorry. I'm sorry.

I'm not sure who I'm apologizing to, but it feels wrong. It feels like a kind of betrayal.

She relaxes her lips and posture, and sadness starts to creep onto her face. That face that I've seen for three years, and I haven't noticed that maybe there are similarities to mine. That the dimple in her cheek is the same, that her blue eyes have flecks of brown in them. It's not fair that she got our dad and I didn't. He looked in those eyes and saw the flecks. Did he see them in mine? Did I even give him the chance? "I heard you stopped by."

I don't say anything back. Not sure what she knows and doesn't, and frankly I want to hibernate in a hole and come out in the spring.

She shifts the books curled in her arm to the other, then back to the original arm. "I think you should talk to him. I know . . ." She pauses, and her eyebrows crease like she's thinking. "You have every right to be mad, but he didn't know about you until recently. I promise. He's the type of dad who would have found you if he could." Her gaze is pleading, and I want so badly to believe her. "He's on meds for the new kidney, but we don't know if they're working or if they will. It was by chance he found you. He's been in a frenzy lately to discover his past and . . . well anyway, he found out about you through your grandma? I guess. He never liked her but he wanted some closure, to tell her sorry or something, and that's when she told him about you. Your mom kept it from him for some reason."

Why didn't he tell me that? *You never gave him a chance.*

"Why?" is the only question I can think of. Why would my mom do that? Was she too young? Did Sam do something to make her angry? Did her parents disapprove of him? What?

"I don't know."

So my mom never told him. I'd found out she was dead last year when I went searching for her, but there was never a dad listed. He was like a ghost. So when I got the letter from him last week, I didn't think it was real.

She smiles, and it's so similar to his it's creepy. Jealousy burns in my veins at that. She can't get his smile, too. Does she have his laugh? Is that something I have to share with her, too?

"Look, I know you're trying and I appreciate it. But I yelled at him. He's not going to want to see me."

She gives me a thoughtful expression, and I have to glance behind me to see if she's actually giving it to me or if someone she *really* likes is standing behind me. She shakes her head and places her hand on my arm gently, soothing. "Come by tonight. Mason's not cooking. It's pizza night." She smiles.

"Okay," I say without thinking again. It's as if my brain wants something my heart doesn't.

I have no idea what I'm doing, if I'm about to make a huge mistake by letting Sam into my life, but I'm willing to take the chance just to see what we can build together.

I don't have to knock this time when I show up. Sam is the one that answers and he's alone. His yellowish skin makes sense now, his slow movement, his awkwardness. My instinct is to help him. To make sure he's not in any pain. I ignored that the last time I was here.

"I'm so glad you decided to come back," he says with Julie's smile.

"I thought I'd give you another chance. That, and I wanted to try some more of Mason's cooking, but I heard it was pizza night. Darn," I say sarcastically.

My laugh pours out of his mouth and I can't help but join him. His posture relaxes and he envelops me in a hug that rivals Mason's. "Thank you," he whispers.

That night on the way home from the Parkers', I pass the sign in front of nothing and for the first time I don't wonder why it's there.

Erica M. Chapman writes dark, emotional YA novels with bursts of humor and lighter contemporaries with smart-ass protagonists. Her first novel, *Teach Me to Forget,* was published by Merit Press in December 2016. She's a member of SCBWI & Sweet16s and a lifetime Lions and Michigan football fan who loves alternative music. She loves to tweet and watch various CW & Freeform shows while typing her next story on a MacBook in a Detroit Lions Snuggie.

"Being a part of a family isn't about blood, it's about love. Love isn't created with genetics—it's made with time spent together, small moments you will always remember, hard times that make you stronger, and so much joy you can hardly believe it's real. I've been so blessed to have my beautiful goddaughter in my life, and I shudder to think what life would be like without her. She is spunky, smart, and empathetic. She brightens the world around her, and I truly believe she is where she's meant to be."

Up by a Million

by Caela Carter

When I sit across this table from my mother, we're transported. She isn't really her. And I'm not really me, either. We're in a different, pretend version of our lives. A version in which we get to live the end of my childhood the way we did the beginning: together.

Prison has become my happy place.

I feel so far away from my other life, my other mom, that I almost stop worrying about what I have to tell this mom today.

Almost.

"You look so beautiful, baby," Mom says, collecting two cards from the pile between us. We're playing our endless game of War. "Who's doing your hair these days?"

"Coach K took me to a new salon last week." The words "Coach K" feel clumsy in my mouth. I haven't called her that since I was here last Sunday. I've been calling Coach K "my mom" on the outside for a long time now. Months. Maybe a year.

But in front of my real mom, she's back to being "Coach K."

"Yeah?" my mom says. "How did you get her to do that?"

"I asked her," I say.

I don't tell this mom how scared I was to talk to Coach K about my hair when I first started living with her. How embarrassed I was to be fourteen with no clue how to take care of my own hair. How I tried to figure it out based on YouTube videos and things my friends were telling me. And how my hair was getting worse and worse every day because I was using the wrong shampoo in the wrong amount and at all the wrong times. I got more and more ashamed of my hair, and the words I couldn't say built and built until finally I exploded and yelled at my other mom that she might be black like me but with her short hair she'd never understand mine anyway and how both of us being black wasn't enough.

"You asked and she took you?" my mom asks. "How's that for easy."

"Yeah," I say.

I don't tell her how Coach K stared at me and said she didn't know my hair was bothering me. Or how she called the most popular stylist in town and when that stylist said she was booked for three weeks solid, she explained that I needed her, that she was parenting a teen who'd never been taught a thing about her own hair. And how once Coach K explained that much, the stylist offered to open the salon early just to give me a two-hour lesson in hair care.

I needed that lesson years ago. Maybe five years ago, when I was first a teen. Maybe I needed it the year my mom went away.

But my hair looks good now.

"I've always trusted Coach K with your heart," Mom says. "I didn't know I could trust her with your hair, too."

"War!" I say.

I'm grateful for the way the cards have laid themselves out on the table between us. Normally, when I sit here across from my mother, we ignore our other lives and focus on the cards. It never fails that a war breaks out to separate us from the real issues as they pop up in the conversation.

We each lay three cards out in quick succession, then flip the last one over.

I flip a queen.

Mom flips an ace.

"Damn!" I say, but I'm smiling.

We look at what Mom has won: two jacks and a three from me. And she recovered another of her aces. Not too awful, but not good.

Either way, now she's smugly collecting cards from me and smiling at me with all of her teeth, and I'm basking in the glow of her smile as I pretend to be upset about two lost jacks.

And five years. Five lost years with her, so far.

Today I might lose the rest of her. But I don't want to tell her. Not yet.

"How's school?" Mom asks as she restacks her cards.

"Fine," I say. I don't dwell on school when I'm with her. I don't bring my mostly-As report cards to prison. I don't brag about my brains to the mom who just earned her GED last year.

I let my other mom hang those report cards on the refrigerator.

"Still on track to graduate next year?" Mom asks.

My face burns. Graduate? I'm on the honor roll.

"Yup," I tell her. I lay out a card. It's a two to her ten.

Damn. I could use another war about now.

"Then what?" Mom asks.

I shrug. I collect a nine from her and lay a pair on the table.

"What's the overall score by now?" I ask, to change the subject.

But I have to stop changing the subject. Coach K says we have to talk about it. She said if I want to talk to my first mom first, today's the day.

She says we need to get the ball rolling if we're going to have it all wrapped up before I graduate.

When I'm talking to Coach K, I want it all wrapped up. Immediately. Now.

When I'm talking to this mom, I'm afraid our whole relationship depends on the loose ends staying loose.

"Oh, the score," Mom says with a dramatic sigh. "You're up by a million, and you know it. It doesn't matter how many wars I win today."

My face burns again. I'm up by a million in our never-ending game of war that we restart each week after the guards inevitably stop us mid-shuffle. But I'm up by a million in life, too.

I have chances she never had. I have people she never had. I have grades and connections and opportunities she never had. I'm up by a million.

Sometimes I'd still rather be with her, though.

Mom puts her cards down and places her elbows on the table on either side of the pile. She rests her chin in her hands.

My heart speeds up.

I'm going to have to say it soon. Now.

I don't think I'll be able to.

I can't be the one who says it.

I'm never the one breaking her heart.

"Tell me about it," she says. "Tell me about life with Coach K."

I bite my bottom lip.

Mom straightens her back so her chin no longer rests in her hands. She's backtracking. She can tell that question pushed me too far. She skipped a step or something.

Mom doesn't ask about my life like that. She hints at it by asking the easy questions about grades and sports and friends.

She never asks about family.

"You still running?" she says. And we're back on script.

"Yeah," I say. "I came in fourth at the invitational last weekend."

Mom beams. "Did you get a ribbon?" she asks.

I smile back at her. I pull it out of my pocket and lay it on the table on top of her cards. She strokes it.

I feel a guard hover close to us. Mom doesn't pick it up. She's not allowed to pick up anything I bring with me. But her index finger gently traces the "4" printed on the purple fabric.

She's allowed to touch my accomplishments. She's just not allowed to hold them.

"That's amazing, baby," she says. "You're going to ride those track feet right to college, aren't you?"

I squint at her, at my mom, because that's exactly what my other mom says. That's exactly how she puts it. "You're going to ride these track feet to college." And my moms are usually so different.

"Well, aren't you?" Mom adds.

I shrug.

There are things I don't tell Coach K. I don't tell her how I'll call her "my mom" but I won't ever call her "Mom" because it seems like the proper noun should refer only to the woman who has been around since the moment I was born, not the moment I was needy. I don't tell her that no matter how hard she's working for me as a parent and as a coach, I'm not going to be off to some big D1 school in a year if that big D1 school is so far away that I can't visit my mom, my real mom, my first mom.

And there are other things I don't tell my other mom. Things I should tell her. Like thank you.

"Let those feet run you straight to college, baby," Mom says. "You earned it."

I put my hand out to grab my cards, but my mom catches it.

"You earned it," she says again. "Go to college." It almost sounds like she's telling me to leave her.

We hold hands and stare at each other for a minute.

"NO TOUCHING!"

The guard's words blast us apart.

What kind of place is this? Where my *mother* isn't allowed to hold my hand?

More things I don't tell this mom: she should be the one standing on the sideline when I'm the fourth girl in the county to cross the finish line and reporters line up to take down the exact spelling of my name.

And she should be the one there on Christmas morning. And Mother's Day. And my birthday.

And it should be her signature at the bottom of my mostly-As report card.

And she shouldn't have messed up so badly that she ended up in a place where she gets in trouble for holding my hand when I tell her I'm the fourth fastest girl in the entire county.

I protect my real mom from that stuff, from all of the stuff my other mom is doing for her.

I want to keep protecting her. I wish today weren't the day I had to stop.

"How's it going in here?" I say.

My mom sighs. "I'm trying," she says. "My roommate got out last week so I have a new one. A tiny girl. Too young. She looks scared all the time. I just want to give her a hug."

I raise my eyebrows.

I wonder if she does hug this new roommate. I wonder if she hugs her the same way she hugs me twice a week, at the beginning and end of these stupid visits. The only time hugging is allowed.

I wonder if she's allowed to hug this other girl all the time.

"What's she in for?"

My mom sighs. "I don't know. But no doubt she'll be in way too long for whatever it is. She's barely older than you, and she already has two babies. Can you believe that?"

No, I think. *No, I can't believe that.*

I'm only eighteen.

"How is Coach K?"

I shrug. I hate to talk to one mom about the other.

"She's good to you," my mom says, like always.

I shrug again.

But I'm grateful, too.

It's another thing I don't tell each mom. How I'll always be more grateful for the second one. How I'll always love the first one just a little bit more.

Too many minutes of silence roll by. We only have half an hour each week, my mom and me. We don't get enough minutes to be silent for this many of them.

Finally she says, "I think you have something to tell me."

I look into her eyes, the ones that match mine in shape and color and depth. I let her see my tears.

"It's okay," she says. "Just tell me."

The words sneak around the tears, but just barely. They squeak and slide out of my mouth, so quiet I'm not sure if my mom will hear them. They line themselves up on the table between the cards of War. They're ready to let my mom declare war against them.

If she does, they'll fall over quickly.

I'll stop. I'll forget about college. I'll give up my other family. I'll forget about my dreams to make sure I'm close to her.

But I can't make the words say all of that. Instead they say the bare, terrifying truth.

"She wants to adopt me."

My mom's eyes spill over right along with mine. We cry for too many minutes. Crying together feels like wasting time the way being silent together does.

I half expect the guard to yell "NO CRYING" the way he yelled "NO TOUCHING."

It's only after too many tears that I realize my mom has been talking right through them. "I know, baby, I know," she's saying. "I know, I know."

"You know?" I say, too loudly. "You know she wants to adopt me?"

"Yeah, I know," my mom says. "She told me when she was here last week."

My mouth falls open.

My moms sat and talked together. About me. Without me.

"She said she waited until you were eighteen, so that you really get to decide if you want her in your life forever. She said she wanted to do it, though, to get you out of the system before you age out at twenty-one."

I nod. That's exactly what my mom—Coach K—said to me.

"She also told you I was going to ride my track feet to college," I say.

Mom laughs a little.

If we go through with this, she'll become my birth mom, this woman sitting across from me. That's what the world will call her. It seems wrong. She's so much more than that.

"And you don't need my permission," my mom is saying, "but it's okay with me. Just know it's okay." The words are like a kitchen knife coming down in the middle of my rib cage. The image of my mother being taken from me in handcuffs springs back to my brain. It feels the same. I go from half of a family to just one person, alone, again. I get sliced right off.

"I have your permission?" I say.

My mom messed up. I get that. But everyone has always told me how much she loves me. Even in the middle of my other mom saying how she wanted to adopt me, she said how much my first mom loves me.

Now I have permission to not be hers anymore?

Mom reaches across the table and lays her hand right next to my arm. It's the thing we do when we want to touch, but we can't. She gets close enough so that I can feel the heat radiate off her finger and into my elbow. Our electrons are touching and the guards can't do anything to stop that.

"I'm your mom," she says. "I love you more than anything. I want . . . I want what's best . . . for you."

As hurt as I am, my brain is exploding with fireworks of possibilities. A college education partially funded by my other mom. A college loan cosigned in her name. A family to come home to during Christmas break and the summer and all the times that kids come home from college. A family to catch me when I fall.

A chance to make what I've had with my second family for the past five years real in a way I thought it could never be.

But my heart is breaking. My heart is going back four years to when my mom was first taken away and I was sure, just so sure, for so long that it was my fault. That if I was a better kid this wouldn't have happened to me. Coach K got herself certified to be a fictive kin foster parent, took me in, and set me straight.

But if I really am a good kid, how could Mom give up on me so easily?

Mom takes a deep breath and breaks the rules again. She strokes my elbow. Enough of electrons, it's her actual fingers on my skin now.

"We're strong, you and me. We're strong, right?"

I look in her eyes. She's not crying anymore; instead her eyes stare at me intensely.

"You were all I had and I was all you had. Until I ended up in here. I'm the one who messed stuff up for us, you know? And even then, as you grew and grew, as you made friends and had that silly boyfriend and had so much to do with school and sleepovers and track meets and dances and parties . . . even with the messing up I did . . . we're still strong. Aren't we?"

I shrug. I don't know what she's getting at.

"You come here every week just for the chance to hug me twice. Don't you?"

Now I'm crying. I nod at her.

"And that means nothing's going to tear us apart," my

mom says. "Prison didn't tear us apart. It didn't tear us apart when you were sent to foster care. It didn't even hurt us when the state took away my official rights as a parent. No matter what they do to us, I'm your mom."

And nothing has ever been more true.

"You can have another mom—you can have thirty moms," she says. "You'll still be the best thing I ever did. You'll always be mine. Another woman loving you the way only a mother can, that's a good thing. And if all that bad stuff didn't tear us apart, I don't think we have to worry about a good thing."

My mom reaches for my hand and squeezes it. I see the guard watch this. I see him decide to let it happen.

I realize he's listening.

My mom squeezes my hand like she has since I was little. She puts her other hand on the table and squeezes both of my hands. We sit like that, holding onto each other, and the realness of who we are is undeniable.

I'm going to be adopted. But I'll still be hers. She'll still be mine.

She squeezes my hands again. I'm surprised she's still holding them. I can't believe the guards didn't come in and break us up yet. But they will. The guards, the lawyers, the courts, the system will always try to come between us—break us apart so we can't even hold hands. But we can hold onto each other.

Nothing can make us let go.

Caela Carter grew up in Basking Ridge, New Jersey, and Baltimore, Maryland. She's been writing since she learned how to pick up a pen, but before the writing thing got serious she spent six years teaching English to middle and high school students in Jacksonville, Florida, and Chicago, Illinois. When she's not writing, Caela is a teacher to some awesome teens in Brooklyn, a Notre Dame football enthusiast, and a happy explorer in New York City.

"As a writer, reader, and foster parent, I'm always searching for stories that explore the complexities of adoption and foster care while honoring the dignity and humanity of all families and family members. I'm honored to be a part of this project."

Mama's Eyes

by Libby Cudmore

I have intense but scattered memories of riding the bus with my birth mother.

In them, she has a high ponytail and crooked teeth. She's laughing as she passes me around to cooing strangers. Clarice was my favorite; she had a glittering broach on her coat that sparkled like a beacon, and she would hold out her arms to me. I was usually barefoot on that bus floor, the aisle rocking as I stumbled toward that glass jewel. Clarice never let me fall, always caught me and set me in her lap, holding out her purse for me to dig through until my mother gathered me up, screamed at me to stop crying, and smacked me hard on the bottom before stuffing me into my stroller.

Clarice and Roger adopted me when I was two.

The story goes that my mother came up to Clarice at the bus stop, dropped a duffle bag at her feet, shoved me into her arms, and said, "You can have her." She got into a waiting car and took off, never to be found. My mom didn't even know her name. And although it was a long, slow process to adopt me, Clarice always said it was worth every second of it. "I like to think you picked me," she used to say.

But I remember my mother's eyes most of all—not really her eyes, but a tattoo at the base of her neck, a flaming monster face that watched me whenever her back was turned, which it usually was. Reading a tabloid, yelling at her boyfriend on the phone, watching TV. Clarice says I'm too young to remember any of this, that my images of her are pieces of stories stitched together to create something I didn't live. But those eyes haunt my dreams, even thirteen years later.

Sometimes I still go into Clarice's jewelry box and get out that broach. It probably saved my life. If my mother had been so willing to hand me off to a stranger, I just as easily could have ended up with a monster instead of a family who made me their own. I had warm clothes and food and birthday parties; Clarice and Roger never spanked me for spilling juice or leaving my toys out.

And I wore that broach for the first time on a cold November afternoon, on the lapel of Clarice's black overcoat as I stood over her grave, tears leaving cold tracks down my cheeks as the minister read his sermon. Even Roger's arm around my shoulders couldn't warm me. His brother held the umbrella over both of us; Roger's other arm was in a cast, the only visible injury he'd suffered in the crash that killed Clarice. They'd gone to dinner while I was sleeping over at my friend Starr's house; around midnight the police knocked on her door and took me to the hospital in my pajamas. Roger was heavily sedated, but Clarice was already gone. Brake failure, the cop told me. Lucky they weren't both killed, he said, as though that would somehow make everything better.

Almost every night since Clarice's death, I dreamed of those monster eyes. Some nights it was enough to wake me screaming, Roger running into my room in his robe as he did when I was a child. He would hold and rock me while I sobbed; sometimes we'd cry together. "I miss her so goddamn much," he would say, holding me so tight that sometimes I couldn't breathe. I didn't mind. I didn't need to breathe as much as I needed to believe that I had one person in this world to cling to.

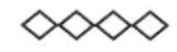

There was a nurse's aide at the hospital where Roger and I went for our grief counseling sessions, a skinny woman with crooked teeth and black streaks underneath her blonde ponytail. Her name tag read Amanda, and she lit up whenever we came in, asked me how school was going, touched Roger's arm. I wanted to hiss at her like a startled cat. No one was allowed that close to Roger except me. I was his protector, his knight, like in the color plates of the big storybooks he used to read me in bed. My grief was our shield; his was as though his skin had been turned inside out, leaving all of him exposed.

One afternoon, Amanda caught up with us in the parking lot. "The doctor forgot to give you this," she said, handing Roger a bottle of pills. Turning to me, she reached into the pocket of her scrubs and pulled out a handful of mini Snickers. "I grabbed these from the nurse's lounge," she said. "Anything you want when you come in, you just ask and I'll get it for you."

"Dr. Hodgeson didn't say anything about a prescription," Roger said.

She shrugged. "He told me to get you before you left," she said. "You can go back in and ask him, if you want."

Roger put the pill bottle in his pocket. "That's all right," he said. "Lord knows I could use it."

I was starving, but I didn't open the candy she gave me. Usually after talking with Dr. Hodgeson, I felt all right, that we really could make it through this. I talked to him about my nightmares, about feeling abandoned by my birth mother; we even spent one session talking about a boy I liked but was too afraid to ask out. But today my stomach had a hard knot, like the day before a test I didn't study for.

◇◇◇◇

We had a tradition, Roger and I. After counseling, we went to Pizza Hut. He used to take my softball team there when we won a game; at the time, the domed red glass chandeliers and the leatherette booths seemed so fancy, not like pizza on a paper plate at a birthday party.

He got a beer and I got a Mountain Dew. These were the nights that he didn't protest my caffeine consumption before bed. I still had homework to do; counseling took up my whole afternoon, and I would be up until midnight doing math problems at the kitchen table. I needed the artificial energy if I was going to solve quadratic equations.

Our pizza arrived and he ordered another beer. He ate a slice, took a pill, and washed it down with a sip of my soda. After a few minutes, he was smiling for what seemed like the first time since the accident. "Despite the circumstances, I like that we have this time together, kiddo," he said. "It's easy to get caught up in school and work and checking email, but these last few months have shown me what really matters." He reached across the table and took my hand, our fingers greasy. "I'm so glad you came into our lives. God, I remember the moment I first saw you. Clarice had taken a cab to the school, and I was just about to go lecture my freshman year bio class on photosynthesis. She came into my office with you in her arms and I couldn't believe a kid could smile that big. When she told me what happened . . ." He paused to take another sip of his beer. "I put a sign on the door of the lecture hall and we went right to the social workers. We didn't want to wait an extra minute to make you ours. It took forever, and there were times I was sure they were going to take you from us, put you in a foster family, but somehow, we prevailed. You made us both so happy."

There was a word stuck in my throat. Until now, I'd always called him Roger; I'd never learned to say "Mama" or "Dada" as a baby—to try and say them later in life was like trying to learn a foreign language. Tears welled up in my eyes. "Thanks," I said. "Dad."

Outside the Pizza Hut, Roger pinched his temples, squinting his eyes closed. He exhaled a long, slow breath and sank down on a bench. "I don't feel so hot, kiddo," he said, his words thick and measured. "Maybe . . . you should call your mom to come get us. We can get my car tomorrow." *Mom? The car?* Clarice was dead, her car totaled in the wreck. I didn't know whether to call a cab or an ambulance. I sat down next to him, fishing through his pockets for the pills. There were no warning labels, just a jumble of letters and Dr. Hodgeson's name, *take one with food three times a day*. I rubbed his back. "You'll be all right," I said. "I'm gonna take care of you. Just hang in there."

I started to go back inside to get the manager, but headlights blinded me. A door slammed, and I saw Amanda, now in a striped hoodie and jeans, rushing toward Roger. "Are you all right?" she asked.

I balled my fists. "What did you give him?" I demanded. Had she followed us?

"I don't know," she said. "They were from Dr. Hodgeson . . ."

She was lying. Dr. Hodgeson never said anything about pills, and for whatever reason, she was screwing with us. "Just call us a cab," I said.

Roger moaned and she touched his face. "You'll be okay," she said. "Come on, I'll get you two home."

"I'm not going *anywhere* with you!" I screamed. "Call us a cab, you bitch!"

Another family approached the restaurant and side-eyed our scene. Normally I would be mortified that anyone was looking at me, but not tonight. Tonight, I wanted to make as big a scene as possible to drive this woman away. She would only hurt us more. She put her hands on my arms, gripping me tight. She looked at me with an expression I'm sure she thought conveyed kindness, but all I saw was malice. "I know you're scared, Zoe," she said. "But he'll be fine. We just need to get him home and into bed. Trust me, I'm a nurse. I know how to take care of a patient. I'll stay with you, don't worry."

How did she know my name? We gave our names to the receptionist, but never to anyone else. Had she overheard? Checked my file? My heart was pounding in my throat, but I knew I had to take care of Roger. I couldn't get him home by myself, and the manager was sure to come out any minute and start screaming at us to leave.

"He needs to go to the hospital," I insisted.

"I can drive you," she said.

I pulled out my cell phone. I called 911. People gawked out the restaurant window as the ambulance pulled up. I was angry and embarrassed for him, scared of her, and scared I might lose the one person left in my life in front of a stupid Pizza Hut.

The ambulance pulled up. The EMTs got him inside. Amanda put her hand on my arm, smiling like Medusa. "I'll go with you."

I shook her off. "Not on your life," I snapped.

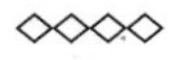

Dr. Hodgeson seemed confused by the pills Roger had taken. He couldn't find a record of prescribing them. "That nurse is trying to kill us," I said to Roger. "I've seen cases like that on TV. She poisons her patients so she can be the hero and save them at the last minute. How else can you explain her being at the restaurant right when you were sick?"

He chalked it up to my imagination, stress from losing Clarice, and too much TV. "Dr. Hodgeson sees a lot of patients," said Roger. "I'm sure it was an honest mistake."

Out in the lobby, Amanda was waiting for us. "Thanks for

getting us home the other night," said Roger. "I'm sorry for the trouble."

"I'm the one who's sorry," she said. "The warning stickers came off in my pocket. I'm just glad I ran into you—poor Zoe was so scared."

"I'm really embarrassed," he said. "I should have known better, even without the warning labels."

"How did you know where we'd be?" I demanded. "Did you follow us?"

"Zoe, please," Roger said, holding up his hand. To the nurse, he said, "Why don't you join us for dinner tomorrow night? It's the least I can do. You've been really great to us."

"No!" I grabbed his coat sleeve. "No, Roger—Dad—she's—she's trying to kill us!"

"Zoe!" He shook me off. "I'm sorry. She's still upset about the other night . . ."

"It's understandable," said Amanda. "Zoe, I'd really like to share a meal with you so we could get to know each other better. I think we'd have a lot in common."

She was talking to me as if I was five. I wanted to punch her in her pink mouth. But before I could say anything, Roger jumped in. "How does 6:30 sound?"

Amanda brought a bottle of wine for dinner. I ate silently, answering her questions with as few words as I could. She touched Roger's arm; the wine—and the pill he took before she got there—made him silly and easily amused. I caught them kissing in the kitchen. I said goodnight early and made an excuse to go do homework.

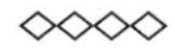

I had that dream again. Those eyes, my mother's evil eyes, were watching Clarice, following her everywhere. I woke up screaming, but Roger didn't come for me. The pills. The goddamn pills. I needed him, and all he cared about was his own numbness. That, and Amanda.

I got up and got a drink of water. I heard moaning from Roger's room and panicked. Was he sick again, crying out for me? I threw open the door.

Amanda, straddling him, broke from her kiss to stare at me. The streetlights from the windows hit her back, illuminating a tattoo of two flaming monster eyes.

My mother's tattoo.

I turned and ran. I heard Roger call out to me, but I was already out the door. I didn't care that I was barefoot. I just had to get away. I heard him yelling up the street. I stumbled over a crack in the sidewalk near the Wasserman's house and fell on all fours onto the leaf-covered sidewalk. Roger gathered me up and I fought like a cat being dragged to the vet. He shouted my name, and lights came on in the neighbors' houses. "Zoe, Zoe, it's all right," he said, rocking me back and forth. I could smell wine on his breath. "It's all right, I'm here."

I tried to push him away, but he was bigger than me. Amanda came running up the walk, hoodie unzipped, shirt on inside out, shoes untied. "Zoe, are you all right?"

"Get away from me!" I screeched. "Leave me alone!"

"I'm sorry, Amanda," he said. "She's had these nightmares ever since she was a child. Her mother abandoned her on a bus, and now with Clarice gone, she's really struggling with those abandonment issues."

He was parroting Dr. Hodgeson. I waited for her to confess, but instead she crouched down. "I know how that must have hurt you," she said. "But I know your mother loved you very, very much."

I broke one arm free of Roger's hold and punched her. Not hard, but it startled her, leaving a small trickle of blood down her mouth. Roger grabbed me and shook me so hard I thought my neck would snap. He had a wild look in his eyes that I'd never seen before, and for the first time in my life, I was scared of him.

"Roger, be careful with her!" Amanda begged, gripping his arm. "She's just a child."

For a moment, I was glad she was there. He softened. "Zoe . . ." he breathed, his grip slackening. "Zoe, I'm so sorry . . ."

Amanda hugged me. I was so dazed I let her. "I'll go," she offered, as though she was doing us a favor.

We walked back to the house in silence. I watched Amanda drive until her lights vanished around the corner. I double-checked that the back door was locked, and Roger poured the rest of the wine into a juice glass. I just stared at him. "I think," he said, setting the glass down, "that you could use an extra session a week with Dr. Hodgeson."

"I think," I said, folding my arms across my chest, "that you should stay away from Amanda."

"You were very rude tonight," he said, taking another drink. "Now I'm sorry I got angry, but your behavior these last few weeks has been unacceptable. What is going on with you?"

I took a deep breath. "That woman," I said. "Amanda. I think she's my real mother."

"That's nonsense," he said. "Why would you think that?"

"Her tattoo," I said. "It's just like the one I keep dreaming about."

"It's a flash tattoo," he said. "I can't tell you how many of my students over the years have had ones just like it."

"I'm scared of her," I insisted. "I'm scared that she's coming to take me away from you."

He got that mean look on his face again. "Even if she was, she wouldn't want you now," he spat.

I felt as if he had stabbed me through the gut. I waited a beat for him to realize what he'd said, but he didn't apologize. Instead, he drank the rest of his wine, glowering at me over the rim of his glass. I mumbled a good-night and went upstairs.

Lying in bed, I reached for Clarice's broach in the darkness. Tears trickled down my cheeks, wetting my pillow. I didn't want Roger to hear me crying.

I must have fallen asleep, because I woke up to Roger's weight on the end of my bed. "Remember when you were little, and on Saturday mornings, you would get in bed with us?" he asked. "I would hug Clarice, and she would hug you, and you would hug that little stuffed bunny we got you for your first Christmas with us." He sniffled, his voice cracking. "That was the highlight of my week. No matter what else happened, no matter what else was going on, I knew I had those few minutes to look forward to."

"I am so, so sorry I hurt you," he continued. "I'm sorry for grabbing you and for shaking you, but what I'm really kicking myself for is what I said. Any parent would be lucky to have you. I know I am, and I know Clarice was too. You're what made us a family." He was sobbing now. "I just miss her so goddamn much, I feel like I'm losing my mind."

I sat up and hugged him. "It's okay," I whispered. "I miss her, too."

"I won't see Amanda again, if you don't want me to," he said. "You don't have to give a reason. We'll switch doctors if you want."

"Please," I said. "I'm scared of her. I really think she's after me."

"You don't have to be scared," he said. "I'll protect you. I promise you. I know I haven't done a very good job in the last few weeks, but I'm going off the pills. No more booze, either, not even a beer with pizza. I want to be alert and ready so you feel safe. No more numbing the pain."

He put his arms around me and kissed the top of my head. "One day, I might be ready to date again, and I need you to promise me that you will be welcoming to her," he said. "But I won't bring anyone home who doesn't love you as much as I do."

"She's going to be tough to find," I said.

"Then she'll be worth the wait," he said.

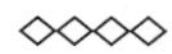

Roger let me sleep in. He made pancakes and we had breakfast together. He dropped me off at school before his 11:00 lecture. I was taking a history test when my teacher answered the classroom phone, hung up, and tapped me on the shoulder. "You need to go to the office," she said. "There's someone here to pick you up."

My heart jumped. Roger had only one class on Friday; maybe he was taking me on a trip for the weekend. I wasn't doing great on the test anyway, and being called out would give me a chance to make it up. I'd lost a lot of time after Clarice's death, and although teachers gave me a wide berth, my grades were starting to show signs of strain.

I gathered up my books and stopped by my locker for my jacket. But it wasn't my dad waiting in the office for me—it was Amanda. Before I could say anything, she jumped in. "Roger OD'd," she said. "They think he took the whole bottle of pills. He's at the hospital now. I said I'd come get you."

I thought I was going to throw up. After all his promises last night to give up booze and pills, he took the whole bottle? I gripped her arm, forgetting that I hated her. "You have to take me to him," I begged. "He needs me—please."

"Of course," she said. "Come on. My car's outside."

She drove a beat-up Kia with too many stickers on the back windows, Tinkerbell and daisies and *If You're Going To Ride My Ass, At Least Buy Me Dinner*. "Throw your stuff in the back," she said. "Sorry about the mess."

But we didn't go to the hospital. She drove us out of town, and we got on the highway. "Where are we going?" I demanded. "We need to go see my dad."

"Your dad's fine," she said.

"But you said . . ."

"I needed an excuse to get you out of school," she said. "I knew you wouldn't come with me otherwise."

I tried to reach for my backpack to get my phone, but she swerved the car, throwing me back into my seat. "I don't know why you even care," she said. "He's not your real dad. Your real dad was some dick I used to buy weed from."

"I knew it," I said. "You're her. The one who abandoned me." After all these years, she had found me, put all the pieces together, and come for me. I thought I should be grateful, feel loved even. But instead, I felt as if I was turning into a black hole, shrinking inward until nothing would be left.

"How about being a little grateful?" she said. "The one who let you have a nice, boring, middle-class life with those people?"

"Please take me back to Roger," I begged. "He'll be worried about me."

"Do you know how long I searched for you?" she said. "Five years. Couldn't go to the cops . . . they had a warrant out for my arrest. For *abandoning* your sorry ass. I didn't abandon you. I didn't leave you at some gas station with a dirty diaper. I picked a nice family to take care of you while I got my shit together. But do they see that? Nope. Hell, *you* don't even see it, you ungrateful little bitch."

"So why did you give me up in the first place?" I asked.

"Because I lived in a shit apartment with no job," she said. "I had a chance to go to Florida with my boyfriend, but he didn't want you around. I was trying to *better* your life. But fuck, Zoe, I missed you. Dumped his ass, moved back here to try and find you. But I didn't even know that bitch's name."

"Her name is Clarice, and don't you *dare* call her a bitch!" I cried. "She *loved* me!"

"I love you, too, don't you see that?" she insisted. "I love you so much I *let you go,* like that shitty Sting song. But now I got a job, we can be together. We'll be best friends. Hell, I can even move in with you and Roger. He seems like a good guy. The pills help. I knew he wouldn't be able to drive after he took one, so I followed you guys to Pizza Hut. Your mom's pretty clever, huh?"

I knew it. I knew she had followed us, set all this in motion just to get close to us. "You stay away from him," I said. "You could have killed him."

"He was supposed to die in the accident," she said with the same casual tone I used to describe a normal day at school. "We would have been able to be together a *lot* sooner if it had all gone as planned."

"You caused that accident?" I said. "You bitch! You killed my mom!"

She swerved the car again. I hit my head on the window. "Don't you raise your voice to me," she said. "You're too big for me to spank, but don't think I can't kick your sorry ass if you talk shit to me. They fuckin' spoiled you."

I was shaking. My head hummed with the blow from the window. She turned the CD player on. Of course she liked Nickelback. She sang along off-key, smiling at me. "Mother-daughter road trip," she said. "This will be fun."

"Where are we going?" I asked. I had to call Roger, call the police, tell them everything Amanda told me. I had to get away from her.

"My mom's house," she said. "It's in New Jersey. You'll like it. They got a T.J. Maxx nearby, and this Chinese nail salon where you can get a mani-pedi for, like, twenty bucks. We'll get matching ones."

"Please just take me home," I said.

"I *am* taking you home," she said. "Don't you remember? Grammy gave you that big teddy bear? Mr. Snuffles? That's where you belong, not some bullshit suburb."

New Jersey. That was hundreds of miles away from Roger, from my life and my school and my friends. I had to get away from her now. "I have to go to the bathroom," I whined.

"Why didn't you go before we left the school?"

"I thought I could go at the hospital," I said. "Please pull over—I'm about to have an accident."

She rolled her eyes and yanked the car to the side of the road. I got out of the car and opened the back door. "What the fuck do you think you're doing?" she asked.

"I need a tampon," I said.

Her eyes welled up with tears. I felt suddenly gross. "My little baby is all grown up," she said. "My little girl is a woman now."

I grabbed my backpack and fled into the woods. I found my cell phone, but there wasn't much reception. I shot off a text to Roger. *Amanda kidnapped me. Killed Clarice. On route to NJ. Please send help. I love you.*

"Zoe, you done?" she called. "Come on, baby, I haven't got all fucking day!"

I stuffed my phone in my bra. It was still on silent from school. I grabbed my hoodie from my backpack to hide the lump. "Thanks," I said as I got back into the car. "I feel much better."

She hugged me. "Come on, we'll go to Burger King, like old times. You used to *love* eating all my french fries; you'd get ketchup all over your little face."

I took my time with my lunch. The more time we were in one location, the more time the cops had to reach us. Amanda chattered for a few minutes, then took to her phone. She made us take a selfie, and I tried to smile. It was all evidence. She'd probably be dumb enough to post where we were.

But her patience grew thin quickly. "Hurry up," she said. "I'm sorry it's not a fancy four-course meal like *Roger* and *Clarice* probably served you, but come on, we've got someplace to be."

"I'm sorry," I said. "It's just that they didn't let me have fast food. Everything had to be organic and healthy." It was a sort-of lie; they cooked at home most of the time, but they didn't freak out if I had McDonald's with a friend. But I knew I had to buy time. Fighting her didn't do me any good. I had to make her think I wanted to be here with her until I could escape.

"Figures," she said. "They fucking thought they were better than us. Imma go outside for a smoke. If you want more, go ahead and get something. My treat." She threw a five down and stood up. "Don't take all day."

As soon as she was gone, I got out my phone. *Called police. Help on the way. I love you. Hang in there.*

I heard sirens. Amanda came in, cigarette still in her mouth. I dropped my phone and she saw. "You bitch!" she said. "You fucking bitch, you called him, didn't you?"

"Ma'am, we don't allow that kind of—" stammered a manager who didn't look much older than me.

"Shut the fuck up!" she snarled. "Don't tell me how to raise my kid!"

The sirens grew louder. I yanked myself out of her hold. She slugged me, and I hit my head on a booth. I stumbled, blackness closing in. The sirens stopped. Had they passed us by?

I thought I heard Roger's voice, but there were so many others that I couldn't be sure. I put my head on the cool tile floor. Someone tried to pick me up, but I weighed a thousand pounds. The voices got farther away. The eyes in my nightmares closed and were gone.

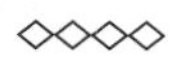

I woke up in a hospital bed. Roger was sitting in a chair next to me. "Hey, kiddo," he said, stroking my hair. "You gave me quite a scare."

"Where's Amanda?" I demanded. "Is she here? Is she watching us?"

"Shh, relax. She's not here. Totally different hospital. The cops took her into custody. You're safe. It's just me. You got a nasty bump on your head, but you're okay."

I started to cry. I thought about Clarice, about the accident, about how much time Roger spent in hospitals. He sat on the edge of my bed and put his arm around my shoulder, kissing my head. It hurt, but I didn't say anything.

"I'm sorry," he whispered into my hair. "I'm sorry for all of this. This was all my fault."

I drifted back into sleep. The doctors sent me home the next day, but I don't remember leaving the hospital. Roger carried me up to bed, and I slept with the sounds of him puttering around downstairs. I woke only to use the bathroom. He promised me Pizza Hut when I felt up to it, but I never wanted to eat there again. We went to Steak 'n Shake instead.

When we got home, there were flowers on the doorstep. "Must be from your classmates," he said, handing me the card. "You'll be able to go back to school tomorrow."

But it wasn't from my classmates. The card had three typed words on it.

Mama loves you.

Libby Cudmore worked at temp agencies and record stores before settling down in Upstate New York to write full-time. Her debut novel, *The Big Rewind* (William Morrow, February 2016), was hailed as "smart, poignant, and addicting," (Kristi Belcamino, *Blessed Are the Dead*). Her short stories have been published *Pank, The Big Click, The Stoneslide Corrective*, and *Big Lucks*. She holds an MFA in Creative Writing and makes all her own notebooks.

"Where we come from is as much a part of our journey as where we're going . . . even if sometimes the answer we find about our past is difficult. I'm honored to be part of an anthology that celebrates the discovery, for good and for ill, and the love of the people who guide us down that road."

A Kingdom Bright and Burning

by Dave Connis

Inside: 2/7/15

Though it was my kingdom, I didn't know the king.

I didn't know anyone in it, really. I'd built everything I saw, but I'd never talked to a single soul. I couldn't be seen. I was too afraid of the citizens. Afraid they'd realize I was the one who built it, and then they'd leave, and then I'd really be alone.

I built the kingdom's first tower out of stones I pulled from a quarry hidden in the deep of the Western Forest, and travelers passing through have always gathered around that tower at night. Something about the stones, maybe their strength and solidity, called to them. The tower gave them a comfort I'd spent my whole life trying to find.

Ironically, I built the kingdom hoping that, eventually, I'd find comfort or belonging in it somewhere. Maybe in the corner of Mickey Cobbler's shop in the village square, or in watching a bard in the Rusted Root Tavern. I thought maybe the correct combination of timber and rock would get me somewhere, but it didn't, no matter how much I built.

After all these years, I'm no closer to finding what I'm looking for than I was when I started. That was why I'd never go meet them. The travelers, I mean. I couldn't bear to look them in the eye knowing they'd found what I wanted. Instead, I just watched them from my favorite tree, an ancient oak. The tallest tree of the Western Forest. The tree told me what the birds said as they rested in his branches, and that day, the birds had been in a heated debate about how the kingdom began.

"And what do they say?" I asked him.

"Fables. A story of a simple man drinking it into existence at a tavern or the sneeze of a wizard while getting off his horse."

"Never me."

"No. Never a boy."

I couldn't remember how I built it, but I did. Every last bit. I even knew what the castle looked like. I knew its secret passages better than I knew myself.

"Mickey Cobbler made that boy's shoes," I said, pointing at a traveler boy.

Oak shivered his leaves, and a few brushed against the nape of my neck. "Mickey does fine work. Very fine. You know, Zeke, you should meet him. If you met him, you could probably get your own pair of shoes."

"I can't."

"You built this place for them," he says, stretching a limb toward the travelers. "You should be with them. What's the point of building an entire kingdom if you can't call it home?"

I plucked a leaf off one of his branches, and he quieted. Minutes later, I climbed down him and made my way toward the Wizard's Guild. They had an unguarded pantry that often kept me fed.

I snuck into the guild through an open window and then ran down a set of spiral stairs. I got to the bottom and saw the pantry door, as it always was, unlatched and open. A baguette hung off the shelf next to a sack of potatoes. I reached for it slowly, sure not to make a noise.

"Your family is coming today," a voice said.

I spun.

A stocky woman, whose black and billowy robes sat on her shoulders with a welcoming grace and lightness, stood behind me. She had a whisper of beard, too, which I found somewhat funny, even though I didn't laugh. I wasn't allowed to laugh in my kingdom. The only thing I did there was travel in the darkness of night and shadow and watch who came, who went, and everything in between.

I was the watchman.

"Are you excited?" the woman asked. I didn't say anything. I was too shocked to hear a voice this close. Never in the years of the kingdom had I been spoken to, outside of Oak, and my ears almost hurt from a tone that was directed only to me. A sound made specifically for my understanding. Did all closeness hurt this much?

"Well, all right, then . . . you'll have to come with me." The woman reached for me.

I ran.

Outside: 2/7/15

Anita Marzipan had the kind of posture that made chiropractors wish they'd gotten a degree in business administration and started a local pub. Her back was more of a crescent than a spine, and her feet were flat, which caused her to walk bent forward with an awkward bob of the head.

So when Anita walked straight into the office of the orphanage director, Mary Detwiler, all these unique faculties were at play in the most dramatic fashion. The night before, Anita had received a call from Mary letting her know that a family had shown interest in adopting one of the orphans. One would think that Anita would be happy for the child, but she felt such bitterness toward childish things that she was only happy for herself. For ridding the orphanage of another whiny rook.

Ezekiel Most sat in the chair in front of Mary's desk. He was silent. Distant. The cold look of someone who'd never had a fridge or pantry door to open without asking.

"So," Anita said, frowning. She hated apathetic children. "The silent one is leaving us?"

Mary frowned. "The Abernathys have signed the papers and will be here to pick him up within the next two hours."

Anita stared hard at the buzzed head of the child. If he'd heard what Mary said, he made no show of emotion. It appeared that that day was no different than any other for the Most boy.

"Who are the Abernathys?" Anita asked.

"They live in Sacco. Own a restaurant in the harbor that's been in their family for years. I Don't Give a Clam, if you're familiar. My sister says they attend her church. Good folk."

Anita snorted. She hated God-fearing folk, especially the ones that adopted apathetic children.

"They do understand what they're signing up for?" Anita asked.

Mary gave Anita a trenchant nod, then turned to the boy and said, "Zeke, Anita and I will be right back."

The boy, again, said nothing.

Mary stood up from her desk and pulled Anita into the hallway.

"Do they know they're adopting a twelve-year-old mute?" Anita was what she considered a safe distance from the boy—barely three steps.

With a sharp flick of her hand and a slight curl of her lip, Mary motioned for Anita to move out of earshot. "He is *not* mute, Anita. The janitor claims he's heard him speak when he's alone."

"That wasn't my question."

Mary sighed. "They are aware his late father's abuse had negative effects on him. They are aware that Ezekiel prefers not to speak, and they are the kind of folk that sign the papers regardless of what they know."

Inside: 2/7/15

Running through the town square was all it took for me to realize something was wrong. Somehow, the townspeople watched me through the walls of buildings. I didn't know how they knew I was there, but they did. Their gaze followed me as I ran back to Oak.

I climbed up and up and up, deep into his branches.

"Did you feel the earthquake?" he asked.

I nodded even though I didn't know that's what I'd felt. I assumed I was responsible for my own trembling. My fear causing my feet to shudder.

"What's happening?"

Oak's bark roughened under my hands.

"The kingdom is under attack."

"How? We don't have any enemies. I never built enemies."

Outside: 8/2/15

Mr. Abernathy pushed his glasses back onto his nose as he watched his wife's fingers grip tighter and tighter around her cereal spoon. He pushed his iPhone aside, though he was one candy away from a new high score, and prepared for what she'd say next.

"I just don't think he hears us," she finally said.

He smiled; it was gentle, understanding, but firm, much like an autumn breeze. "For some, love takes a long time to hear."

"We love you, Zeke," Mrs. Abernathy said, but Zeke said nothing.

A few minutes later, Mr. Abernathy broke the painful silence with the rustle of his coat sleeve, soaking up a tear from his wife's cheek before it fell into her cereal.

Outside: 3/19/19

"I love you, Zeke," Mrs. Abernathy said on the drive home from the latest emergency delivery. She always asked to deliver more lobster if the kitchen ran out because it gave her the chance to sneak a few spoonfuls of Chef Mematiane's lobster chowder while he and the bulk of the staff were busy unloading.

Zeke, as he had for the last four years, said nothing.

Mrs. Abernathy didn't notice the reciprocated glance. A glance so small it could've fit within an atom.

Inside: 3/19/19

It had been years since the attack started.

Everything was dying. The buildings were in a progressive decay, crumbling more and more with every pass of the sun. The streets were filled with expanding sinkholes, their foundation attacked by something I couldn't see.

"Any news?" I asked Oak.

"The birds have found nothing and no one. The land around us is empty."

I groaned. "What do we do?"

The oak shook his leaves. "We should consider surrender."

Surrender? To an unknown enemy? The whole kingdom? The place where I've lived my whole life? The safest place?

"Most of the citizens have left, Zeke."

"This is how it was, you know. Before the king and the citizens. I don't mind fewer people."

From the branches of Oak, I saw another building collapse.

I knew that one. It was Mickey Cobbler's. It toppled with a plume of dust, and before it settled, another earthquake shook the ground. It was like every quake that had come before. Small and sturdy. It was as if the fault line was directly under me.

Another stone shook from its place in the massive wall surrounding my kingdom. A beam of bright light poured through the hole, punching the ground below with a glow as noticeable as the red flames of a fire.

Thousands of those thirsty beams existed, rays of sun shimmering through clouds of dust, and their number grew every day. I knew that the shadows I used to travel in wouldn't last much longer.

I thought about the danger of surrender, the intense heat of the light coming through the new hole in my wall. I slid down Oak and stood by him, watching the dust of all the lost buildings float through the sea of speckled blazes.

I slowly walked toward a ray of light, and then, when I was only a few inches away, I reached toward it, curious as to what kind of light could be so bright and pure. So hot. Was it a trick from the Wizard's Guild? Some casting to find the missing architect of their dying city and enlist his help?

My finger was swallowed by a brightness I felt in the innermost marrow of my bones. A sear both cold and hot. Tearing and melting.

I cried and ran back to Oak.

I settled in his branches. "Nope. We can't surrender."

Outside: 8/9/19

"Are you ready for your first day of high school?" Mrs. Abernathy asked Zeke as she readied his lunch: a bag of thinly sliced apples and a turkey sandwich on a pretzel bun. She knew this was his favorite lunch ever simply because he looked at her when she made him these things.

"I bet you are," she continued. "You get to see Mrs. Bailey again. She moved up from the elementary school to teach English. Stand up."

Zeke stood, and Mrs. Abernathy fingered his shirt collar and fidgeted with a tuft of hair sticking toward heaven on the back of his head. "Okay, you look good. Ready to go? All right, let's go."

Inside: 10/2/19

There was nothing left.

Nothing but the walls, and even they were filled with holes.

"They will collapse soon," Oak said, his leaves the fiery red of fall. "You can either choose surrender or have it forced upon you. There's no hiding from it anymore."

"We can't. I'm alive here. If I surrender, I'm afraid I'll die."

Oak stayed silent, and his silence confirmed it.

"It's safe here," I added, though it was as obvious as the skin on my body that it wasn't.

Oak took a deep breath. I felt his bark expand under my feet. "It has never been safe here, only comfortable. Why do humans always assume that those are the same thing?" He paused. "Answer me something, before I die. Why do humans assume that isolation means safety?"

"You won't die, Oak. I planted you."

"Answer my question."

"If I'm alone, I won't be hurt."

"Then why do you hurt when you are alone?"

I looked at him, his question coursing through my veins, and that's when his leaves began to drop. It was fall, but his leaves weren't dropping because the season commanded it. It was obvious by the way they fell, straight down as if they carried weight instead of a calm flutter, that they were falling like the rest of the kingdom. Was I the only one who refused to believe that falling was the only choice?

"You're choosing this. Don't leave me here," I begged. "Please, Oak."

"I'm confident in my choice. The king will die soon, Zeke, and when he does, will you die with him? He will die paralyzed. His life a hostage to fear. Will you follow him?"

"I don't know the king," I said. Tears streamed down my face, watering the Oak's dying branches. "I've never known the king. You know that!"

"Of course you have," Oak said. "It's you."

The last of his leaves fell to the ground, and immediately I felt the spirit of his company fade like the warmth of the sun as it dips below the horizon. For hours after he left me, all I could do was sit in his branches and cry.

Eventually, I climbed down him, but I didn't leave. I sat underneath him and watched as his limbs decayed, each one snapping from his trunk and falling to the ground like an earthen icicle. As time passed, all that wasn't limb and branch—his stump, his roots—turned into dust and blew away.

In the hours I spent watching Oak die, I realized three things:

I was alone. I was the king. And I still hurt.

Outside: 12/29/19

Mr. Abernathy threw another log on the fire. The rest of his family had abandoned him to the flames hours ago in search of sleep. He sat and stared at the blaze with a heavy mind. He considered picking up the Xbox controller to play a silent game of FIFA, but he was too distracted with processing the "whats," "whys," and "hows" that plague most humans when they reach the New Year.

Would Zeke speak by the time his sister, two years old, began to bring boys home? Why could Zeke hear so well, and do everything asked of him, yet never find words? Would the coming year be the year he spoke? Was he, Mr. Abernathy, hoping where hope didn't exist?

Maybe love and time *couldn't* fix the most collided of collisions.

In the midst of his fervent hoping, Zeke came out of his room and sat next to Mr. Abernathy on the couch.

"Can't sleep?" Mr. Abernathy asked.

Zeke didn't answer.

"I just put another log on the fire. You can hang here for a while. Maybe that will help."

And then, much to Mr. Abernathy's surprise, Zeke began to cry.

Inside: 12/29/19

I was in the center of the kingdom, where it was darkest, but even there the beams of light swallowed most of the space around me.

I sat in the spent ashes of my oak's limbs. He'd kept me warm, but I'd just thrown his final limb on the fire. It went up in a quick flare of heat, and just as quickly turned to smoldering coal. The fire was dying, and as the light waned, I knew I'd die there. In that ever-present darkness. I also knew that my wall wouldn't fall unless *I* asked it to.

My enemy had stopped shaking the stones loose. That way, the decision to surrender would be mine. I knew I'd die either way, in the dark or in the light. I knew because I was the king. I was alone. I hurt. I thought of the kinds of death I'd meet in the darkness, and they all frightened me. Starvation. Slow and painful. Pneumonia. Slow and cold.

Every death slow.

As my fire's coals turned to black and crumbled with one final puff of smoke, I knew what I had to do.

I stood and walked toward the west section of the wall, but I did not stand in the beams of light. Their brilliant forms rested on burnt grass only inches from my feet.

In the dark, I'd die forever. In the light, I'd only burn for seconds.

I wiped my cheeks and took my last breath.

"Walls, fall," I said, voice trembling.

With an ancient rumble, the earth beneath me began to shake. Stones clattered against themselves before falling with heavy thuds to the ground. And then, all at once, the walls fell and what had kept the light at bay was nothing more than a pile of ash. The light screamed through. The burn I'd felt on my finger before wrapped around me hot and fiery.

In the light of my last moments, I saw buildings past the crumbled line of what was my wall. It was a new kingdom bright and burning, and the more of myself died in the light, the bigger the kingdom became. And right before there was nothing left of me, I knew the burning kingdom hadn't come to end my reign.

It had come to bring me home.

Outside: 12/29/19

Mr. Abernathy held his son and cried with him too, even though he knew they weren't crying for the same reasons. Despite these reasons, he knew that moment meant something. The last four years of Zeke's silence had been broken not by words, but by sobs, and though Mr. Abernathy was sad that the silence wasn't put to death with audible verse, he was aware of humanity enough to know that tears were just as complex and loud.

"Ezekiel," Mr. Abernathy said, his tears seeping into the

couch cushions. He asked the question he'd asked every day for the last four years. "Do you hear me?"

The fire crackled. Mrs. Abernathy snored in the bedroom. The clock ticked as it always had. Mr. Abernathy loved like he always had.

It was the most normal of evenings.

"Yes."

Dave Connis writes words you can sing and words you can read. He is the author of *The Temptation of Adam* and *Suggested Reading*. He lives in Chattanooga, Tennessee, with his wife, Clara, and a dog that barks at nonexistent threats. When he's not writing YA or MG, he's probably working really strange part-time jobs and doing other things that actually give his family the ability to eat food.

"For some, love takes a long time to hear."

"Even for people who've had one, 'home' takes a lot of time to parse out. Putting roots to the concept, physical and emotional, is never easy and rarely as obvious and simple as just a structure with four walls. Adoption attacks the complexity and baggage of what 'home' means with pure love, in all its forms: ornery, unconditional, hard, easy, and chosen. Adoption invites all involved to love and be loved, to fight to be a home outside of ourselves, whether or not we know what that means. I hope to join that fight someday."

The Inexplicable Weight of Mountains

by Helene Dunbar

It began with Joey's mother asking Mom how much she paid for me.

It began with Aunt Susie whispering behind her hand that four "in-country" families would have had to reject my file before Mom and Dad could have seen it.

It began in middle school with Jordan Lee asking where my parents got me, since I obviously wasn't "theirs."

No, really, it began with the family tree project in art class. That collection of construction paper and photos and glue that was just one more deadline to meet for the rest of the kids, but which kept me up for two straight nights trying to remember who my parents' great-great-whatevers were.

And it didn't matter anyhow, because all I saw when I closed my eyes were mountains from a grimy second-floor window. Mountains I've never visited, would never visit, but mountains I stared at every single day for six years. European snowcapped mountains. I didn't know why their image came back to me so often. I wasn't even sure that they were memories and not something from a book. It felt like cheating.

My parents never hid the fact that I was adopted. I mean, they couldn't have. My mom is a pale redhead who burns every time she looks out the window. My dad has brown hair that gets pastel in the sun. Next to them, I look like a cookie left too long in the oven.

When I was little we even talked about how I was from Eastern Europe. I loved to hear about how my parents brought me home. And then, just like the story of Santa Claus, I outgrew it and was more interested in Star Wars.

And then I didn't think about it again.

Until I did.

◇◇◇◇

To: Yuri.Guryev@birthsearch.ru
From: MountainBoy@me.com

Mr. Guryev: I read on the Internet that you can search for people's birth families. Can you tell me how that works?

Thanks!

◇◇◇◇

"You'll be careful, right?" Mama whispered from bed. She held the car keys out with a shaky arm. Migraines always hit her hard.

I raised my eyes and tried to look confident.

"Marin?" she whispered.

"Yes, Mama, of course."

Given my lack of an official driver's license, I understood her concern. I had my birth certificate—two certificates, actually—the European one that listed Marin Avelin as the son of Kirill and Darya and the American one that listed Marin Simon Frazier as the son of Frank and Melissa—, but somehow my citizenship certificate had gone missing. We'd reapplied, but the letter we got back said it was going to take six months. That meant that while I'd passed Driver's Ed, the state wouldn't give me a license or even a permit until we had all the paperwork.

Mama sighed. If she didn't need her meds, if Dad weren't traveling for business, if there was anyone she could call to pick up her prescription, she wouldn't let me drive on my own. I got it.

"It's okay. I'll just go to the drugstore and come right back." I looked away. Mama was uncanny about reading a lie in my eyes, and I didn't want her to see the other plan lurking behind them.

I took the keys and jingled them, not noticing I was doing it until Mama winced. I shoved them in my pocket.

The room grew cold with the chill of the snow covering the tops of mountains so far away. It felt as though a part of me was trapped there in the orphanage, staring out the window, and I didn't know how to get that part back.

"Marin? Are you sure?" Mama asked. I usually told my mother everything.

But not about the mountains. And not about stealing time that I was supposed to be using to finish my summer reading list in order to see Lisa.

I leaned over the bed. "Of course, Mama," I whispered, and kissed her before heading to the door.

"Take care, polar bear," she croaked.

"Must disembark, aardvark," I replied as I had hundreds of times.

I drove slowly. Sticking to side streets. Thirty miles an hour tops. I didn't even turn on the radio.

Lisa Kilkenney's house was in the subdivision next to ours. Her door was pale green like the color of her eyes, and her mom's old car that sat dusty with end-of-summer pollen in the driveway.

She was just finishing washing the wheel wells when I drove up. I rolled down my window and called out, "I can ask Mom to let me help you with that after we get back."

She shook her head and said, "It's okay. I got it," just like I knew she would. She loved old cars and caring for old cars, and, though we hadn't said it yet, I kind of hoped she loved me.

She dried her hands and got in the car, and then all was right with the world.

They don't teach you how to drive one-handed in Driver's Ed. They don't teach you how to focus on the road when the girl you're falling in love with is sitting right next to you and her perfume is making your head spin back to mountains and mountains and mountains.

"I only have an hour," I reminded her out loud, but really I was reminding myself. "That's fifteen minutes there, and fifteen back. And I can say there was a line."

"It's better than not an hour." Lisa squeezed my hand. My stomach, or maybe it was my heart, lurched as if I'd eaten something that was looking for escape.

Morris Grocery was out on Smithton Road. There were closer pharmacies, but I was lucky that Mom had been using this one since it was closest to her office.

When I thought about it later, I didn't know if I had seen the family that was begging at the edge of the parking lot when we pulled in. I think maybe I saw the streetlights, the kids riding their bikes on the grass median, the way it looked like it might rain but then again like it might not.

All I know is that my attention was on the heat of Lisa's skin, the way my heart was beating frantically out of time, the too-fast tick of the watch on my wrist—a present from Dad on my sixteenth.

In the store, I dropped off Mama's new prescription.

In the produce aisle, we tried grapes that tasted like cotton candy and apples that tasted like grapes, and I took a small toothpick of sample cheesecake and placed it in Lisa's mouth like a sacred offering.

We talked about school. An upcoming dance. The latest episode of our mutually favorite TV show.

I looked at our hands, hers so light in mine, and wondered: if we had kids, what color would their skin be? Would they have her green eyes, or was it only possible that my darker features would take over? We'd talked about dominant and recessive genes in bio, but I didn't remember how it worked.

Too soon, my name came over the intercom. Too soon, we paid for Mama's prescription and wandered back to the car. Too soon, we were leaving.

"That's so sad," Lisa said, pointing out the window at a family of beggars hanging out near the side of the parking lot. A woman sitting cross-legged under a tree with a baby on the ground propped up against the trunk.

Blink.

"Do you ever wonder what it'd be like? To have to ask other people for all the things you need?"

Blink.

I slowed the car to get a better look at the mother. She was staring at a cell phone and fumbling with a cigarette. The baby was crying, but no one was paying attention.

Blink.

Lisa grabbed the wheel and twisted it. I slammed my foot on the brake before I had time to think about it. A boy had jumped out in front of my car, but I didn't even see him.

Now he stood in front of my hood laughing.

I jumped out of the car. "What the hell are you doing?"

He smiled a lazy smile, the type I'd seen on some of the kids at school. Leering. Slow. Deliberate.

"Hey, can you help us?" he asked, only his tone made it

more of a demand than a question. "My mom needs money to feed my little brother."

I looked over the boy's shoulder. The woman I assumed was his mother smiled at me from where she sat, looking unbothered about the fact that her kid had just run in front of my car. It wasn't a "please help me" smile. It was a challenge that wrapped itself around her face like her lips wrapped around the cigarette in her hand. Next to her sat a full, stickered carton. I didn't say the obvious, that she could feed her kids with what cigarettes cost these days.

Oblivious, the baby stuck a handful of dirt in its mouth.

"Sorry, I can't," I said. "Not today. But . . ." I rustled through my pockets and came up with a hard mint I'd taken from the little glass bowl at the pharmacy counter, "Can he have this?" I asked the woman.

She gestured for me to give it to her, so I leaned over and placed it in her dirty palm.

She held it up by the plastic and examined it before throwing it in the grass.

"What we really need is money," the boy said. He'd taken a step toward me and was standing too close. I moved back. Now I could see that he was around my age. Older maybe, but only just.

"That's all I have," I shrugged. From my pocket, my phone buzzed. "Sorry." I moved toward the car where Lisa waited. I had to get her home and then get the car back before Mama freaked.

The boy gave me the finger as I pulled away.

◇◇◇◇

To: MountainBoy@me.com
From: Yuri.Guryev@birthsearch.ru

You are correct. We do birth family searches using

local investigators. You have not told me what region your search would need to occur in, or even your name. Please be aware that we do not operate in the United States.

Our fee is $500. For that, we hope to supply whatever data we can find, including video interviews with family members.

Best,
Yuri

◇◇◇◇

After I gave Mama her medicine and made her a cup of tea, I sat in my room, staring at my phone. It wasn't the $500 that had me freaked out—every birthday and Christmas, I'd divvied my gifts into piles: Spend, Donate, Save. I'd put aside the money I'd made shoveling snow and mowing lawns and running errands. I had more than $500 in the bank.

What got to me was "video interviews." The idea that I would not only get photos, but also hear the voices of my Eastern European . . . I didn't know what to call them. Family felt wrong. But out there somewhere were people. People I was related to. A woman who had walked around pregnant with me.

Mama and Dad hadn't shared details about why I was put up for adoption. But I'm sure they knew. I caught the look between them when I asked a few years ago, and I suspected then that they'd never tell me.

There were sites on the Internet that showed pictures of available babies. I didn't understand how you could give up a kid regardless, but the one thing Mama had talked about when I was eight and trying to wrap my head around it all was how different cultures had different superstitions and forms of discrimination about unwed mothers as well as disabilities.

I wasn't disabled, and my faults weren't unusual. I sucked

at algebra. My room was a mess. I spent too much time dicking around on the Internet. I played my stereo too loud.

But my birth family wouldn't have known about any of those. Maybe they weren't married? Were too poor? Too young?

I'd been wondering about these things for so long, and now I finally had the chance to get answers.

But I was afraid, too. What if there were things wrong with me that were just waiting under the surface? Things I didn't even know about? I'd read that there were forms of mental illness that were hereditary but didn't show up until you were an adult. I'd read that eighteen is like some magic age for the onset of schizophrenia, and my birthday was only a couple of months away.

I could already be sick and not even know it. Maybe that's what the whole deal with the mountains was.

That was part of the reason I'd never mentioned my plans to anyone. There was no way I was going to tell Mama and Dad that I was even considering this. And my few close friends just didn't, couldn't, get it. I mean, how could I even expect them to? Danny's parents and grandparents and most of his aunts, uncles, and cousins, all lived within a fifteen-minute drive of each other. Louis's parents were divorced, but that just meant that he spent the school year here with his mom and stepfather and his two brothers, and vacations and summers in Seattle with his dad, *his* wife, and her daughters. Even Lisa . . .

The weird thing was that Lisa was adopted, too. But when her moms decided to have a kid, they put an ad in a magazine and found a couple who needed someone to raise their baby. Then they had a "semi-open adoption," which meant that her moms and her birth family exchanged Christmas and birthday cards, and they all got together at the beach once a year in the summer.

I loved Mama and Dad. And they loved me; I'd never had a reason to doubt that. So I didn't understand this unshakable curiosity. This hole in me. These dreams of mountains.

Did I have family—brothers and sisters, maybe—who were looking at those snowcapped peaks right now? Was anyone out there wondering what had happened to me? Would I ever know?

◇◇◇◇

To: Yuri.Guryev@birthsearch.ru
From: MountainBoy@me.com

My name is Marin and I was adopted from Eastern Europe, but . . . is it okay if I don't tell you more until I hire you?

◇◇◇◇

That night I dreamt about the family of beggars. In my dream, the boy grabbed my arm and shoved it next to his, saying, "Look, we're the same."

I couldn't say anything back because he was right. Our skin colors matched. And when I looked into his eyes, I saw that the shapes were identical.

In the morning I texted Lisa to ask if she would take me back to the store. To the lot. To the family.

I told her about the dream I'd had. Then I told her the part of my fear I thought I could talk about. I asked while she drove, "What if I'm related to them? To this family?" even though that wasn't really something I thought possible. "I mean, they're kind of awful."

Lisa shrugged, and her hands tightened on the wheel. "Yeah, but . . . I don't know. Maybe they just need help?"

I thought of the boy jumping in front of Mom's car. The sneer in his eyes. The mother tossing away the candy.

"Well, they sure have a funny way of asking for it."

Lisa was quiet until we pulled off the freeway. "Believe me, I get why you want to find your birth family," she said. "But I don't understand how these people have anything to do with that. And you need to be careful, Marin. This stuff is harder than you think. I grew up knowing my birth family. I still get angry at them for giving me up, even though I wouldn't change anything now." I squeezed her hand and said, "I know," although I wasn't sure I really did. I loved my parents. My grandparents. My life. Wanting answers and wanting to change things were totally different.

The family was in the parking lot, just like last time. I asked Lisa to park in front of the store while I ran in and grabbed a couple of sandwiches, some bottled water, and a banana for the baby.

When I came out, Lisa looked at the bag in my hand. "I get what you're trying to do. I really do. But maybe it would be better to give them info for a shelter or something? That's what my moms tell me to do."

"It's just food." My muscles tensed. The bag was suddenly impossibly heavy. I shrugged. "Besides, I already bought this stuff. I might as well give it to them."

The boy saw me coming and walked over. Swaggered, really. "You bring us some more candy?" he asked.

I closed my eyes. Inhaled to get my bearings. What if my birth family was poor? Begging. What would I want someone to do?

I thrust the bag toward him. "I brought you some food."

His mother sucked on another cigarette. She didn't look interested.

The boy dug his hand into the bag and pulled out an orange. "You really aren't getting this." He bounced the fruit up and down in his hand.

I could hear his accent now. His mother yelled something at him and he responded. I couldn't figure out what language they were speaking, yet somehow it sounded familiar.

I leaned in and grabbed the fruit from him before it bruised. "Where do you live, anyhow?"

"I didn't know that I invited you over for dinner . . ." he said.

Next to me, Lisa quietly said, "Marin, let's just go. I don't think they want your help."

She was probably right, but I couldn't bring myself to walk away.

"The world, man. We're citizens of the world," the boy said, his eyes slowly traveling across Lisa's body.

And that's all it took. I turned and walked away. Taking the bag with me.

◇◇◇◇

To: MountainBoy@me.com
From: Yuri.Guryev@birthsearch.ru

Marin, in this process you should feel free to tell me only the things that you wish to share. If/when you decide to hire me though, I'm sure you'll understand that the more information you share, the more we will have to go on.

There is, of course, no guarantee that your birth family will be found and if that happens there will be no fee. People move. Change their names. There are many ways to stay hidden.

◇◇◇◇

June 22 was our "gotcha day." At least that's what my parents called it in honor of the day they "got me." Every year, we celebrated the day the same way. My mom made a giant crème brûlée and dragged out the photos they'd taken at the orphanage.

"I wonder what happened to Simon," she'd muse about the little boy with the toothy grin who had been my closest friend, even though I didn't remember him.

"Should we send a photo, Marin?" my dad would ask.

For the first couple of years after I was home, my parents had to file a report letting the orphanage know that I was being well taken care of. They hadn't needed to do that in a long time. But some years we still sent a letter, photos, news about the first (and only) all-A report card I earned, a photo of me on my junior high baseball team.

I wasn't sure what I had to prove or whom I was proving it to. I didn't remember much about the staff in the orphanage or whether they were even still there. But the whole thing seemed to make my dad happy and proud. And some years that was reason enough.

But this year, I wasn't sure. As I flipped through my mother's scrapbook ("Look! Here's the plane ticket you used to come home." "Here's you and that stuffed elephant we brought. Do you remember?"), I noticed the background more than I had before. The peeling paint on the door of the orphanage. The Soviet-era statues, covered in graffiti around town. The mountains.

And in a few of the city scenes, the beggars. Obviously, it wasn't the boy and his family. I got that. But it could have been. It could have been my family. Birth family. Maybe.

"Marin?"

I looked up at my father and his concern. I didn't know what to do. Not about the photos. Not about the begging family. Not about the search.

He looked at me as if he could read my confusion. "We can skip the photo this year," he said and closed the album. "Let's go set fire to the brûlée."

I thought about the phrase the investigator had used: *ways to stay hidden*. Maybe my birth family wouldn't want information about me anyhow. Maybe they wouldn't want to share their own. After all, they had to figure that they'd never hear from or about me again when they gave me up, right? Maybe that's what they were counting on.

But then I thought of Lisa's birth family. Her birth mom had been just sixteen and already looking out for a younger sister because her own mom worked two jobs. Back then, her birth dad didn't even know he'd gotten someone pregnant.

Now, everyone claims to love those summer mixed-family trips together, although Lisa admits they're kind of strange. She has a stepbrother on her birth mother's side and two little twin sisters on her birth father's, but she only sees them once a year, so . . .

Maybe something like that happened with my birth family. Maybe they wanted to keep me, but couldn't.

And I love my parents, so maybe it doesn't matter.

Maybe.

Regardless of what I was doing—summer reading; helping Mom build a raised garden bed; riding my bike to Lisa's and sitting on her back porch, making out until we lost track of time—I couldn't get that boy, that family out of my head.

Every time I spaced out; every time I forgot to pick something up that my mom had asked me for; every time I dreamed of those damned mountains, I wondered what type of screwed-up inheritance might be waiting for me.

It was a vicious circle, the wondering and the fear.

I told Mama I was okay. I told Dad I was okay. But when they both sat me down and gently suggested that maybe, perhaps, we might want to "talk to someone" about how distracted I'd been, I knew I had to act.

I needed to go back and see that family. I couldn't figure out how to wrangle the car from Mom, and I didn't want to ask Lisa, but eventually I had no choice. And I think Lisa got it, because she didn't question me when I asked her to drive, except to ask what I planned to do.

I couldn't explain the dread and fear that something might be wrong with me. I couldn't explain how this boy made me feel like I was looking into some sort of twisted mirror.

So I shrugged and asked her to park and wait while I ducked into the store.

I hesitated as I started to walk out. The $260 (the ATM only gave out twenty-dollar bills) felt conspicuous and surprisingly heavy in my pocket.

I didn't hear the boy come up behind me until he whispered, "Looking for me?"

I turned and stumbled. "No. I mean—"

He laughed a sound tinged with something other than amusement. My stomach clenched.

"Look. I was going to use my money for . . ." I stopped. No way was I going to tell him. "something else. But . . . I'll give it to you if it will help. I mean, you could get a hotel room for a couple of nights or some real food or—"

The boy cocked his head at me. "Why?"

"Why what?"

"Why do you want to help so bad? You got it good. You feeling guilt or something?"

If I couldn't tell Lisa the truth, there was no way I was going to tell him. And the more I thought about my fears and how they were tangled up, the more I realized that I couldn't have told him even if I wanted to.

I took a deep breath and closed my eyes, my hand wrapped around the money in my pocket. If I gave this boy my money, I wasn't going to be able to hire the investigator. Not for a long time, anyhow.

And so I wouldn't know if I was going to be okay. But then I might not know anyhow.

I took out all the money except for one twenty. "I just want to help," I said. "Like my parents helped me."

The boy looked at the bills in my hand, one eyebrow raised, and licked his lips. Greedy. Predatory. Challenging.

I pushed it toward him. "Take it."

He hesitated.

"Take it," I said again, and then, "and stop jumping in front of people's cars."

He grabbed it quickly and shoved it into his pocket. Then he turned and walked away without even a thank-you.

I went back into the store and spent my final twenty on two bouquets. One for Lisa and one for Mama. Then I went home.

◇◇◇◇

To: Yuri.Guryev@birthsearch.ru
From: MountainBoy@me.com

Mr. Guryev—I've decided not to look for my birth family now. I thought I wanted to. I thought I needed to. I thought . . . well, I just had a lot of questions. But right now, I'm not sure they're questions I really need answers to.

If it's okay, I'll hang on to your address in case I want to look for them later.

◇◇◇◇

That night, I didn't dream of mountains. I dreamed something I thought I'd forgotten a long time ago. The plane ride to the United States from the orphanage. Mama sitting on one side of me. Dad on the other. The sound of the engines starting up, and Mama whispering quietly in my ear, "This is it. This is the start of the rest of your life. You are loved."

Helene Dunbar is the author of *These Gentle Wounds* (Flux, 2014), *What Remains* (Flux, 2015), and *Boomerang* (Sky Pony, 2017). Over the years, she's worked as a drama critic, journalist, and marketing manager, and she has written on topics as diverse as Irish music, court cases, theater, and Native American Indian tribes. She lives in Nashville with her husband and daughter and exists on a steady diet of readers' tears.

"As an adoptive parent to a daughter from Eastern Europe, I am a firm believer that families are created by the affection in your heart and not only by the DNA in your blood. Love is love is love, and you are blessed by its gift, regardless of by which means it finds you."

Webbed

by Julie Eshbaugh

Miranda held the sealed letter loosely in her fingers, trying not to let her damp palms dimple the paper. The sea breeze stirred her hair, raising goose bumps at the back of her neck. She'd dragged a beach chair to the edge of the boardwalk, and her feet were propped on the railing, the thongs of her hot pink flip-flops—her first-ever pair—wedged between her newly separated toes.

Miranda hadn't always known her feet were special. It wasn't until she was four years old, clutching her dad's hand and splashing in the tide pools with a girl she had just met, that it first came to her attention. "Why are your feet weird like that?" the girl—red haired and smudged with freckles, reeking of coconut sunblock—had asked. Miranda had peered through the warm puddle and seen her webbed toes as if for the first time.

She hadn't known how to answer, so she'd flicked water with her weird foot at the girl's gaping face and run away.

"You inherited your special feet from your birth mother," Daddy had said, once he'd coaxed her out of the gloom that blanketed the sand beneath the boardwalk. She'd hated it under there—it was cold and damp and smelled like a pail of fish—but she had always been stubborn. She would have stayed there all day if Daddy hadn't offered to buy her a cone and tell her a story. As they sat on the picnic bench outside the DQ, she'd glanced down at the pink bead of melted strawberry soft serve that had dripped onto her big toe, a membrane of skin holding it tight against its neighbor. "It's a secret, and you must not tell anyone, but your birth mother was a mermaid princess. She fell in love with a common land dweller, and he loved her, too, so much that you were born. But the mermaid princess couldn't stay on land, so she had to give you to someone who would love you and take care of you. That's how Mommy and I came to adopt you."

Miranda licked a long drip from the side of her hand. "Is that the truth?" she'd asked.

"It can be a kind of truth, if we want it to be," Daddy had said. "It can be our truth." Miranda had heard this, but she would not remember it. She would remember only that Daddy had said it was the truth. Her weird feet weren't weird at all. They were a mark of her royal mermaid birth.

And so began the mermaid years.

Miranda's adoptive mother, an art school grad who had once harbored dreams of a career as an illustrator before earning her master's in mechanical engineering, painted blue waves capped with white seafoam on the walls of Miranda's room. When Miranda was eight, there were seashells on her bedding. When she was twelve, there was swim team practice every day before dawn. Miranda was a star swimmer. She could hold her breath longer and extend her kick farther than any other girl Coach had ever trained.

"It's those webbed toes. She's more adapted to the water than the other girls," Coach would joke, gripping Miranda's shoulders with two large scaly hands. The other girls would turn quiet and tense, but Miranda would shake it off.

"I guess I am," she would say.

At night, Miranda would take out a secret journal decorated with the words "Miranda the Mermaid" written with an aquamarine gel pen in her best curly script. Most of the pages were covered with small grids she'd drawn to fill with her times at practices and larger grids in red pen for times at meets and what ribbons she'd won, but a few pages in the back were reserved for drawings. Miranda would spend hours creating detailed images with colored pencils: coral reefs, schools of fish, and a woman with long, soft hair that floated like a fan around her face. Miranda treasured the secret of the mermaid mother because it was hers alone—never spoken out loud, not even to Daddy—and so the secret was left undisturbed, unchallenged, and unexamined, even as she grew older.

Until the day the letter came.

Her father was the one who appeared at the door of her room with the ivory envelope in his hands. It looked delicate and small in his large palms, like it was made of eggshells. When he handed it to Miranda, though, it transformed into something big and weighty. Though the outside was completely blank, it was somehow ominous, and she let it tumble onto her desktop, where it landed with a thud.

"What's this?" Miranda asked. Yet somehow, she knew.

"It came from the agency," he said, staring down at the envelope as if it were an animal playing dead that might spring up and attack. "They forwarded it on behalf of your birth mother."

The envelope—clean, dry, common—lay on her desk like a silent accusation. Miranda wanted to yell at her father, *How can this be from my birth mother?* But she stayed silent. She didn't need to ask, because she knew. The answer had been there for a long time. Miranda had simply turned her head and looked away whenever the shadow of the truth crept into view.

That night, with only the plastic seashell night-light illuminating the room, Miranda lay on top of her covers and studied the silhouetted shape of her naked feet. The room was frigid cold—the AC was blowing hard through the vent—but she would not climb into her bed or even pull on a pair of socks. Her feet somehow appeared different than they had appeared every night before that night, as if they had somehow betrayed her and become something strange and unfamiliar while she'd been distracted by other things.

In the morning, Miranda tucked the letter—still unopened—inside her swimsuit drawer. Her feet were now covered in socks, and as she walked to the breakfast table, she noticed that the socks felt too tight, as if her toes were bound and she ached to stretch them. She poured a bowl of Frosted Flakes and said, without looking up, "I'd like to see a doctor about my feet."

Her parents agreed without argument, causing Miranda to wonder if they'd expected this day to come all along.

It wasn't until the night before the surgery that Miranda spoke to her father. It was raining hard outside her window, an early summer soaking, and she'd gotten out of bed and crept to the family room. She'd found her father sitting beside the aquarium in his pajamas, watching the plastic mermaid bob up and down in the bubbles.

"Can't sleep?" she asked. "Me neither." She settled down on the arm of the big leather chair he sat in.

"If you're scared, it's okay. You can still call it off. No one's making you do this."

"But I want to do it," Miranda said. "I'm ready." Then she added in a whisper, "I need to let go of the mermaid mother." To Miranda's surprise, her voice broke on the last word. "But it's so hard. I've held on to her so long."

"Have you opened the letter?"

Miranda shook her head. "It wouldn't be fair. I need to let go of the lie first."

Miranda's father wrapped an arm around her. He smelled like fabric softener. "I didn't mean to lie. I'm so sorry."

"It wasn't a lie," Miranda said. "It was a game." She said

this, though she didn't really mean it. Like him, she was lying to protect someone she loved.

Her postsurgical limitations weren't very restrictive, though she found them almost intolerable. *No swimming in the ocean* and *no flip-flops* until her toes were healed. She spent too much time in her room, glaring at the waves on the walls and the still-sealed envelope on her desk. Her father knocked at the door one day and found her sitting, staring at the ivory square. He handed her a few sheets of pale blue stationery and a navy blue envelope.

"In case you want to write back," he said, and then slipped away.

Miranda stared at the paper. Her father was right. She needed to write a letter. But not to the woman whose letter still lay sealed on her desk. She dug into the drawer that held her journal, neglected since the day she decided to see the surgeon, and pulled out an aquamarine gel pen. She would write a practice draft in this book before copying it onto the pretty paper from her father.

Sitting up tall at her desk, she turned to a page beside the colored pencil drawings of the mermaid world, and the words poured onto the page.

Dear Mermaid Mother,

I'm writing to say good-bye. And to say thank you.

Thank you for the time I beat Brittany O'Neal in the 100-meter freestyle when no one thought I could.

Thank you for the time Ryan Kimble called me a freak and stomped on my bare foot at the playground, and I didn't even cry, and Alyssa Anderson said that I was really cool.

Thank you for every other time I was scared and

wanted my parents but they couldn't be there. Thank you for being there when no one else could be.

I'll miss you so much.

Love,
Miranda

◇◇◇◇

From her chair on the boardwalk, Miranda gazed over the navy blue envelope at her bright pink flip-flops. She climbed to her feet. The thongs felt odd between her toes, but there was no pain. Her feet were healed.

The beach was empty except for one man with a dog and a ball. The season wouldn't start for another two weeks. The water would be almost unbearably cold.

Almost.

Miranda placed the sealed envelope on the seat. The breeze gusted as she slid out of her shorts, folded them, and left them on the chair with her flip-flops and towel. Taking the envelope with her, she climbed through the railings, hopped off the boardwalk, and ran across the sand to the water's edge. She was in the waves, the letter still in her hand, before she could give the plan a second thought.

The water was cold—so cold her heart pounded in her chest, but the farther out she swam, the warmer she felt. She dove into wave after wave, her eyes opened to the green murky darkness, searching. She saw nothing but tangled seaweed and the sandy bottom and broken seashells stuck in the ocean floor.

She swam a long time, until the waves no longer crashed over her head. The water around her shoulders was quiet and calm when she finally stopped to tread water and look back.

Something in Miranda's stomach wriggled when she saw how far out she'd swum. She was startled but not scared, though she knew she was farther out than she'd ever gone before. The letter was still in its navy blue envelope, still clutched in her cramping fingers. She tipped her head back to let the water cover her ears and listened to the hum of the sea as the sun warmed her face. Then she drew in a huge breath and swam down, far under the surface, and opened her eyes.

At first it was as it always was: green water, the sun-brightened surface, the shadowed sea floor. A fast-moving fish too far away to see. As she stared through the gloom, straining to make out its silver scales, Miranda's lungs began to burn. She ached to kick for the surface. She almost did.

Then all at once she saw it.

A castle of coral loomed up from the bottom, its spires reaching through the darkness. Its sudden appearance didn't frighten Miranda—it was as if she'd always known she would find it. Every color from her pencil box was there in the castle walls—blue, pink, lavender. A garland of aquamarine fluttered from pillars that framed the round door.

The open round door.

Like the mouth of a cave cut in rock, the door stood gaping wide, waiting for her to come home. Home to her heritage in the sea.

Home to her mermaid mother.

Miranda stared at the open door, marveling at the way light seemed to glow from inside. Her lungs strained, and cold soaked into her bones. It would be warm inside. Miranda swam farther down, kicking hard. She had wanted this for so long, and now it was so close.

One final time, Miranda turned her eyes up to the surface. Far above, the sun was a smear of gold. Her pulse pounded in her ears. Miranda remembered the letter, soggy and soft, still held in her tight fist.

She looked at it. Remembered what it said. And let go.

For a moment it hovered, suspended in the sea right in

front of her eyes. Then she kicked as hard as she could for the surface, never looking back at the letter or the castle below.

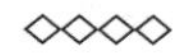

Air had never tasted as good to Miranda as it did when she broke through and drew her first breath. The touch of it was warm and soft. Breathing it in felt like coming home.

Climbing out of the waves a few minutes later, Miranda found her legs were weak and wobbly, as if they were new. She stepped carefully up onto the sand. For the first time since she was very small, she was happy to get out of the water. To let the sea shed from her skin.

Back at her chair, Miranda slid into her shorts and slipped the flip-flops back onto her feet. She wrapped the towel around her hair to keep the cold drips from running down her neck. Before she sat, she pulled a second envelope from her shorts pocket.

She propped her feet back on the railing. They glowed white with cold, and she watched as warm color returned to her toes, threaded once again through the thongs of the bright pink flip-flops.

She turned the ivory envelope in her damp hands and slid a finger under the seal.

Julie Eshbaugh is the author of *Ivory and Bone* (HarperCollins, 2016). She used to have trouble staying in one spot, having lived in places as varied as Utah, France, and New York City. Julie eventually returned home to the Philadelphia area, where she now lives with her husband, son, cat, and dog. Her favorite moments are when the unexpected happens, and she cheers loudest when the pitcher gets a hit.

"The first line of Anna Karenina says, 'Happy families are all alike; every unhappy family is unhappy in its own way.' That's a great line, but I disagree. All families are unique! In my experience, adoptive families are just as varied as other families, with all the love, devotion, sacrifice, guilt, and every other good and bad thing that comes along with being part of a clan. As an adoptee, I'm grateful for what adoption has done for me. I'm also grateful for the opportunity to be a part of this anthology, to help share the many unique stories of adoption."

Life: Starring Tallulah Grey

by Lauren Gibaldi

I feel him behind me, hovering closely. I hear the soft sound of his arm stretching out to grab me. Before his dead fingers have the chance to graze my skin, I whip around, stake in hand and ready to strike.

"You wouldn't," he sneers, blood still trickling down his lips from his last meal. I didn't know her, but she didn't deserve to die the way she did. No one does.

"I would," I respond, and in one swift move I punch my stake into his heart, ensuring he won't strike again. He falls to the ground, and as I wait for the explosion of dust and remains, I stare at him. I watch the entire time, not once giving in to the lump rising in my throat, the strain in my heart.

"Cut!" Michael calls from his director's seat. "Perfect! That's a wrap for today."

Exhaling with relief—and feeling that quick transition from character to actor—I reach down and help Oliver up. He's covered in fake blood and now has my stake sticking out of his chest.

"Nice stab," Oliver says, wiping some blood off his mouth and removing the stake.

"Nice death," I respond.

"Well, for now," he says with a smirk. His character has died seven times since the first season started, including the initial time when he became a vampire. He'll be back soon enough. That wasn't even the season finale.

"Tally, Oliver, great job. You guys are good until Monday," Michael calls to us. "Wrap for Sebastian and Ariel for this episode," he announces to the rest of the room.

"Awesome," I call back, giving him a thumbs-up. "Shall we?" I ask Oliver, signaling toward the exit. He nods in response, and we walk out of the fake forests of Savannah, Georgia—deep, impossibly green trees and the occasional sound of cicadas, all re-created by an actual Georgia transplant—and into the not-as-magical Los Angeles soundstage.

We round the back of the studio to our trailers and stop just in front. He raises an eyebrow at me and I shake my head, smiling. Every day he jokingly tries to get me back into his trailer; every day I remind him to keep it professional. I mean, as professional as vampire-slaying, on-and-off-screen lovers can be.

"Fine," he sighs dramatically. "What are we doing tonight?" He pushes his black hair back, smearing the fake blood along his forehead. My heart still flips at the "we" because it's still so new.

"I don't know . . . I mean, I'd like to go out, but . . ."

"Yeah, I know." He looks down, and then back up. "Wanna try?"

"It's a Friday night," I point out, leaning back onto my trailer. It's the one thing I've struggled with since being cast in *Thirst.* I love it, I love every minute of acting in it, but my life outside TV has taken a dive. Every time I go anywhere, I'm swarmed with paparazzi or fans. I love the fans, and I can handle them—I mean, they make my career possible—but the paparazzi are infuriating. I can't even buy milk from the grocery store without them making some sort of a story about it. *"Is she gaining weight? Is she pregnant?"* Oliver has it just as bad—if he's even talking to a girl, he's automatically dating her. Once they linked him with his cousin. HIS COUSIN. I mean, it was bad before we were dating. Now it's worse.

"Come on," he says, leaning up against his trailer next to me and taking my hand in his. "It could be an adventure." He grins, and despite the graying makeup that makes him look dead, I can see the spark in his black eyes. And I know before I say anything that I'm going to give in.

"Oh, fine," I relent, shaking my head. "But if I'm chased out of a bathroom again, I'm ratting you out."

"Oh, yeah? And what would you say?"

I think quickly. "That you snore."

"Too ordinary."

"That you sleep with a night-light on."

"Girls would find it adorable," he grins.

"That you've got a big personality, but a tiny—"

"I hate you."

"No, you don't." I push myself off the trailer. "Okay, give me an hour to shower and get your blood off me."

"Admit it—you love being caked in my blood," he taunts.

"You are so weird."

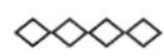

Thirst started a year and a half ago, and almost instantly it became a hit. We weren't sure if it would, with all of the other vampire competition, but somehow ours worked. I think it's the satirical nature of it. We've got great effects and scary moments, but it's still pretty funny. Like, we know how ridiculous the whole thing is—vampires in high school and all. And it's been a fantastic experience playing Ariel, the vampire slayer to Oliver's vampire. They're doomed lovers of sorts, since she frequently has to kill him. I mean, he's a bad guy, after all, and no amount of steamy make-out sessions can let her ignore that fact.

I pick up my phone before leaving my trailer and see that I have a missed call from The Number. My heart jumps, as it always does, but I click it off and shove the phone in my pocket, ignoring the call as I have the last seven hundred times or so. I still don't know what to do about it, so I'm ignoring it until I do. It's easier that way.

Oliver is scrolling through his phone when I step out, and even after all this time, I still get excited to see him. Not like the other girls, the fans who think he's just hot—and he is—but in a different, more personal way. He knows me better than most people, which I suppose is expected since we work together every day, but still. It's gotten to the point where we'll drive and he'll know where I want to go without me telling him.

He catches my eye as I meet him by his trailer and smiles. "Where do you want to go?"

"Um . . . how about that new Mexican place Michael told us about? It's not cool yet."

"Which means it'll be dead or slammed."

"Let's hope for dead?"

He nods, adding, "I can always go for burritos."

He puts his arm over my shoulder, and we walk to the parking lot behind us. "I'll drive." He lets go of my shoulder and opens the door to the passenger side of his jeep. The sky is just starting to change as he pulls out, deepening from the light blue it was to a purple hue, and though I try to wipe the thought of The Number out of my mind, it keeps coming back. I roll down the window to let out my thoughts as we drive in silence. It's one of those evenings where talking isn't required; the sound of the wind blowing in through the windows is enough. I look at Oliver and know he's thinking the same thing when he smiles and slows down. A song plays on the radio. I can't place it, but its quietness speaks volumes.

We park in a lot a street down, and look up. A billboard for *Thirst*'s second season hangs above us, showing Oliver embracing me from behind, leaning down to bite my neck, while I look straight out with a smirk, holding a stake close. The session went for two hours, and it was the first shot they ended up going with. We started dating two days later.

"I still can't get used to that," Oliver says, putting his hands in his pockets as he looks up at us.

"Yeah." Taking in the billboard, I feel so visible, so out there. For everyone to see. For everyone to find. No matter how much time has passed, it still seems surreal to me. "Me either."

We cross a small street, and once we hit the sidewalk, we hear our names called out. I instinctively look back.

"Oliver! Tallulah!"

Oliver swears, then grabs my arm, pulling me forward. "Already?"

"Ol, let's just pose quickly, get it over with. Then they'll leave and we can eat."

"No, because then they'll call their friends. Just keep walking." He lets go of my arm, careful not to be too touchy in public. We never confirmed dating rumors, but people assumed, especially when photos of us kissing in a secluded area of a beach surfaced. We thought we were alone. We were wrong.

We swing around the corner, and in front of the restaurant is a slew of photographers taking pictures of the newest YouTube singer turned pop star who's posing with fans. Apparently, we aren't the only ones who thought of going for Mexican food.

"I told you this was a bad idea," I sigh, frustrated and feeling exposed.

Behind us, the other photographer catches up. "Tallulah, what do you think about—"

"And I told you there'd be an adventure," Oliver says,

cutting off the photographer, but not before I heard the word "mom."

"Wait, what did—"

"In here." Oliver grabs my arm and pulls me into a Vietnamese restaurant.

We burst through the doors making much more of a scene than intended. My face flushes from embarrassment, and I guiltily slink to a table in the corner with Oliver following and chuckling as quite a few eyes follow us, and phones start to light up.

"I think our cover is blown," he says when we sit down.

"We were doomed from the start," I say, picking up my menu and then putting it back down. "Hey, did you hear what that photographer said?"

He sighs. "No, probably something to get a rise out of us. Like always."

"Yeah," I say, nodding, but something still doesn't sit right with me. Did he say "mom?"

"Let's just eat and get this over with."

I glare at him. "Glad you're looking forward to eating with me."

He looks up and his face softens. "You know what I mean."

"I do." I smile, shaking away the previous questions. I look around and see the gaping looks, hear the whispers, and note the texts being sent. I know that if I check Twitter now, there'd be mention of us here. There might be photos and details about every movement we make. The visibility is startling. I consciously pick up my phone and see a missed call from my agent, but no message, so I assume it's not important. Then I see that The Number called again, too. She never calls this many times in a row. I shake my head and then look up at Oliver.

"All okay?" he asks.

"Just looking." I shrug, leaving my phone on the table. If she calls again, I'll decide what to do. Maybe.

"Welcome to Pho 22." A waitress says as she materializes beside us and greets Oliver, not me. "Can I get you anything?"

"One Coke, a water, and spring rolls to start," I say, ordering for the two of us, trying to see if she'll, for a second, look away from Oliver. She glances quickly, and then meets my eyes again and recognition crosses her face. She nods, then backs away, disappointed I'm sure that Oliver brought a date, and the date was me.

"I think you have an admirer," I say, not sourly.

"I love that you ordered for me," he says.

"Sorry. Just trying to get her attention."

"Don't be sorry. The assertiveness . . . it was hot."

"So it really is my vampire-slaying skills that attracted you?" I lean forward on my crossed arms, and he smiles. I sometimes wonder what he sees in me, compared with Every Other Girl that wants to be with him. Why me? But then I see that look and I shake away my worries and thoughts because for some reason he made up his mind, and I like the decision.

My phone rings again and I see that it's my agent. Again.

"It's Tracey," I sigh, and he gestures for me to take it because he understands.

I pick up my phone, hoping for good news but knowing it's probably not that. "Hey, Tracey."

"Dammit, Tally, there you are."

My pulse speeds up in fear. "What's going on?" I look at my phone and see that it wasn't one call I missed from Tracey, but several. Seven, to be exact.

"Where have you been? Why haven't you been answering your phone? Doesn't matter. I'm going to ask you a question and I need you to be honest with me."

Dread comes over me as I slowly answer, "Okay. . ."

"Are you adopted, and if so, has your birth mother been contacting you?"

My heart jumps as I gasp. I flick my eyes to Oliver, but he's looking down at his phone. I try to slow my racing pulse, but I can't. So I breathe in and slowly nod, answering, "Yes. To both."

She sighs, disappointed. "Why haven't you told me?"

"It's kind of personal." With that, Oliver looks over at me, worried. "Wait, how do you know?"

"Everyone knows. Your mom just went to TMZ."

"My mom? Wait, what?"

"Your mom, your birth mother, that woman trying to contact you. She went to TMZ and now everyone knows. She said she's been trying to get in touch with you for *months* and you're ignoring her. It's on all the blogs; they're all wondering why you don't want to talk her. Do you know how this makes you look?"

"No . . ." My heart starts racing again and I think back to the photographer. He did say "mom." I never thought it would come to this. This is something small, something personal, something I haven't wanted to deal with, which is why I haven't answered the calls. Why did she go to the news? Why has she needed to see me so badly, after all this time?

Tracey sighs again, frustrated. "To mothers you look like someone who's giving up on family. To adopted children, you look like someone who's embarrassed by that, which is why you've never mentioned it. To everyone, you just look like a liar."

"What? Why? I mean, this is *personal*, this isn't . . . this isn't . . ." I start to panic. My breath is coming in short bursts, tears springing up in my eyes. It was one thing for everyone to question my relationship with Oliver, but another for them to question and dissect something *I* don't even want to question and dissect. Something I kept private for a reason. I catch Oliver's eyes across the table and he mouths, "What is it?" but I can't answer. I can't even shake my head. I know I'm making a scene, but I can't calm down. I can't even think. I feel Oliver's arm around me and impulsively shrug him off, not wanting to be touched or comforted. Not wanting to be seen or heard or known. My eyes are blurry with tears.

"So you haven't spoken to her?"

"No! Not in about a year." I shake my head, as if she can see. "Why?"

Tracey sighs, as if bracing herself. Instinctively, I do the same. "It gets worse." She pauses. "You should probably hear this from her, but . . . she's sick. That's why she's contacting you."

I shake my head again and realize I haven't stopped, shock and weariness run through me.

"Wait, what?"

"She's severely sick. Apparently that's why she's been trying to see you. I don't know. Call her. Let her tell you."

"Tracey . . ." I start. I try not to let my mind go into the *what ifs* of it all. What if it's all a joke? What if it's not? What if, what if, what if.

"Let's meet in the morning and find a way," she says, her voice measured. "I'm only upset because I didn't know. And you know when I don't know about something, I don't know how to react right away. If I knew, I would have been prepared."

"I know," I say, sniffling. "I know."

"It'll be okay. We'll figure it out. And I'm sorry, for what it's worth."

"Okay."

I hang up and cover my face with my hands. I know she's going to be up all night, trying to spin this so I don't look like the complete jerk I'm being made out to be. I know she's going to work hard. But it's almost secondary to what she said. *Severely sick*. I've suddenly lost my appetite.

"Are you going to tell me what's wrong?" I take my hands away and look up. Oliver's still sitting beside me, and I'm reminded of shrugging him off, pushing him away when I needed the comfort. His arms are crossed and his eyes squinted, looking at me wearily. There's motion and action in the restaurant all around us, but it's as if we're frozen. I shake my head, then nod. I need to tell him. I need him to hear the whole story from *me,* not the press, not his agent, who I'm sure is about to call him. I feel naked, exposed. I can't imagine how I look in the photos people are taking now. How I'll look online. Honestly, at the moment, I don't care.

"Something personal about me leaked. . ."

He raises an eyebrow and sits up. I quickly backtrack. "About *me*, not *me and you*. And not me and someone else, don't worry."

He breathes out and drops his arms. "Sorry. When you start things like that, I'm just waiting for you to say you're seeing, like, seven other dudes or something."

I shake my head. Normally I'd quip back, but I don't have the energy. "It's a long story."

He leans forward, and I turn to look at him so our knees are touching. With his elbows perched on his knees, he gently touches my arm. "I've got all night."

"Okay," I brace myself, knowing I can trust him, but I still feel uncomfortable sharing. Because it's not how I wanted to tell him, not how I wanted it to all unfold. I wrap my hands in his. "I haven't really told people about this . . . not that I'm embarrassed by it, I'm just . . . I don't know, I don't like talking about it." I breathe in. "You know I was adopted, but you don't know the whole story. When I was two, I was put in foster care."

"Oh. Oh, wow."

"Yeah . . . um, I don't remember anything from then, but I know I lived with my mom before, and . . . it was a bad situation. Like really bad. So the state took me away and I lived with another family."

"Oh . . . Tally . . ." He squeezes my hands.

"No, it's okay. It was great, because that's my family now, you know? The ones you met. They became my parents; their kids became my siblings. I was welcomed in. I mean, I guess it was hard for them, I'm sure it was, but, yeah, I don't remember. I just know that I was happy there, and I still am. My family is great."

"Yeah, they are. So . . . what . . . that's what got out? That you're adopted? That's not bad."

"Yeah, that—which isn't bad—but also . . . my birth mother's been trying to get in touch with me."

"She has?"

"Yes."

"Really?"

"Yeah. . . ."

"What're you doing about it?"

"That's the thing. I've been ignoring her."

"Well, that's your right."

"Right, I know. That's what I thought."

"But . . ." he starts.

"But she went to TMZ."

"Are you shitting me?"

"No, that's what my agent just called to tell me."

"What the f—"

"I know," I cut him off.

"Why the hell would she do that? What does she want? Does she want money?" Anger starts to flood his face.

I breathe in, and tell him what Tracey told me. "Apparently she's sick. . ."

"Oh . . ." His face falls and mixes in a way that's undecipherable. Kind of like my feelings. "Is she okay?"

"I don't know. I don't know anything."

"What are you going to do?"

I sigh. "I'm terrified. I mean, I wasn't planning on talking to her. At least not until I knew what I wanted to say. But now I kind of have to."

"Screw that. You don't have to do anything you don't want to. Especially after this. What if she's not sick?"

"What if she is?" I shake my head, taking the thought away. Because what if she really is—what if I lose her before ever getting to know her? Or what if she isn't, and she's just lying to get to me? Which would be worse? "Apparently people are pissed."

"Like, fans and stuff? Why would they be pissed?"

"Fans? I don't know. Moms are mad I'm ignoring her. Adopted kids think I'm ashamed. It's all—"

"You're kidding? They're giving you crap for this? Do they even know the story?"

"No, and I don't want them to. This is my past. I don't want it on TMZ. And it already is. And I hate that." My face flushes.

"I'm sorry . . ." He calms down when he sees me start to panic, squeezing my hands again and pulling them toward him. Our knees bump, and if we were alone, I'd curl up in his lap, but we're not. So instead he cradles my face and kisses the top of my head. "I'm really, really sorry. What can we do?"

"I don't know." I sigh, sinking into his touch and then straightening up. "What is there to do?"

"Have you even met her before? I mean, uh, re-met her? Since you were a kid?"

I nod. "Yeah. I tried . . . I tried talking to her when I was younger, just starting high school, but she never got back to me. I figured she just didn't want me in her life, and that . . . really hurt."

"Yeah, I could imagine."

"And then I was cast on *Thirst* and she got in touch with me. My parents warned me it was because of money, but I didn't want to believe them. I wanted to believe she came back because she missed me." I shake my head. "It was stupid."

"What happened?"

"I mean, they were right." I shake my head. "I met her for lunch. I was so nervous; I think I changed my outfit, like, seven times. What do you wear to see your biological mother, you know? For the first time since . . . I mean, I couldn't even remember her. Anyway, she came and basically asked me to pay her rent."

"Seriously?" He looks angered. He looks the way I feel.

"More or less. She was proud of me, excited for the show and whatever. But was under 'hard times,'" I say, using air quotation marks, "and needed help."

"You didn't help her, did you?" I don't answer. "Oh . . ."

"What was I supposed to do? She looked just like me. I think that's what freaked me out the most. She looked just like me."

"So what happened after?"

"Nothing. I left, angry, and swore I wouldn't see her again. And I haven't."

"But now she's contacting you. Again."

I sit up straight and admit this to the front door, the restaurant's ceiling, to anywhere but him. "She has been. For over a month. I didn't want to go back to that whole . . . thing, to me getting excited and her letting me down. So I ignored it. And now . . ."

"Now you can't, really, anymore."

"Exactly . . ." I say, turning back to him.

He's silent, because there's no answer. I can talk to my mother and see what she wants, see if she's lying, see if she's not. Get this feeling out of my chest. But am I ready for that? Am I ready to be disappointed again? Or hurt? Why would she do this—why would she go so public?

Oliver's phone rings, breaking my thoughts. He looks down and shakes his head.

"Your agent?"

"Yep. I'm sure I know what this is about."

"Go ahead and answer it." I lean back, away from him, and can tell instantly the call is about me because he rolls his eyes and looks pointedly at me.

I think about that last time I met her and remember why

I was hurt so badly, I mean, besides the whole money issue. It was because my plan worked and, yet, it didn't. I wanted to act, to have a job like I do, so I could be visible. So I could be found. And I was. I wanted her to see me and know that I turned out okay, despite her. I wanted her to see me and remember me. I wanted her to think about me. I *did* want her to reach out to me, so she could see all that I had done. But in the end, she just came for her own selfish reasons.

But maybe I was doing it for a selfish reason, too.

Oliver hangs up and looks at me. "Yeah, it was about you."

"What'd your agent say?"

"She wanted to get the full story, but I didn't tell her. That's your story to tell."

I nod at him and say, "I don't know what to do."

"Screw it."

"I can't just screw it."

"Yes, you can. At least the TMZ part. People will judge. Who cares? They judge us on everything else. The Internet is full of people lashing out at us for one reason or another. It sucks that this stuff happens, but people who like you? Like the show? They won't care. They're behind you."

"Um, excuse me? You're Tallulah, right?" I turn around and see a girl, about ten, looking at me. She has dark skin and big, puffy hair and this amazing smile. I can't help but smile back.

"I am, yes," I say.

"I'm Shae. I love your show. I watch it all the time. You're my favorite." Then she looks at Oliver and says, "Sorry."

"No big deal," he shrugs good-naturedly.

"My mom said for me not to bother you, but I wanted to say hi." She points across the room, and I see a very pale blonde woman running over to us.

"Oh, my gosh, I'm so, so sorry," the woman says. "I told her not to go over here and disturb you."

"It's okay, really," I smile.

Shae smiles up to her mom and then back to me. "What's going to happen? Is Sylvester going to come back?"

"I can't tell you that," I say, sadly, but add, "but I can tell you this—he's never *quite* gone, now, is he?"

She grins at her mom again, then jumps around and hugs me. I gasp, surprised by the movement, but hug her back. After everything tonight, it's like she knew I needed a hug. When she lets go, I ask, "Would you like a picture?"

We say "cheese" and smile, and she happily bounds back to her mom, giving me a wave before leaving.

"You made her day. Thank you," her mom says, and they walk back to their table.

"You think she's a bit too young to be watching our show?" Oliver asks.

"You're just jealous that I'm the favorite."

He smiles. "Feel better now?"

I shrug and look down. That girl just went against her mom's wishes to see me. She wanted to see me that badly. Maybe that's how badly my mother wants to contact me. Enough to go against what I told her the last time. Enough to give up all her dignity and come back. Enough to go to a website to get my attention. Maybe this time she wants to get to know me and not just ask for something. Maybe she wants to know what she missed out on, learn who I am. Maybe she's finally realizing that that's what I wanted last time.

Like looking at the billboard earlier, I feel so visible to her. Maybe it's a good thing. It's what I wanted, after all.

"Let me ask you this." Oliver says, rubbing his hands together and looking at me with these eyes he never uses on the set—the ones reserved only for me. "Do you even *want* to see her?"

I think for a second, because I never actually answered this for myself. I always pushed the calls aside. I always thought I'd handle it later, too nervous or confused even to think about it at the time. But do I? Do I want to see her and hear what she has to say? See if she really is sick?

I close my eyes and think about it. I have no connection to her at all, but sometimes it's as if I can feel her. I can feel her pulling me, tugging me. Telling me I need to go. So I nod my head. Because, yes, I do want to see her, I just never knew *when* to do it. Or what to say. I didn't want to until I was prepared.

But now I don't want to be too late.

I remember being thirteen and just wanting to know if she knew I still existed. I remember being seventeen and just wanting her to know I was okay. And now, I'm eighteen and want to know if *she's* okay.

Looking back to Oliver, I answer, "I think I do."

My phone buzzes again and I sigh, already knowing who it is. I take a deep breath in and look at the text. I know it's time.

"What's up?" Oliver asks.

"Nothing. Hang on. I'll be right back," I say, standing up.

He stands up with me. "Where are you going? Everything okay?"

"Yes." I reach down to squeeze his hand—no public displays of affection—and say, "Give me five minutes."

He cocks his head to the side. "You wouldn't."

I show him my phone and smile, thinking how the scene we filmed just two hours ago feels like two days ago. Or two years. "I would."

The front door is packed with photographers, so I head to the bathroom and see a back door. I look out the window. It's empty outside. Opening the door, I feel the fresh air and once again see my billboard. It's weird and eerie and big and perfect. It's everything I wanted when I started out and maybe didn't even know. Back then I wanted to be seen. I wanted to be seen by her.

So when I see a woman standing a few feet away, shuffling

from foot to foot, and tentatively raising an arm, I know it's her. And I know it's time.

I step forward and say, "Hi."

Lauren Gibaldi is a public librarian who's been, among other things, a magazine editor, high school English teacher, bookseller, and circus aerialist (seriously). She has a BA in Literature and MS in Library and Information Studies. She lives in Orlando, Florida, with her husband and daughter. Her books include *The Night We Said Yes* (HarperTeen, 2015), *Matt's Story* (HarperTeen, 2015), and *Autofocus* (HarperTeen, 2016).

"Teen years are both exciting and scary because everything feels important, and, honestly, everything is. You're figuring out who you are and what you want out of life. You're figuring out who you'll become. But for a select few, you may also be figuring out where you came from. There are so many different types of teenage journeys, and I'm incredibly honored to be in an anthology that celebrates these."

Salvation

by Shannon Gibney

I. A fly landed in the middle of Sully's mid-sight, and he swatted it away. He anxiously repositioned the rifle, working to get the small boy and the *desgraciado* into focus. They were standing about fifty feet away, lifting their small tote bags out of the back of the Buick. Jacqui's worn Star Wars shirt was ripped on the side, and Sully wondered if that was the result of some kind of scuffle. The large, sweaty man was smiling at the boy uneasily, saying something to him. Sully didn't dare take off the trigger guard, as he didn't trust himself not to shoot if the *desgraciado* tried anything. He was officially there just to scope out the scene, make sure nothing funny happened before backup arrived. No one back at the station even knew about his "borrowing" the rifle. Through the front sight, Sully watched the man lift his arm to pat the boy on the back. Jacqui jumped, and it took all of Sully's self-control to steady his jumpy shoulders and steady his grip on the gun. *Calm down, asshole. And get that bottom-feeder back into focus.* He moved the rifle to the left, as the man who was reputed to love young boys walked toward the entrance of the broken-down motel. "Say cheese, motherfucker," Sully snarled.

II.

Jacqui knew that he was lucky, but he still couldn't shake the feeling that his luck would run out. Like the earthquakes that had destroyed his family's small shack in Cité Soleil, Jacqui knew that sometimes the earth felt its only recourse was to swallow bodies whole. The disaster had critically wounded his younger brother, Nico, and annihilated the modest kiosk his mother sold goods out of to keep them alive. And the way things were going, he wasn't convinced that the ground had been satisfied yet.

He stepped off the jetway in Miami and shivered, even though the adoption agency had given him a warm, wooly sweater to wear on his trip. There were so many white faces in the crowd—far too many, really. Honestly, it reminded him of home, where the streets were crawling with them. He could never make out one from another, would never feel easy near them. And besides, how could he even take a step without Nico's soft face buried in his side?

"Jacqui? Jacqui?" someone shouted, a woman, he thought.

He scanned the crowd anxiously, looking for "Kelly," the blonde-haired woman in the photograph he had been shown so many times at the agency. But there were at least six other white women with blonde ponytails that he could see, and none of them looked anything like the image he had tried to burn into his brain. Kelly had cool, gray eyes, and her smile was inviting, as if to say, *Welcome home!*

Someone grabbed his arm then, and he was pulled off-balance toward a short white man with balding hair and a wrinkled plaid dress shirt. "Frank! It's Frank Bolden, Jacqui, your adoptive father. Kelly's right here."

And then she stepped forward, the lady in the picture. Except that she *wasn't* the lady in the picture; she was both weightier and less substantial. The woman before him was solid, like his Aunt Roseline, and wore ugly plastic shoes on her wide feet. Her plump hands rested on an enormous, doughy white baby that she had somehow managed to fasten onto a carrying contraption on her chest. Her eyes were a dull gray, not the bright blue the photo had somehow conveyed.

"Jacqui," Kelly said, "I can't believe you're really here."

The sound of his name was unfamiliar to him from her mouth, all hard and angular—not at all how it sounded from his mother: light and crisp, like the breeze from the beach at dusk. *My boy, I am dying now. But I have prepared a new family for you, in Miami.* She had given the instructions on her deathbed in the Red Cross tent two years ago.

Jacqui blinked and forced himself to come back to the present. He tried to smile but he could feel how awkwardly the attempt sat on his face. "Hello, Kelly," he said. It came out almost in a whisper.

The woman laughed, a loud, sharp sound that made him jump. "Kelly?" she said. "Jacqui, after all this time and correspondence . . . after everything, you can call me Mother." Then she took another step toward him and placed a cool palm on his flushed cheek. "My 'son.'"

Jacqui flinched. How he wished Nico were here, with his half-leg and tiny crutches. What would happen to him now? Initially, the plan had been for the Boldens to adopt both Jacqui and Nico, but after they had finally understood the extent of his injuries from the earthquake, they balked at taking on two children with "special needs." Jacqui had been diagnosed with PTSD, having seen Uncle Stanley and his cousin David killed before his very eyes by a falling pillar. He had no idea what "PTSD" was, although he did understand it had something to do with the nightmares that plagued him and the endless nervous jiggling of his right knee when he sat down. "PTSD" also meant that he had to converse with a smelly old white lady at the adoption agency every week and talk about his family, his friends, his home, and what he hoped for in America.

If the Boldens had noticed his reaction, they didn't let on, and Jacqui was relieved when they abruptly headed away from the gate and toward the baggage claim. Kelly chatted all the way there and all the way to the house, asking him silly questions about Haiti and the rebuilding efforts and his flight. He tried to answer all of them with the same eagerness she displayed toward him, but when she got to the questions about Nico, he just shut his eyes and laid his head back on the plush leather seat of the truck. He wanted to say, *If you had bothered to bring my brother here, you would not have to ask. And I would not be all alone in this cold, white place.* But since he knew he couldn't say that, he thought it best to say nothing at all. Instead, he clasped his chapped hands together tighter and told himself that God would forgive him for leaving his little brother behind.

III.

When Kelly Bolden saw the fallen-down buildings, the city turned to rubble and dust, the post-apocalyptic nightmare that Port-au-Prince had become just after the earthquakes, she knew she had to do something. She immediately phoned the Red Cross emergency fund and donated five hundred dollars from their savings. She walked down the street to the neighbors, who had come from Haiti more than twenty-five years ago, and asked them if their family there was OK. They told her that they were still working to account for everyone, but that most of their family was from the other side of the country, which had not been hit by the quakes, so they were not really worrying about it. When Kelly asked them what else she could do to support the relief efforts, the dour-faced woman simply said, "Nothing. There is nothing more to be done from this side, if you have already given money."

Kelly had smiled stiffly, thanked them for their time, wished them and their family well in the crisis, and walked back to her house twice as quickly as she had come. Then she sat at her desk and pulled on her hair absently. There had to be something she could do. She got out her laptop, and halfway into an email to her pastor, she realized why this issue was bothering her so much, why she couldn't seem to let it go no matter what she did: God was calling her to act. And what He was specifically asking her to do was to feed, clothe, shelter, and love some of these Haitian children whose lives had been upended by the disaster. She and Frank had been trying to get pregnant for years and were currently in the middle of their second round of IVF. Suddenly, she understood why nothing had worked, why they had been made to suffer simply for their common desire to have a child and raise a family. God was calling them to something greater than just ordinary family-making. Yes, she could see it now: In making their family, He was calling them to save those who, by no fault of their own, had gotten in harm's way. In a matter of minutes, it all became clear to Kelly. The way forward. How she would approach Frank to convince him. Where she would begin looking for the children and making ready their collective salvation.

IV.

Two years and five months later, Jacqui crouched behind the wall that separated the kitchen from the living room. He could hear Kelly bawling on the other side. "We have to give him up. I know that." She sniffed. "You know it, too."

Jacqui's stomach fell, and he pressed his eyelids together.

God, what is this talk, now? His adjustment to the Bolden household had certainly not been easy, but he thought things were getting better. He wrung his hands absently. That *he* was getting better.

Frank's voice: "Give him up? Give him up? He's our son, Kelly. Not a carton of milk that's gone sour. For God's sake!"

Yes! Frank always stood up for him.

Kelly cried harder. "There's no need to swear."

"Oh, there's a need. There's definitely a need," said Frank.

"Shhh! He'll hear you!" she said.

Behind the wall, Jacqui shook his head. She still thought she could protect him, even from themselves.

"I hope he *does* hear," Frank yelled. "I hope you at least give him the decency of looking him directly in the eyes when you tell him that he came all this way and survived that hell in Haiti just so he could be thrown away again."

Kelly's voice changed then, went back to its usual evenness. He heard her labored breathing come back to normal. "We're not throwing him away. We're sending him somewhere where they can deal with his outbursts better. Somewhere where he can get the help he needs, the help he deserves." Then, almost in a whisper: "Somewhere where he can't hurt Katie."

Jacqui's eyelids flew open.

"That was a mistake, and you know it," said Frank. "He didn't mean to do it. He just needs some help regulating his emotions. You heard what Dr. Frasier said."

"It doesn't matter if he meant to do it or not. The fact is, he could have seriously hurt her." Kelly's words were cold and deliberate.

Jacqui resisted the urge to punch the wall. Two weeks ago, they had caught him in the act of slapping Katie in the face in the living room as they played with the Star Wars Lego set Frank had let him pick out. When Kelly confronted Jacqui and asked him why he did it, he did not have an answer. It had just been a reaction: His hand had flown of its own volition.

He hadn't commanded it to do anything of the sort. The child was as greedy as she was impetuous and had taken the X-Wing fighter he had spent all morning assembling. He knew that if he did not retrieve it, she would break it, and he did not want that to happen. So he had gotten it back. That was all.

Frank sighed, which worried Jacqui. He was usually Jacqui's fiercest advocate in the face of Kelly's endless lamentations. But his one weakness was Katie.

Kelly had become pregnant while finishing up all the adoption paperwork—the shock of her life, she often said sheepishly. And though she tried to hide it, Jacqui had a sneaking suspicion that she had really wanted to stop the whole process of bringing him here once she had discovered she would be having her own baby. She would never admit it, of course, but that was what he felt.

"I thought you said that God spoke to you," said Frank, "that He called you to take on this ministry of Jacqui's salvation by bringing him into our family. Were you wrong? Was that all a lie?"

Jacqui took a chance then, and stuck his head around the wall. Frank was looking at Kelly imploringly.

Kelly walked slowly up to him and touched his right arm. *That woman. She will break him. Break us. She has no regard.*

"No, it wasn't a lie," Kelly said. "God's call to me wasn't wrong. I've prayed about this, believe me. His call was for us to bring Jac here. That is *his* salvation. And we've done that. We've taken him out of that cesspool and brought him somewhere where he really has a shot."

Jacqui wanted to laugh. It was absurd, really, her notion that she knew anything about his home. The streets, teeming with people, buying, selling, moving, laughing, fighting amidst the broken-down buildings and dilapidated kiosks. The easy comfort of his mother's cornmeal with herring. Tears came to his eyes, as he realized he would probably never taste it again.

Frank again: "Will he, though? Will he really have a shot without us?"

Jacqui wiped at a tear with the back of his hand. He was really crying now. *Yes, they are really considering letting me go! Who are these people, again, that I should ever have called them Mother, Father?*

Kelly cradled Frank's chin in her hand. "Yes," she said, but it came out crooked, unsure. "Yes," she said again "these are good people, Frank. They love children, and desperately want one of their own. Mrs. Webster sent me a copy of the home study that DHS did, and it was glowing, positively glowing. Said that they could provide any child with a stable, clean, healthy home. Said that she and Mr. Webster are also phenomenal with special-needs kids. They're an older black couple, so they'll be able to provide for his cultural needs better. He needs to be with people who are like him. People who understand him. We can't provide that."

Jacqui ducked his head back around the wall, worried that they would discover his indiscretion soon enough. He needed to creep carefully back to where they had last seen him sitting in the living room and pretend he was thoroughly engrossed in the Angry Birds comic the school librarian had checked out for him. But who were these Websters the Boldens intended to dump him with? And how had Kelly even found them? He sucked on his teeth. Probably through one of those adoption Facebook groups she was always on. Posting and reading and responding at all hours.

Jacqui could hear Frank crying openly now. Jacqui hung his head. It was done, then. "I know we can't go on like this, but I just . . . wish there was another way, Kel. It doesn't seem right, you know?"

"It'll be okay, you'll see. You just have to trust me, honey. It will all work out," said Kelly.

V. Frank had made him memorize his cell phone number before he left, and told him to call if anything looked shady or if there were any problems, but Jacqui still felt adrift in this strange place, with these strange people. Mr. and Mrs. Webster were nice enough, and they led him to what would be his new room in their small apartment right before the Boldens left. It had a modest double bed in the center and what looked like a fresh set of sheets across the mattress. They had even gone to the trouble of installing a twenty-inch television in the room, as well as an Xbox game console. That was more than the Boldens had ever given him. Sure, they had fed him, clothed him, and even bought him a few toys, but there was always the sense of withholding with them. As if they were carefully measuring how many objects, how much affection they could afford to give him. Jacqui didn't feel that way with the Websters at all. After a week of contemplating using the Xbox, a week of awkward exchanges between him and the old couple, he finally sat down on the worn carpeting and began loading *Call of Duty*. After Jacqui had lost to the Xbox four times, Mr. Webster called him out to the living room.

"You ever been to a dogfight, boy?" the old man asked him. He was sweaty and he smelled funny. Jacqui didn't know why, but his instinct was to stay as far away from him as possible. It was something about the way the whiskers around his pale brown mouth twitched when he looked at him. As if Jacqui was a delicious peppermint stick he wanted to lick.

Jacqui shook his head and looked at the floor. He wished Kelly had not taken away his cell phone. He wanted to call Frank now, but it didn't look as if the Websters had a landline or cell phones of their own.

"Speak up, boy!" Mr. Webster barked.

Jacqui jumped at the sound, and then said "No," weakly. He glanced sideways and saw that Mrs. Webster, who had donned a dirty *The Heart of Louisiana* apron in preparation for cooking dinner, had come out of the kitchen to watch the exchange. A dopey grin was plastered across her face, and he wondered what she was thinking.

Mr. Webster stood up from the couch and clapped his hands. "We going, then. Right now. Get your jacket, boy."

"Right now?" Jacqui asked. "But I'm in the middle of a game."

Mr. Webster laughed, but it wasn't a funny laugh. "Yeah, and now we going somewhere. Let's get to it." He ambled over to the small table by the front door and grabbed his keys. Jacqui noted that his jeans were too large and landed about halfway down his butt.

Jacqui shook his head. This wasn't the way it was supposed to go—any of it. The Boldens were supposed to keep him, love him forever. *You will have a new life and a new family on the other side, and you will make something of yourself*, his mother had said. That was the way it was going to be. Not this drop-off with these strange and probably perverted people, who wanted to take him God knows where.

"Boy, you better get a move on!" Mr. Webster yelled. His face became clouded with anger, and there was meanness there, something that frightened him. Like the few memories he had of his father, grabbing his arm to take him away from his mother right after Nico was born, under the pretense of helping to provide for the family, when really, all his father had wanted him to do was beg the expats for money that he would end up using to get drunk.

"I'll have supper on by the time you all get back," Mrs. Webster said from the kitchen. "Burgers, Mr. Webster's favorite!"

Jacqui grabbed his jacket from the hook where he had hung it barely two hours before and stumbled toward the door. *God, please. Be with me now. Keep me safe.* It was a prayer he had made up and said to himself at least once a day since the earthquakes, and he had been saying it all the time since arriving at the Websters'.

"You gonna love it, I promise," said Mr. Webster. Then he pulled on Jacqui's arm, his thick, greasy fingers grasping at his shirt. He finally got hold of its side, and it ripped, just as the front door closed behind them.

VI.

The boy and the *desgraciado* exited the motel reception area and began to walk down the sidewalk, presumably toward a room. Sully's grip on the gun shaft tightened, and he felt a kind of rage bubble up from his stomach as he watched Webster gesture for the boy to follow him. *Motherfuckers. They always get the children. Always from the places no one gives a shit about.* His mind went back to the small village in Guatemala he could barely remember, to his mother handing him off to the middleman, to his adoptive family in Cleveland who had never stopped beating him for speaking Spanish. He had read Jacqui Dabrezil's file, knew all about Kelly and Frank Bolden and their despicable rejection of their Haitian son to a child molester and convicted felon. "Yeah, well, the tables are turned now, aren't they, *hijo de puta*?" Sully released the trigger guard, moving his index finger into position on the trigger. He saw the shiny expanse of Webster's forehead beyond the front sight, and he began to pull back the trigger.

"Sully!" someone yelled from across the parking lot.

The *desgraciado* and the boy both stopped and turned to look at the commotion.

"Fuck!" Sully yelled, as Webster moved out of his sights. He almost had him.

"Recruit Ricardo Sully, I am ordering you to stand down,"

a voice boomed from beside him. Then someone knocked the rifle out of his hands.

Sully recognized the voice as Lisa's. He turned toward his friend-in-training, who had had his back these past ten months when no one else had, who was a regular addition to dinners with his family and one of the only Latino higher-ups in their department. "Lisa, what the fuck?"

Lisa pointed her gun at Sully. "I could ask you the same thing, Sully. What. The. Fuck."

Lisa was one of the few people in the world who knew his full history. She had sat through his diatribes on the rampant corruption of the international adoption system, had, over many beers, stomached his obsession with following stories in the news of adoption disruptions. But looking into her tired, disappointed face now, he could see he had broken through to some other untouchable space with this act, and that she would no longer try to talk sense into him, to bring him back to the world of "positive solutions," rather than tragedy and revenge. Yes, Sully knew what he had almost done. And he knew it would be an abrupt end to his budding career and get him kicked off the force at twenty-one. The worst part was that he couldn't even bring himself to care enough to stop it. It would have just felt so *good* to kill that predator, to make sure he didn't destroy even one more life.

"That *desgraciado* was about to violate that innocent—"

"Shut up, Sully," Lisa said evenly. "Shut up *now.*"

"Evans, cuff the man, then put each one in a car," she said into her com. Then she lowered her gun.

Sully turned and watched Evans lock a set of handcuffs on a shocked Mr. Webster and then walked each of them to a different squad car.

"Get up," Lisa told him. "Take the rifle, and put it away. We'll take it back to the station and sneak it back into the weapons locker. Evans will agree that it's not worth it to tell anyone about this little incident. And you're taking the rest of the week off and getting some help."

Sully blinked. She understood. Of course she understood. She was his friend, almost family, and would protect him.

Sully got up and grabbed the rifle. "I'm not talking to a goddamn headshrinker."

Lisa got up in his face. He couldn't remember another time he had seen her like this. But then, he had never been on the verge of executing someone before. "Those are my terms. Either take them or leave them. I'm so done with this shit, Sully. Don't test me." Then she turned and walked to Evans, helping him process Webster and the boy.

Sully walked slowly back to the car with the rifle. His hands started to shake as he imagined the boy staring at the dead man beside him, slowly engulfed in a pool of blood. Yes, he had really almost done it. He half screamed at the air, the sound both feral and muted. Then he walked back to Lisa and Evans.

"Okay," he said evenly. "I'll do it."

Lisa smiled. "So glad to see you can be reasonable." Then she pointed to Webster. "You. We're taking you in on child pornography charges."

"What?" he asked, incredulously.

Sully resisted the urge to punch him then and there.

"And you," Lisa said, pointing to Jacqui. "You're going back to your family."

A wide smile spread across Jacqui's face, and then disappeared just as quickly. Sully surmised he was thinking of his Haitian family, his real family back home, until he realized what Lisa truly meant.

"No, I can't," he said, in a small voice. "They . . . they . . . they gave me up."

Lisa opened the car door and motioned for him to sit down. "Yes, I know. But they're gonna take you back." Jacqui frowned, but he got into the backseat of the car. Sully tried to make eye contact with him on the drive back to the precinct, but the boy just stared blankly out the window, his right knee bouncing relentlessly the whole way there.

Shannon Gibney was born in 1975, in Ann Arbor, Michigan. She was adopted by Jim and Sue Gibney about five months later and grew up with her two (biological) brothers, Jon and Ben. Shannon is currently at work on her second YA novel, *Dream Country* (Dutton, 2018), about more than five generations of an African-descended family crisscrossing the Atlantic both voluntarily and involuntarily.

"We need to talk about adoption, family-building, and dissolution. We need to see it on the page and wrestle with both its joys and its difficulties so we have a clearer lens through which to look at what's happening to us and our loved ones. Adoption is everywhere."

Twenty-Seven Days

by Jenny Kaczorowski

When I was ten, my gramma took me to Arizona. The roads there were smooth, like gliding on glass. That's how I know we're still close to home. These roads rattle my bones.

The social worker's car hits another rut in the gnarled, pitted streets of Los Angeles, slamming my shoulder against the door of her busted-up Honda. It smells like stale cigarettes and grease.

I stretch my shoulders back. I don't slump. Gramma didn't teach me much, but she taught me to hold my head high.

The social worker slows and puts on her blinker. I wiggle my toes, as if I can carve out more room in my cramped boots. Eighteen months ago, on one of her clean streaks, Mama held them out for me—a priceless gift to memorialize my first day of high school.

She never made it past eighth grade.

But that day, when the August sun burned my brown shoulders and the reek of the dumpsters behind our apartment burned my nose, I was as proud of her as she was of me. She clutched my shoebox in one hand and a bright purple nine-month sobriety chip in the other.

Doc Martens. Genuine, authentic, oxblood leather Doc Martens.

These boots cost her an entire paycheck, but my mama is a good worker. At least when she's straight. Those boots were supposed to be the start of something.

Then Gramma died.

The car lurches to a stop. I pull off my headphones while I wait for the social worker—I think this one is named Jessica—to wrench herself free from the worn grooves in her seat and shuffle onto the street.

"Are you ready, Aprillia?" she asks with a smile.

At least she didn't have to check my case file to remember my name.

I grab the trash bag from the seat beside me and slide it across. I feel safer clutching it to my chest as I follow her up the front path.

A scream rips through the neighborhood, and I jump.

The social worker places a cool hand on my shoulder.

It's just kids playing. My brain knows that, but my body doesn't and I can't stop it from reacting. Where I come from, screaming means something bad. Every time.

The front door opens and a middle-aged Latina steps out. Her face is creased with laugh lines, and her forehead is knotted in concern. "Oh." Her worry morphs into a soft smile. "You must be Aprillia."

The social worker nudges me forward, and I stumble, holding my bag up like a shield. I force a smile for the strange woman who is supposed to be better at taking care of me than my own mother.

Not that the bar is set very high.

I try to follow what she's saying, but she's trying to

welcome me while she handles the business of foster parenting with the social worker.

I'm something between a person and a case number, wherever I am.

The house is big, and everything echoes. I don't know where to look, where to turn my attention. What can hurt me. I'm clinging to this stupid plastic bag as if it can keep me afloat.

This is it. This is my home. Unless they can find a relative in the next thirty days, I'm here until my mama can pull herself together. Again.

Except I don't know if she'll make it back this time.

"Aprillia." The foster mom—Mrs. Beckett—tentatively puts both of her hands on my shoulders and I allow it. It helps me bring my eyes to hers. "Would you like something to eat? Or would you rather see where you're going to stay?"

"I need . . ." I hold up my bag, not quite able to get the words out. I need to move. I need to hide. Anything to get out of this space and somewhere I can maybe think again.

But my stomach grumbles, and no matter how much I want to hide, I need to eat. There isn't always another chance. "Dinner." As if Gramma is slapping me upside my head from beyond the grave, I tack on "please."

She nods and steers me toward the kitchen. She's a pro. I'm not her first rodeo, and she's not mine. That should make it easier.

"I'll take your things to your room," she says. "I didn't have a lot of time to put it together. . ." She trails off, but we both know what she's talking about.

Emergency Placement.

It might as well be stamped across my forehead. Each time CPS has pulled me, it's been without warning. I'm old enough now to know when Mama is losing it. I know it will be only a matter of time before a neighbor or friend or the security guard at the mini-mart calls to report that she's using again.

I try to keep things together, to cover for her, but there's only so much I can hide.

She's the adult, after all.

"We can pick up anything else you need," the foster mom says, reaching for my trash bag.

I relinquish all my worldly goods—a hoodie, a couple of books, a pair of jeans that are too big. But I hold on to my phone. Mama stopped paying the bill, so it's useless for making calls. But I have my music.

The front door flies open, and a handful of kids tumble inside.

I stagger back, straight into Jessica.

My eyes catch on a girl about my age. She doesn't look like me—with dark skin and her hair twisted into dozens of tiny braids—but there's something about her. Something about the way she looks at me. A flicker of recognition that tells me we're alike in some way.

Or at least that's what my heart dares to hope before my brain shuts it down.

Her mouth twitches into a smile and she manages a "hi!" before the other kids bundle her off into the kitchen.

"Take your seats, kiddos," Mrs. Beckett calls down the stairs.

The kitchen is loud and crowded, but weirdly controlled. The smell coming from the stove makes my stomach rumble so hard I'm sure they all can hear it.

Except they're all engrossed in conversation. Each kid looks so different that I have no idea how everyone fits together.

"The three on the left are mine," Mrs. Beckett says. "Zeke is my oldest." She inclines her head toward a boy with rich, olive-toned skin, just a shade or two lighter than mine. "He's seventeen now, but he's been with us since he was ten months old."

"Next is Xavier." She nods toward the one with his back to

me. "He'll be fifteen next week. He's been with us for almost eleven years." He's a big kid, at least as tall as Zeke, but broader, too. He has a soft, coffee-and-cream complexion.

"And last is Gabriel." He looks enough like Mrs. Beckett that I wonder. "He's thirteen now. We got him when he was about two."

Three foster brothers about my age is a lot to take in.

I tilt my head up, waiting for an explanation for the other kids.

"Oh." She laughs a little. "The others are the Jacksons. They live next door. Elijah, Jeremiah, and Olivia. They're all together a lot."

Five boys and the girl. No wonder she's staring at me with excitement bordering on desperation.

No wonder I feel it, too.

Mrs. Beckett hands me a plate heaped with food and points me toward an open chair. "They're all used to visitors," she says. "Kiddos, this is Aprillia."

"'Sup," Xavier says as I take the seat across from him.

"Where you from?" Zeke says.

"Boyle Heights."

"Nice." He jerks his head toward Gabe. "He's got some family out there."

I want to ask why he's here if he has real family, but instead I keep my eyes on the plate.

God, this woman makes homemade garlic bread. I want to be grateful, but this resentment is forcing its way up. Why can't my Mama keep it together to make me spaghetti and meatballs? Why did these kids get out and get this life?

I don't want this life. I want my life. I want my life to look like this. I shouldn't want this life. I should want my mama. But this spaghetti tastes like heaven, and I haven't had anything fresh to eat since the last time I went to school.

I might as well enjoy it for the next thirty days. Or however long I'm here.

I risk a peek at the girl—Olivia—but she looks away every time our eyes catch. Just as awkward as I am.

If she's half as cool as the thick earrings, braids, and nerd glasses lead me to believe, this placement might not be terrible.

But hope is a jagged thing and cuts deep when I hold too tight.

And it's not as if I can say, "I love your vibe. Can we be besties?"

So rather than answer the questions burning in my gut, I push my dinner around the plate while she does the same and we occasionally exchange self-conscious glances.

One of the boys shoots a spit wad at her and she jumps up from her seat. "Gross!"

"Wasn't me," Eli says.

She glares at her brother, but he just points at Zeke.

"I suck at spitballs and you know it," the oldest of the Becketts says.

She rolls her eyes. "Whatever."

"Everything okay?" Mrs. Beckett asks, sticking her head in from the living room, where she's still talking with Jessica.

"Fine." Olivia gives her a tight smile.

Mrs. Beckett shoots a withering look at Zeke. "I hope you're being welcoming to our guest . . . making her feel like part of the family."

Olivia snorts.

"I'm fine," I insist. "Thank you. For dinner. Mrs. Beckett."

She smiles. "Let us know if you need anything." With a final warning glare at the boys, she glides back into the living room.

"It was Eli," I say, making a split-second decision. I should be making allies with the kids I'm actually living with, but I have to side with her.

"I knew it!" She turns on her brother.

"So?" He glares back at her. "What are you going to do about it, Liv?"

"Wouldn't you like to know?" I interject, folding my hands on the table and smiling serenely.

Eli lowers his fork.

Olivia stifles a snicker, and we exchange a look that almost makes me giggle, too.

The boys hurry to finish and drop their plates in the sink. The dishes clatter together and they just get louder. The back door slams shut, and quiet descends.

It's just me and Olivia.

"Boys." She rolls her eyes. "You know?"

I chuckle. "Yeah. I definitely know." I can't quite suppress a shiver of fear. "They okay?"

Her face falls. "Oh, yeah. They're obnoxious, but they're good guys."

I flick my eyes up, and there's a moment when we both completely understand without having to speak the unspeakable.

God, this girl *knows* me.

"Aprillia . . . that's pretty," she says, her eyes roaming the room.

"Thanks. My dad rode Aprillia motorcycles."

She crinkles up her nose. "That is so freaking cool."

"Sure." My smile fades. "Mama says the only thing he loved more than his bike was me. I just wasn't enough to keep him off it. And I'd rather have him than a cool name."

She blinks, reeling a little. I'm about to apologize when she clears her throat.

"I was named after my grandma Olivia," she says. "But everyone calls me Livie. Not like anyone would mix us up. She died before I was born."

The awkward, too-full silence falls again. I can't take whatever this thing is between us.

"Okay." I take in a deep breath. "I have to ask. Your shirt? Do you actually know The Classic Crime?"

She snaps her head up. "Are you kidding? They're my favorite band ever."

"No way!" I practically jump out of my seat. "I cannot believe you've even heard of them."

She adjusts her glasses. "*Phoenix* got me through a lot of things."

"*Closer Than We Think* is my anthem," I say. "Makes me feel less alone."

Her eyes settle on mine for the first time, really, truly looking into my soul. "You're not alone." Her words rush out. "You've got me."

"Sure." My smile falters. "For as long as I'm here."

She slides over next to me. "As long as you're here."

Suddenly, thirty days doesn't seem like very long.

"How are things going?" Jessica asks, looking up from her folder. My file is way too thick for fifteen years.

I shift in my chair. Mrs. Beckett gave us the kitchen, shooing the boys into the backyard. I appreciate the privacy, but I don't know what to do with myself while this strange woman, who knows far too many personal details of my life, tries to assess me.

They always tell me it's okay, that I can relax. But I'm literally being judged. These people who are caring for me are being judged. My mama is being judged.

How are things going? So simple, and yet . . .

"Good." I force the single syllable out.

She gives me a look. Not the patronizing pity I usually get. Or the disinterested apathy from the seasoned vets. No, this is the kind of sass my mama gives me.

I break into a smile. "I'm really good. How is my mama?"

Jessica sets down her pen. "I wish I could tell you."

I pull my eyelids shut. I knew this would be a bad one. "She's not coming back, is she?"

"We don't know that." Her tone is clipped, and she folds her hands on the table.

"Can I at least stay here?"

She looks away. "You know we always prefer to place you with family."

"Yeah, but my grandma is dead. Who are you going to stick me with?" How can I explain to her that these people, these kids I've known less than a week, already feel like family? That I finally feel like I'm home?

"Aprillia." She sets her hand over mine. "You know I'm looking out for you, for what's best for you. That's my job. That's all I'm trying to do."

I let out the breath I'm holding hostage. She's right. She's one of the good ones. "I just want to stop moving."

Twenty-three days left. If they can't find a relative willing to take me in twenty-three days, I can stay.

Jagged, jagged hope.

"I know." For a second, it sounds like her voice is cracking, but she clears her throat and picks up her pen, all business again. "All right. Things are going well here at home. How is the new school? Are you settling in?"

And there we go, diving into the mundane minutia of my life, because no detail is private anymore. That's what happens when your worst moments are preserved in a case file. Kind of hard to define boundaries after that.

"Things are good," I reiterate.

Now I'm waiting for the other shoe to drop. Twenty-three days.

I'm not entirely sure how this friend thing is supposed to work. I've gotten by figuring out which kids will help me survive and which ones will hurt me, but it's not as if I'm inviting people over to watch my mama shoot up. Foster care rules don't even allow sleepovers.

But Livie is on her way over to watch a movie while the boys are all next-door.

I don't even know what movie to watch. The odds of us actually having the same nerdy taste in movies are slim to none.

She knocks on the kitchen door, and I jump up from my spot on the couch.

I take a couple of deep breaths. *This* is normal. It's not my normal, but it's normal.

"I brought cookies," she says, holding up a plastic-wrapped plate. "What are we watching?"

"Well . . ." I nod toward the giant, overly bright screen. I've highlighted my favorite of The Lord of the Rings movies. It's a stretch, but maybe, just maybe, she's into long, epic fantasy.

"Perfect!" She flops down beside me and grabs a cookie.

"I know it's long," I say, trying to give her an out. "We could watch something else."

"No way!" She shakes her head. "These movies are flawless. I just can't get anyone to watch them with me anymore."

I place my hand against my heart. "I will always watch this movie with you. Anytime. Anywhere." Then my stomach clenches. Sixteen days left. "As long as I'm here."

Livie gives me a weak half smile. She too knows that this won't last.

From the first epic swell of the score, the vast sweep of towering, snow-capped mountains, I'm lost in this world again. A world where good and evil make sense and villains can be defeated and even the most insignificant characters matter.

Livie sighs. "The costumes in this movie make me so happy."

"I'm still jealous of all the Elvish braids."

"I can braid your hair."

"Seriously?"

She points to her own head. "Seriously." She pauses. "If that's okay? I remember one of the Becketts' kids couldn't take his locs out, even when they got itchy. His bio mom didn't want them cut."

"Oh, yeah." I look away. "Foster rules at their best. But my mama doesn't care."

She chuckles and I try to laugh, too, but it's forced.

"Anyway," she looks at her hands, "I like doing hair."

"Cool." I slide to the floor in front of her, and she lets my lackluster locks loose from my ponytail.

I relax as she runs her fingers along my scalp. She works at my hair in sections, parting, twisting, and twirling it into braids. I don't even know what she's turning it into, and I don't care. It seems to take forever, while armies battle and hearts break.

"Is this what normal kids do?" I ask, when she taps my shoulder to signal she's done.

"I don't know about *normal,*" Livie slides down beside me and nudges my shoulder, "But it's what I do."

"I like your normal better than mine."

"Maybe this is it." She wraps her arm around mine. "Maybe you'll get to stay this time."

"Maybe." A slow smile drifts across my face. "Just sixteen more days."

"Hmmm?"

"CPS has sixteen days left to find a relative. If they can't find anyone within thirty days of placement, I get to stay here."

She leans her head against my shoulder. "Sixteen days."

The front door bangs shut and I pause my folding, staring at the shirt as Livie thunders up the stairs.

She skids to a halt in my doorway, braids in chaos and eyes wide. "No." It comes out as a whimper.

I meet her eyes, resignation weighing me down. "I don't get a choice."

"But you've never met these people."

I roll a shoulder. "They're my dad's cousins. They're family."

Like that's supposed to mean something.

Livie drops down beside me and takes my hands. "You've never even met them. *We're* your family."

I squeeze my eyes closed, and my whole body crumples. "I know, Liv." There's so much pain. I don't know what to say or what to do.

"Twenty-seven days. I thought you were clear." She hugs me so hard, like if she clings to me hard enough, Child Services can't pull us apart.

My gut twists. I don't know what I'll do without her.

"Okay." She straightens up and brushes aside a tear with the heel of her hand. "Okay. We'll be okay."

I make a sound somewhere between a laugh and a cry. "I've made it this far."

"God, this sucks." She shakes herself. "What do you need?"

What do I need? Time. Home. Livie.

But I nod toward the trash bag beside me. "I have to pack."

Livie frowns. "This is a trash bag."

"It's what I have."

"No." She jumps up. "No way. I am not letting my best friend leave with a trash bag."

"It's what I came with." I scramble to my feet, all my defenses flaring up.

She swallows hard. "You're taking all of us with you. So you're not packing your stuff like it's trash." She starts digging through the top of my closet.

"I don't need you fixing things, Liv."

She rolls her eyes at me. "It's not charity. Mrs. Beckett got this for you." She shoves a purple duffle bag into my chest.

I sigh, and she grins, like she's won. Maybe she has.

"So, packing?" She plants her hands on her hips and glares at me.

"Yeah." I hold the duffle bag for a second before kneeling again beside my stack of clothes.

We set the last pair of socks inside, and I zip it closed with a deflating sense of finality.

Twenty-seven days. All we got was twenty-seven days.

For a moment, a brief, shining moment, I had a friend. And that moment gives me strength. That moment gives me hope. With all its jagged edges and beautiful pain.

Hope hurts, but I'd rather hurt than be hopeless.

And maybe that's the point.

Jenny Kaczorowski is the daughter of a social worker and grew up on stories of neglect, foster care, and adoption. As an adult, she's still drawn to stories about the search for home, in all its many forms. She likes her heroines smart and quirky, her heroes nice, and her kisses sweet. Her Oceanside High series —*The Art of Falling* and *The Trick to Landing*—is published with Bloomsbury Spark. Apart from writing, Jenny is an avid photographer, loves music despite no discernible musical talent, and harbors a deep-seated fear of goldfish. She lives near Los Angeles with her husband, son, and daughter. The four of them are always on the lookout for their next adventure.

"This story is inspired by one little girl. I grew up surrounded by adoptive families and saw many sides of adoption and foster care through my dad's career as a social worker. But it was this one little girl and her special friendship with my daughter that really brought it home for me. While we knew her for only a

short time, the impact she made on our lives will last forever. I hope she finds this anthology someday and remembers how much love we have for her."

Ink Drips Black

by Julie Leung

There is a legend, whispered among the women who live near the Nan mountains, one that has been passed down for generations from mothers to daughters.

If the child is male, he belongs by the hearth.

If the child is female, she belongs to the mountain.

When the woman saw that she had given birth to yet another squalling girl, ill-colored and unwilling to suck, she shed four tears of bitterness. Where they fell upon the child's cheek, black moles appeared. The woman knew then that her daughter would be an unlucky one.

She called out for her mother-in-law to come and take it away. Take it away before she could feel anything past the disappointment.

Upon seeing the girl-child lying on the floor, the old woman sighed. The baby's throat had grown hoarse from screaming for food and warmth. She scooped the infant up and placed it into a basket that she would bear upon her back. She paid no mind to the mother, who lay silently curled in her bed, facing away from the door.

It was a hard journey to the mountain temple, perched

high in the fog-laden tip of the highest peak. The old woman began early in the morning, climbing poorly carved stone stairs. She tiptoed across rotted bridges draped across canyons. Occasionally, she would step over a delicate set of bones, bleached white by the sun. Her own bones creaked in protest with every step. Many bearers had grown too tired or impatient. And the girls were either given to the river or left out to the elements.

Along the way, the infant stopped crying. Her eyes opened and took in the majestic surroundings with silent wonder. The light feeding her in the ways her mother wouldn't. The woman stifled a small smile at this. Perhaps, one day, the child might see more than the village had to offer.

By the time she spied the temple's brick roof tiles above the bamboo groves, sweat drenched the old woman's clothes. Her feet were bloody from open blisters, her back strained and stiff. The straps of the basket she had been carrying cut deep grooves into her shoulders. She limped forward toward the open doorway, her eyes stinging with tears of relief.

Inside, she was greeted by a large golden bell suspended from the ceiling. Scores of fish meticulously carved on its surface, forming a never-ending swirl of scales.

Below the bell, a burbling hot spring fed a small pond.

She walked closer to inspect it. Instead of water, the spring spewed forth a steady, thick sludge of black ink. It bubbled and flowed away from where the woman stood, forming a steady stream that disappeared into the mouth of a cave. She could not see beyond.

The old woman knelt by the spring and unstrapped the sleeping child from the basket.

She tried to remember her own mother's instructions when she had first become pregnant. But her memories held only wordless echoes. Luckily, she had always been blessed with a son.

She spied a wooden mallet sitting at the edge of the pond.

Picking it up, she rang the bell twice. A deep, rich chime reverberated into the cave, and the whole temple seemed to shake. The inky water began to churn.

The woman waited, whispering a quick prayer to the Goddess of Mercy, Guanyin, between her lips.

From the darkness, a slithering creature emerged from the cave. He looked half-fish and half-man. Iridescent scales covered his serpentine face, and long slits along his neck opened and closed like gills. He glided forward, his milky eyes roving around the temple until they fell on the baby.

San Mo-gwai, they called him—the mountain's monster, the Fate-eater, the transporter of souls to lands beyond their reach.

The woman averted her eyes quickly and held the child out in offering.

The creature took the baby into his barnacled hands. Like a spider's limbs, they curved around the slight body. He sighed. And when he sighed, a mournful wind whistled down the mountains.

"Does she have a name?" he asked. His voice came out as a multitude of whispers.

The old woman shuddered and shook her head no.

He sighed again. Far down in the valley below, a woman felt a chill wind. She clutched her blanket closer to herself. In that moment, she felt the absence in her womb like a gnawing chasm.

The creature gently submerged the child into the pond, letting the black liquid pour over her. The grandmother held back a cry. Did she bring the baby all this way only to have a monster drown it?

Just when she was about to protest, the creature lifted the child up again. A length of red thread emerged, tied to her right hand. He took the thread and pulled and pulled until a scroll of red paper also came out of the black abyss.

He handed the grandmother the scroll, and with a sharp fingernail, he cut the thread.

"What is this?" the old woman whispered, gingerly unrolling the paper.

The *mo-gwai* clamped a hand over hers, staying it. Its clammy skin clung to hers like a wet rag.

"The part of her that is always yours to have, whether you want it or not," he said. "Keep it, give it to the mother, or burn it. I care not."

The creature turned and began to depart with the child cradled between his arms.

"Where do you take them?" the old woman asked. Her throat suddenly tightened around a small regret that died on her tongue. The scroll burned like a heated brand in her palm.

"Where they are wanted," came his reply. With that, the nameless girl disappeared inside the cave.

The grandmother gripped the slip of paper for the length of five breaths.

She wanted to call after him, but she held back.

She knelt back down at the pond. Dipping a tentative finger into the ink, she began to write. When she was done, she folded the paper into the shape of a small boat and placed it on the pond. She watched the eddies carry it away into the cave, trailing its original owner like an albatross.

Later, she would try to wash her hands in the nearby river.

To her surprise and secret relief, the ink stains would not wash from her hands.

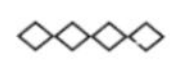

For eighteen years, I have lived as a changeling child.

When the therapist looks down at her clipboard, I see her eyes scan over the name I've written in neat, capped letters on my form.

"Stacy Duchamp?"

My head rises, and my hand floats up to acknowledge her. I see the split-second readjustment she makes as the girl she expects disappears. The girl with the paler complexion fades into my sallow tones. Her rounder eyes reshape to fit mine. The brighter hair is spirited away, to be replaced by a blanket of black. But her ghost is always there, hovering behind the therapist's compensating smile.

I don't know who that Stacy Duchamp is. All I know is that I've stolen her place. And I've become accustomed to erasing this girl from other people's minds.

I sit down on the sticky pleather chair on the other side of the desk. The air is desert-dry and stifling hot, as two space heaters war with each other in the corner. I eye the multiple tissue boxes laid out on the coffee table.

So this is a challenge.

"Comfortable?" the therapist asks. She wears a cowl-neck sweater that swallows her bird-thin frame. Behind her horn-rimmed glasses, there is a severity as sharp as broken glass.

Not in the least, I want to say. But I only nod politely. I lean back on the couch but sink too far back into the soft cushions. I elbow myself upright and try to find a neutral position instead.

"I see you come as a referral from Lenox Hill," she remarks, as if this were a particularly interesting fact, like I'd just returned from an exotic tropical island and not a psychiatric ward.

"Yeah," I respond. Already my mind is racing elsewhere, preoccupied with the unread email burning a hole in my inbox.

"I've gone over your records prior to our meeting, but I would like to hear everything from your perspective. I think it would help me understand how best to approach your treatment."

The hands I've rested on my knees instinctively turn into fists, but I keep my voice calm.

"I'd rather not talk about it. I thought I made that clear in my exit interview."

"That's not how mental health works, Stacy," the therapist says. "Recovery is both a biochemical and an emotional process. Your psychiatrist will prescribe you what you need in terms of medication, but with me, I'm here to listen."

I stare at my fingernails, turning white from pressing so hard into my palms.

I let the silence gestate; it feeds on the discomfort crackling in the room.

"Your parents are worried about you," she continues. "I understand they were the ones who set up this appointment. They want you to get better."

Guilt slithers around the insides of my chest like a many-tentacled parasite. Giving up was always the easy part—my grades, my friends, my life. They slipped from my fingers as if they had never belonged to me. Everything that bound me to this world belonged to a girl named Stacy Duchamp. Hers was an identity I could wash away like face paint.

I think about the cold water of the East River enveloping me and the pressure building around my ears when I sank. I think how hard it was to make my body stay still, to stop the swimming lessons from kicking in.

But then to resurface an even bigger failure than before? To learn that a passing kayaker had fished me out? I woke to my mother's worried face and red-rimmed eyes, my father clutching my hand. They loved their Stacy very much.

How could I tell them that their daughter was a husk? She had been replaced by a charred little creature that always lurked underneath her skin.

"Okay, let's try it this way. We don't have to talk about anything you don't want to," the therapist says. "Why don't you fill me in on your background. Does anyone in your family have a history of mental illness?"

"I'm adopted," I say. "So I wouldn't know."

"Ah, I see, that explains your name." By the tone of her voice, I can tell that the therapist has flagged this as a significant note. She scribbles some words on her clipboard. I know she'll want to come back and unpack this later. And if she's very lucky, I'll cry.

"Often, depression can manifest in feelings of not belonging and can trigger emotional crises. . ."

I want to kick over the coffee table and scream.

But instead, I say, "I'm sorry. May I use the restroom?"

Standing in front of the greasy restroom mirror, I close my eyes and collect my heartbeats. I open my eyes and look at my reflection, half expecting the other girl to reappear. But only my small dark eyes glare back.

The tidal wave rises up from afar, and I can see how my hateful thoughts will try to drown me where I stand. Like the time before, when I let my gremlin heart drag me to the bottom.

I count the four moles that dot my cheek like a reverse constellation. This is a face that does not belong to a Stacy Duchamp, but to that *other* one, lost in an unrealized timeline. This body was made to house her, its construction built according to an entirely different blueprint than the one I had lived.

Like a treasure hunter, I scour the landscape of my skin for a clue—some remnant that might remain of a mapmaker's mark.

I stare until my vision blurs.

"Why does it cry, dear changeling?" a raspy voice sing-songs in my ear.

I stifle a scream. In my peripherals, I can make out the humanoid shadow of the creature lingering at my side. My mouth fills with the taste of stagnant water and oily fish. I try to turn and face it, but my muscles won't cooperate. My eyes are frozen on my reflection.

"Why are you here?" I hiss, still staring at myself. The slippery shape moves to my other ear.

"I don't understand." The creature sounds perplexed, as if trying to solve a logic puzzle. "I brought you to where you were wanted. Why don't you want to stay?"

"I did not want myself," I say. "I did not want my pain."

The shadow is silent, his head nodding. "I have something for you, then."

Two pale, calcified fingers appear from the folds of shadow. They hold out an origami boat folded from bright red paper. I gingerly grab it without touching the creature, surprised that the paper feels heavy and real.

I regain control of my arms and began to unfold the panels.

"She dipped her own fingers into the fate pond to write it," the shadow muses, "even after I severed her thread to you."

"What is it?" I ask, studying the fluid calligraphy filling every corner of the page. The ink dripped black, splashing hieroglyphs against the red paper.

I run my fingers over the symbols, feeling hooks inside me latch on to the strange characters. My heart clings to this paper. And though I cannot read her words, her intentions flow into me like a gentle tide of music—a song of sacrifice, guilt, and blind hope.

"Mind yourself, changeling," the monster whispers. "She wanted you. She wanted you to go far."

Julie Leung was raised in the sleepy suburbs of Atlanta, Georgia, though it may be more accurate to say she grew up in Oz and came of age in Middle-earth. By day, she is a senior marketing manager for Random House's sci-fi/fantasy imprint, Del Rey Books. She is also the mother of FictionToFashion.com, where she translates her favorite books into outfits. In her free time, she enjoys furtively sniffing books at used bookstores and winning at obscure board games. Her favorite mode of transportation is the library.

"To adopt and become someone's family is to alter that person's fate in the most fundamental way. Family, for good or bad, is a pillar of one's identity. In my story, I wanted to explore the issue of cultural identity through this lens. Moved by an article I had read about a girl searching for her birth mother in China, I wanted to explore this life-altering severance from not only a birth family, but also one's original culture."

Upon the Horizon's Verge

by Sangu Mandanna

"Between two worlds life hovers like a star,
'Twixt night and morn, upon the horizon's verge.
How little do we know that which we are!
How less what we may be!"
—Lord Byron, Don Juan

I fall asleep on the bus and miss my stop, so I get off at the pier instead. The salt and vinegar smell of seaside chips tickles my nose, and the baby kicks me pointedly in the ribs, the greedy little goblin, so I buy a cone of chips and walk to the fairground. I expect bright lights and cotton candy and shitty music, but instead the fairground is dull and quiet and looks as it has for years, a motley collection of rusted rides and seagulls.

This is weird. I was here only last year, and the rides were alive with noise and color then. When did they shut the fairground down? Why didn't we hear about it?

The gates are open. There's not a soul in sight. Just gulls and rust and the creak of old metal in the wind. It's unnerving, but it's also peaceful, the kind that draws you closer and shuts the rest of the noisy, messy world away. The baby kicks, *hard*, so hard I have to stop and kind of push back on her foot so that it goes back to a sensible place. And then it's a battle, of course, her foot against my hand.

She wins. I let her win. I do that a lot. Probably out of some irrational hope that she'll remember this and won't think quite so badly of me later. *Yeah, my mother gave me up*, she'll tell people, *but she used to let me kick her however hard I liked, so that's something.*

I find the old carousel, relatively free of broken pieces and rusty edges, and pull my chips, my giant pregnant belly, and myself up onto a dusty white pony.

"That's brave," a girl's voice remarks.

I *am* somewhat precariously perched on this horse, but I'm a dancer. I have an excellent sense of balance, even seven months pregnant. I look around to find the source of the voice and see that there's a girl tucked into a ladybug's hollowed-out body close by. She's about my age, sixteen or seventeen, and she pops little white balls out of her ear. At first I think they're cotton wool, but then I realize they're headphones, some kind of supercool wireless type that I've never seen before. I think of my lame headphones with their perpetually tangled wires and feel instantly envious.

"I didn't see you there."

"I know," she says. "I didn't mean to startle you." Her eyes drift again and again to my belly in a way that I've gotten used to over the past few months, only it's not the usual rude judgy look I see in her eyes. It's something else. "Can I have a chip?"

I hold out the cone, and she reaches over the ladybug's head to take one. Her eyes are bright and clever, and they remind me of someone, but I can't put my finger on whom. They dart to my belly again.

"Yes, I'm pregnant," I say.

"Sorry," she says sheepishly, and then, in a rush to explain herself, "My birth mother got pregnant with me when she was sixteen, so I can't help noticing when I see people my age with, you know, a bump. It always makes me think of her."

"Oh." I pause, hesitate. "Were you adopted?"

She nods.

"Do you know her?"

She shakes her head, then says, "But that's fine, because I don't think I want to know her."

"Oh," I say again.

"I have a family already," she says, rushing once again to explain herself. Killian. That's who she reminds me of. Killian, with his bright, clever eyes and the smile that melts my heart to a puddle and that earnest desire to be liked, to be understood. "A big family, all messy and daft and really annoying sometimes. My parents split up when I was six, so I have stepparents too and a stepbrother and new cousins and about twenty grandparents." She smiles, but this time there's something brittle and forced about it. "I mean, my family annoys me sometimes, and they don't always get me, and I really, really wish my dad would stop trying to convince me to become an architect like him, but you know what? They love me; I know they do. There's not one drop of blood shared between them and me and they love me anyway. So why would I want to know someone who never loved or wanted me just because we've got some of the same DNA?"

As she speaks, I reach absently for the pendant around my neck. Hidden under my oversized sweater, it's a gold ballet slipper on a delicate gold chain. I run my thumb over it, one, two, three times. I watch the way the girl's face softens when she talks about her family and how that softness vanishes when she talks about the birth mother who didn't want her.

You see, I can almost hear my mother say, *this is how your daughter will feel if you let her go. This is what I've been warning you about. You'll regret it if you give her up—you know you will.*

She's a broken record these days. Five and a half months since I found out I was pregnant, five and a half months of my mother and sisters and everyone else telling me what I should and shouldn't do. Five and a half months of my own doubts nagging and scratching at me, keeping me up at night, telling me I'll regret it if I keep her, I'll regret it if I give her up, I'll regret it twenty years down the line when I wonder what became of her.

I've been quiet too long. The girl blinks at me, then awkwardly changes the subject. "So do you know if you're having a boy or a girl?"

"A girl."

"Cool! Do you know how you're going to juggle everything once she's here?" Her face brightens. "My cousin had a baby last year, and he drives her *crazy*, but she's so happy. Do you think you—"

"I'm not," I say. Bite the bullet, get it over with.

"Sorry?"

"I'm not going to juggle everything. I'm putting the baby up for adoption."

Silence. So much silence I can hear the whistle of the wind from the sea, the caws of the seagulls, the thrum of my own heart. The baby kicks again. Fireflies twinkle across the fairground, which is odd because I've never seen fireflies here before.

I dare a look at the girl's face. I can see she's replaying everything she said to me and feeling embarrassed because of the way she spoke about her birth mother, but I can also see she almost feels betrayed too, as if she thought I was someone she could like and then I turned out to be just like the girl who left her behind.

She clears her throat. "Can I . . ." She hesitates. "Can I ask . . ."

"You want to know why," I finish for her.

She nods.

We can't possibly have the same stories, her birth mother and I, and there are a million and one reasons to keep a baby or to give one up. But maybe she feels that this is the closest she'll ever get to understanding why her mother gave her up. All I can do is give her my truth, and maybe it will give her a piece of hers too.

"I don't think I'd do it right," I say.

She frowns. "But no one does it right at the start, do they?"

"It's not that. I know that. It's *me*."

Killian told me he'd support whatever I wanted to do, that he'd stick by me. And his voice is the one I've relied on when I've had my own doubts, his voice and my body, the body on hundreds of videos, dancing, always dancing. I've watched them a thousand times, and each time I dream of getting back on a stage again. I know you can dance and have a baby at the same time, I know people do it, but I don't think *I* can. I don't think I could do both *well*.

I don't think I *want* to do both.

I try to explain. "I don't think she's the life I want," I say, "so it feels like it would be unfair to her to keep her despite that. I love her, but she's not right for me and I'm not right for her. A broken condom doesn't mean either of us should have to be shoehorned into lives that don't fit."

"What if it's what she wants?" she asks. "You're not exactly letting *her* choose."

That's kept me up at night too. It's true; this baby doesn't get to make a choice. Do babies ever get a choice? Isn't that the point of a parent, to be the person who makes the choices even when it's hard? This may be the only choice I'll ever make as her parent. And it's the right one. I know that. I trust that. I just—

Regret.

—I just wonder sometimes.

"I don't get it," the girl says, quieter now. There are tears in her eyes. "I don't understand why she doesn't matter more to you than that."

My temper flares, but I stamp it down and try to be gentle

to this girl who is so happy in her home and so happy with her family and yet has carried around a small, secret pain for so long. "She does matter," I say. "That's why I want to give her up. She's not my dream, but she is somebody else's. She deserves to be there, with that somebody else. She deserves to be the dream."

The tears spill out of the girl's eyes and run down her cheeks, but she wipes them away. "Sorry," she mumbles, pink and awkward.

"Don't worry about it."

"And I'm sorry I was rude. What you do with your baby is not my business. I don't have any right to judge."

"It's okay. I know why you said it; I don't blame you."

She takes a minute to look across the empty fairground, and her tense, unhappy expression eases away as she calms down. She takes a couple of more chips from my cone. "Do you think maybe my mother felt like you do?"

"Maybe," I say, "or maybe not. But it doesn't matter unless you want it to. I mean, you're happy. Your birth mother can't make or break that, no matter what." I hesitate. "You *are* happy? Aren't you?"

And then suddenly I'm the one with tears on my face. I look out at the sea, at the horizon of gray water and silver sky. My feet itch, dancer's feet desperate to run to the horizon and soar over the edge into a life full of dreams and color. And yet I'm leaden, grounded, afraid to go over the edge.

"I don't want to break her heart," I whisper. "I don't want to break her world."

The girl's hand creeps into mine. We both look at the sea, two girls, an unborn baby, and creatures on a ghost carousel. "Is that what you're afraid of? That you'll choose badly and the world she ends up with won't be so great?"

"If I could only *know* . . ."

The girl nods. "If I could only *know*," she repeats. "I've said that too. Story of our lives, I suppose? If we could only know."

The baby kicks again, another big one, and it knocks the rest of the chips right off my lap. We both laugh. The girl climbs out of the ladybug and crouches down to pick up the box. As she does, a pendant falls out of her coat and glints gold in the weak spring sunlight.

My heart kicks harder than the baby. The pendant is a gold ballet slipper.

I slide off the pony. My voice breaks. "Where did you get that?"

"This?" she frowns. "My birth mother sent it with me when she put me up for adoption." An odd look crosses her face. "I suppose she must have cared about me a little, mustn't she, if she gave me this?"

There's a roar in my ears, louder than the sea. I look at the fairground, alive and vibrant and tacky last I saw it and yet inexplicably deserted and disused now. Fireflies and rusty metal and dreamlike quiet that shuts the rest of the world out. I look at the girl with Killian's bright, clever eyes. I look at the necklace my grandmother had made for me, around my neck, and somehow around hers too.

"What year is it?" I ask.

"What sort of daft question is that?"

I wait.

She huffs. "2032."

My world teeters, but I try not to cry. "When I fell asleep on that bus today, it was 2016."

She gives me an odd look. "If you say so."

"Look," I say. I pull out my own necklace and show her the ballet slipper. Her eyes grow wide. "The back of this slipper, see? It's engraved. Just one word."

Soar.

She turns her own pendant over. And there it is, worn down by the years but still clear.

Soar.

"This is impossible," she breathes.

"Maybe it's a dream."

"Yours or mine?"

"I don't know. Maybe both. Maybe neither. I don't know."

She stares at me, eyes enormous and incredulous. "So you're my—"

She stops. She can't say it. Neither can I.

"Let's go for a walk," I say, "until one of us wakes up."

So we do. *If only we could know*, we said, and now we can. We tell each other everything. I talk about Killian and that first time we kissed and how his eyes grow bright like the sun when he watches me dance; she talks about her parents and stepparents and how she has this best friend and they want to go on a road trip together like in old movies, and I tell her those movies aren't "old" for me, thanks very much.

We stand on the pebbly beach with the sun turning hard and red on the horizon. Her beach is no different from mine sixteen years ago, just perhaps a little more worn down. The sea looks the same, but then maybe the sea is always the same no matter which side of the horizon you approach it from.

"I won't pretend I completely understand why you're going to let me go," she says. "I won't pretend I don't get pissed off about it sometimes. Maybe I'll understand one day, maybe I never will. But I know you care. I do see that. And that means the world to me."

"Are you okay?"

She looks at me, and she smiles, *my* smile. "Yes," she tells me. "I think so. You don't have to be afraid. It's like you said: I wasn't your dream, but I was someone's else's. You grew me, but they made the shape of me. And I *will* soar."

"I know you will," I say.

"And so will you."

"Just not with you," I say, and it's funny how much that hurts. I'm okay with this choice, I am, but she's in my heart and I'll never get her out. "Come say hello one day. If you want to."

I look out at the water again. There's no question it will break my heart when I give her up. There's no question it will break hers every time she wonders why we weren't right for each other. But that's okay because you can soar with a heart that's been broken and mended so many times you've lost count.

When I look back, my daughter is gone and the fairground is alive with lights and music again.

Sangu Mandanna was four years old when an elephant chased her down a forest road and she decided to write her first story about it. Seventeen years and many, many manuscripts later, she signed her first book deal. *The Lost Girl*, a YA sci fi novel about death and love, is available now. Sangu now lives in Norwich, a city in the east of England, with her husband and kids.

"I was very young when I first realized families come in all shapes and sizes. The choice to give a child up is as valid as the choice to keep one, and the choice to welcome a child into your home makes you as much a parent as someone making the choice to carry a baby to term. I'm so excited to be involved in an anthology that celebrates all those choices and all the different loving, messy families out there."

Lullaby

by Matthew Quinn Martin

"There is a mark upon a stone. And in this place a life was written, And there a stain was laid where I was born."
—Michael Gira, from My Father Will Guide Me a Rope Up to the Sky

What would you say if you knew that tomorrow you would leave Earth, never to return?

The question was centered on a single sheet of thick paper hand delivered to me by a member of the Defense Courier Service. He stood there, waiting and watching, as I sat on my barracks bunk pondering what it meant. The envelope was addressed to me: Marine Corps PFC, Ibrahim Walker. But other than that, and what was printed inside . . . nothing.

"What am I supposed to do with this?"

"You are to verbally answer, private," the DFC man said with the curtness of all career military. "If your answer is deemed acceptable, you will be given an opportunity for reassignment."

"Reassignment? Where?"

"Classified."

There was no making sense of this. But then again, very little of my life had ever made any sense. *Sense* and *fairness* were luxuries reserved for others. Not for orphans. Not for foster children.

All the foster kids I'd ever known carried with them the same two dreams. There is the public dream, and there is the one we keep secret—only occasionally sharing it in hushed tones with other members of the loose cabal we'd been drafted into. The first dream is simple. We wait—some of us for years, some of us until we are grasping adulthood—to be adopted, to be welcomed into a family that will love us not for the genes we'd received, not because of which sperm made it to which egg, but for us—and us alone.

Then there's the secret dream. The mythic dream. The one we all go to bed wishing for until we're so old that our wishbones have grown ossified and arthritic, ready to snap. We keep it secret because we know how fragile it is. If you've spent your whole life trying to angle, to wheedle, to tap dance, or to flat-out lie to get what most children take for granted, the last thing you want is to watch that one last hope burned to cinders by the cruelty of others. Other orphans. Other adults asking you to manage your expectations. Other experts, other "care" takers, and that sly *other* that lives inside your head.

The secret dream goes like this: One day, the orphan, the throwaway kid, the stepped-on stepchild, the street urchin—honestly, take your pick—will wake to find out that there was a *reason* why they were abandoned, something beyond random chance or selfishness. Grave circumstances, as it turned out, forced his or her noble parents to make the hardest choice imaginable in order to protect their beloved child from an evil beyond measure. That dream whispers to us the impossible: that the suffering we've endured was not without purpose. It was, instead, a purifying fire. And that what happened to us was not a tragedy—it was destiny.

◇◇◇◇

You know this story. From Moses to Harry Potter, it's always the same. You know it in your head, but it takes an orphan to hear that song—that lullaby—singing in his blood.

I joined the Marines hoping to find some foundation. Always a good student, despite the hardships, I graduated from high school early, with top honors, at sixteen. The day after my seventeenth birthday, I shipped out for boot camp. Four months later I found myself here—Camp Dwyer, Afghanistan, a desert hell pretty much exactly how you'd picture it. What I'd hoped to find in the Corps was a surrogate family—not a perfect one, just one I could call mine. Just one that would call me theirs.

What I found was dust.

Acres and acres of dust.

What I found were bullets, blood, and the dubious honor of being able to call myself a murderer—a government-sanctioned murderer, but a murderer just the same. Still half a year shy of being old enough to vote and I'd already racked up three confirmed kills along with all the backslapping that comes with it.

I read the question again. The paper felt as heavy as a stone tablet. "And I just tell you my answer? That's it?"

"Those are my orders, private. Mine *and* yours."

Reassignment. The word ricocheted in my mind. Any place would be better than this. I'd made exactly zero friends since my deployment—forget about family. I wondered what this reassignment would mean. "Last day on Earth?" Space? NASA? Something else? Something stranger?

My head filled with the kind of pabulum a high-ranking bureaucrat might want to hear.

—I'd feel like a proud pioneer! I'd wear that badge with honor. I'd hold fast, like the mariners of old who'd tattooed that edict across their knuckles.

—I'd miss my home. But nothing of value is gained without great sacrifice.

—I'd feel terrified. But only by conquering that all too personal terror would I be able to play some part—no matter how small—in ushering humanity into its next golden age.

Bullshit. All of it bullshit. I'd spent my life spinning out line after line of bullshit and always in the name of survival. And yes, I'd survived. But is that all my life would ever mean? Surviving? I didn't want to *survive* my life. I wanted to *live* it.

I looked up at the man still hovering over me, hands clasped behind his back as he stood at ease. "The world has showed me nothing but indifference on my best days," I told him. "Flat-out cruelty for the rest of them. If I had a chance to go someplace else, even if it meant never coming back, what would I say?

"I'd say, 'why did it take so long?'"

The man smiled. He held out his hand. "Welcome to Project Nephilim."

The flight to the port of Karachi took less than an hour. The time we'd spent at sea took more than a week. There were roughly four hundred souls packed in that floating sardine can. All of us, it turned out, had been presented with the same single question. And while our answers differed, each of us had been extended an invitation to join this probationary phase, as they called it.

Some were like me, culled from various branches of the armed services—and not only the US military, but from all over the globe. Many more had been pulled in from other areas. PhD candidates in various specialties. Engineers. Ballet dancers. Agriculturists. Doctors fresh out of medical school. Linguists. Artisans. Musical prodigies. You name it. We were headed to Port Foster. Ironic, as it turned out, for every single passenger was an orphan. Ironic, but no coincidence, as I would later learn.

No one told us which organization or government had brought us here. No one told us anything else about the enigmatic Project Nephilim. The word, while obscure, was known to enough of our number that competing definitions soon spread through the ranks. Some said they were giants. Others, demigods. Still others, a race of watcher angels. Many pondered the significance. Those of us who were familiar with code names pointed out that they usually amounted to jack shit, nothing but smoke screens.

There were more tests. More questions. Interviews. Evaluations. We ate and lived together. Fights broke out. Flames ignited. We formed cliques, knowing they would be short-lived, but hoping some would continue if we reached the next phase. And then we docked at Port Foster. Like all short but intense periods, it felt like a lifetime . . . and it felt like a dream.

We assembled in the main hold. One of the mariners stood on a catwalk, clipboard in hand, staring down at us. "If you hear your name read aloud," he said, "proceed up the ramp and you will be directed from there."

Name after name was called out. There were cheers from the elect. High fives delivered to friends who'd made it on that list together. There was no order. No waiting for the letter of your last name to pass by. There was simply the litany and a steady emptying of the hold until the mariner put down his clipboard and turned to leave.

I looked around. Fewer than thirty of us remained. I didn't know a single one of them. "What about us?" I called out, saying aloud what we all wanted to know, trying not to let it get to me, that all-too-familiar feeling of being left behind. "What do we do?"

"You . . ." said another voice from behind us. We turned to

see a man whose name I would shortly learn was Dr. Ramirez. He wore a white lab coat and a grin. ". . . have made the cut."

The base looked just like an ice-locked hut no bigger than a fishing shack, dimly backlit by the Antarctic dusk, wavering in and out of view as the wind kicked up scrims of biting snow. We were told that the bulk of the facility lay hundreds of feet below the surface. This was simply the access port. The only access port.

We were ordered not to speak with each other. We were told not to speculate on what we were doing here, or about the project, or why we were chosen. We were informed that there would be one last test, if we chose to take it. But until then, we would be isolated from each other.

We descended, eight at a time, in a cargo elevator. I was shown to a comfortable, but sterile, cinderblock cell. It had a bunk, a television and video player, a toilet, a sink, an intercom—and a door that had a handle only on the outside. That's where I spent the bulk of the next month. Meals were delivered to me whenever I requested them. I was given access to the workout room for an hour every day and my pick of whatever was in the library—provided I took it right back to my quarters. But I was forbidden to speak with anyone, even the staff.

"Why don't you want us talking to each other?" I once asked the guard stationed outside my cell.

He didn't answer.

He didn't answer the next time, or the next twenty times, for that matter. Then, finally, scanning in both directions to make sure we were not watched, he whispered, "Personal attachments—especially either strongly held or newly formed personal attachments—can negatively affect the process." He cleared his throat. "It seems to get jealous."

"It? What it?"

"You'll see."

And those were the last words I'd heard spoken for nearly a month.

By the middle of the second week, I'd taken to lying on my twin bunk for hours, just imagining what it would be like to have a conversation with another human being. When the third week had rolled over into the fourth, I'd grown to enjoy the silence and the solitude.

I was staring at the ceiling when I heard the magnetic seal on my cell door clack open. There were footsteps. I felt a shadow hanging over me. "Private Walker?" came the voice I'd recognized as Dr. Ramirez. "I'll be taking you through the final phase of your testing."

We walked down the same stretch of hallway I'd traversed twice daily on the way to my workout sessions. We went past that door, as well as the one to the library, and into uncharted territory.

"Ibrahim," said Dr. Ramirez, as if he were chewing the syllables rather than speaking them, "Do you prefer to be called that?"

No one had ever called me that—no one who wasn't sounding my name off a roster or a manifest. "When I was a kid they all called me Raheem," I told him. "Now everyone just calls me Walker, or Private, or . . . Hey You."

"And what do you prefer?"

I thought about it and told him straight. "I don't care much what other people call me."

"Interesting," he said, more to himself than me.

We stepped into another elevator, and down we went. I wondered just how deep this place extended—and just how deep I had gotten myself.

◇◇◇◇

It swirled, the thing on the other side of the glass. No, that wasn't quite right. It *danced*. I stared at it, rapt. The closest I could ever hope to come to describing it was *like a dust storm with a mind . . . no, a soul.*

Dr. Ramirez stood behind me. I watched his ghosted reflection as that reflection watched me and *it*. I tentatively held my palm to the glass. The particles began to coalesce against the pane. They seemed drawn to my hand like iron filings to a magnet, growing ever thicker, mirroring me. I twisted my wrist, and they followed. I slid my palm over, and they followed. I drew my fingers together until only the tips remained in contact. They tried to follow, maintaining cohesion for a little over an inch before collapsing back into the tumbling whirl.

"What is it?"

"We're still not entirely sure. Our best guess is that it's a colony of chemo- and photo-autotrophic archaea that possesses, if not consciousness, at least a rapid reactiveness—not unlike the way a plant will grow toward the sun, only much, much faster."

Apparently.

"That," he continued, "and . . ."

"And?"

"And the ability to act as a kind of communicator."

"Communicator? For whom?"

"Someone—something—very, *very* far away from here."

I felt the weight, the solidity, of the silence between us. My mind scrolled back to the question that had set this whole machine in motion.

What would you say if you knew that tomorrow you would leave Earth, never to return?

"You're telling me this is from outer space?"

"Not exactly. The organism originated on Earth. The general consensus is that until its recent emergence, it lay dormant in a lake about a mile beneath us—trapped in the ice and completely sealed off from all other life on the planet for eons."

I had no words, and I could tell I was not the first to react this way.

"About thirty years ago," continued Dr. Ramirez, settling into an obviously well-worn patter, "some of our satellites noticed anomalous energy discharges in this vicinity. We sent in a team—or at least, the organization did. I was still watching Saturday morning cartoons back then.

"They discovered this." He nodded to the helix of particles still swirling on the other side of the glass. "Seems something in the energy discharge, well . . . told it to wake up, and to . . . evolve."

Evolve? Things weren't just commanded to evolve. They evolved to fill a niche. That's how evolution worked. And it took millennia, not days. "How is that possible?"

"We've been trying to figure that out for three decades. We believe that the organism responds to messages coded in those energy discharges, and that they are coming from another consciousness."

"Messages?"

His voice grew quiet. "Messages and commands."

"But where? Consciousness from where?"

He talked slowly and calmly, as if he were explaining how to drive a golf ball and not revealing the cold truth that we were not alone in the universe. "This entity, or entities, is approximately fourteen hundred light years past the rim of the solar system. The energy discharges are one-way dispatches sent superluminally. How they get here, we don't know. We believe it has something to do with harnessing the earth's magnetic field. That's why they have always been here, near the pole."

"And what has it been saying?"

"We can't just talk to it—to them—whatever. Look how hard it us for us as a species to communicate with *each other*. Now imagine trying to do that with an entirely alien mind. One that had an entirely different evolutionary path. One that experiences time at a different rate, in a different way. Most of what we receive gets hopelessly lost in translation, and the fact that we've been able to communicate at all is a miracle." He took off his wire-rimmed specs and nervously started polishing them with the end of his necktie. "A lot of it has been decades of guesswork, but we think we know why they reached out."

"And?"

He looked me square. "Are you familiar with the Gaia Hypothesis?"

I shook my head.

"Watch this, then," he said, clicking a fob clipped to his lab coat. The lights went dim, and a film was projected onto the far wall. It reminded me of educational videos we would watch in grade school. Archival footage showed a much younger Dr. Ramirez and his staff. The graphics were dated, but the message got across.

Gaia theory, simply put, posits that the earth is a living system—a meta-organism. This meta-organism interacts with the inorganic material in the planet itself and eventually develops a consciousness of its own. And that consciousness is humankind.

"So this other consciousness?" I asked when the presentation was over. "You think what? It's trying to talk to us?"

"We more than think it . . . we know it. And the overwhelming sense is that it—or they—want to help us grow."

"Grow?"

"If you follow the logic that this planet is a living thing . . . that this meta-organism that we are a part of has now reached, for lack of a better term, *adulthood* . . . then what's the next logical step for any living thing?"

I shook my head. Logical step? None of this was logical.

"Reproduction." His voice had grown rhapsodic, almost giddy.

I found my mind pulling back. Reproduction? *Planetary* reproduction? "Hold on. Are you saying this other world, this other meta-organism, it, what . . . wants to *mate* with us?"

"Not exactly," he said. "There are ways—yes—that you could see it that way. But I think a better term might be . . . midwife. This other consciousness has recognized another like itself and it wants to help us reach our potential. It wants us to join it in becoming more than we are. It wants, well . . . to adopt us."

That hit like two boots to the chest. "Adopt us?"

He broke off quickly, knowing what a word like that meant to someone like me. "Or at least welcome us into some kind of . . . galactic family."

I tried to get a grip on what he was saying, and what it might mean for me. "How can you be sure? What if it's some kind of game? What if that . . . that . . . *consciousness* just wants to invade us, to take us over?"

"Trust me," he said, his usually cheerful tone slipping into a grave and minor key, "this thing is advanced far beyond what we can even imagine. It's mastered faster-than-light communication. It has the ability to alter life on this planet from a distance we can barely comprehend. If it wanted us dead, we'd be dead. If it wanted anything we have on earth that isn't already abundantly available throughout the rest of the Milky Way, it would have taken it.

"No . . . it wants to help. It wants us to grow. If there's one single concept we've managed to home in on, it's that." He turned back to the glass and the dervish behind it. "And where you come in, perhaps."

"How?"

"We've already detected at least a dozen planets less than twenty light years away that are all within the circumstellar habitable zone. In order for Earth—for Gaia—to reproduce, it must replicate itself using one or more of these worlds as a platform. We've been at work designing a fleet of ark ships that will carry human beings, as well as a wide enough sample of Earth's biodiversity for a viable ecosystem to take hold. These ecosystems will, of course, adapt and evolve in their own right, sure, but they will be—in a very real sense—Earth's offspring. Gaia's children.

"We can reach these planets. We have the technology. But even at the outer limits of our projected velocity it will take centuries, if not millennia. Every living thing on the ark ships will be kept in stasis. They'll need someone to watch over them. And that's what it . . ."—again, he gestured to the glass—"is providing for us."

Watchers. Nephilim. It wasn't a smoke screen at all. "How?"

"It chooses certain individuals to bond with. It infiltrates them and combines with them at the cellular level, drastically altering their physiology so that they will be better able to withstand the rigors of interstellar travel."

"Bond with? Like a parasite?"

He shook his head. "More of a composite organism. Similar to lichen. We're not entirely certain of all of the parameters, but other subjects who have bonded uniformly developed immunity to extremes in temperature, drastically increased strength and mental prowess, the ability to spend extended periods of time in a complete vacuum, and an extended life span."

Superpowers, that's what he was talking about. This thing gave you superpowers and perhaps even immortality. "How extended of a life span?"

Dr. Ramirez spread out his hands. "Centuries, if not millennia. If not more."

Again I looked at the thing as it swirled. I could swear it was beckoning to me. "You said it chooses. How?"

"You go into that chamber and find out. It's the final test."

"What happens if I fail?"

"Bad things," he said. "I'm not going to lie. I'm not going to go into the details either. But I will tell you this: we've managed to achieve a 90 percent success rate. The whittling-down process you underwent on the boat, it was all part of the plan. The organism favors a certain type of person to bond with."

"Orphans."

"Yes. But not just orphans. Ones who seem to hold at their heart a deep love for this world, but at the same time avoid all personal attachments. Think about it. Do you have a girlfriend? A best friend? A blood brother?"

He knew the answers better than I did.

"What about a favorite TV show? A football team? You don't, do you? You are a cypher. Every candidate who makes it this far is. What we're offering you is a chance to become something more."

A 90 percent success rate, I thought. Those were solid odds. But I knew all too well that there were seventy-three million children in the United States, and only 0.5 percent of them ended up in foster care as I did. I was used to pulling long odds and getting burned by them. "And if I'm in the 10 percent that doesn't make it?"

"You probably won't die. It will be . . . unpleasant." He paused. "I need to be clear about this. The sense of loss, of abandonment, that we've observed in rejected candidates is so pervasive that none have been able to live functional lives afterward. And it will be painful. There is a strong likelihood that you will beg for death if the organism chooses not to adopt you."

Death did not scare me. Death is at the end of the line for all of us. But there was that word again . . . *adoption*. Here it was, staring at me, my last chance to be *adopted*. And not just that, but to have the secret dream come true at last. For all of this to mean something.

"The choice is yours," Dr. Ramirez said finally.

I took one last look at the miniature cyclone whirling hypnotically behind the glass partition. I could swear it wasn't just dancing; it was singing. It was singing to me. Dr. Ramirez was wrong. The choice was never mine—not alone.

I awoke on a hospital bed. My mouth tasted like melted wax, and my head pounded. Machines flanked me, and I'd been hooked to more wires and tubes than I'd thought possible. By my bedside sat Dr. Ramirez.

"How long have I been out?"

"About three weeks."

"And the process . . ." I tried to remember what had happened after I'd entered the chamber and came back empty.

"The process went smoothly. You have nothing to worry about."

"I don't remember it."

He shrugged. "Do you remember your birth? Why would this, your second birth, be any different? You've become someone—something—else. Some subjects even choose new names for themselves."

It was my turn to shrug. I'd meant it when I'd told him I don't care much what people call me. "Now what?"

"Now we wait. Eventually, when the ark fleet has been completed, you'll be assigned to one of the ships and help shepherd in the next phase of Terran evolution."

"There will be training, I'm assuming."

"In time."

"Can I see the others now? The others who have also been bonded?"

"You will soon enough." Something about the way his eyes suddenly slid to the floor troubled me.

"And the ark ships . . . when will they be ready?"

Dr. Ramirez's eyes stayed on the floor. He tugged off his glasses and once again began to polish them. "Current estimates put the launch date somewhere in the middle of the twenty-second century.

I shook my head, not sure I'd heard him correctly. "But that's more than a hundred years from now."

"Yes."

That's all he said, damning me with a single syllable. "But what will I do? I can't go back to the regular world. Not like this. Not as a . . ." As a what? A freak? A god?

"No, of course not. You'll stay here. You'll stay here and you'll sleep," he said. "You'll sleep with the rest of them."

"Sleep?" I'd just been asleep for almost a month. The last thing I wanted to think about was more sleep. "I don't want to sleep."

"Want is irrelevant. You'll sleep. You all sleep."

I sat bolt upright. "What are you talking about?"

I could see that, again, he'd dealt with these questions before, maybe countless times. "Think you're up for a walk?" he asked.

I nodded.

"Then come with me," he said, already unhooking me from the machines.

We traveled down another elevator. It opened up on onto a vast chamber. And that's where I saw them. A field of statues. Except they weren't statues, and I knew it. They stood, fixed and at attention, stretching back in a grid until they disappeared into the gloom.

I remembered seeing a picture of an army of terra-cotta warriors that had been buried with the Chinese emperor Qin Shi Huang. This is what they looked like. A buried army. One that was alive. One that was immortal. One that I would soon join.

"How many of them are there?"

"One thousand one hundred and twenty-two," he said. "You make it -twenty-three."

Standing here, I could tell that he hadn't been lying to me. I would sleep, and that sleep would be long. "And when will this happen to me? When will the sleep take hold?"

"Most likely in the next twenty-four to forty-eight hours. But it could be sooner. Much sooner."

"Have any of them ever woken up?"

"Not a one."

That night, lying on my bed, I didn't think I'd sleep, not in the normal sense. But I did, wondering if it would be the last time I did. Wondering if I would have my last human dream, or nothing but blackness.

And sometime in the night, the lullaby came to me. It sang to my new body from someplace far away. It sang in a voice that I recognized in the core of my being, in my DNA. It was the most beautiful thing I'd ever heard. I rose from by bed and followed it. I followed it down the hallway, to the elevator, and out into the open air.

They were all outside waiting, my brothers and sisters, my family. Like me, they'd been called by the same voice, the same song. The one that is beyond words, and beyond worlds. They'd been waiting for me to join them, and I would be the last. We gathered in the blackness of the long Antarctic night, knowing—knowing it all.

It was all so blindingly clear. We were never destined to leave this world. Instead, we would protect it. They had it wrong, the people who brought us here. They were right about the earth being a meta-organism. They were right about it having developed a consciousness. But it was not the adult consciousness they'd thought it was. The earth had the consciousness of a child—a misbehaving child.

The entity we were in contact with on a level that no pure human could comprehend, it wasn't some cosmic cheerleader rooting for us to make it to the next level. It was a thing so vast, so ancient, that it could not be reduced to a word as simplistic as "consciousness." And in that lullaby it sang to us the truth of it all. *It* was what had created us. *It* was our parent. Our father, and mother, in heaven.

And it had been watching. And like all good parents, it wanted only the best for its child. Did it want to help us grow, as Dr. Ramirez had thought? In a sense. But he was only half right. What it wanted was for us to grow *up*. And for a child to learn, sometimes that child must learn the hard way.

We never spoke, but we all knew what would come next. From here we would spread out, my brothers and sisters, all one thousand one hundred and twenty-three of us. We would bury ourselves deep in the ice, in the earth, and we would wait. Dr. Ramirez's ark ships would never be built. Long before that could happen, humanity would reap the devastation it had caused to the planet. The seas would rise. Wars would break out. Civilization would collapse.

And we will wait. We will wait until the advancing glaciers of another ice age destroy all traces of this version of humanity. We will wait until the humans who remain talk of this world the way we did of Atlantis. We will wait, rocked by the lullaby only we can hear. And when the time is right, we will come back.

And we will watch.

Matthew Quinn Martin was born in Allentown, Pennsylvania, and raised in New Haven, Connecticut. However, it wasn't until he moved to Manhattan that he realized he was a writer. He's the author of the *Nightlife* series (Pocket Star/Simon & Schuster) and screenwriter of the original script for the feature film *Slingshot* (Bold Films/Weinstein Co.) These days, he lives on a small island off the North Atlantic coast of the United States where it gets quiet in the winter . . . perhaps too quiet.

"Not every adoption has to be some big legal thing. Every time you offer up any part of your life to a child who needs you, you've become a part of that child's life. These 'small' adoptions add up to big things. I know they did for me."

Census Man

by Mindy McGinnis

They said the census man was comin' and that means something special, I guess, 'cause we got extra time in the bathroom this mornin'. Not enough to make the water any warmer, mind you, but I don't make much noise 'bout that. Some of the other girls like to brag how where they come from there was a hot water tap, but I don't much see the point in talkin' up something you lost. Me, I been in this here orphanage a year, and not a day goes by I don't thank the Lord for the flush toilets. Nobody appreciates a crapper 'til they've had to use an outhouse.

Laura elbows her way in next to me to give herself a good look in the mirror. She pulls up a perfect curl to hang against her face real pretty. "How you doin' yours, hon?"

I shrug. I don't have so much as a bounce in my stick-straight hair. What there is left of it, anyway. The last lice check left a good part of it in the trash bin.

"Aw, c'mon now, Mary Ann," she says, turning me toward her real gentle. "You've still got the baby fat in your cheeks, looks real sweet with that short cut. Somebody's gonna spot you and say—that, 'That one, right there, the one with the cherub face.'"

She points at me like she has a hundred times before, play-acting the day when I walk out of here with a new family, easy as spit. I seen it happen for a few, mostly the littlest ones, some of 'em so small they got to be carried away crying, too young to understand this ain't home, just a stopping point on the way.

"What's a sin-sus man do, anyway?" I ask Laura. My mouth was all awkward around the strange word. She wets her fingers and tries to smooth out what's left of my hair. "He write down things we done wrong?"

Her eyebrows come together like I said something funny but she doesn't laugh at me like the others. "Not sin like the kind they talk to us about in chapel, Mary Ann. C-e-n-s-u-s." She spells it out real careful, her fingers brushin' against my ear as she tries to cover up the top bit that's all wiggly from where I got up against the stove one time.

"He comes to count us," she goes on.

"Why? He have to practice his numbers or somethin'?"

"No, not exactly." Laura takes me by the hand, and we find our step on the long stair, each of us standing on the one that's got our named chalked on it. She's one below me, so when she turns to answer me it's like we're the same height.

"He counts us 'cause the government wants to know how many people there is," she says, patient as ever. "So the census men, they go out and write down the names of all the people in the houses, and who's the parents and who's the kids and how old they are."

I scuff the toe of my too-big shoe against the step, rubbin' out part of my name by accident. "That'd take an awful long time," I say as I change my name from Mary Ann to plain Mary. "Not as long as writin' out everybody's sins would, I guess."

Laura laughs, and that gets us a whack with the headmistress's hazel switch. Our calves are smartin' as we go down to breakfast to the sound of a hundred borrowed pairs of shoes marching down stairs in a house no one lives in.

"You know an awful lot 'bout it, the census," I say to Laura around a mouthful of eggs.

"I remember the last one. They do 'em every ten years," she says, touching away a line of milk above her lip with her napkin. "I was only six, but momma made a big show, put us all in our Sunday clothes."

My throat tries to close up around my eggs, but I act like hearing her say *momma* don't bother me none. Laura's far enough away from hers that she can say it casual like that, 'cause it don't mean nothin' to her no more. And maybe it's easier, too, 'cause hers wanted to stay with her. Laura's told me more than once how she fought the fever, swearin' up and down her girls weren't goin' to no goddamn charity house. But the sickness thought otherwise, and Laura's been here longer than most.

Laura always gets a little shiver out of me when she says the swear word in her story, coming down real hard on that *goddamn* like it's the best part. She thinks that's why I ask her to tell it over and over, her words whispered tight and low so we don't get the switch after lights out. She don't know it ain't the bad word but the good ones I'm dying for, and the thought of a momma that tried.

I gulp my milk down fast, chasing the ball of tears that wants to find its way up to my eyes. I don't know if it's a bad thing to be mad at my parents or not, or even if that's allowed. But there's one name that won't be on this census and wasn't around for the last one. My little sister Luella died with a bellyful of lye after momma mixed it and left it on the counter, too soused to put it up high where little hands and a curious mouth couldn't reach.

I try not to think about Luella too much, how I couldn't

get her to uncurl from around her tummy, how I tried to wake up momma even though I knew if the sound of Luella's screaming wasn't going to do it there was no way I could either. The headmistress tole me when I got here that what's past is behind me, but if that's the case I must have eyes in the back of my head, 'cause I can see the look on my momma's face plain as day when the court lady came to get me.

I reach up to itch my scalp and Laura eyes me real hard, so I drop my hand. I been thinkin' so close on Luella and momma that I took no notice of the hall gettin' quiet around me. Everybody's sittin' up straight and proper and using their polite voices, so I know the headmistress musta come in with some people who want a kid and here we are a whole room full of kids who want people. I'm one of them, and dang if there isn't a tickle on my head that needs a scratch like the dawn needs the sun.

"Laura, Mary Ann, this is Mr. and Mrs. Ocker." The headmistress's voice is right at my elbow, and the two of us look up, me trying to seem like a good and pretty child and Laura not having to try at all. We nod and say "good morning," and Mrs. Ocker smiles at me, answering with, "*Guten tag.*"

The German sounds like a coiled-up spring next to our English, a wild word that bounced around inside her mouth before finding a way out. Reminds me of the Richstein boys who would walk the train tracks with me, looking for coal that mighta blown off the cars so that we could heat our houses.

"Mary Ann is a good, clean girl," the headmistress says. "She's been with us for a year, and I can personally attest that daylight can't get in between her hand stitches."

Mr. Ocker waits for the headmistress to finish, then speaks to his wife in German. She nods, and they're about to move on when Laura pipes up.

"She's a good cook too, Mary Ann is," she says. "Knows her way around the kitchen real well."

The headmistress frowns at Laura for speaking out of turn,

and I give her a kick under the table for stretchin' the truth. I can boil water, but that's about it.

Mr. Ocker repeats what Laura said to his wife in German, and she reaches out to tuck my stubby hair bits behind my ear. Her fingers are soft and cool, and I feel the slightest waver in them when she sees the damage the stove done. But she keeps her face still and says something to me in German, eyes on mine even though Mr. Ocker does the talkin'.

"She says you must be from strong stock," he says, his English thick and heavy.

I feel those tears coming back hot and fast, because if I'm strong it's by my own right, and nothing to do with a father who knew the inside of a jail better than his own home or a mother who only loved me when I brought her a bottle. But I can't say that, so I dig down deep for the one thing those Richstein boys taught me, other than to look for coal where the track curves.

"*Danke*," I say.

Mrs. Ocker could keep her face straight at the sight of my ruined ear, but the one word of German I know breaks a smile out like I just recited the whole Bible in her language.

"Go along then, girls," the headmistress shoos us. "The census man is waiting." And even if she is a bit quick to flick her switch hand sometimes, I swear the headmistress tips me a wink as I clear my place.

There's a line of girls in the hall waiting to file in to the front room. Laura's in front of me, scratching the back of one leg with her foot.

"Didn't know you speak German," she whispers over her shoulder.

"I don't," I tell her. "And I don't cook none, either."

"I betcha you could learn," she says before she goes in the front room, the door clicking shut behind her.

"I bet maybe I could," I say to no one.

She comes out a few minutes later, squeezing my hand as she passes by.

I don't know what I thought the census man would look like, though I was expectin' something like the judge who banged a hammer and said I couldn't live at home no more. But this guy looks like anybody else, lines around his eyes and a smudge of ink on his hand. He glances up at me as I sit on the stool, crossin' my feet at the ankles like the headmistress says to.

"Name?" He asks, teeth clenched around a pipe that isn't lit.

"Mary Ann Hummel, sir," I says, and he scratches my name into the biggest book I ever seen.

"Age as of September 1 this year?"

I know my age, but he found a way to make a simple question hard. I fold my hands in my lap and realize they're sweaty. I clear my throat and look up to find he's still waitin' for an answer, but he don't look mad or nothin'.

"How old are you, sweetheart?"

"Eight, sir."

"Mmm," he says, and I hope it's the right answer because he writes it down in his book and that makes it official. He doesn't ask me anything else, but his pen keeps going, like he knows things I don't. So I lean over a bit to see.

There's rows and rows of names, some of them girls I know pretty good, some I don't. Laura's is above mine, her age—sixteen—looking big and grown-up over my little eight. The names look all confused piled on top of each other, like if I tried to read them they'd come out in a jumble. The ages, too, look like some kind of arithmetic problem I'd never be able to figure out. But the line after that's the same word over and over, and my eye goes to the neat stack of letters even if I don't know what it says.

"What's . . ." I pause, my eyes tripping over the census man's script. "What's *inmate* mean?"

"It means you're a ward of the state, kid," the census man says.

I slide down off the stool when he excuses me, thinking about that long row of inmates, written with ink that don't fade. And I'm walking down the hall wondering if maybe for the next census it can say *daughter* next to my name instead, when the door to the headmistress's office opens.

"Mary Ann," she calls to me. "Mr. and Mrs. Ocker would like to meet you."

Mindy McGinnis is a YA author who has worked in a high school library for thirteen years. Her debut, *Not a Drop to Drink* (Katherine Tegen Books, 2013), a postapocalyptic survival story set in a world with very little fresh water, has been optioned for film by Stephanie Meyer's Fickle Fish Films. The companion novel, *In a Handful of Dust* (Katherine Tegen Books), was released in 2014. Her Gothic historical thriller, *A Madness So Discreet* (Katherine Tegen Books), won the Edgar Award in 2015. Her newest releases, *The Female of the Species* (Katherine Tegen Books, 2016) and *Given to the Sea* (Putnam's Childrens, 2017), are available now!

"My grandmother spent a few years of her childhood in an orphanage, and as a kid I always asked to hear those stories. She always kept them light and appropriate, but looking back I can see the gaps where things she chose not to share with us fit."

Invited

by Lauren Morrill

The drive is almost two hours, most of it on the interstate. I spend the time watching McDonald's restaurants and BPs and Dairy Queens whiz by every few miles. I'm hoping it lulls me into something like a hypnotic state, which both distracts me from my nerves and keeps me from getting carsick. Mom, in an effort to avoid conversation or distract us from our destination, queues up a book on tape. The volume booms through the car as if it's being read by God himself, though I doubt God has much use for romance novels. Not that I would know, since we've always been an Easter-and-Christmas kind of family.

Miranda is preparing to leave Jonathan at the altar when we pull up in front of the house, a beautiful white brick home with black shutters, a red front door, and elegantly creeping ivy that practically screams, "HAPPY! FAMILY! HOME!" Mom pulls up behind a line of cars at the curb, parking behind a shiny silver minivan. The stick-figure family on the back window consists of a mom, a dad, three children of decreasing heights, two dogs, and what I think is a cat but might be a possum.

"Are you sure?" Mom asks.

No. "Yes."

"Because we can leave right now."

Yes, please. "It's fine."

She looks at me for several seconds, and I can tell she's doing that mom-intuition thing where she's trying to decide if she's going to believe me or not. She sighs.

"Okay, well, I'll just be at a coffee shop somewhere nearby. There's got to be a Starbucks or something. I brought a book." She pats her purse.

"Don't watch me walk to the door. It'll make me nervous. You can just go," I tell her. She raises an eyebrow, and I can see that this is one request she's thinking about not granting me, but she finally nods.

"Okay. Out you go, then."

I climb out, then duck my head down and give her the closest thing to a real smile I can muster. "Thanks, Mom."

"I'll be just down the street. Call me if you need anything."

As I watch her drive away, I know she won't read a single word of whatever book she brought. She'll be spending the entire time sipping on a rapidly cooling latte while she engages in some Olympic-level worrying. About me. It's what moms do.

I know that now.

The stone path up to the front door is perfectly manicured and devoid of weeds. I pass a red plastic baby swing hanging from a branch in the front yard, swaying slowly in the light summer breeze. The sight of it sends my stomach directly into my throat.

I'm standing on the doorstep, staring at the brass door knocker shaped like a lion's head, wondering if this is a knock or a let-yourself-in kind of gathering, when the door opens. A tall, athletic black man is standing there holding a bag of trash, and when he sees me he does an almost-comical double take. His muscular shoulders hunch for a fraction of a second before relaxing, an overeager smile spreading across his face. I remember reading that he played football in college. A knee injury ended his chances at going pro, so he'd gone to law school instead and is now some big-shot attorney. It's why he's leaning more on his right side, supporting the weight of the trash bag. He calls it his lucky knee. I remember liking that when I read it in the file.

"Corey! You're here!" He drops the trash bag on the mat and steps forward, then back and to the side in a funny little waltz. He can't decide if he should hug me, and in the end he just gestures for me to come in.

"Hi," I say as I step into the foyer. The house is beautiful, as if it was recently staged for a *Southern Living* photo shoot. It couldn't be more perfect if Hollywood had designed it.

"Neill, Corey's here," he calls, then gestures down the hall. I don't want to lead the way. I want to follow, preferably ducking safely behind his broad back.

My shoes, a pair of brown leather ballet flats that I borrowed from Mom, click on the hardwood floor. We pass an arched entry, through which I see clusters of party guests sipping lemonade and chatting.

"We have the same couch," I say of the overstuffed white sectional that flows seamlessly into the immaculately decorated room.

"Oh yeah?" he says, as if I've just said something profound about the state of peace in the Middle East. "We had that before Ella. I doubt it'll last much longer. White upholstery plus tiny human is *not* a good combination."

I inwardly flinch at the mention of her, which is a thing I absolutely cannot do. I'm here now. I chose to come. I need to act normal.

Neill pops his head out of the kitchen at the end of the hall.

"Corey! I'm so glad you came. I'd hug you, but I have

guacamole hands." He wiggles his fingers, which are covered in green goop.

"That's okay," I say, thankful I've managed to dodge a second hug.

He glances over my shoulder at Bryan, a quick look that seems to telegraph something I can't read, before focusing his piercing blue eyes back on me. "She's in the family room. Bryan will take you."

And in that moment, I know I'm not ready. It's a feeling I know well, not being ready. But after the last two years, I know that not being ready is not at all correlated to experiencing the thing. The thing is coming, whether you're ready or not. That's what she taught me. Of course she'd remind me now.

The family room is apparently not the same as the room with the big white couch we passed. The family room is designed for, well, family. The couch is a soft, fluffy leather (easily wiped down, easily crashed into), there's no coffee table (to avoid head bumps), and the rug is brightly colored and patterned (to hide stains). There are bins and baskets in every corner overflowing with brightly colored toys, blocks, and stuffed animals. There are small children playing amid a cascade of those giant, toddler-sized Legos with parents hovering nearby carefully trying to pretend they're *not* watching their children like hawks.

And then I see her, standing and holding on to the arm of the couch with one chubby hand while with the other she flings a Lego across the room.

"Ellie-bell, no throwing," Bryan says, bending down to scoop her up. She's so much bigger than the last time I saw her, which was almost a year ago at the lawyer's office. She was only a few weeks old, and she slept in her carrier the entire time. But despite the obvious growth, she still looks tiny in his muscular arms. She grabs his cheeks with her little hands and blows a raspberry right in his face, sending spit and drool in every direction. He laughs, and she laughs, and

I want to sink into the floor or teleport back to the front seat of my mom's car.

"Ella, look who it is!" Bryan points at me. Her eyes scan the room, looking for what he's pointing at, before settling on me. I brace myself for some kind of recognition, but there's nothing. Just a blank toddler stare and more than a little drool.

Bryan swipes at her chin with the sleeve of his shirt. "She's teething," he says, and I nod as if I know all about that. I don't. That's the point of this.

"It's Corey!" he says to her with all the enthusiasm of a child's birthday clown. Oh god, is there a clown here? Please don't let there be a clown here. "Let's go out back."

I follow Bryan out a set of French doors into a beautifully landscaped backyard. He sits down on a wooden bench, Ella balanced on his knee, and I take the spot next to him. I wave and smile at her, but she mostly ignores me in favor of pointing at two squirrels chasing each other across the lawn. I'm sure some girls would know how to talk to a one-year-old, but I'm not one of them. I wasn't one of those girls who babysat for extra money or worked as a camp counselor. I spent summers filing and compiling mailings in my dad's dermatology practice. I have absolutely no idea what to say to a person who enjoys throwing Legos and spitting in people's faces. So instead I talk to the grown-up. That's what I'm good at, usually.

"Does she know who I am?" I ask.

"No," he says, and I must recoil, because he quickly continues. "Not because we haven't talked about you, but because she's one, so she doesn't get it. Plus, she doesn't see you that often. Her world basically consists of me, Neill, her nanny, and Neill's mother, who lives in town. Otherwise, everyone is a stranger. She probably thinks you're one of our friends."

"I don't want to, I mean, I'll just—" I say, but he holds up a hand to silence me.

"Corey, you just try to make yourself comfortable. We'll go at your speed, okay?"

I let out a long, slow breath. I hadn't realized that I'd been breathing as if I'd just finished a marathon, but now that I'm focused on it, I realized that I'd been wound up like a top.

"Thank you," I say.

"Of course."

As if she can tell we've reached an awkward impasse, Ella starts squirming until she slides off Bryan's lap, then takes off in a wobbly sprint, like she's just stepped off a cruise ship and still has her sea legs.

"We can go back inside," I tell him, as he rises to chase her. "I'm happy to just, you know, watch."

He nods, and the three of us head inside. Almost immediately Bryan disappears with Ella to change her diaper, and left alone for the first time, I decide my safest bet is the buffet table. Most of the other adults in the room are laser-focused on their children, but a few give me furtive sideways glances. They know who I am, if only by process of elimination (they don't know me, so they *know* me). Most everyone gives me a wide berth while I fill a Sesame Street plate with mini quiches and crudité. But as I'm filling a cup from a glass jar of pink lemonade, a woman corners me.

"I'm Cecilia," she says, offering me a manicured hand, which I can't take since my hands are occupied by Sesame Street party dishes. When I give her the international gesture for "nice to meet you, but my hands are full," she gives me what looks like a sort of tense smile. "I live down the street. That's my Noah over there." I follow her finger to see a chubby little redhead boy who is currently trying to relieve a Barbie of its head.

"He's adorable," I say, because I'm pretty sure that's the only acceptable response.

"So you're the birth mother."

Despite my best efforts to plaster on a smile, this drops it like it's been slapped off my face.

"Um, yes."

"Well, I just think what you're doing is amazing. The generous gift you've given Neill and Bryan." She continues talking, her hand resting delicately on her heart like she just can't bear the wonder and beauty of me. But I'm not listening. I've heard it before, of course. It's the same best-of-Hallmark platitudes I've been hearing since the moment I walked into the adoption agency. *Precious gift*, as if Ella is a quilt handed down by my grandmother. *Strong and brave*, which are words best reserved for people whose jobs involve them getting shot at. Hero? Not me. Not even close. Most of the time I feel like a coward, like the rest of my life is going to be an elaborate game of duck and run. Because that's what I want to do right now, while Cecilia is blathering on, already giving me a third *bless your heart*.

"And to have the strength to know you're giving that child a better life—"

"Excuse me," I practically bark at her, my lemonade sloshing over Elmo's face. Cecilia breaks off her stream and blinks at me. "I need to, um, find the restroom."

And with a final glance at Ella, who has toddled back into the room, I bolt for the nearest exit, tossing my plate in a trash can as I flee.

Some hero.

I head back to the bench in the backyard. I sit and take several deep breaths. I can tune out most of the platitudes, but the one that won't leave me is the whole "better life" song and dance. Like I'm some kind of poor, pathetic charity case who's just looking for someone to take a chance on me. I can feel my blood pressure rising when Neill steps out on the lawn.

"I saw Cecilia cornered you. I was about to come rescue you," he says, rolling his eyes. "She can be a lot to handle."

"Yeah."

"Are you okay?"

Yes? No? I have no idea? And because my thoughts are spinning around in my head like one of the light-up toddler toys in the family room, I open my mouth and things just start spilling out.

"I don't know how to be this person, the one they keep making me out to be. The person I'm absolutely not. People keep saying that I'm giving her a better life, as if that's supposed to make me feel better. But it just makes me feel 100 percent selfish."

Neill looks like I've just told him that I feel like a serial killer. "Why?" he asks, horrified.

"Because I could have given her all this," I say, gesturing to the house and the yard. "My parents are *doctors*. We're not destitute. She could have grown up in a beautiful home and gone to the best schools and had everything I had, which was *everything*. I didn't give her up so she could have a better life. I gave her up so *I* could have a better life."

Neill stares at me for a long time before speaking. "And you think that makes you selfish?"

"You don't?"

"Look, you're never going to get me to say anything bad about what you did, because that decision created my family." His voice becomes deep and gravelly, and I realize his eyes are welling up. Then he blinks hard and turns his whole body toward me, until his knees are touching mine, and he stares me straight in the eye. "You putting yourself first meant you *were* putting Ella first," he says. "And it's not as if you abandoned her. You're here. This is still a family if you want it to be."

When the party's over, I leave with a stack of pictures of Ella, a piece of cake covered in tinfoil, and the satisfaction of having cornered that awful Cecilia woman and told her all about my plans to study political science at Wesleyan, where I'll be headed in just over a month. Mom is idling by the mailbox, and when she spots me coming down the driveway I can practically see her unwind.

"Everything okay?" I ask as I climb into the car.

"I was about to ask you the same thing."

"It was good." I pass her the stack of pictures. The top one shows Ella, a smudge of pink icing on the tip of her nose, a birthday hat askew atop her nearly bald head. Neill practically mowed down his party guests en route to the office to print it up moments after snapping it. As soon as she sees it, she gasps, her fingers to her lips, her mouth slightly agape.

"She looks just like you," she whispers, then grimaces. She didn't mean to say it out loud. There's a heavy silence that hangs in the car.

Finally, I break it. "I told them I'd come by over Thanksgiving break," I say.

Her head whips in my direction, a mixture of shock and relief on her face.

"Are you sure?"

"I'm sure," I say. And I am.

We're a family.

Lauren Elizabeth Morrill is many things, including, but not limited to, a writer, an educator, a badass roller derby skater, a former band nerd, an aggressive driver, and a die-hard Mac person. She also watches a lot of TV, eats a lot of junk food, and drinks a lot of Coke. It's a wonder her brain and teeth haven't rotted out of her head. Lauren is the author of *Meant to Be, Being Sloane Jacobs, The Trouble with Destiny,* and the forthcoming *My Unscripted Life* (October 2016), all from Random House.

Empty Lens

by Tameka Mullins

Empty Lens: A Mother-Daughter Photography Project
Blog Entry 15—June 7, 2015

Pictured: Jill (mom) and Jessie (daughter). The mom's hazel eyes are red, but twinkling. She looks like she had just been on vacation as her tan is still visible but wearing off. I can tell she had a long day at work. Her skirt is wrinkled from sitting at a desk all day and there are small sweat stains poking through her green blouse. Jessie is wearing a school uniform and attempting to create a Snap of me with her iPhone that she can share on Snapchat. She's asking me more questions than I'm able to ask her. She's twelve. She and her mother are coming out of a McDonald's on 72nd Street. After asking Jill for permission to take their photo and my interview question she lets out an exhausted sigh.

Interview Audio: "I cherish my daughter because she almost didn't make it. I had a complication during my pregnancy, but here she is all energy, arms, and legs. She's going to be tall like her father." Jessie breaks in with, "I want to be a fashion model that creates science experiments. That's possible, right?" She looks at her mother and smiles. I take the shot.

I think these images are touching other people too because I get new followers every week. I find this to be like therapy, but without the glaring eyes of judgment and weekly appointments. Shrinks claim they don't judge you, but I know their gears are turning as they sit with their legs crossed trying to appear objective. The last one I had was infuriating. I wanted to slap her so bad. Something about the way she looked at me made me uncomfortable. Her eyes were too perfect, too green, like looking through the ocean floor straight to the bottom. Her dark brown hair was casket sharp. Not a strand out of place. How could someone so put together understand my scattered thoughts?

"Eva, are you going to share anything today? I can't help you if you don't share what you're feeling and why you're hurting."

That's the day I got up and walked out. My mother was pissed, but she didn't force me to go back. Talking to that head doctor was like talking to a dead fish. Blank eyes, no emotion at all. Maybe that shit works for some people, but it doesn't work for me. All that clean antiseptic sharing is for white folks.

Yes, I am a POC who has white parents. How that happened was that I was adopted. I'm sure most of you didn't know this. Actually, I wasn't sure if I would ever share this part of my life with you, but since I no longer have a therapist's couch to purge on, I'm gonna use this space to clear my head and share my art.

The whole reason I created this blog was to share my photography, and then I found that over the past year I had become more interested in taking pictures of people. Namely, mothers and daughters. I never liked photographing people as

I am more of a nature girl, but something in me shifted after my short stint with that shrink. I'd never admit it to her, but she did touch a nerve with me, and it was then that I realized I wanted to find my mom. My real mom.

Donna and Gene Westminster are my parents and they are the only ones I've ever known, but they are the whitest white folks ever. When we go out, we look like those Golden Oreo cookies with a chocolate middle. I know they love me, but sometimes, well, a lot of times, I don't think they get me. Loving someone and truly being connected to them and understanding their struggles are two different things.

A lot of my friends would really question whether I have any struggles. I live in an amazing brownstone on the Upper East Side of Manhattan, my parents are rich doctors, and I have never wanted for anything. Not anything material, anyway.

Blog Entry 23: July 21, 2015

Pictured: Brenda and Virginia. They were both scurrying out of the light rain that had just begun to fall and into Red Rooster, a soul food restaurant on 125th Street in Harlem, where celebrity chef and owner Marcus Samuelsson often mixes and mingles with the guests and guides them through the menu. I went once with my mentor, and that dude that hosts *Chopped* was there. He looks taller on TV. Anyway, back to the photo subjects. They both were wearing sporty attire, but with fancy shoes. I learned that they were tourists from Atlanta who were in town on vacation. Brenda looked to be in her late forties or early fifties and her mom was probably in her seventies, but she looked young, like one of those grandmothers you see in Facebook videos dancing to hip-hop music. Older mothers and daughters always fascinated me. Especially moms and daughters of color. I actually got off lucky that day because, due to the bad weather, no one wanted to talk to me.

These two were thrilled and probably were going to tell their friends back home about this.

Interview Audio: Brenda said about her mom, "If someone would have told me that I would be on vacation in New York City with her," she pointed at her mom, "ten or fifteen years ago, I would have laughed at them. We were never that close when I was younger, but time and God worked it out."

Virginia smiled and added, "Raising a headstrong daughter is never easy, but neither is living with a Southern mother. I knew we would work it out. Now, can we get something to eat, gal? You've done dragged me all around this city. I'm hungry!"

Interview over.

Thinking about the issues that this mother-daughter duo had overcome made me think about my dad. I had a fight with him last night. Not a big blowup, but he snapped at me and I'm not used to that. He hurt my feelings really bad. I was telling my mom that I should be getting some information soon about my biological first mother. I was taught in therapy not to refer to my natural mother as my birth or biological mom. I am still kinda confused about this because that's what she is, isn't she? Anyway, the statue in a skirt of a therapist explained that saying biological or birth mother is like reducing the mom to being a baby-making machine, kinda like she was only on Earth for making babies. She said that a mother's bond with her child goes beyond birth, so we shouldn't put that negative title on them. Like I said, I'm still getting used to talking about this adoptively correct stuff. I always knew I was adopted. My parents told me when I was little. I thought it was cool at the time until I started wondering why my original parents didn't want me.

Anyway, my dad overheard me and my mom talking, and he freaked the fuck out. We all had a talk as a family about me wanting to search, and even though he didn't say much at the time, I thought he was cool with it. Now he's acting like an ass, like I'm trying to punish him. It's like he thought I was joking around when I said I wanted to know who my mom was. I don't care if he reads this either. I was always raised to speak my mind and I'm not stopping now. One day I want to be a full-fledged reporter, so he needs to get used to me writing about real things. Well, I actually want to be a photojournalist and go to war-torn countries and expose their bullshit. Ours here at home, too.

Back to my dad. Now, when I asked about my natural parents, my mom was the cool one. She said she expected that I would ask someday. My goal is to find my parents before I graduate from high school. Being that I love investigative work, I treated it like a journalism class assignment. I did my interviews (my mom and dad), got them to give up some sources (information about the adoption agency), reviewed my research notes, and went to work. Initially, sometime after contacting the adoption agency, I was told that the office building they used to work in burned down in a bad fire and my records were misplaced. When I told my parents, my mom looked sad for me, but my dad looked relieved. It hurt my feelings, but I guess he just doesn't want to deal with it. I don't know why he's so concerned. I'm the one who has to deal with everything anyway. My dad comes from a close family. My granddad still falls all over him when we see him. "My son, the doctor," he says, all loud when we're out in public so everyone can hear him. He doesn't know how it feels to always wonder why you weren't wanted.

My mom's family is mad dry. They are cordial and semi-friendly, but very aristocratic. Everything is a show. My grandma Ruth always has to list my educational achievements and any applicable awards first before she ever introduces me as her granddaughter to anyone. She probably thinks she is being complimentary, but I always wondered if I were white if she would bother. Probably not. People expect white kids to be smart.

Yup, I keep it real around here, folks, so please don't get in your feelings.

In a world of lies, I need to tell my truth at all times.

My mom gets along with her mother, but at times they act more like friendly socialites than like mother and daughter. Sorry Mom, but you know it's true, if you're reading this. That's why I think she is okay with me searching. She is a good mom. I can talk to her about a lot of stuff, but there are times that she is lost when it comes to my blackness. But she does try her best. Even though I'm annoyed with him right now, I have to admit that my dad puts in a decent effort at times too. One day I came home and my mom was making dinner (a rare thing), and she had some Kendrick Lamar playing! Granted, it was turned down as low as humanly possible. I asked her how she knew about Kendrick's music, and she said she didn't, she just knew I liked hip-hop and found a SiriusXM station that played it. My dad smirked a little before greeting me and giving me a hug that day.

My dad can be a sweetheart, so that's why it was so hard to take him being mean to me yesterday. I had received a call from the court intermediary, the person who worked with the local court to help me find my parents, and she told me that my adoption records had been found and that she was a step closer to finding my natural parents. When he heard me telling my mom, he interrupted us and asked if my mother had forgotten about a work dinner they were invited to. When my mom said she was discussing something with me and that she'd get ready afterward, he huffed. When I tried to include him in the conversation, he said he didn't want to hear it and that I should leave my mother alone so she could get dressed. He raised his voice and everything! I don't usually cry easily, but I bawled before going to sleep last night. I think I was sad and upset and scared. Sad and upset about my dad being foul to me and scared of what the rest of the search process would bring. Things were already changing. We had a nice family. Everything wasn't perfect, but I was loved and content. Why did I go looking anyway? Shouldn't my parents have come looking for me instead? Enough about me and my woes. I'm not running through the 6. I'm just trying to get through my days in the 212.

◇◇◇◇

Blog Entry 31: August 8, 2015

Pictured: Marilyn and Jenna (James) Dean. It was hard not to notice Jenna. Her mom still calls her by her given name, but she said that she prefers to go by Jenna, which is a name she chose for herself. I ask why and she says, "I am the modern-day rebel without a cause." She is growing into her pretty, but I can still see the boy in her. She is sixteen years old, tall, lean, and muscular, and her long hair is curly and black and shaved on the sides with pink highlights. It's a Mohawk that Nicki Minaj would love. Her makeup is flawless—bright pink lips against ivory skin and perfectly drawn-on eyebrows that frame soul orbs that are lined for the Gods. Her mom, Miss Marilyn, probably won a lot of beauty pageants and has a sweet face, but she looks like she doesn't play and that she's still coming to terms with the fact that her son identifies as a girl.

Interview Audio: Miss Marilyn shifted to one leg and held her shopping bags in front of her and shared this about Jenna: "What can I say? When someone feels differently than they look, you have to support them. I love my child. Period. I'm still trying to understand it all, but I want my kid happy and if this is what makes (she pauses) her happy then I'm all for it. Jenna looks at her mom like this is the first time she's hearing her say this and gives her a hug. Photo finish.

◇◇◇◇

Acceptance, admiration, and love are definitely dope, aren't they? Speaking of, this boy is my whole heart. Well, when he's not working my nerves. He's a nerd who tries to be street. He's sitting right under me as I write this. I ain't scared. He knows my pen is savage. This is one of the few places I can totally be me, and I never allow a word unthought-of to be unwritten if I think it works. People better be glad this isn't a vlog. Okay, he's gone now so I can really talk about him. We're meeting up later to go to the movies, but I needed my fix before then. Thankfully my mom and dad like him, which is kind of rare. They usually don't like my boyfriends, but Eric knows how to talk to them and highlight all of his scholarly ambitions rather than his hood dreams. I still don't know why he tries so hard when his parents are just as rich and privileged as mine. He kind of looks like Evan Ross—he's just a tad darker. He has tats, but he keeps them hidden whenever he visits me. I met him at Central Park. Lame, right? I was sitting on a park bench when he came up to me and sat down. I was annoyed at first, but his smile wiped the side-eye off my face. Then when we started talking, I was actually enjoying it. He was funny and chill and that's what I like. If I want serious situations, I don't have to look that far for them in my own life. Having someone to make you laugh takes the pressure off sometimes.

When he first met my folks, he gave me a look, but he didn't freak out. That made it easier to share stuff about my adoption. He knows that I'm waiting on news about my natural parents, and he's been mad cool about it. He asks me how I'm feeling, but he doesn't press too much. He gives me space to think. It's that perfect mix of concern without being obnoxious or acting like he doesn't care at all. Yeah, he's cool. I'm keeping him.

Now, my girl Jayla is another story altogether. We've been

best friends since grade school, but she likes to act like my adoption doesn't exist. After so many conversations about it, I thought she would be more supportive. It hurts my feelings, but I keep it to myself. If I complained, she'd just say I was being butt-hurt, so why bother? Just like that time when I tearfully confided in her that when I asked to get my hair twisted, we had to have a family meeting. I had to sit between my two white parents and discuss whether wearing the hair that grows naturally out of my head would cause me issues at school. I was angry that I couldn't just go and get my hair done like other black girls. Being the brown daughter in an affluent white family was always so damn political. Jayla thought I was being a spoiled brat and said she wished her parents cared enough to question her choices. She didn't get it. I'm very sensitive when it comes to people who feel misunderstood so that's why when I saw this mother and daughter a while back when I was hanging out, I knew I had to get a picture and hear their story.

Blog Entry 45: September 4, 2015

Pictured: Donna and Evangeline. I never thought I'd get my own mom to appear on this blog or take a selfie with me, but today she did both. Normally she has what some call RBF, but in this photo she's radiating something warm in her eyes even though she's still not smiling. I'm not smiling either, but I like how our heads are almost touching. Most people will see my brownness and her whiteness, and that is what I used to see too in our pics, but here and now, I just see my mom.

It's been a few weeks since I received the news, but I needed some time to be alone with it. The court intermediary reported back like she said she would and told me that my natural mom and dad died in a house fire a few years ago. My mom and dad were in the room with me when I found out, and I'm glad I didn't have to face the news alone. My dad gave me the longest hug in history, and my mom kept asking me over and over how I was doing that day. They usually are very controlled people so it was weird seeing them so helpless. I was hurt, but I didn't want my parents to think I loved two people I hadn't met before more than them, so I just held a lot of my feelings in. I didn't even cry until I went to bed that night. Actually, I cried all night off and on. I fired up my computer and blasted Beyoncé the whole time so my parents wouldn't hear me. I didn't even recognize the sound of my cries. I sounded like a hurt animal. I have never known pain like this, and it's confusing. Why am I so hurt even though I didn't know them?

The next day my parents asked me if I wanted to go do something special like go to the outlet malls or take a trip, and I told them that I just wanted to be left alone. I didn't say it in a mean way. I just wanted to get up and walk around when I wanted to, or if I wanted to get in my car and go for a drive I could. I didn't want to be stuck in a car with anyone else or on anyone's airplane. From minute to minute I felt different. I was either angry, weepy, or pissed off, or I felt nothing, and I needed room to move around while I was feeling all of these things. I loved them for wanting to make it better, but you can't shop away the fact that your natural parents had died and you never got a chance to know them. I felt like a weird organism floating around. I had Donna and Gene and they were as good as parents could be because no one's parents are perfect, but . . . I need to write this to get it out. I was not born to them. I don't know how that feels and now I will never know and it's ripping me up inside. Oh, and the guilt. Even just typing that makes me feel like shit. Of course Donna and Gene are mine, but not tied by blood like the moms and daughters I speak to for this blog.

I also went back to a shrink. But a new one. He specializes in helping others who are dealing with adoption issues. I immediately felt more comfortable with him because he told me that he was adopted, too. I've never met anyone else who was. My mom told me that she's not letting me get out of going this time around. She said she'll even come with me, and my dad said he would, too, and for him that is huge because he doesn't like sharing family business.

I plan on doing my therapy and spending more quality time with my parents, Eric, and even Jayla. We haven't spoken too much about what's going on, but she texts me every day now, and she brought me some books and t-shirts the other day. I have a feeling I'm going to have a lot to write about after processing all of this, so stay tuned.

Bonus Photo: Stacey Fullerton and William Payne Jr. These are separate photos I found online of my natural parents after I received more information from the court officer. I cropped them together so it looks like he's holding her. I look a lot like my mom. She looks a little like Sanaa Lathan but edgier, and my dad resembles a football player that I can't remember the name of. He's huge, like a big teddy bear. They look to be in their early twenties in these images. When it comes to them, I will forever wonder how and why and what, although I may be getting some more information as I asked the court intermediary if she could help me connect with more family members. Maybe that can be my next blog project.

Tameka Mullins is a writer, poet, blogger and author of *12 Hours of Daylight – A Jason Jules Novella* (CreateSpace/BookBaby, 2017) who spent the first half of her life in Detroit and now resides in Brooklyn. Her work has been featured by NPR's Tell Me More during National Poetry Month. A social media professional with over ten years of experience, she enjoys live tweeting shows like *Empire*, *Scandal*, and *Game of Thrones*. Join her at @tamstarz. She currently works as a digital marketing consultant during the day and pursues her creative passions as a hybrid author at night. You can learn more about her at tamekamullins.com.

"Talking and writing about adoption will always be important to me because even though I reunited with my natural family, I still feel fragmented. Processing my broken past through discourse, essays, and stories helps to heal me and possibly may help others heal, too. I've accepted that this mind-, body-, and soul-mending is a lifelong dance, and writing is the music."

A Lesson in Biology

by Sammy Nickalls

Let me tell you something that may or may not make you think less of me. I mean, okay, I can't imagine you'd *actually* think less of me. I hate something, but it's not like I hate cute puppies or deep-dish pizza or world peace.

I hate trees.

Okay, yes, I understand they are essential to life on Earth as we know it—not only for us, but for millions of cute little woodland creatures who make trees their home. Before you jump to any conclusions (ugh, like stupid Shelby Rigley did two years ago during our ninth-grade class field trip to the state park), let me clarify that I do *not* want said little woodland creatures to die a terrible death. Got that? *Not* a crazy genocidal maniac who specializes in exterminating chipmunks.

Cool, moving on.

Yes, I know that trees can live a ridiculously long life, which is great and all. In fact, I know very well that there's a bristlecone pine in White Mountains, California, that is over 5,000 years old, meaning it's one of the oldest living organisms in the entire world. Trees can stand the test of time. Many of them can weather even the worst of storms. They are majestic, strong, and beautiful.

Yes, yes. I get all of this.

But I still don't like them.

Stupid Shelby Rigley said (or rather, screamed obnoxiously, as she tends to do) that my hatred for trees automatically makes me some anti-environmentalist jerk, as if I'm some evil villain in a Pixar movie. But I'm not a monster or anything.

I hate trees because it's totally inconceivable to me that these majestic, practically ancient organisms *don't have the ability to move.* From the moment they're planted until the day they die, they're lodged in the same place, rigid as my great-great aunt Mildred, who has had the same ugly living room furniture for the past seven decades. It's all a putrid shade of chartreuse with a way-too-busy floral print. Like, *why?* Who in the hell thought *that* was a good idea?

Yeah, sure, trees grow—upward, and maybe a *little* outward. Other than that, when a tree is planted, that's where it stays. Forever. And there's no changing it, unless you cut it down and make it into paper. Or houses. Or more of that horrible furniture that my aunt loves so much. So why do we glorify them? Seems a little overrated to me, because what's the use of living for five thousand years if you're not willing to change—to adapt?

Now, as I sit in biology class studying the paper on my desk in front of me, I can't help but be darkly amused by the sight of an illustration of a healthy, vibrant tree . . . printed on a sheet of dead tree.

"For tomorrow," Mr. Stohler tells the class, taking long, purposeful strides around the classroom as he passes out the rest of the papers, "you are to fill out this entire tree. Not its biological parts, because as you know, we studied trees last semester. Rather, you are to fill it out with your family members of the past four generations, ending with you and any siblings or first cousins at the bottom."

What amusement I once felt instantly evaporates. I glower at my paper as Mr. Stohler continues.

Okay. So maybe there's another reason why I hate trees.

They . . . remind me of things I don't have.

"I also want you to write down three genetic attributes for every blood-related family member you include: their eye color, whether they have a widow's peak, and whether they are double-jointed," he explains, adjusting his wire-rimmed glasses. "I understand this may be difficult for any family members who are no longer with us, but ask the relatives that are. Fill it out to the best of your ability. And if it's not totally complete, that's okay."

He glances over nervously at Ted Hitz, who everyone knows just lost his dad last month.

Whatever, Ted. My tree is going to be a hell of a lot barer than yours.

I consider my options. Obviously, I won't raise my hand in class and announce to my classmates that I'm adopted. I mean, they probably already know it, judging by the fact that my parents are blond, blue-eyed, and as pale as can be, and I'm, you know, *not*. But still, I'd strongly prefer not to draw attention to myself. I may have been born in Guatemala, but I'd like to maintain the illusion that I belong in Albion, Indiana, even if I'm well aware that it's a blatant lie.

But I also don't want to approach Mr. Stohler at the end of the class like some sad little puppy-eyed child. He'd just assign me something else, or—worse—excuse me from the assignment entirely. Knowing him, he'll probably have us talk about our findings in a class discussion, and being excused due to extenuating circumstances is the social equivalent of standing on my desk and screaming, "EVERYONE FEEL BAD FOR ME BECAUSE I DON'T KNOW WHO MY REAL MOMMY AND DADDY ARE." Yeah, not happening.

Mr. Stohler dismisses us, and as I trek down the hallway toward creative writing class, I decide that I have only one real option: to totally make this shit up. If I don't know anything about my real tree, I will adorn my paper tree with lovely leaves that don't exist. I'll hand it in, then feign sick for the discussion so I can go to the nurse for the class period. Mr. Stohler has seen my parents during parent-teacher conferences, but he sees hundreds of parents every year; he won't remember.

I take a deep breath. *This will be fun*, I tell myself. It will just be like another creative writing assignment—an exercise of the imagination. I try to put it out of my mind as I walk into creative writing, my last class of the day, and sit next to Trish, my best friend.

"Hey, girl!" she exclaims, grinning happily at me. "You look beautiful, as usual."

Trish is the human embodiment of a ray of sunshine. It's one of the many things I love about her, but right now, I just can't match myself to her energy. I give her a half-hearted smile as I toss my backpack on the floor next to the desk.

"Eves," she says, nudging me, "What's wrong?"

Normally, Trish would be the one person I'd confide in, but as I watch her pull her straight blonde hair into a perfect ponytail, I can't bring myself to explain it to her. "It's nothing. Didn't sleep well last night."

Just then, Ms. Thatcher hushes the class to begin the lesson. Trish makes a pouty face and writes something on her notebook, pushing it toward me. "Let me know if you need anything!" it reads. I nod and make a heart with my hands.

Sometimes I paint my imaginary biological parents in my mind. It's addicting; I can't stop myself.

My mother has eyes that are so dark they look almost black, but they're warm and kind, and have the uncanny ability to make anyone feel understood. She isn't double-jointed, but she does have a widow's peak where her hairline begins, her big black curls cascading down her shoulders just like mine.

In fact, everyone says she and I look just alike, except for the eyes. I have my father's eyes—big, wide, a deep rich brown. He's not double-jointed, nor does he have a widow's peak, but he does have a big, luminous smile that can brighten even the most frigid of rooms.

They aren't millionaires or celebrities or secret government officials with complicated backstories regarding why they had to give me up.

They love each other so much, I think to myself as I stare out the school bus window on the way home. *And I love them.*

Even if they're not real.

When I get home from school, my parents—who *are* real—are still at work. But my grandma is home. She moved in with us after my grandpa passed away from lung cancer a few years ago. I miss him dearly, but at least we have Gran around 24/7. Her awesomeness is unparalleled.

Gran has her frizzy gray hair tied up in a bun on top of her head, her bedazzled reading glasses on the tip of her nose as she studies what looks like a magazine laid out in front of her on the kitchen table.

"Whatcha reading?" I ask as I toss my backpack on the table and sit in the chair facing her.

Gran places a bookmark in the magazine and closes it. "A fascinating study," she responds brightly, pushing her reading glasses on top of her head. "It's about the genetic variation of *Galax urceolata.*"

"Cool, cool. And that is?"

"A lovely evergreen perennial plant, my dear. White flowers, glossy leaves that are shaped like hearts. Not a very flashy specimen, but beautiful in its simplicity." She winks at me. "Beauty is everywhere, if you know where to look."

I smile weakly. Gran was once a researcher, quite renowned

in her day. Though she retired when my grandpa got sick, she still subscribes to several journals to keep up to date. She is always regaling me with trivia on the latest and greatest in the botany world, which I'm normally interested in. Well, maybe I'm more interested in the *way* she describes it; she could make watching paint dry seem like a grand adventure. I love hearing about all the plants she adores (as long as it isn't *that* one). But now, seeing the way her bright blue eyes shine in the daylight streaming from the kitchen window, I'm suddenly overcome with that same exhaustion I felt earlier.

And, like Trish, she can immediately tell. "Eva, honey. What's wrong?"

"I'm just . . . ah, hung up on a creative writing assignment," I blurt out. "You know how I get before I come up with an idea. It's very frustrating." My stomach twists with guilt, the profoundly uncomfortable sensation that can come only from lying to my grandmother. I can probably count on one hand the number of times I've done it.

"Hmmm, yes," she muses, chewing on her pen. "Well, do you have a general theme? Perhaps a vague concept? We can spitball from there, yes?"

Great. This is why I never lie, I think. "Er, yeah. I thought I could write about . . . um, trees."

"Well, you've come to the right place. What about trees? Any particular species?"

"No, no. About all trees. Trees in general. Maybe . . . about what they stand for. As a symbol. In writing."

"Ah, yes." Gran furrows her brow and chews on her pen some more. "Well, that extends beyond my area of expertise, but there's the biblical meaning—temptation of the forbidden fruit. Also, trees can stand for self-growth. And they're often planted to mark a turn of events . . . a creation of something new, such as the birth of a child. Ah, and of course, family trees."

"Yes—that. That's what I was thinking. Family." Lying or not, I'm starting to think this could be a really good side project for my writing endeavors.

Meanwhile, Gran's expression has changed. She's studying my face fervently. After about thirty seconds of this, she says carefully, "What do you want to write about trees and family?"

"About . . . I don't know. I don't know, Gran." Well, at least *that* isn't a lie.

She nods, then places her hand on mine and gently squeezes. Her fingers are covered in rings, which feel cool against my skin. We stay like this for another thirty seconds in total silence; then, in her abrupt Gran fashion, she suddenly stands up and briskly walks over to the kettle on the counter.

"You know, Eva, as much as I love trees, I've never found them to be a good representation of a family." She fills the kettle with hot water from the sink and flicks on the switch. "And I would know, kiddo. Because I know all. Tea?"

"Yes, please," I respond, staring at the flowering dogwood in our backyard, its pink flowers waving at me in the spring breeze. "And why do you say that?"

She grabs two mugs from the cabinet and places them on the counter; they make a little *clink* noise against the granite. "Well, if you consider a tree as a metaphor for genetics, sure, it makes sense."

My heart sinks in my chest. "Yeah. Yeah, it does."

"But that's the *only* thing the metaphor takes into account," Gran continues, grabbing various boxes of tea from the cabinet. "Chamomile again?"

"Yes, please. And that's not true. Trees can be really old—some going back thousands of years. Like family legacies. And they're strong—it takes a lot to knock down a tree, just like a family. It all makes sense."

Gran rips open two packets of chamomile and places the teabags in the empty mugs. "Plenty of things in the universe are old, my dear. That's like saying Florida is a metaphor for hell because they're both hot—though your grandfather would agree wholeheartedly with that, I suppose."

I giggle. When we went on vacation to Florida back when I was in middle school, my grandpa hated the heat so much that he stayed in and worked on a puzzle all day while the rest of us had a blast at Disney World. "It's not a vacation if you break a sweat!" he insisted.

My grandmother smiles, and I can tell she's thinking about him. "Anyway, yes, trees are strong. Stronger, perhaps, than families."

"Wait—*what*?" Gran has always been a vocal advocate for family loyalty and togetherness; "stronger than families" is the *last* thing I'd expect to come out of her mouth.

She laughs as she fills up the mugs with the water from the kettle. "Eva, families aren't *naturally* strong. How many families do you know that are broken? Cousins no longer talking because of some fight they can barely remember, brothers and sisters arguing over an inheritance, children separated from a parent after a nasty divorce."

She walks back over and sets my tea mug in front of me. It's covered with little blue and brown hearts. Gran puts her hand on mine and squeezes again, a bit tighter this time.

"Genetics may link two people together, and that link will always exist, but that link is made of fishing line, not bark and wood," she says. "Genetics are not the definition of a strong family, and that's why trees as a metaphor don't work—because it's love that's the *true* bonding material between a group of people. Love, and love alone. And love is work. But it's the best kind of work there is."

I look at Gran, her face swimming a little bit in my vision as my eyes begin to water. She reaches over and wipes away the tear as soon as it falls onto my cheek.

"Shhh, dear. Take a sip of your tea."

I blow on it first, then take a sip. She takes a sip of hers as well, then looks at me over the rim with those vivid blue eyes.

"Trees are beautiful, Eva. I've spent most of my life adoring them, studying them, poring over them. But a tree is not a family. Plants are one of my deepest passions, but they cannot love me back. Not like you can."

"But that's not the point, Gran. It's just a metaphor."

"Metaphors can only go so far. And the reason they're used so often is because it's tempting to try to find meaning in the complexities of life by comparing them to what's around us. But that can be dangerous. Families come in all shapes and sizes, and we cannot define them with such cookie-cutter terms." She looks at me for a few seconds, her eyes softening as if she's remembering something. "You know what *is* family?"

I shake my head. She cups my face with her hands, gently brushing away my tears with her thumbs. "*This*. This is family, my beautiful girl. *You* are this family. You have been ever since the day your parents took you home. Lord above, you were such a beautiful baby, which is why your mother has covered every damn inch of this house with your baby pictures."

I laugh through my tears and wipe my eyes. "I love you, Gran."

"I love you too. Don't forget that. Our family is stronger than anything in this world. And it's all because of love—we sure have a lot of that going around." She grins at me and puts on her reading glasses, flipping the botany journal back open.

We sit in silence. As she reads and jots notes, I think about telling her that she should be a teacher, because she's taught me more than biology class ever can. But instead, I glance over at my backpack, then stare at the dogwood's flowers outside. I'll email Mr. Stohler and explain why I can't do the assignment.

One day, I'll try to find my biological parents and see if they're anything like my imaginary ones. But at this moment in time, all I need is *this* family. Not one I made up inside my head.

My real family.

Most important, *my* family.

Sammy Nickalls was born and raised in Lebanon, Pennsylvania, though she currently resides in Brooklyn. She has worked as a writer and editor for numerous publications, including *HelloGiggles* and *Esquire*. Sammy is a mental health advocate and started #TalkingAboutIt, a Twitter movement that encourages users to talk about their mental health as openly as they would their physical health. Follow her on Twitter @sammynickalls.

Tunneling Through

by Shannon M. Parker

My therapist's office is in a cave.

Okay, not exactly. But his office is the closest you can get to a cave and still be in an actual building, so that's cool. One wall is solid rock. Like the dude who designed this building two hundred years ago didn't want to excavate the huge stone outcropping, so he built around it instead. Dr. Richard painted the granite wall institution-white, maybe to make it look like a regular wall. But his paint can't hide the rock's rough surface, the way water and time carved grooves into its face. I see the stone underneath.

Dr. Richard welcomes me in with his smile. I hang up my masks on the coatrack. Not all of my masks, but I shed a few:

The Attentive Student
The Good Daughter
The Peace Seeker

Okay, that last one isn't really a mask. I am a peace seeker.

It's pretty much all I am. Dr. Richard tells me my peaceful disposition is rare for a trauma survivor. He says I have to go to the "hard places" underneath. He still doesn't get that all my underneath places are hard. Harder than that boulder face.

I sink into the deep couch and face the rock wall. Pieces of me are tattooed there. I mean, not literally, obviously. Still, I see the words I leave behind, the ones I let only Dr. Richard hear. I imagine some of my words scrawl themselves across the white granite face; I admit *fear,* and the word paints itself in thick, black strokes.

I say other words, too.

Only here.

When the knock sounds, my spine straightens. Mom pokes her head through the door and I stretch on the mask made for her: Daughter.

"Hey, Mom."

"Hey, kiddo." She sits at the opposite end of the couch, but not before giving my knee a quick squeeze. She tugs her workbag from her shoulder, asks me how my day at school was. All typical Mom stuff.

"I'm glad you could join us today," Dr. Richard says.

"I'm always happy to be invited."

And I know this is true. Mom does like to come here.

I move one hand under my thigh so I can feel the rip of my hangnail catch against the rough couch fabric. Pain sears the tender skin, and I scratch again, hungry for this slice of hurt.

"I think we've been making some great progress lately." Dr. Richard is trying to prepare my mom, even though there is exactly no preparing a person for what we've been talking about. It takes all the strength I have not to run out the door, high-fiving the rock wall on my way past. Dr. Richard must sense my escape plans because he asks, "Are you feeling scared?"

I nod.

"Maybe you could start by telling your mom about another time you felt deeply afraid."

I know exactly what he's talking about. That first time with Mom, the dark closet. Sometimes this story is the only thing I can see clearly. Sometimes it's what helps me fall asleep at night. Okay, most nights. I don't even pretend like I'm trying to call the memory up. I owe Mom that much. "Do you remember when I was five? When I first came to live with you?" The quiver in my voice betrays me.

Mom smiles softly, and the memory presses its weight down, sits on the couch between us. "I do."

"Do you remember the first time you got mad at me?"

Mom smiles again, though this time her eyes squint with suspicion, which she doesn't try to hide. "I do."

"I don't remember what I did but you sent me to my room." The reason I got punished has never mattered.

Mom nods. Waits.

"You sent me to my room and went outside to rake leaves in the front yard." I twist a lock of my long, painstakingly straightened hair around my finger. "I watched you from my bedroom window. I was so mad."

"You were pounding on the glass. Screaming at me." Mom's being kind. I was throwing a full-on tantrum.

"I beat the window so hard the pane shattered."

Mom's hand moves to her heart. I don't think she knows it's even happening. "I never ran up a set of stairs so fast. I was petrified of what I'd find."

"What did you find?" It's Dr. Richard. I'd almost forgotten he was here.

"Nothing," Mom says. "The room was empty."

The air stills for a beat of time, long enough for the office to morph into a closet. My bedroom closet. Dark and hidden away. I am tucked in tight, cowering and hiding again.

"But your closet door was open a couple of inches," Mom says.

"Do you remember what you did?" I want her to remember. I need this to be the most important moment in her life too.

"I sat outside of the door and asked if you were okay."

"You reached your hand in."

"I did."

"You held my hand."

"I did."

"I was breathing so hard."

"You were."

A tear starts in my eye now, threatening to ruin my makeup, my most trusted mask. "I was so afraid you were going to hate me for breaking your window. I thought you'd send me back. Ask for a new kid."

"I know," Mom says.

"But you didn't."

"I didn't. I told you that my love was like a train. That it could never stop. It traveled on a loop of track with no beginning or ending. It would continue on forever."

The plates inside me shift then. Readjust. Because she remembers it perfectly. I steel my insides. Prepare. "That minute. That very second was the first time I believed maybe I could love someone. You know? Trust them."

"I know," Mom says, her voice hiccups.

I look down and realize she's holding my hand. Just like that day. Her skin still so warm and soft. Her grip so dependable.

"I think it's important that you hear what your daughter is saying here."

I hear the word *daughter*, louder than all the rest.

"I hear her," Mom says.

And I know she does. My mom hears how impossible it was for me to trust. She remembers how hard she had to work to soothe me, settle me during those first years. Even now, if I'm being honest. Mom's still working to overcome the damage another woman did to me. I hate that. I hate that my mom has to pay for someone else's cruelty.

So how can I burden her with more? Tell her about The Me under my masks?

"Good," Dr. Richard says. He makes a note in his book. I wonder if it says "good" in tight, underlined script.

I see my words on the wall. The ones I've told only Dr. Richard about:

Boy

Alone

Boy

The letters of these private words are carved into the stone, etched with a dark coal against the glimmering white boulder face.

"So I think we can all agree that we are working from a place of trust."

My mom nods.

I nod.

"Are you ready to tell your mom about some of the things that we've been talking about over this past year?"

I see Mom's posture ripple. A year is a long time to keep a secret. She knows this.

But I know it's been way longer than a year.

And the thing is, I'm not ready. Not even a little bit. *Boy.* The word is darker now. Pulsing. Taunting. I want to scrape it from the rock's surface. Bury it.

I'm so good at burying shit. I should get an A+ in Life for burying the shit I've buried.

"This is a safe place," Dr. Richard says.

Sometimes I think he's an idiot. He can't possibly know what a safe place means for someone like me. Someone who remembers what it's like to feel unsafe. No, scared. Scared All. The. Time. When I heard footsteps coming to my room. When the woman who called herself my mother screamed at nothing, at everything, for hours that bled into days and then years. The men she brought home. The needles multiplying on the tabletops. The gun at my head. The hunger in my middle. Dr. Richard with his framed degrees can't understand how I carry that scared kid's baggage around inside of me, my suitcases crammed with memories that I want to dump on the side of the road.

I want to leave all of it behind.

Start over.

Start my life.

And I know that's what Dr. Richard wants me to talk about now. What that life would look like. If I could really own it.

My mom waits. She's patient like that. I sort of envy it and hate it. Today, I hate it. I wish she'd get frustrated at the silence that fills the room. I wish she'd walk out so I wouldn't have to say the words. I could scrub them from the walls, and Dr. Richard could never tempt me to say them again.

But then my mom does the dumbest thing. She whispers, "Choo *choo*," and squeezes my hand—softly, but in a never-letting-go kind of way. It's so beyond ridiculous the way she makes this baby *choo choo* sound, and I laugh at her. Except laughter isn't what leaves my lips; it's a giant sob, like all the wind has been punched from my gut. Hurt escapes from the jagged cracks inside of me where I hide stuff. I crumple into her words, into myself, and I feel so real in this moment. So me. So alive and loved that I don't even try to keep my mask from slipping. I just let it fall, hit my lap, careen onto the floor. I squeeze my mother's hand as I say the words that I know will make her walk out the door.

"I think sometimes I don't feel like I belong in my body."

I see my mom break a little, her posture falling. Her eyes latch onto mine in a way that makes it impossible to look away even though that's pretty much the only thing I want to do.

"What does that mean?" Mom's voice is velvet soft as it presses against the dark clamoring in my head.

I pull my hand from hers and shove it under my leg, let pain screech along my hangnail. I scramble to cover my mistake. "I'm not saying I want to be a boy."

"You're not?"

No. Yes. Maybe. "I don't know." It is the truth. "I think . . . I think sometimes I feel more masculine maybe."

"Good," Dr. Richard says, and I want to cram the word down his throat. Because honestly? Who is he to tell me I'm good?

Mom doesn't even register Dr. Richard. Her eyes are all on me. Over me. Around me. In me. Seeing the dark thing. "But this doesn't make any sense."

She leans back on the couch.

She is pulling away.

"You always hated boy toys when you were a kid. Just last year I asked you if you wanted to cut your hair short and you protested so violently. You said you didn't want to look like a boy."

I look to Dr. Richard now, hating how much I need his support. "Good. Go on," he says.

"I think I was afraid."

"Of a haircut?"

I hesitate, the fear strangling. "I wanted that haircut." I was afraid of how much I wanted it.

"I don't understand," Mom says. "That was your decision."

Short hair. It's such a dumb thing. Scissors. A few snips. But what if the haircut made me look like who I was meant to be and then there was no turning back?

Mom leans in, brushing a long wisp of hair from my face. I see the way her eyes linger on the small constellation of freckles on my forehead. The freckles make the shape of a heart. When I met Mom she told me the freckle heart looked like it was drawn with a fine-tipped paintbrush. Right there on my forehead so the whole world would know how big my real heart was.

My heart is the reason my mom is my mom. Not the heart on my forehead, but the one inside my chest. I begged her to tell me our birth story at least a thousand times when I was little. I loved hearing about that cold Easter day eleven years ago when we met, how she helped me hunt brightly colored plastic eggs in the straw-yellow grass. How she'd cleared her throat when we stumbled upon one and I couldn't even see its bold color through the haze of my excitement. How she let me bend down, pick each one up. How we pretended we were princesses collecting jewels. And at the end, how I dumped out all of my treasure on my foster family's driveway, making two equal piles of pennies and Tootsie Rolls.

"This one's yours," I'd told her, offering her a heap.

"Mine?"

"You helped me find our treasure, so you should get half."

"That's so nice of you," she'd said.

"It's the easiest thing in the world to be nice," I'd said.

Every time my mom repeated this story, she told me that this was the moment she knew I was her daughter. When I'd offered her half, even though I had nothing. It was the moment she knew I was born from her heart, she always says. She knew our hearts were family. I want her to tell me our birth story again now as we sit in the therapy cave. I want her to tell me that one unchanging story that makes me feel safe.

"Is there more you want to say to your mother?"

No. I don't want to say more. I want to stay protected in my adoption story. But then I see my words on the wall, hieroglyphic pieces of me. My past. My now. I want to tell my mom so much, but I dare only this: "I'm not sure what I want."

Mom's chest hiccups, but not with sadness exactly. Her lips form the words long before they pass her lips. "What are you really trying to tell me?" I feel the softness in her question, her patience no different than when she sat outside of my closet, holding my five-year-old hand. She on one side, me on the other. We were connected then. Even through all that darkness. I took her hand, heard the song of her soothing voice. I close my eyes, and I'm there again. In the darkness. Five years old. Scared—so fucking scared—but tired, too. Beyond tired. I tell myself I will let my voice close the distance between us. The way she did then. I will let my voice, my haunted, mixed-up voice, say the thing I have always wanted to say. From the day of the train. From the Easter egg hunt. From back beyond that, maybe. Beyond my earliest memories. I will let my voice tell my whole truth.

I'm surprised when I look to Dr. Richard. "She picked me. Out of all the kids, she picked me. She picked a girl." My words are words and tears and fear in such a jumble that I wonder if he can understand me.

I turn to my mom. I let the echo of my voice crash around us because it is its own train, and I can't stop it now. My voice has no beginning or end. "I'm afraid you won't love me anymore if I'm not in a girl's body."

Mom exhales, her shoulders moving away from mine as they deflate. I close my eyes. I go to the part of my brain I can control. A compartment. I pack my clothes. I leave this place. Because I've always been alone. Will always be alone.

"Oh, baby. I didn't choose a girl or a boy." My mom's voice pierces through a thousand layers of doubt. Of fear. "Don't you know I picked you for your heart? Your heart is the most beautiful thing I have ever known." Her soft tone fills the space between us, hovers. "Only you get to decide how you want to carry your heart through the world."

And somewhere in the dark, faraway compartment where I stuff all my shit, I swear I hear a whistle blow. The kind of whistle trains have. The loud roar of a whistle that tells people to look out. Move away. I am coming through.

Shannon M. Parker lives on the Atlantic coast in a house full of boys. She's traveled to more than three dozen countries and has a few dozen more to go. She works in education and can usually be found rescuing dogs, chickens, old houses, and wooden boats. Shannon has a weakness for chocolate chip cookies and ridiculous laughter—ideally, at the same time.

"Adoption means my sons found their forever home. Our hearts found forever love."

Broken Stars

by C.J. Redwine

Everything I own fits inside a burlap sack no bigger than my pillowcase. I fold my summer dress, smoothing the fraying fabric with shaking hands, and slide it into the sack, followed by my spare chemise—a treasure found in last winter's charity bin—and the comb Ms. Adelaide gave me when I turned sixteen last month.

"Don't forget your stockings, Bellana." Ellie swings down from the bunk above mine and drops to the floor. "Ms. Adelaide would never forgive you for going out into the world stockingless."

She gives me a bright smile, blue eyes flashing in her freckled face, but her cheerful tone sounds forced.

I reach for my stockings, still respectable though I had to darn them after I caught my legs against a prickly bush on the way back to the orphanage from the first of many apprenticeship interviews Ms. Adelaide scheduled for me.

Have you any experience with tutoring children?

Do you have an aptitude for balancing columns of numbers?

What skills do you bring to the discipline of alchemy?

The interviews were a misery. A never-ending parade of

questions to which I'd fumbled my answers, vainly searching for ways to stretch the truth into something that would persuade someone to offer me an apprenticeship upon my exit from Ms. Adelaide's Home for Orphaned Girls when I turned seventeen, as the kingdom's law required.

I'd had no luck, though Ms. Adelaide had briskly assured me that I must be qualified for *something,* and that every "no" brought me one step closer to a "yes." One step closer to having a roof over my head and food in my belly once I was on my own.

None of that matters now.

My heart flutters in my chest, a bird trapped in a cage of bone, and a pit of icy black fear opens within me. I draw an unsteady breath as I stare at the chest of drawers that I've shared with my roommates—Ellie, Karis, and Solana—since the day I was left on the orphanage steps at the age of four. I still catch glimpses of the woman who left me when I see myself in the mirror, but her voice has long since disappeared into the shadows of my memory.

"Did you get everything?" Ellie is still using her too-bright voice, though it shakes at the edges now. She tugs my drawer out as far as it will go and sweeps her hands inside.

"Better wear the stockings today. You'll need to make a good impression." Karis speaks from the bunk beside mine, her nails tap-tap-tapping against the polished grain of her bedstead.

"She already made a good impression." Ellie's hands emerge from the drawer full of winter socks knit with my clumsy stitches and the apron she'd made for me last Winter's Eve. "Otherwise they wouldn't be adopting her."

"No, I didn't." I take the socks and the apron and fold them into the sack. The pit of fear sends shivers across my skin. I hadn't made any impression on the people who'd be arriving today from the far edges of the kingdom to collect me and my meager belongings. They'd simply written to Ms.

Adelaide and said they wanted to adopt an older girl. Ms. Adelaide had done the rest.

She could've chosen Ellie with her quick wit, or Solana, with her gentle smile. She could've chosen Karis with her fierce confidence, or one of the fourteen-year-old girls who shared the room beside ours. Instead she'd chosen me, the shy one who'd daydreamed through every class and barely managed to master the basic skills necessary to find employment outside the orphanage. If I still believed in wishing on stars, I'd call it luck, but the stars I used to wish on are broken, and luck doesn't happen for girls like me.

Solana climbs down from her bunk and wraps a soft arm around my shoulders. "Don't worry. They'll love you." She squeezes my shoulder and then turns to plait my unruly brown hair into a tidy braid. "You're lucky to have a family."

A family. It's what I'd wanted since the day I obeyed my mother's command to wait on the steps of Ms. Adelaide's until someone came for me. What I'd yearned for as I lay on my bunk at night those first few years, staring at the star-swept sky and wondering if my mother, with her wracking cough and her nervous fingers, stared at the same sky and thought of me.

It's what I'd wanted, but time is cruel and hope is a fragile creature.

Karis stops tapping her fingers and looks at me. "You're sixteen. You'll be used as their governess or their maid. Or *worse*, if the man of the household finds you attractive. People don't adopt sixteen-year-old girls because they want them in their family."

"Karis." Solana frowns, while Ellie thrusts her hands onto her hips and glares.

"People do too adopt older girls because they want them in their family." Ellie's voice trembles, and twin spots of pink burn bright against her pale cheeks.

"No, they don't." Karis sounds weary. "If they did, none of us would still be here."

Ellie opens her mouth, but I beat her to it.

"It doesn't matter. I have to go with them and hope . . ." I swallow hard against the pressure building in my throat and gather my sack of belongings close to my chest.

Ellie flings her arms around me. "Don't forget about us." Tears spill down her cheeks.

The pressure in my throat sends a sharp ache along my jaw. "I won't."

"They'll love you." Solana wraps her arms around me as well.

I lean into her embrace without answering.

Karis gets off her bunk, pries Ellie and Solana off me, and looks me in the eye. "No matter who they are or where you go, you'll be fine, Bellana. You're stronger than you think, and you know how to find your way back to us if you need us."

Before I can speak, there's a sharp rap on the door, and then Ms. Adelaide comes in.

Her gray eyes are steady as she assesses me in one swift glance. "Good. You're ready. She's waiting in her carriage. Say your goodbyes and come along."

I cling to my friends for one long moment, my chest aching as the pit of fear within me grows until I think it might swallow me whole, and then I slowly follow Ms. Adelaide out of the room.

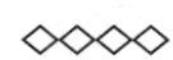

The carriage rumbles over the cobblestoned streets, and I sway against the seat as I clutch my burlap sack with white-knuckled fingers and stare at the woman seated across from me. She's darker than me. Darker than most Veracians with her golden-brown skin and curly black hair. Noticing my gaze, she smiles.

"My mother was from the kingdom of Therill. I resemble her."

My voice is a breath of its former self as I say, "I resemble my mother, too."

"So you remember her?"

"I remember her leaving." I turn and stare out the carriage window at the gray-bricked storefronts with their brightly painted flower boxes and fancy iron doors. My mother used to love the marketplace. We'd trail our fingers over the velvet-smooth petals of the peonies that bloomed in front of the bakery, and she would smile at me like the big, wide world was ours.

My chest aches again, a sharp pain that pierces the memory with bitterness.

"I'm sorry." The woman's voice is gentle.

I dig my fingers into my burlap sack and watch the marketplace give way to a wide avenue that cuts directly through a neighborhood of gracious homes built with pale stone and dark roofs. Is she sorry that my mother left me? Or that she'd decided to adopt a girl with no family, no apprenticeship, and no prospects beyond Ms. Adelaide's determination not to have any of her wards end up as beggars on the streets?

Silence stretches between us, and the pit of fear gnaws at me as my thoughts tumble into chaos.

She was going to decide that a girl who barely speaks wasn't acceptable.

She was going to take me to her home anyway and make me teach her children their sums.

She was going to pity me and show her friends what a good person she was for taking a girl whose own mother hadn't kept her.

She was going to bring me back to Ms. Adelaide's and choose someone else.

I should feel relief at the thought of going back to my friends. To the only home I truly remember.

Instead, my stomach aches and my palms grow damp.

"I brought you a present," she says, her voice still gentle. Still careful. Like I'm a broken thing and she doesn't want to damage me further.

She lifts a small rectangular package wrapped in purple cloth and tied with twine and leans forward to hand it to me. I reach for it, the manners drilled into me by Ms. Adelaide stronger than my reluctance to let go of my burlap sack, and hold it in my palm. It's heavier than I expect, and I nearly drop it.

"Go on. Open it." The woman smiles.

My fingers shake as I fumble with the twine with one hand while clutching my sack with the other.

"Here, let me hold that for you." She reaches for the sack, and I jerk it out of reach.

"It's mine." It's all I have left, and I can't bear to part with it. Not even for a second.

My heart thuds against my chest at the way her mouth forms a little "o" of surprise.

"I know it's yours," she says, the kindness in her voice unwavering, though she's watching me carefully now. "I just wanted to help."

"I don't need help." I speak quietly as I drop my eyes to my lap and study the knotted twine.

I don't need help. Not from a woman who doesn't love me. Who doesn't even know me. Not from a woman who will surely bring me back to the steps of Ms. Adelaide's once she realizes that I can't be the governess or the maid or the daughter she hopes I'll be. The pit of fear that opened inside of me at the orphanage yawns dark and wide.

The woman is quiet for a moment. Then she says, "What *do* you need?"

I shrug my shoulders and pick at the twine.

"Bellana, I'm your mother now, and I—"

"You aren't my mother." The words escape before I can hold them back. "My mother *left* me."

"Oh, Bellana—"

"I can hold my own things." My voice trembles. "And I can unknot some twine. I've learned how to do a lot of things without a mother."

Tears prick my eyes, and I turn to the window, blinking rapidly as we pass through the city of Berasford. The white-washed brick exteriors of shops with their filigreed iron shutters and their hand-painted wooden signs give way to wide streets lined with peach trees and bushes with pale yellow blooms. In the distance, the spires of the king's Berasford castle pierce the sky, the scarlet flag of Veraci fluttering in the breeze.

My breath hitches in my chest as silence fills the carriage. I don't dare look at her, though from the corner of my eye, I see her hands clenched tightly together in her lap. I've been rude. Worse, I refused her help, and I'm still struggling with the twine. So much for making a good first impression. Solana would've found a way to gracefully accept this woman's help. Ellie would've had her laughing by now. And Karis would've ripped off the twine like it was string.

I draw in a deep breath and try to ignore the fear inside me. Maybe this woman will decide I'm not worth keeping. Maybe she won't. But she gave me a present, and in my experience, only those who care about you take the trouble to do that. The least I can do is open it and thank her properly.

As the gently rounded hills of Berasford flatten into plains, I turn away from the window, place my sack at my feet, and push the twine to the edges of the rectangular object it hides. The paper tears, the twine catches on the corner and then slides free, and I'm left holding a book.

The cover is worn, its edges frayed, and the golden letters that spell out *Tales of Valor* are dull as if rubbed often over the years. I lift the book and catch its scent—the musk of aged paper and the sweetness of ink—and then I gently open the cover and see a list of names written on the inside. Each name looks to have been written by a different person, and at the bottom of the list I see *Bellana Shriner* written in elegant letters.

My heart beats fast as my fingers slowly trace the name, and then I look up at the woman. "Thank you."

She smiles, though tears shimmer in her dark eyes. Quietly, she says, "It's been passed down for generations in our family, from mother to daughter."

Something tingles up my spine at the weight she gives to the word "daughter."

"I'm sorry I was rude," I say as I slowly hug the book to my chest. The light streaming in through the carriage window is diffused with gold as the sun begins to set.

She leans toward me. "You weren't rude. And I'm so sorry your birth mother left you. I know it's going to take time for you to trust that I won't do the same." She pulls a handkerchief from her pocket and hands it to me as tears fill my eyes. "Relationships take time to grow. I'd like to get to know you. Ms. Adelaide says you like stories. So do I. I've collected hundreds of books. So many books, I decided to turn my dining room into a library."

I choke on a half-laugh, half-sob and say, "You turned your dining room into a library?"

"I did."

"But where do you eat?"

She smiles, warm and generous. "In a chair with a book balanced on one knee and a plate of food on the other. Much nicer than a big, lonely table. I might have some stories that you'd like to read. If I don't, then we can plan trips to booksellers across Veraci to find them. And along the way, we'll get to know one another. We'll learn how to be a family with each other."

"You aren't married?"

"I was for a time, but he died years ago, so it will be just the two of us." She reaches for me, and I let her take my hand. "We can take all the time we need to figure things out, Bellana. I'd really like to try, if that's all right with you."

I stare at her fingers, golden brown against my pale skin. At the way she holds on to me like a gift she doesn't want to lose. At the precious book she passed down to me.

"I'd like to try too," I say.

Her hand remains over mine as the carriage passes through fields of ripening wheat, golden stalks painted crimson beneath the dying rays of the sun. I search myself for the icy pit of fear, but find in its place a tiny kernel of warmth slowly unfurling into something I haven't felt since the last time I stared into the night sky and wished upon a star.

Hope.

C.J. Redwine loves fairy tales, Harry Potter, and watching movies at the theater. She is the New York Times bestselling author of *The Shadow Queen, The Wish Granter*, and the *Defiance* trilogy. C.J. lives in Nashville with her husband and children. If the novel-writing gig ever falls through, she'll join the Avengers and wear a cape to work every day.

"Adoption is the heartbeat of our family. We adopted two of our children from China and we will be going back to adopt another within the next few years. It's the most heartbreaking, beautiful, challenging, amazing journey we've ever been on. Our daughters are so precious to us, and getting to watch them blossom is one of the best parts of my life. I love encouraging others toward adoption. Every child deserves a loving home!"

The Snow-Covered Sidewalk

by Randy Ribay

I'm not sure I should open it here. The café is too public, too busy. It's practically buzzing. Every table's taken up by people chatting or reading or staring at their phones as they sip their lattes and take a break from Christmas shopping. The air is thick with afternoon conversation, punctuated by the bursting hiss of the milk steamer or the sudden growl of the coffee grinder.

Sure, everyone seems to be doing their own thing. But I can't be sure some creep won't read my screen over my shoulder. You just never know with creeps.

Besides.

It just doesn't feel right to read it here on my phone. That's, like, pretty unceremonious. Like maybe I should read it at midnight by the glow of a candle with some dramatic music playing in the background. Or on a ship at sea as the sun sets and Morgan Freeman narrates. I don't know. Something like that.

Or not.

I should at least be by myself. I'm sure of that. After all, I know I'm going to lose it, and I don't want to have a freaking nervous breakdown in public and then have everyone staring at me thinking something stupid like I just got dumped by a boy or I didn't get into my top college choice. And, of course, someone would recognize me and then end up asking my parents if I'm doing okay. I'd have to tell them what I've been up to, and I'd probably die of awkwardness or shame or awkward shame.

Still. My heart's racing. It's taking everything in me not to click on the little envelope icon that indicates I have a new message. The need to know what it says is consuming, but I slip my phone into my backpack at my feet. Not now, not here.

I drag my right index finger down the side of my iced coffee's plastic cup to wipe off the condensation and repeat the motion all the way around while taking a few slow, deep breaths. After there's no more condensation to wipe, I let my eyes drift outside the window to the failing light and falling snow. It's not much of a view, just the strip mall's parking lot. But it's still kind of pretty, and after a couple of minutes I feel my heart slowing. I take one more deep breath and pick up the book I was reading before I got the message notification. Except I end up reading the same sentence a million times because I can't get my freaking mind off that freaking unread message. Those are the words I want to be reading.

Screw it.

I mark my page, close my book, and reach for my bag.

"Excuse me, m'lady," some guy says in a really terrible mock-English accent.

I look up. A boy's standing on the other side of my table with a gloved hand on the opposite chair. He's maybe a little older than me. White. Smiling. Short. Wearing all black—black jeans, black shirt, black winter coat with snowflakes still melting on the shoulders. Even his hair—which is a tangled mess—seems like it's dyed black. He's got these really long, scraggly sideburns that look like wings, and around his neck hangs a necklace with a yin-yang pendant, which makes me imagine he's got a shelf full of anime and a samurai sword on the wall at home. Not my type.

"Mind if I sit here?" he asks, dropping the accent and already starting to pull out the chair. "It's pretty crowded up in this place."

I shrug. "Sure. I was just leaving."

"Cool." He pulls the chair out the rest of the way and sits down. As he struggles out of his coat (I'm not sure why he didn't remove it while he was still standing), I catch a whiff of winter and smoke. Not like fire-in-the-fireplace smoke, but like giving-himself-lung-cancer-via-cigarette smoke. Definitely not my type.

"Great book," he says, as I'm slipping it into my bag. "But I don't know about that ending."

"You've read it?" I ask, surprised not only that a guy would have read this book but that a guy would publicly admit to having read it. It's widely considered "girly" by the general public. Whatever that means.

He nods slowly, as if that was a really dumb question. Because how else would he know it was great but with an unsatisfying ending if he hadn't read it? Go me.

"Cool," I say, tucking it the rest of the way into my bag.

He pulls off his black gloves and shoves them into his coat pocket. "How far are you? Did you get to the part where she catches her boyfriend with her mother?"

"Um," I say. "Just started."

"Oops," he says. "Spoiler alert."

"You're supposed to start with that."

He musses his own hair, shakes his head like a dog trying to dry off. "Sorry. I have trouble doing what I'm supposed to. It's pretty much my life story."

"Cool," is all I say, even though I can tell he wants me to ask him more about that. "Well, enjoy the table—it has a great view of the parking lot." I zip up my bag, stand, and pull on my coat. I feel his eyes on me the entire time, like some creep, and think about calling him out, but whatever. I've got better things to do.

"Wait," he says. No, *pleads* is a better word. He *pleads*. And his voice hits just the right note of pathetic-ness that it triggers some instinctual concern inside my brain. I pause, fingers lingering on my coat zipper. Our eyes meet, and there's definitely some genuine desperation behind his. Like he wants to say something but can't work up the courage.

"What?" I ask, trying not to sound bitchy but kind of failing.

"Um," he says, mussing his hair again. "You don't have to leave. We can share the table."

"I've got somewhere to be," I say, thinking about that message sitting in my inbox, waiting to change everything.

"Oh." He lowers his gaze. Uses the nail of his forefinger to scrape some piece of dried food off the table's surface and then smooths his palm across to brush it clean. "Have a good evening then, m'lady," he says, returning to that terrible English accent that sounds more like a mix of Irish and Australian. Then he leans forward, puts his arms up on the table, and rests his head in them like he's going to take a nap.

It's pretty damn sad. Makes me feel like I just kicked a freaking puppy.

I sigh.

I've waited my entire life trying to find anyone biologically related to me, so I suppose I can wait a few more minutes to read that message. Or maybe he's just an excuse to put off what scares me about it. Whatever.

I slip my coat off and sit back down.

He lifts his head, and his lips lift in a small smile. It's all I can do not to walk to the nearest drugstore, buy a razor, and shave those ridiculous sideburns off his face. Muttonchops, I think they're called.

"You're staying?" he asks.

"I guess," I say. I want to note that he looks pretty damn sad, but I'm guessing he probably feels sad enough that that wouldn't be a very helpful observation to share.

He sits up all the way and scoots his chair forward. "Are you . . ." he starts to ask, but hesitates. Then it's like he just gives up and sits there like some malfunctioning robot. So despite the hum of conversation and movement all around us, we just chill out in this awkward bubble of silence.

"Um," I say, wiping off the condensation that has reappeared on the side of my cup even though it's mostly just ice now. He's still not saying anything, leaving me to wonder about the rest of his question: Am I what?

"Are you . . ." He stalls again. "Never mind. Iced coffee in winter, eh?"

"Yup."

"That's kind of weird." He nods outside in the direction of the still-falling snow.

I shrug. "Aren't you getting any coffee or anything?"

He fidgets in his chair. Looks away. "I don't really have the money."

I laugh. "For a cup of coffee?"

He shakes his head, and I immediately feel like the world's biggest asshat for laughing.

"You want to borrow a couple of dollars?" I ask.

"Nah, I'm cool," he says. "Really." He starts scratching at something on the table again. "I didn't actually come in here to buy coffee."

I raise an eyebrow. Here we go. "Oh?"

"I saw you in the window . . . and I . . . well, I wanted to talk to you."

Ah. There it is. Just another dude who wants to hit on me. My eyes go back to his yin-yang pendant. Probably another one of those white guys who's really into Asian stuff. Maybe he's about to mention that he knows how to use chopsticks and that he took karate lessons for a year in fourth grade. Maybe he'll compliment me in Mandarin. I rotate my cup. "Why did you want to talk to me?" I ask.

"You're Emily Johnson, right?"

I narrow my eyes at him. He knows my name, but I have no idea who he is. I'm hoping this is just a consequence of being, like, one of the only Asians in this town and not because he's been stalking me for months and wants to take me to the secret torture room he's prepped in my honor.

Okay, maybe I watch too much *Law & Order: SVU*.

Still, it's too weird for me.

"Well, I'm going now," I say as I pull my coat back on.

He starts fidgeting hardcore. Scratching at the table again, mussing his hair some more, even rocking back and forth a bit like it's time for his meds. I really need to get out of here.

"I'm sorry," he says. "I'm really sorry. That was creepy."

I wrap my scarf around my neck. Avoid making eye contact. "Agreed."

"I graduated two years ago," he says, speaking quickly. "You were a sophomore when I was a senior. That's why I know your name. Warren Lucas. That's mine. That's my name."

That explanation makes this situation a little less creepy, but only a little. It doesn't completely rule out the torture room possibility. I don't remember ever hearing the name "Warren Lucas" before, and my eyes slide back to his face and it still doesn't trigger any memories. Only about four hundred kids go to our school, so you actually end up knowing who most of them are even if you never talk to them. Especially if you're in student council like I am.

He tugs at the sideburns that make him look like he stepped out of a Civil War portrait. "I didn't have these back when I was in school." He must notice the lack of recognition that remains on my face because a moment later he adds, "You probably didn't know me. Most kids didn't. I kept to myself mostly. Still do."

And I know I should really get the hell out of there, but I take my time putting my hat and gloves on because there he goes again making me feel sorry for him with that kicked-puppy vibe he's rocking.

"Are you still in student council?" Warren asks.

I nod. "I'm president this year."

He nods. "That's awesome. Congratulations. I bet that looks really good on college applications."

"Yeah," I say and sling my bag over my shoulder.

"Finished with your applications yet?" he asks.

I nod, and I almost ask Warren what college he's going to. But if he can't afford a cup of coffee, he's probably not even at Community.

"Cool," he says.

I pick up my cup and toss it into a trashcan next to the table. "Well, bye."

"Wait," he says, and before I can walk away, he reaches out and grabs my wrist. He doesn't grip it hard, and it doesn't hurt at all. But still. I pull away. Heat rises to my face. My pulse quickens. I feel people at the nearby tables look up from their books or phones or computers.

"Don't—" I start to say.

"You're adopted, right?" Warren asks, interrupting me.

I freeze.

That question. Of course he asks *that* question. Everyone always asks *that* question eventually. And even though the answer's yes, I'm so damn sick of *that* question because—no matter how well you do in school, no matter how unaccented your English is, no matter if you're student council president and get along with everyone—if you're a Chinese girl with white parents and don't resemble anyone else in this town full of white people, everywhere you go that question is always in everyone's eyes, always on the tip of everyone's tongue—even though they already know the answer to *that* question.

So his asking it lights a fuse inside of me. As it burns

down, I try to decide if I want to scream at him to get the hell away or if I want to cock my arm back and slap those damn sideburns off his face and send them sailing across the continent and into the goddamn Pacific Ocean.

"It's just that—" he starts to say, but I don't let him finish.

I push in my chair so hard it slams into the table, making Warren jump back in his seat a bit. The people who weren't looking before are definitely paying attention now, but I don't even care.

"Why do you think it's okay to ask me *that* question?" I ask, leaving him no space to answer. "You must be messed up if you think you have the right to ask me *that* question when you don't know me beyond whatever Facebook stalking you've done. Just leave me alone, okay? Just go back to whatever bridge you live under or whatever dumpster you crawled out of. Leave me alone."

As I'm giving this kid the death stare and he just sits there like he's about to cry, I hear someone coming toward us past the crowded tables.

"Emily, is this guy bothering you?" a guy asks, touching my elbow.

I pull my elbow away and turn to him. He's a balding middle-aged guy in a suit with a face like a turtle. It takes a moment, but I recognize him. It's one of my dad's coworkers. I forget his name, but I'm glad to see him in this moment. "Yes," I say.

He turns to Warren. "All right, buddy. Time for you to go."

"Sorry," Warren says, real quiet. "I wasn't trying to cause any trouble. I just . . ." He trails off. He stands up. He grabs his black coat, not bothering to put it back on, and walks away while my dad's coworker follows close behind like my personal bodyguard. Our eyes meet one last time just before he steps out into the early darkness, and there's something so sorrowful and so familiar there that I feel a knot form in the pit of my stomach.

Or maybe that's from his question upsetting me. I'm also shaking, adrenaline still coursing through my veins. I sit back down at my table, without taking off my coat, to try to calm down for a moment. I hate that I'm feeling like some stereotypical damsel in distress, but whatever. I'm just glad he's gone.

The people sitting nearby go back to whatever they were doing before all of this went down, and a few moments later, my dad's coworker reappears. "Are you okay? Did he hurt you?"

"Yes," I say, eyes on the table where the boy was scraping at the encrusted food. "I mean, yes, I'm okay. Not that he hurt me. He didn't hurt me. Just said some stupid things."

He shakes his head and makes a sound of disgust. "Boys. Some of them can just—they just don't know how to respect women anymore."

I shrug.

He lingers.

"I'm really okay," I say. "You can go back to getting your coffee. I'll be fine. Just a bit shaken up."

"Are you sure?"

"Yes."

"Do you need a ride home or anything?"

I shake my head. "I drove."

"Okay," he says. "Did you want anything? Another coffee or a scone? Maybe a muffin? It's on me."

"I'm good," I say. "Thanks, though."

"Sure thing." He hangs around for a few seconds longer than he needs to and says, "Tell your father I said hi," and finally walks away.

I sit at the table for a few minutes longer. I don't even take off my hat. I just sit there staring at the table until I stop shaking, until my heart slows down, until the burning fuse fizzles out.

Finally, I get up and walk out. I leave behind the warmth and the light and the scent of coffee and push through the door into the quiet cold of the evening, the early darkness making it feel later than I know it is. It's stopped snowing, and a few inches of fresh white blankets the world. Suggestions of the sidewalk, the parking lot, and the cars sit under the pale light of the parking lot lamps. Only a few tire tracks and footprints disrupt the white, but the plows haven't come through yet.

The world is silent except for the muffled crunch of the snow under my boots. Gloved hands buried in my pockets and my head still in some strange space, I make my way to my car—or at least the buried form that sits in the place where I think I parked.

When I get to it, I find something strange: a folded square of paper sticking out from the snow that covers the driver's side door. I pluck it from the ice and unfold it. It's a page torn from a book with something written in pen. It takes me a moment of struggling to figure out what it says before I realize that I'm looking at the wrong side. The pen has bled through from the other side of the page. I turn it over, angle it under the parking lot lamp, and read:

I'm sorry. I was also adopted. I just wanted to talk to someone about it. —W

My heart drops.

I'm an asshole.

Warren Lucas was just trying to reach out to me, and I blew up on him. Shamed him in public when he was just trying to find someone to talk to, someone who knew what he was going through. Wasn't that the same thing I was trying to do when I sent that stupid swab with my saliva to that stupid company so they could match my DNA against their database to find any of my biological relatives? Isn't that the connection I wanted when they gave me the name of a second cousin and I tracked her down and messaged her? Isn't that all any of us are looking for—someone who understands us in a way nobody else can?

But how was I supposed to know? Shouldn't he have

opened with this vital piece of information? Instead, he just awkwardly fumbled through a conversation as if he was hitting on me. How else was I supposed to take it? Besides, what is he to me?

Bah. I should find him and apologize, at least. Maybe it's not too late. He couldn't have gone far. I tear my eyes away from his sad three sentences and scan the parking lot, but there's no sign of him. I trudge through the snow back to the entrance to the coffee shop, clutching his note in my gloved hand. I look down at the snow-covered sidewalk and see my set of footprints and then a second set heading in the opposite direction. I follow them down the strip mall, past the closing stores, and around the side of the building.

But then the tracks disappear into a patch of damp cement that leads all the way down the rear of the long building where it must have been blocked from the wind. Still, I follow the patch, hoping to find where the tracks pick up again or even more so hoping to find Warren propped up against one of the dumpsters smoking so I can apologize, or if not apologize, just talk about things, about everything.

I reach the other end of the building without finding either, though. No tracks. No damaged boy with sideburns self-medicating with cigarettes.

I sigh.

Oh, well. I tried. I can probably find him online later.

Slowly, I cross the snow-covered lot back to my car. Without brushing off any snow, I pull open the door and slip inside, knocking a few flakes from around the doorframe onto the driver's seat. I slam the door closed, throw my bag in the passenger seat, and just sit there trying to make sense of the evening.

I watch my breath puff out in front of my face in small white clouds. The snow still covers all the windows, blocking out the light from the parking lot lamps, encasing me in my own little world.

Finally, I dig my keys out of my pocket and slip the car key into the ignition, though it takes me a few tries since I keep my gloves on. The engine rumbles to life. I turn the heat all the way up and switch on the defrosters, even though the vents are still blowing cold air.

This.

This feels like the right moment.

I slip off my right glove and dig my phone from my bag. I pull up the message from my long-lost supposed second cousin, the only living person in the world I know of who shares my blood.

But I still can't bring myself to read it.

Warren Lucas, with his two first names and his mutton-chops and his yin-yang necklace, keeps popping into my brain. I was so caught up in my own thing that he wasn't even real to me. I wonder what he would have said if we had actually talked, what I would have said. I wonder if he knows any of his biological relatives and, if so, if that makes him feel any less alone. It's not that I'm not loved by the people who are actually in my life, but it's just—it's hard to explain. Even to myself.

My thoughts are interrupted by the rumbling scrape of a passing snowplow. After the sound fades, I click on the windshield wipers. It takes them a few swings, but the snow isn't as heavy or as frozen as it can sometimes be, so it's not long before I have a clear view of the parking lot. Several other cars sit encased in white, and I wonder if there is anyone else sitting within any of them.

A light flickers at the other end of the strip mall. A mini-van rolls along a freshly plowed path in front of me. The snow begins to fall again.

I read the message.

Randy Ribay is the author of the contemporary YA novels *After the Shot Drops* (Houghton Mifflin Harcourt, 2018) and

An Infinite Number of Parallel Universes (Merit Press, 2015). He's also a high school English teacher, reader, gamer, watcher of great TV, husband, and father of two dog-children. He can probably be found somewhere making lightsaber sound effects with his mouth.

"Every single child, without question, needs and deserves unconditional love."

Deeply

by William Ritter

Obsidian waters roiled beneath the cliffs of Hartkin. Scarcely a breeze stirred the air in the quiet little town, and yet, far below, buoys rocked madly and fishing boats strained against their moorings, clattering together like heavy wind chimes. The ocean was angry. It churned up seafood and sediment and the briny stench of something else. Something old.

The rain had not yet begun to fall, but from his position atop the bluff, Jay could feel it coming. He didn't mind. He hadn't even bothered to zip up his jacket. Jay enjoyed the rain. He enjoyed the hot sun and the biting frost. He enjoyed the smell of pine needles and even the taste of dust. He just enjoyed being in the world.

Mostly, if he was being honest, Jay enjoyed not being in school. His new classmates were fine, all except the Patterson twins—who were jerks—and Henry Hinkler—who always sat too close and smelled like warm bologna. His new teacher, Ms. Espinoza, was okay, if a bit dull. She had assigned Jay's least favorite project on Friday, though. Every teacher got around to it eventually. It made Jay's stomach turn in knots. The Family Tree.

There was nothing about real families that looked like trees. His was less a tree and more a complicated mess of broken branches, of limbs grafted on at odd angles, and of other trees that had grown tangled with his own. And then there were all the branches that mattered to Jay, but didn't properly connect to his tree at all. Branches that he only wished were a part of his tree.

Last year, Mrs. Winslow had given everybody premade charts with tidy little boxes to fill in, but the handouts left room for only one mommy and one daddy. Jay had stared at the boxes until he wanted to cry. And then some other things happened, and pretty soon Mrs. Winslow was squawking at him for flipping over his desk and Jay was yelling and there may or may not have been biting. That was when Mrs. Winslow said she was going to call Jay's mother, which only made matters worse.

That had been at Jay's last school. Before the move. Before the adoption. Before, well, before *complicated* got *more complicated*. Nobody seemed to understand. Family was weird.

Jay sat with his feet dangling over the edge of the cliff and pulled a ragged, faded yellow duck from his backpack. Yucky Ducky was stained and had been inexpertly repaired along one seam with mismatched orange thread. Jay could not remember a time before Yucky Ducky. The plush doll was dingy and juvenile, he knew, but he kept it with him at all times.

Once, last year, stupid ugly Oliver Hampton saw him with it and told everyone at recess that Jay played with baby toys. Jay's face flushed red hot with embarrassment, and he had thought about throwing the duck away right then and there—but he couldn't do it. Yucky Ducky had been there for him. It was broken and frayed and it had been left, forgotten in the dark, countless times. But so had Jay.

Let them laugh. Yucky Ducky had been through it all with him, which was more than anyone else in the whole wide world could say.

The ocean heaved. A great dark shape welled beneath the surface, impossibly vast. Jay watched as the remaining seagulls abandoned the rocks below and soared toward calmer waters up the shore. The smell was almost tangible now. Something was rising.

"Your momma never teach you to stay away from the cliffs, dweeb?" jeered a voice behind him.

Jay groaned. Not one but both of the Patterson twins were sauntering across the clearing toward him. Marcus and Lucas—not that Jay could ever tell them apart—were the tag-team bullies of Hartkin Elementary. Jay pulled himself to his feet to face the thugs. The twins were each a foot taller than Jay and built like sacks of cement with skin.

Jay had met plenty of boys like the Patterson twins before, kids who just liked to cause trouble wherever they went. His foster parents had called kids like them "troubled youth," which Jay had always thought was a backward sort of way to describe totally obnoxious jerks—until one day he overheard his caseworker call *him* a "troubled youth," while she was on the phone and thought he couldn't hear her.

Jay didn't want to be a troubled youth. He didn't want trouble.

The Patterson twins, on the other hand, appeared to have embraced trouble with both meaty hands.

"I don't think he heard you, Luke," said one of the twins. "You should say it again—harder."

"You don't wanna get too close to the edge," warned Lucas. "It's dangerous!" As he said it, he pretended to lunge at Jay, who was smart enough not to back away. Behind him was a fifty-foot drop to the tumultuous black waters of the cape.

"What do you buttheads want?" Jay asked, trying to sound tough, even as his eyes searched for an escape. All he needed was an opening to dart past the twins and run away. The Pattersons might have been slabs of raw muscle, but they were *slow* slabs of raw muscle. He could outrun them any day if he could just . . .

The twins seemed to read his mind. They closed in, blocking Jay with his back to the steep cliff.

"What'd you call us?" said Marcus. "Your momma never teach you no manners, neither?"

"I heard he doesn't even have a mom," said Lucas.

"Naw, he's got parents," said Marcus. "I heard his mom is, like, crazy or something, and his dad's some kinda deadbeat." Jay's entire body clenched as he glared at the Patterson twins. He wanted to run away and fight and barf all at once.

Lucas did not respond right away. Something else had caught his attention. "Dude, Mark," he said, his eyes shooting over Jay's shoulder. "Look."

Marcus ignored his brother, not finished toying with their victim yet. "Whatcha got there, dweeb?" With a quick swipe, he grabbed Yucky Ducky out of Jay's hand.

"Give it back!" yelled Jay.

"Or what?" Marcus dangled the toy just out of reach above Jay's head. "What is this, anyway? Are you in preschool?"

"Mark, dude, look at the water!" Lucas had gone curiously pale, but his brother still wasn't listening.

"Your crazy mom give this to you?" Marcus sneered.

Jay was shaking with anger now. "Yes." He could feel the hot tears welling in his eyes. He clenched his fists. "She *did*. Now give it BACK."

"Wha . . . what is that thing?" Lucas stammered. He stumbled backward and tripped, falling onto his back with his eyes still fixed on the ledge.

"It's a stupid dolly," said Marcus. "I think it's supposed to be a duck."

"It's MINE," said Jay.

"If you want it so much," Marcus snarled, "go get it!" He

whipped Yucky Ducky up over Jay's head, high into the air and then down, down, down, tumbling toward the salty waves.

The sneer left his face as his eyes followed the duck.

Jay took a deep breath. "You think my *mom* was crazy?" he said quietly. "You should meet my new dad."

The wet hell that erupted from the inky sea below has no name in any human tongue. Tentacles writhed like a mountain of snakes. Somewhere within them there might have been a body, but if a body there was, it was coated with untold eons of barnacles and strange weeds that draped and clung to its dark flesh.

The Patterson twins stared, dumbstruck. A great glistening tentacle slammed into the hillside to their right. The tallest, oldest tree in Hartkin could not have fallen with a heavier crash. The tendril was like a slimy, meaty hillside.

Marcus leaped aside, tripping gracelessly over his brother as Lucas attempted to get back to his feet. The twins righted themselves just in time to see a second tentacle, as broad as a house and long as a railway train, come hammering down to their left. The walls of dark, undulating flesh now cut them off completely from the rest of the world.

And then came the voice.

THEIR EMPTY HUSKS SHALL SINK INTO THE DARKEST DEPTHS, AND THEIR BONES SHALL BE SCATTERED TO THE FURTHEST CORNERS OF THE UNDERSEA.

The voice echoed inside their heads. The voice was everywhere and nowhere. The voice was wet and poisonous and deep beyond measure.

DO YOU WILL IT? asked the voice.

The Patterson twins began to cry.

"No," said Jay. "It's fine."

THEIR MINDS SHALL CRUMBLE TO SALT WITHIN THEIR SKULLS AND TORMENTS UNCEASING SHALL ASSAIL THEIR WAKING DREAMS.

"Just be cool, Dad," said Jay.

THEY SHALL LIVE. FOR NOW.

The heaving hillsides of grimy muscle retreated. The Patterson twins tripped and stumbled over each other in their rush to leave the clearing. Neither would return to the waterfront for the rest of their lives. Lucas would one day move to central Kansas where he would avoid swimming pools, bathtubs, and large bottles of water, and Marcus would come to find that even a whiff of seafood from then on would send him into a cold sweat.

Jay stood alone on the bluff, looking into the fathomless face of the horror from the depths.

YOU CALLED US *DAD*.

Jay nodded. "It's a thing people call their guy parents sometimes."

HUMAN GENDERS HAVE NO MEANING TO US. The dark, convulsing shapes that comprised the leviathan's body wriggled constantly.

"I guess you don't seem like a 'mom,'" said Jay. "Is that . . . okay?" This whole situation was still very new. Family was weird.

TO POSSESS OUR TRUE NAME WOULD BURN YOUR MORTAL BEING APART FROM THE INSIDE OUT, said the voice. YOU MAY CALL US *DAD*.

A long coil whipped through the air and snapped above Jay with a spray of salt water. Yucky Ducky landed at his feet. Jay picked it up, briny foam dripping from its little yellow tail. "Thanks."

THERE WERE MONSTERS IN THE DARKNESS, said the voice. THEY WERE YOUR MONSTERS. THEY WERE YOUR DARKNESS.

Jay swallowed. The first droplet of rain hit his cheek. He nodded.

THEY WILL NOT HURT YOU NOW. NOR EVER AGAIN. WE HAVE MADE IT SO.

"I know."

THAT TRINKET. IT WAS A GIFT FROM THEM.

Jay looked down at the soggy duck. He sighed. He had been through this conversation with enough caseworkers and counselors already. "I don't know why I like it. I just do."

There was no sound but the gentle patter of rain beginning to fall in earnest before the voice spoke again. WITHIN THE DARKNESS, WITHIN THE MONSTERS, IN THE BLACKNESS OF THEIR HEARTS, THERE WAS LIGHT. THERE IS ALWAYS LIGHT, EVEN IN THE DEEPEST DARK. WE UNDERSTAND THIS. THAT TRINKET KNOWS YOUR DARKNESS. IT IS A REMINDER THAT THERE WAS A GLIMMER OF LIGHT EVEN THEN—THERE WAS LIGHT IN THE DEEPEST DARK. The nameless beast paused. IT IS GOOD.

Jay felt a weight in the pit of his stomach lift just a fraction. It was a weight he had almost forgotten was there, a private weight he had locked away deep down inside himself. *There had been happy times.* He held the thought tenderly in his mind now, like a fragile bird with a broken wing. Sad memories had stained them and covered them up and crowded them out, but there had been happy times—and it was okay to remember those, too. He had been protecting them for so long he had almost forgotten what it felt like to let himself remember them. The rain fell softly around him. Beams of sunlight cut through the clouds beyond the creature, lighting up the calmer seas in the distance. This storm would pass.

Jay looked down at Yucky Ducky, dripping onto the grass—and, in spite of himself, he smiled. It was nice to have someone else doing the protecting for once.

THAT GLIMMER OF LIGHT IS ALSO THE REASON WE DID NOT RAZE THE TOWN IN WHICH WE FOUND YOU AND EVISCERATE EVERY MONSTROUS HUMAN THERE.

"What was that last bit?" Jay looked up.

NOTHING. DAD STUFF.

William Ritter is an Oregon educator and the author of the NYT bestselling *Jackaby* series. He is a loving husband, a giant nerd, and a proud father to two outstanding young boys. Adoption made his family complete.

"Adoption taught me that there are many ways to find who you're missing, and many paths to find your way home together. Families are weird. Adoption made my weird family complete."

Meant to be Broken

by Stephanie Scott

Five years of nothing, and now this. Five years of no answers and empty Facebook search results, and then my childhood best friend Becca showed up in a box overflowing with unfiled paperwork.

This was crazy. I was staring at a file in an *adoption* agency. Becca already had a family. What was her name and information doing here?

Her name in bold font, Rebecca Sampson, marched across the top of a form with the Little Hands Adoption Agency logo. My heart stuttered, caught somewhere between exhausting itself and failing entirely. I'd been focused on logging my National Honor Society volunteer hours by sorting through boxes in the agency's neglected storeroom. Grunt work easy enough to hand off to a student. I'd never expected to, you know, *recognize* anyone. A photo slipped onto my lap. A twelve-year-old Becca stared back. Stringy brown hair, a smile hinting at mischief, and tanned skin from a summer tearing up the neighborhood on our bikes. *My* Becca.

A knocking sounded. I jumped nearly out of my skin and flipped the file facedown.

Shay, the agency program director, stood in the doorway. "Everything okay, Hannah?"

"Sure!" My voice boomed, too loud for the small room. I adjusted my glasses. "I mean, yes. Just sorting away!"

Volunteering at a human services organization was like frosting spread on top of extra credit. At least, that's how it should look in my portfolio: Hannah Malone, NHS Leadership Initiative Candidate, followed by a nice long list of activities. Things like caseworker meetings, visitations, and support groups. I hadn't exactly envisioned a windowless room sorting scattered files, but here I was.

I also hadn't envisioned seeing Becca's name among the files. It was so weird even thinking about Becca after five years. I couldn't picture what she looked like beyond sixth grade. I wasn't sure I'd recognize her if I saw her today.

Shay's smile was laced with sympathy. "I'm sorry we have you stuck going through these boxes, but it's a real help for our state audit. Let me know if you need anything."

I nodded. After she left, I looked back at the file. The page was more like a cover sheet. What I needed was the rest of the file.

Becca hadn't simply moved away. She'd vanished. One day we were having a sleepover, and the next, she was gone. Becca never came back to school again. It was as if the whole family had picked up and left without a word. I'd tried to find answers. I really had tried.

And then you stopped looking.

The cold truth hit me square in the chest. I *had* stopped looking.

I stared at Becca's name until the letters blurred together. I may have stopped looking, but I was still in the same place. Becca never bothered to find me either.

Back when we were friends, Becca never missed school. Even when she had to pack her own lunch and help her younger brother get ready because her mom was too tired, she made it to school. And when she was sick, she called or texted. She *always* contacted me.

So when Becca hadn't shown up to school for two days and my texts piled up with no answers, I got worried. Nobody answered her door in the morning, so I walked to the bus stop alone. Nobody was home after school either. No lights on in the house, no figures shadowed the windows. No cars in the driveway.

No phone calls.

"Did her family leave on vacation?" my dad had asked when I'd brought it up.

I shook my head. Her family didn't take vacations.

Maybe there was an emergency, like a grandparent dying. But then why wouldn't Becca let me know?

I stayed behind after Earth Science, Becca's favorite class, to ask our teacher, Mrs. Gallagher. "Do you know where Becca is?" I explained she couldn't be sick because then she would have texted. I told her how her house looked empty.

"Hannah, I'm sorry. This happens sometimes. Families move and don't tell anyone."

"But this is Becca. She would have told me." She *definitely* would have told me she was moving. Best friends shared everything. *We* shared everything.

Mrs. Gallagher said she'd ask around. She'd said she was sorry. Sorry didn't mean much to me. She didn't have answers.

I went back to my parents, but they said the same thing as Mrs. Gallagher. "Becca's mom has been troubled for a while. Maybe they moved in with a relative. They might have needed a fresh start."

Troubled? "What do you mean?"

My mom looked at my dad. "Money troubles. Becca's older brother. It could be any of those things."

"That's stupid." So what if Becca's family didn't have a lot of money? That didn't explain why Becca wasn't calling me. And her older brother didn't even live with them anymore. Only her younger brother and sometimes one of her mom's boyfriends.

The fourth day Becca didn't show up to school, kids started talking. Some said her dad got out of prison and came for the family. Except her dad had a life sentence. He sent cards at Becca's birthday and they were always late. Her mom would say what a waste it was, making contact, since he'd never see the outside of a cell.

They were only rumors.

Anytime I brought up Becca to friends at school, they'd say, "It's so weird she disappeared!" Maybe they'd make a few guesses about what happened, but eventually, they'd go back to quoting their favorite online videos. I'd laugh with them, but the pangs of hurt never strayed far. *Becca left me. She left, and I don't know why.*

Days and weeks passed. Each day could have been the day Becca contacted me. Each day, the lights might have been on at her house, with her mom's old truck parked in the driveway.

Each day, my laugh grew steadier with my friends at the lunch table. These were my friends now. Anger at Becca leaving shifted to anger at myself for caring so much. If she'd wanted me to know her family was leaving, she would have told me. Each day, that truth planted itself deeper. Each day, another branch of memories withered and snapped. That's all I had now—memories. Becca was gone.

If everyone else could forget Becca so easily, maybe I could too.

◇◇◇◇

I was supposed to be racking up service hours, but the more I thought of Becca being connected to the adoption agency, the more I wanted to find out what happened to her. I needed the rest of her file.

The problem? The upstairs offices with the file cabinets required a key card. I didn't have one.

Footsteps sounded in the hall outside the storeroom. A bearded man paced, talking on his cell phone. His badge was very much not on a lanyard, but instead clipped to his jacket. All loose and vulnerable.

He turned the corner.

I followed.

This was definitely not on my day planner's To Do list. *Steal badge. Break into files!* Probably no cutesy Kawaii sticker for that task.

I wasn't a rule-violating type of girl. I was the type to read the fine print on user agreements. Rules were my currency. I followed them and was rewarded. Well, there was that one time I shushed my British Lit class when they cracked up at Mrs. Vanwellen's over-the-top dramatic reading of *Jane Eyre*. Obviously, it did nothing for my popularity.

My shoulders sank as the man disappeared into an office. Moments later, he left again, jacketless, headed toward the restrooms.

Every nerve in my body lit up. Now or never.

Every step felt deliberate. *I am doing something wrong. I am taking property that does not belong to me.*

It was so easy. The open door, the jacket hung on the chair back. The badge, a simple click to unclip.

Seven Years Ago

I wanted to run. Either run or melt into a puddle and seep into the sidewalk cracks. Anything but stand here and face Diamond Martino and her diva crew.

"Aren't you going to say anything?" Diamond, with her shiny, long dark hair and bejeweled platform sandals, stood beside the playground swings with arms crossed, flanked by three girls in our fourth-grade class.

They'd been whispering all day. Walking the long way around my worktable, making faces at each other as they passed. Now, the impossible question. I would lose any way I answered.

I'm not ugly! I wanted to shout. Who asked a girl *why* she was ugly? If I said I wasn't, they'd call me stuck-up for thinking of myself as pretty. And I didn't. They'd made sure I didn't. But if I gave a reason, then I admitted I was ugly and gross. My cheeks flamed. My feet wouldn't move, and my mouth sealed shut as if glue lined my lips.

"You're a loser," Diamond said. "Ugly fake-brand jeans. Ugly face."

I felt like a monster. My hair and my clothes were hopelessly uncool. My glasses not trendy enough but too strong a prescription to go without. The last time I'd told the teacher on Diamond, she'd lied that it was all a misunderstanding. Then she'd posted a video to her friends how I was voted ugliest in class by secret vote. I cried for days.

"Hey there, Sparkles," Becca breezed in. She was supposed to be with her learning specialist this recess period. "Your pedicure can't hide your toad toes. I can't *believe* you actually wear sandals."

Diamond started to retort, but Becca stepped forward. "Call Hannah ugly one more time and I'll tell everyone how you peed your pants during the Frontier Days assembly."

Diamond's mouth dropped open. The girls beside her tittered. One of the recess monitors came by, too late as always, and the girls scattered.

"I didn't even *do* anything." My tears let loose. "You shouldn't have said that to her. Now she'll be after you too."

Becca steered me away from the approaching teacher. "I already threatened to jump Diamond after school. I told her my brother and his friends would be there."

"You'll get suspended if you fight!"

"I'm not going to fight anyone. Diamond is too scared to fight. She's afraid of me already." Becca shrugged.

No one seemed to scare Becca. And she was right, some kids were afraid of her. Maybe it was because of her older brother. Some kids said he sold drugs—that he was a dealer. I'd met him a bunch of times. He was nice, but tough. I didn't believe the rumors.

After school we walked from the bus stop to her mom's salon. When it was warm outside, the door was propped open and people came in to talk as often as to get their hair cut or nails done.

All day I'd felt like the word *ugly* was written across my skin in permanent marker. Now that we were miles from school, I relaxed. "You said Diamond had *toad toes*. That's so weird."

"I heard her say once that she hates her feet." Becca grinned as we sifted through the sample polish jars. "For real, though, Hannah. If she says anything to you again, let me know."

This hadn't been the first time Becca stood up for me. "You can't get into a fight. You'll get in so much trouble."

She twisted shut a bottle of nail polish and gripped it in her fist. "I've got your back, okay? I won't let anyone talk to you like that."

"I don't know what I did to make them hate me." Tears sprang back, hot and fast.

Becca's mom walked over, and Becca told her everything.

"That's just girls acting jealous," her mom told us. "Mean girls. Come here. Let me style up your hair."

"And I'll paint your nails with *this*." Becca held out a bright pink shade my own mom would hate for sure.

I nodded, wiping my tears. The *ugly* label didn't disappear, but it faded enough. I had a friend I could count on, and that was what mattered.

◇◇◇◇

Thankfully, the agency's upstairs offices were dim and silent since it was the end of the workday. Being the rule follower and all, I had to note I hadn't been *specifically* told not to go upstairs. Only that a badge required access.

A badge that I had not been given, but I couldn't dwell on that now.

I wound through the cubicles, then let out a slow breath and zeroed in on a row of cabinets. A label on the closest one read "Adoption Files."

Before I lost my nerve, I opened the drawer for "S" and searched the files. Nothing.

Wait—this was good news. Just because this was an adoption agency didn't mean Becca had actually been adopted. The file could have been for another reason, like counseling or something.

I should just go. This was ridiculous—me standing here by a file cabinet trying to piece together a childhood mystery. I sighed and let my attention drift to the window, to the street beyond. A dash of coral sliced the horizon as night settled in. Two kids raced by on bikes. Two girls, one with a bushy ponytail, the other with her unzipped coat flapping in the wind. Tearing home before dark, just like Becca and me, back in the day.

I stared at the closed drawer. Opened it again. My fingers flipped through the "R" section. My breath stalled. There it was—Rebecca Sampson. The file was missing the cover sheet, which I held in my hand.

This was it. I was about to find out what happened to my friend.

Inside: a police report. *Unlicensed guns. Drugs. Illegal possession. Drug trafficking.*

No. *No, no, no*. This had to be wrong. I would have

known. I'd been in Becca's house so often I dreamed about it sometimes. I would have noticed these things going on.

Her mom's boyfriends. A stirring built up inside me so fierce I growled out loud. Some jerk brought drugs into their house and busted Becca's family. He should be in jail!

I skimmed the report. The only names noted were Becca's brother and her mother. No mention of the boyfriends.

The next page listed the name MARTINEZ in capital letters. Beds: six. Foster care placements: five. Specialization: teens, preadolescents, and emergency placements. Open to adoption. An address.

The page blurred. I wiped my eyes with the back of my hand. A sick feeling churned in my gut. It didn't make sense. Becca's mom loved her. She wouldn't give her away. Becca's younger half-brother wasn't in the file. What about him?

Right now, I needed to get out of here. Wait, I should make a quick copy of the report. I slipped my phone out of my back pocket and snapped a picture of the page.

"What do you think you're doing?"

I froze. My heart, oh, my poor heart, hated me. Standing behind me was Shay, who knew where I was supposed to be, and where I wasn't.

Busted.

Program Director Shay Kingston stared at me unflinchingly from across her desk. "Well, Ms. Malone. You want to explain why you had this girl's file in your hand?"

I could invent a reason. I could say I was trying to file the misplaced folder in the right place. But I wouldn't get to touch that file again. I couldn't give up as if I'd never found this missing piece to the mystery of losing my friend.

That was the thing. How do you erase someone who used to be your other half? People talked about love as being two halves coming together. No wonder people were a mess when they broke up. If fractured love was anything like a broken friendship, I never wanted to fall in love.

"She's somewhere safe?" I asked Shay.

"Yes."

"What about her mom? Her brother?" I had so many questions.

"You understand this is information that cannot simply be shared. It violates laws."

I tried to squelch the panic rising up. I would lose service hours, and Shay could report my violation to the school. To the police. To my *parents*.

"I have to tell your parents."

I cringed, the shame and panic now fully alive and pulsing inside me. "I'm sorry. It was stupid what I did. I was just so freaked out and I thought I could . . ."

All I had left was my trusty rule-following. "I know her. *Knew* her." I stared at my hands, folded in my lap and clenched together. "She was my best friend, and just like that she was gone." I kept talking, telling Shay how I'd begged my teachers for information, how for two years I detoured by her house, just in case, even after new renters moved in. "I can't believe an agency like this would take kids away from a mother who loved them."

Shay watched me. Her expression changed. Not kind, but softer. "You wanted answers. Is that why you signed up for this internship?"

"No. I swear. I didn't know anything until I found her name and picture. Then I needed to know more."

She considered this. "You were young. You would have been, what? Twelve? People get themselves involved in bad things for all sorts of reasons. Oftentimes the drug-running starts small—make a little extra money to keep the lights on. To feed the kids. Things escalate. You didn't know what was going on because your friend and her family didn't want you to."

Like a switch, my shame at breaking into the files vanished. "You didn't know Becca. She wouldn't have kept this from me. I didn't even get to read the file. Can you tell me what happened?"

She gave me a steady look. Then she picked up the file again. "It says here your friend's family ran a drug house. The night of the arrest, the kids were taken into foster care." She skimmed the pages. "The police were watching the house. They had an informant looking for the drug stash, but the stash was moved. Drugs and a large amount of cash. A few days later they found it. They questioned some teachers at the school."

All of this information was coming together too fast. The police report. The drug charges. Her mom's in-and-out salon clients. The skeevy boyfriends.

"Which teacher?" My words barely surfaced. "Please, can you tell me?"

Shay gave me a conflicted look. She let out a breath. "Marissa Gallagher."

Mrs. Gallagher. She'd known! I clenched my fists, fighting to keep myself together. "She should have told me. I asked her so many times, and she never told me." All this time wondering and my teacher already knew Becca had been taken.

"Hannah, your teacher could have jeopardized the investigation. She could have risked your friend's safety if she gave you Becca's location. Besides, chances are she didn't know."

This still didn't feel right. "Becca wasn't in danger. I would have known."

Shay returned to reading the file. "It says here a backpack was recovered, which led to the arrests."

"A backpack?" Icy horror raced through my veins. "I need to go." I stood, shaking, as the memories flooded back.

"Hannah, I'm contacting your parents," Shay said. "You were found in a secure area with someone else's security badge. I can't let this violation go."

I nodded, not even caring about the volunteer hours for once. "That's fine. Call my folks. I just need to get out of here."

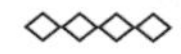

I only told my teacher the one thing. That one time when Becca and her brother stayed the night at our house on a weeknight because their power had been shut off. Becca's mom stayed with her boyfriend.

When Mrs. Gallagher asked about Becca's homework in class the next day, Becca said she forgot it, but that wasn't true. I told Mrs. Gallagher Becca had the homework in her backpack. We'd worked on it together at my house. I was so excited we'd had a midweek sleepover, I couldn't keep my mouth shut about it.

The report said the stash had been moved. *The backpack.*

"Just leave it alone," Becca had said to me after class. "I'll get a new one."

That wasn't like her. Becca wasn't careless with her things. "Someone stole your backpack. With your homework!"

Becca shrugged off my shock, so I'd gone to Mrs. Gallagher later to have her report the stolen backpack. That's what friends did for each other.

Two days later, Becca was gone.

For all the times my best friend had my back, I should have protected her. The cops were looking for a drug stash and I'd tipped off our teacher about the stupid backpack. Of course she'd tell the police about it when she was questioned. I'd led them right to it.

I was the reason Becca was gone. Her family had been arrested and I couldn't breathe. The memory pressed sharp points into my skin.

I stumbled through the back door at home, barely able to keep from crying. My parents, being of the hovering variety, demanded to know what happened. Hiding what happened was useless. Shay would be calling them about my violation.

So I told them. Everything.

"First of all, you're grounded for this trouble you caused at the agency," Mom said, looking to my dad, who paced the kitchen. "Second, Becca's mother and brother were arrested on drug charges. They were breaking the law. You seriously think you have any blame here?"

"Obviously I didn't cause *that*. But if I'd only—"

"What? Not said anything? People only get away with crimes for so long. Eventually they get caught. It's not your responsibility to protect anyone. Even we were duped. We didn't know what Becca's family was involved in."

Dad nodded. "It sounds like her mother knew the house was under surveillance and used Becca to get the drugs out of the house." He blew out a breath of air, probably realizing those drugs may have briefly been in *our* house before some kind of transfer.

Which meant Becca knew. She had to have known. And she'd chosen not to tell me. I would have kept any secret for her. I desperately wanted to believe I would have.

Mom rested her hands on my shoulders. "You did the right thing by telling your teachers what you did. It's unfortunate what happened to Becca. Her mother must have lost parental rights." Mom's eyes softened and she pulled me into a hug. "I'm so sorry, Hannie. This can't be easy."

I let myself cry. A cry that drained my anger and left me hollow.

I tried to forget about Becca all over again. I wrote an apology to the staff person whose ID I'd taken, and I signed off on an incident report to the honor society. So much for my pristine school record. But even that didn't deter my endless questions. What happened the past five years? Was Becca happy? Maybe she'd wanted to contact me back when everything went down, but it was too dangerous.

I'd never know.

Knowing Becca was adopted simply wasn't enough. So many holes existed in this story. I was only now beginning to fill them.

◇◇◇◇

Of course it was a school night when I realized I had Becca's address captured on my phone. When I was grounded.

I had to find Becca or I'd never be satisfied. It was as if Becca herself reached out to me through that file. Her past called out and I had to know more. I *needed* to know.

Mom was out at an evening meeting, and Dad wore headphones while he worked in the den. I slipped out unnoticed.

I cranked the music in my car. I drove fast. I didn't think.

A seamless string of houses and businesses passed by with cross-streets leading into new towns. I dipped my hand into my pocket and pulled out the chain I'd grabbed. One half of a broken-heart that read "Friend." The inside of my lip was dented from my teeth clenching the sensitive flesh between them. If I turned back now, I'd never know.

My GPS instructed me to turn. These houses were nothing like the worn brick homes in my neighborhood. These houses were built in this century and had three-car garages. I stopped in front of a house no different from the rest of the block. Lights on both downstairs and upstairs. Two cars in the driveway. One with a sticker stretched across the back window reading Central High.

I scratched at my skin. Took a few breaths. This was a whole lot of stupid to come here. Someone could call me out for stalking. Becca, if she even lived here, could slam the door in my face. She could call the cops.

Maybe she wouldn't know who I was. A heaviness dropped in my gut. That would be worst of all. To be forgotten. As much as I'd pushed Becca aside in my thoughts over time, I'd never truly forgotten her.

A door between the garage and the front of the house opened. Someone in a hoodie pulled out a garbage bin on wheels. A guy.

I had two choices. Throw my car in reverse, or ask him about Becca.

Or a third choice: I ducked down, out of sight.

I'm a coward. Why am I even here? This is ridiculous. I'm leaving. As soon as this guy is back in the house, I'm out.

After waiting so long, my neck started cramping, I finally unfolded myself and peeked up. The guy was gone, but someone else stood beside the garbage bin, mere steps from my car. A tall, lean girl with hair the color of autumn leaves. She wore a Central High sweatshirt with shorts, even though we were past shorts-wearing weather.

Becca never cared for seasonal fashion rules.

She looked up and our eyes locked. My head grew light and fuzzy until everything focused again.

Before I could talk myself out of it, I opened the car door. I stood, one leg still in the car, the other tentative against the pavement stretching toward my long-lost friend.

"How did you find me?" Her face, a mixture of shock, confusion, and a strong shade of guarded. She did not trust me being here. Not at all.

I swallowed. All the anger, the hurt, the confusion swirled up again. Years of it, thick and hammering to get out. The tears came fast and all at once. "You were there, and then you were gone. Just like that. Gone."

Becca still held the trash bag by the drawstrings. She gathered it in front of her, as if for protection. "Things got weird. I didn't think you'd understand." She shook her head, as if not believing I stood in front of her. "Why did you come here?"

If I couldn't make sense of the answer myself, I would never be able to convince Becca.

"I couldn't forget." The words tumbled out. "I wanted to say I'm sorry. I never knew what happened until now. You're right. I didn't understand." I took a breath, needing to say the rest as much as I didn't want to. "And I'm sorry I told."

Becca's face scrunched in confusion. "What do you mean you told?"

I explained about the backpack and what I'd said to our teacher so many years ago. "I'm sorry. I guess I wanted to let you know I'm still here. I've always been here."

Becca studied the ground. Her toes spread over her flip-flops with nails painted a rainbow of polish colors. "I didn't want to bring you into my mess. I cut you out on purpose, Hannah. You don't deserve to have a friend who asks you to lie."

"But you didn't—"

"I asked you to lie all the time. My whole life was lies."

Tiny knives stabbed along my skin. Her words hurt too much to bear. "Not your whole life. Our friendship? Not a lie."

Her expression softened. She jammed the trash bag into the bin, then walked toward me, stuffing her hands into her sweatshirt's front pocket. "I missed you, you know. A million times I almost called your house, but I was scared."

"I'm sorry, I know I blurt things out sometimes—"

"Not scared you'd tell on me. Scared you'd hate me. I'm not good like you." She swallowed hard, seeming more vulnerable than I'd ever seen her back when we ran our corner of the neighborhood.

"I don't hate you."

"And don't go thinking any of it was your fault."

I wanted to believe her, but that icy hurt still clung to my insides. I let down my friend when she needed me. I would have broken any rule to protect her, but I didn't know how then. "Don't go thinking you're not good either." I pulled the necklace from my pocket and handed it to her, hopeful that somewhere inside her huge and beautiful new house she'd kept the second charm that read "Best."

She looked the charm over in her hand. The silence of the

fall night wrapped around us, swirling with possibilities. A hundred questions arrowed through my brain, but I couldn't grasp a single one.

"I like my family," Becca said, barely above a whisper. "They're good people."

Her *new* family. "What about your mom? Your brother?"

"My younger brother lives here. He was adopted with me. Mom, she's in jail. I can see her if I want."

"Do you ever?"

Her hands disappeared back into her pocket. "I was mad at her for a long time. I didn't know back then what I was doing was wrong. Keeping her secrets. Stashing drugs. I was trying to help, you know?" She shook her head. "No, you wouldn't. You shouldn't."

I wanted to understand. I wanted so many things, but maybe it was too late. Maybe too much time had passed. Becca had been my friend in another life, one far past expired by now. I'd done what I'd come here for. She was happy, I'd said I was sorry, and now I could move on. "Thanks for talking. Again, I'm sorry." I turned, heading for the solitude of my car.

"Hannah." Becca caught my sleeve. I turned, seeing the face of my old friend, but with years of maturity. "Hang on to this." She held out the necklace. "I still have the other part."

She'd kept the other piece! So she hadn't forgotten. *I* hadn't been forgotten. I shivered from the night air and the emotions coursing through me.

"You want to come in?"

The question was more than an invitation out of the cold. It was an invitation into Becca's new life.

"I should probably go. I have a curfew."

Becca tipped her chin. "Have you ever broken it? Like, ever?"

"Actually, I'm grounded."

She laughed, then I laughed. Her grin sprang to life, mischievous as ever. For a moment, it was as if nothing had changed between us. No years of separation or police procedures or court hearings. No worried nights or failed Facebook searches.

I had so much to tell her. So much I wanted to hear.

"I'd love to hear why you're grounded," Becca said.

"I almost got kicked out of honor society."

Becca stopped midway up the drive. "You? A misfit in the honor society?" A twinge of pride crossed her face. "We really do need to catch up."

Five years, and now I had answers. Those five years gave us time to grow into who we were. And now we were here together, with all of life waiting to be filled in.

Stephanie Scott writes young adult books about characters who put their passions first. After college, she worked in a foster care and adoption unit where all her best and saddest stories come from. She lives outside of Chicago with her tech-of-all-trades husband, but you can more easily find her on Twitter and Instagram at @StephScottYA. Her debut *Alterations* is a 2017 finalist for the Romance Writers of America Best First Book RITA® award.

"I took a job out of college in a foster care and adoption unit, following in my mother's footsteps. It is by far my most memorable job and where my best and saddest stories come from. The kids I shuffled to and from visitations and doctor's appointments were remarkable in their resilience. I believe human services is a calling in addition to being a profession. My greatest respect goes to those working with children and families in need."

Moving the Body

by Natasha Sinel

Mom and I buried him in the woods by the reservoir. Everything happened so fast. We had no idea whether we'd picked a good spot or dug deep enough. Maybe one hard rain would be enough to uncover it. I didn't know. I'd never buried a body before. Neither had Mom. And there wasn't anyone we could ask.

Afterward, I collapsed on the family room couch. Mom stood behind me and threaded her fingers through my hair, scratching my scalp like when I was little. A seventeen-year-old guy wasn't supposed to need his mom's affection, and on any other day, I would've pulled away and rolled my eyes, but not today.

Her fingers stilled and her hand rested heavily on my head. She stayed like that for so long I wondered whether she'd fallen asleep, but then she sighed.

"Mom," I said, for the thousandth time. I wanted to ask what comes next, but I couldn't.

Mom lifted her hand and looked at her watch. She's worn that watch forever. Dad got it for her when he first became district attorney. They joked it was a pre-apology gift for the long nights he'd be working.

I tried to guess what time it was. Two o'clock? Three? Even though it had been only a few hours ago, it felt like ages since Mom had called me. I'd never forget the way her voice sounded—panicked, terrified.

"Jonah . . . something happened, and I need you to come home," Mom said, out of breath. "Hurry."

But now, as she looked at the watch Dad gave her, she didn't seem as scared. Just sad. And defeated.

"Evan and Hannah will be home soon," she said. "We should get cleaned up."

I moved away from her so I could see her face. Tears made streaks in the dirt on her cheeks.

"I can't believe I got you involved in this." She swiped at her tears with shaking hands. "I wasn't thinking."

"Mom. It's my fault."

"That's ridiculous, Jonah. Don't ever say that. You weren't even here."

Mom was strong—opinionated, honest, a disciplinarian with a low "I mean business" voice when she needed it. But I'd never thought of her as physically strong. She was short, forty pounds overweight, in high-waisted mom jeans and baggy sweaters. Her hair was usually up in some sort of bun or ponytail, and no makeup unless she was going out at night. She was just Mom. But when we heaved him into the trunk of her car and then lifted him out and dragged him to the spot we'd picked to bury him, she had some seriously crazy super strength. Determination and protectiveness completely took over her whole being like in one of those stories about a mother lifting a truck to free her trapped child. I'd only seen her like this once before.

I'd just turned ten, so Evan was nine, and Hannah was eight. Fourth grade, third grade, second grade. Three peas in a pod, Dad called us. Evan once commented that we weren't like three peas in a pod at all because if Mom's belly was the pod, I'd never been in the pod to begin with. I didn't think much about the fact that Mom hadn't given birth to me, but Evan did. More than I knew.

We'd gone for haircuts that day, but as soon as the hairdresser started cutting Evan's hair, she found lice. Then she checked Hannah and me, and then Mom too. We all had it. She sent us to the back room where the "lice lady" would treat our hair with special shampoo and comb out the nits. None of us really cared except it meant we'd have to wait even longer to get home and play video games. But the lice lady put on the TV, so at least there was that.

After she was done with the three of us, she started working on Mom. Since Mom's hair was thick and tangly, I knew it would take forever. My brother, sister, and I settled in to watch *SpongeBob*. But *SpongeBob* didn't distract me enough to tune out Mom's conversation.

"They're so sweet and well-behaved," the lice lady said.

"Thank you." I could hear Mom's proud smile. She loved it when people commented on the behavior of her children, as if it was a mark of her success.

"The girl and the little boy—they're twins?"

Mom got asked that a lot, so I knew her answer by heart.

"No, but close. He's fourteen months older. And Jonah, my oldest, is just eleven months older than him."

"Really? He seems much older!"

"He's tall for his age."

"He must look like your husband, then. He's so big, and with the light hair and blue eyes, so different from you and the little ones with the dark brown."

"We adopted Jonah," Mom said.

Usually when people pointed out how I looked different

than my siblings, or when they asked where I got my blue eyes, Mom would wink at me, then shrug and say, "Who knows?" People had a tendency to say stupid things.

But maybe she sensed something in the lice lady that made her feel safe. Or maybe she was bored and in the mood to talk. Who knows why on this day she decided to share?

"Really?" The woman paused her combing and looked at Mom's reflection. And then she said what most people say. "So after you adopted him, then you got pregnant with your own—what a miracle! That always happens, doesn't it?"

Mom's jaw tightened. She hated it when people talked like that—*it always happens that way . . . You could finally have your own.*

"It rarely happens, actually." I wondered whether Mom would tell *the story of our family*, the story that started with "No miracles. Just real life."

But before Mom could even begin, the woman said something no one had ever said before.

"Doesn't it bother you to take care of someone else's child? When you have two of your own?"

The silence was thick as the words sunk in. Of course I'd seen Mom angry before. She yelled at us so often to get our shoes on, to bring our dishes to the sink, to stop fighting, we'd almost become immune to it. But this was different—the flash of anger I saw in Mom's eyes was venomous.

She cleared her throat while the woman continued to comb through her hair, oblivious to the fact that she'd just conjured the Incredible Hulk.

Then Mom spoke slowly, annunciating each word.

"These. Are. My. Three. Children. What the hell is *wrong* with you?"

Mom stood, pulled the black cape off, letting it drop to the floor, and grabbed her purse. Her hair was wet, half up in a clip.

"Let's go, kids," she said, working to make her voice sound

normal, but I heard what was underneath. Mom definitely could've lifted a truck right then.

"Not now, Mom. *SpongeBob* isn't over," Evan whined, his eyes glued to the TV.

"Now," she said. I grabbed Evan's hand and pulled him out of the chair. He hadn't seen Mom's eyes. If he had, he would've forgotten *SpongeBob* immediately and obeyed. I pulled at his hand as he kept looking back at the TV, and Hannah trailed after us, muttering about the lollipops we didn't get.

After that day, I didn't hear Mom talk to a stranger about adoption again. Sometimes I told friends if I felt like it. But, surprisingly, kids didn't say as many stupid things as adults did. They mostly asked questions: How old were you when you were adopted? *Hours*. Do you ever want to find your real mom? *Birth mom*, I'd correct. *I have some information and pictures. Sometimes I think I'd like to know more, but not enough to do anything about it. Not yet, at least.*

Lately, I'd seen hints of that same look Mom had given the lice lady—whenever Evan brought up *Tribal Combat*. Mom thought he was on the verge of an unhealthy obsession with the computer game. The few times Evan sat at the dinner table for more than five minutes, he'd complain that he was missing out on a crucial battle and letting his tribe down.

The other night, Mom, Evan, and I were the only ones home for dinner—with our schedules, it was rare for all five of us to eat at the same time.

"I'm sure your tribe will do just fine tonight without you," Mom said, scooping rice onto our plates.

Evan's face turned sour and he practically spat out his words.

"Shut up. You don't understand."

My eyes widened. No one tells Mom to shut up.

Her shoulders tensed, but her voice stayed steady.

"What I understand," she said, "is that it's a game, and I see you treating it as something more important than that. I would like you to put your energy toward something more productive."

Evan pushed his chair back suddenly and loudly, making his fork clatter to the floor.

"It *is* important. The tribe, Tim—they're my friends, my *family*. At least *they* care for and appreciate me."

Evan stormed upstairs.

I reached down to pick up his fork, but before I could, Mom grabbed my wrist.

"Do you know anything about these people he's online with?"

"Not really," I said. "It's just one of those multiplayer games where you chat while you're playing. I mean, Evan's being a di—a jerk, but everyone does it."

"You don't."

I shrugged. "I've played. It's just not really my thing."

"Exactly."

"But I've got basketball. This is, like, his team, I guess."

Evan and I didn't have the same lunch period, but when I walked by the windows of the cafeteria on the way to Physics every day, I always saw him sitting alone, headphones on. High school wasn't treating him well, and it didn't help that he was known as Dunk's little brother. He hated that. He hated sports, basketball especially, and I was starting to wonder if he hated me too.

"That guy Tim he's always on with," Mom said, "He sounds *mean* when I hear them talking."

"Well, they're battling. It can get kind of intense, I guess."

"I don't know," Mom said. "I feel like there's something off about him."

"I wouldn't worry, Mom. I'm sure it's fine."

But I knew what she meant. My room shared a wall with Evan's, so I could hear them sometimes. There was a lot of

Tribal Combat yelling and cheering, but there were also some quiet conversations that I knew were just between Evan and Tim once the other tribe members had logged off. And I guess, yeah, something about the guy's voice, the way he talked, seemed chilling. Like he was capable of beating Evan in a game that Evan didn't even know he was playing.

Mom squeezed my wrist and then let go.

"I *am* worried." She swallowed hard, and the look—the truck-lifting look—crossed her face. "Will you talk to him? He listens to you, he looks up to you."

Evan, in fact, didn't listen to me, and he definitely didn't look up to me. The last few months, he'd been making dumb-jock jabs at me, and saying dickish things about Britney, the girl I was hanging out with—comments about her rack and her ass. Evan and I hadn't fought that much as kids, but when we did, Mom had always said, "I know the two of you can work it out on your own. Either do it quietly, or do it outside." Lately we'd been working most things out in the driveway.

I didn't think it would help, but I went into Evan's room after dinner. He was at his desk with his headphones on.

"What?" He slid the headphones down to encircle his neck.

"Can you look over my Lit paper? I've been staring at it so long I can't even tell if it makes sense anymore." Evan did better in school than I did, so I often asked him to read my papers before I turned them in.

"Did Mom send you?"

"No," I lied.

"I'll read your paper, but stay out of my business."

Just then his computer made a sound like a tiger growling, and a *Tribal Combat* message popped up on the screen that said *timstheshite64*. Evan clicked it open and Tim's face appeared. He wore a *Tribal Combat* baseball cap low over his eyes.

"Hey," Tim said. "You done with your useless high school shit and ready to kick the spunk out of some of those red-tribe assholes?"

"Yeah, man, let's do it," Evan said. Then he turned to me. "Gotta go, *bro*."

Evan had never called me "bro" before. The way he said it made it sound like an insult.

"Who's that? The famous Jonah?" Tim asked.

Evan tilted his laptop so Tim could see me.

"Hey," I said.

"Heard a lot about you, Jonah. Or should I call you *Dunk*?" He said my nickname with a condescending smirk. "A pleasure to make your acquaintance. You ever decide to quit being a jock mama's boy and murder some dudes with us, just give us a holler."

Evan's eyes shot me a warning that I read as *Don't even think about it. This is my thing.*

I dropped my Lit paper on his bed. "Thanks for reading this."

"Later," I said to Tim on the screen.

Evan kicked the door shut after I walked out.

I sat at my desk, but I could still hear them through the wall.

"So that's Mr. Fake First-Born Son, huh?" Tim said. "He waltzes in all high and mighty like he's the legit crowned prince, doesn't he?"

What? What did Evan tell him about me?

"Nah," Evan said. "My brother—"

"He's not even your *real* brother, dude. I'm just as much your brother as he is. So your parents scooped up some orphan before you were even born, and he gets the pity vote every time. You never even had a chance, E. He gets everything, and you have to pay the price."

Evan was silent. I waited for the words that would defend me, the words Mom and Dad would say—family is everything, and blood has nothing to do with it. But the words never came.

"You deserve better than that," Tim continued. "You have mad skills, E. You could be a first-class gamer, pulling in cash, getting the respect you deserve. I know people. We can hook you up. But you can't do it while you're still in that house with *them*. They're holding you back. And they always will, man, because they don't get it. They don't get *you* and what you're all about."

I closed my laptop so I could focus.

"I was the black sheep too," Tim went on. "I fucking *hated* my family. And it was mutual. Leaving them was the best thing I ever did for myself. I never looked back."

"I mean . . . I don't *hate* them," Evan said.

"Believe me, you hate them. They think he's better than you, and he's not even their own kid. They don't understand you. When you're ready to leave, you let me know. We'll show you what real life is, what freedom feels like."

I froze, waiting for Evan's response, but he mumbled something too quietly for me to hear.

"Yeah, that's all I'm saying," Tim said. "Just think about it. We'll take care of you, man."

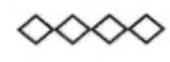

I spent the rest of the night researching Tim. Mom didn't let us use our full names online, but luckily Tim didn't have anyone like Mom protecting his identity. His *timstheshite64* profile on *Tribal Combat* listed his name as Tim Wallace, and even though there were tons of Tim Wallace Facebook profiles, his wasn't that hard to find. His page was public and his photo was a close-up, with the same light blue eyes I'd just seen on Evan's laptop. He'd posted a few concert photos, *Tribal Combat* YouTube videos, and some random memes. He was twenty-three, and some more investigating led me to his ex-girlfriend's page—Renee Byrne. Her account was private, but some of her older posts were still visible. The last messages on Renee's page were about Tim:

tim's 3-month sobriety party friday cancelled L

And then, a few weeks later:

friends: prayers needed for tim. he's back in lock-up. we've lost him to a very dark place.

That post was from a year and a half ago. I shivered. Great-grandma used to say a shiver meant someone had just walked over your future grave, which never made any sense to me. But right then, as I looked at Renee's last post, I felt as if I understood for the first time.

I went back to Tim's page and clicked on Work and Education. Gianpapa's Pizzeria in Clifton, where he worked, was twenty minutes away. I'd thought—hoped—that he'd be halfway around the world. But he was practically in our backyard. His eyes, the "dark place," the things he said to Evan as if he was trying to get him to hate us—hate *me*. As if he was trying to lure him away from home.

Mom's instinct about him was right—there *was* something off about him. She wanted to know more. And now, so did I.

The next day, I told Coach I had to leave early for a dentist appointment. Even though he was pissed I'd scheduled something that conflicted with practice, it was my first time, so he let me go.

As I drove on the highway toward Clifton, my pulse throbbed in my throat. The GPS was off by a block. I circled slowly until I found it—a hole-in-the-wall pizza place in the middle of a strip with a Subway, a generic wireless store, and two empty storefronts with For Rent signs. I parked in front of Subway and got out, careful to lock the car. It was my car just for a few more weeks until Evan got his license, and then I'd have to share it with him. He was obsessed, already making a schedule for Saturday nights months away. Now I wondered where he was planning to go.

Gianpapa's was one of those slice places, though a menu board above the counter showed that it offered more—chicken parm, pastas, salads. No one was at the counter. An older man sat at one of the small tables, scarfing down pizza and Gatorade. He noticed me and nodded.

"Timmy!" the man shouted, but it sounded like Tim-MAY. "You gotta customer."

I heard some rustling and then Tim appeared from behind a tall cart of dishes, wiping his hands on his jeans.

"Hey," he said. His voice sounded deeper than it had through Evan's laptop. A man's voice.

I hadn't planned anything to say to him. I hadn't planned anything at all. I'd pictured a big place where I could sit in a corner booth and spy on him, and then talk things over with Mom and decide what to do. But not this. Not this one-on-one thing where I had to look him in the eye and speak to him.

He sauntered to the counter. Colorful, elaborate artwork started at his wrists and disappeared into the short sleeves of his t-shirt. His white-blond hair was cut close, and he had about a week's worth of beard growth that was a slightly darker blond. He looked at me blankly. If he recognized me, he didn't show it. There was no reason he'd expect me to show up here anyway.

"What'll you have?" he asked.

"Uh . . ."

He looked at the oven behind him.

"Pepperoni's about to come out. You want that?"

"Yeah, sure. I'll take two slices. Um." My voice sounded funny. Like someone else's.

"Drink?"

I shook my head no.

He tapped the screen on the cash register in front of him.

"Seven seventy-nine."

I pulled a ten out of my wallet.

Now I just wanted to leave. I had no idea what I'd been thinking coming here. I stared at the rusted napkin dispenser while Tim went to the oven to pull out the pizza. He put two slices on a paper plate and dropped the plate on the counter in front of me. He took my ten-dollar bill. He tapped on the screen and just as the register drawer popped open, he abruptly pointed at me.

"Hey, I just figured it out. You're Evan's bro, right?"

My pulse raced.

"Yeah," I said.

He stared at me, and I couldn't keep my eyes on his. I knew I looked guilty.

He sighed dramatically, then leaned on the counter and lowered his voice, like he had a secret to tell me. "I think I see what's happening here. You came to spy on me for Mommy. I'm a bad influence on poor little Evan. That sound about right?"

I knew I was turning red, the way I always do when I'm nervous or embarrassed—I could feel the heat rising on my skin.

"You have something you want to say?" He stared at me. "Speak up, *Dunk.*"

Suddenly he was in front of me, leaning over the counter, his face right in mine. I was much taller than him, and bigger, but he was meaner and tougher. He reminded me of a coiled snake, ready to attack. Poisonous. Deadly.

I shook my head no.

"Right," he said. "That's what I thought."

I was frozen in place.

"Run along," he said, flicking his hand at me like he was shooing away a fly. "Go back to your *mommy* now."

I turned to leave, but he stopped me.

"Hold up," he said. "*Rosenberg?*"

I'd forgotten I was still wearing my basketball uniform. Rosenberg was spelled in big white letters across the back of my red Langford Basketball jacket, just above my number—8. For all of Mom's Internet security precautions, it never occurred to her—or me—that I'd been running around town announcing my school and last name on my dumb team jacket for years.

"*Rosenberg?* Evan is fucking *Jewish?* I don't believe this shit."

Jewish? The word, so repugnant the way he said it, replayed in my head.

And then he twisted his left hand to reveal the tattoo on the underside of his wrist. A swastika. Small, but unmistakable.

I'd seen plenty of graffiti with swastikas and the n-word. Since Dad's announcement last year that the district attorney's office would be cracking down hard on hate crimes, there were photos all over his desk at home. But still, when I saw Tim's tattoo, I had to fight the urge to let everything I'd eaten that day make its way back up.

Tim's eyes flicked up to mine, and even though the blue was so pale, his seemed like the darkest eyes I'd ever seen. He thrust toward me suddenly like he was going to head-butt me. He laughed when I flinched.

I turned and smacked the door open, ran down the street, got in my car, put it in gear, and drove. As I went by the pizza place, I saw him—Tim—holding the door open with his hip, watching me, my ten-dollar bill still in his hand.

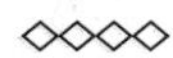

That night, Mom took Evan out to practice parallel parking. When they got home, they were yelling at each other—their new norm.

After I heard Evan stomp into his room and slam the door, I went downstairs to find Mom. Typically, I'd steer clear of Mom after one of their arguments—her fuse was extra short, and I'd end up on the receiving end of her residual anger. But I had to risk it tonight.

She was in the kitchen leaning against the counter, typing fast on her phone, probably updating Dad on her fight with Evan.

I noticed Evan's phone on the counter next to her, which meant the argument had been bad enough for her to take it from him.

"Mom?"

"Hmm?"

"About that guy in Evan's tribe. Tim."

Mom put her phone on the counter. I had her full attention now.

"You were right," I said. "I looked him up and he's really bad. He's some kind of addict and he was in prison—I don't know what for."

She stared at me, her eyes wide. I'd convinced myself that telling her I'd gone to see him would distract her from the real issue, so I left that information out.

"And," I continued, "he has a tattoo on his wrist. Of a swastika."

Mom gasped. "What did you just say?"

"He has a swastika tattoo."

She closed her eyes for what seemed like a full minute. Then she opened them and speed-walked to the electronics cupboard in the living room, fumbled around, and yanked out the cord to the Internet router.

She turned to me.

"I want you to keep this to yourself until I've had a chance to talk to Dad."

We heard Evan's door open, and then he shouted down the stairs.

"Mom, the Wi-Fi's out again. Jesus. Why doesn't anything ever work in this house?"

His door slammed again.

I'd never be able to get the image of him out of my mind. His arms splayed, the tattoo on his wrist hidden beneath his jacket sleeve, his palm open, and next to it a ten-dollar bill—*my* ten-dollar bill. Alexander Hamilton's face was barely visible underneath handwritten numbers and words. In blue ink: our address. Below that, scrawled in all caps: *game over, Rosenberg.*

"He was going to blackmail Dad," Mom said, shaking, one phone in each hand—one hers, one Tim's. "But I didn't . . . it was an accident. I tried to take his phone and we fought . . . and the table was there. I didn't mean . . ."

I did what instinct told me to do. I said, "It's okay," over and over, and I helped her to the couch. When she started breathing normally, she showed me what was on Tim's phone.

Even though the video was dark, the kid in it was unmistakably Evan. At first it was just his back, a close-up of his arm spray-painting red on a gray background. Then the picture zoomed out to show what he'd made—a red swastika on the front door of a little white house. Then the video cut to a Muslim woman walking fast down a sidewalk, as if she suspected she was being followed. In the background, Tim's unmistakable voice said, "Now! Go!" Then Evan was in the shot, moving quickly toward the woman. He grabbed the hijab from her head, pulling some of her hair with it. She screamed and ran, and Tim called after her, "Go back to the desert! You're not welcome here anymore!"

Tim cackled, and Evan turned toward the camera. Even though the video was too dark and grainy to see his eyes, I looked for Evan inside them, hoping he was still in there, that he'd had no choice, that he'd been threatened. It was the only way any of it could make sense.

Suddenly I realized what I'd done.

My fault, my fault, my fault played in my head. I thought I'd been helping, but I was the reason Tim found out our last name and who Dad was. I was the reason he was able to find out where we lived. I was the reason he was lying dead on our floor.

Now Mom and I moved slowly, exhausted from dragging, digging, lifting. When we got to the top of the stairs where we would split up to wash away the hell of the last several hours—her to the master bathroom, and me to the hall bathroom that I shared with Evan and Hannah—we paused.

I leaned on the wall because I wasn't sure how much longer my legs could hold me up.

I had so many questions—Would she tell Dad? What if Tim had sent the video to someone else already? What would happen to Evan now? But I knew she couldn't answer those yet.

"Why me?" I asked instead.

Mom looked at me blankly.

"I mean, why'd you call *me*?"

She put her hand on my cheek and held it there for a second.

"Because you're the person, Jonah."

"I don't understand."

"You're the person I'd call to help me move a body."

She turned and went to her room.

I showered off the sweat and grime and let the water run until the last of the dirt swirled down the drain. After I dressed, I heard the front door open, and I closed my eyes. Evan's and Hannah's voices filled the house.

Natasha Sinel is the author of young adult novels *The Fix*, which was the YA Fiction winner in the 2016 Independent Publisher Book Awards, and *Soulstruck*. She graduated from Yale University and University of Michigan's Ross School of Business, and was a director of business development at Showtime Networks. Born and raised in Washington, D.C., she now lives in Westchester, NY with her husband and three sons.

"My son, whom we adopted, does not have my eyes or the shape of my face, but he has everything else—my heart, my soul, my love. My other two sons, to whom I gave birth, do not

have my eyes or the shape of my face, but they have everything else—my heart, my soul, my love."

In Pieces

by Eric Smith

Arcas felt crushed.

He was surrounded by people on all sides. They pushed and shoved, the mass of them ambling forward, the occasional foot stepping on his. Even if he wanted to turn around, to push his way back through the throngs of frustrated voices, it was hardly an option anymore. The only way out was forward.

People pushed by, screaming demands, madly smashing buttons on the keypads that lined the teleportation platform, entering the hub. It was clear to Arcas that many of his neighbors had things to wrap up before everything went dark. He recognized many of them, carrying boxes and containers of all sizes, anxiously waiting along the walkway leading to the large, squared-off area.

To Arcas's left, a man in a long burgundy trench coat cradled a wailing infant in one arm while he leaned over, awkwardly pressing several buttons on the teleportation kiosk with his free hand. To his right, a woman looked over her station toward the platform, her eyes wide and smiling as she bolted toward the unloading ramp.

A large man struggling with a nailed-up crate slammed

into Arcas as he ambled by. The man stumbled, his large arms grasping the wooden box almost angrily. He glared at Arcas, and Arcas squinted at the box, which appeared damp on the bottom, stained with some kind of liquid. Any other day, he might have said something. Maybe turned to somebody. But not today. There was no time.

"Watch it, kid!" the man barked before stopping to look at him. "Hey, where are your parents?" Before Arcas could make up an answer, the man shook his head and rushed off, clearly eager to secure his place in line, scrambling toward the shipping ramp that led down to the platforms.

Arcas tried to peer over the people in front of him, to no avail. He could feel the heat pulsing from the glimmering golden orbs that lined the thick sheets of titanium suspended above the hub. Every few minutes, like clockwork, he'd wince, squinting as bright blasts of light burst from them, sending an expanse of white energy down upon the hub. As quickly as the energy blasts happened, they vanished, dissipating with a soft hum.

People continued to bolt by, running up to the teleportation pads to pick up items of all kinds, as he glanced at the signs that hung around the transport hub. The messages were bold red and screaming yellow. A mixture of old and new signs, the fading ones made of makeshift materials, protesting against the use of the technology from citizens ahead of their time, while the new ones were sheet metal, hung around the hub with purpose.

Arcas looked down at his feet. His sneakers were grimy, his socks mismatched, and he looked about, his feet shifting, embarrassed by his appearance. He'd had to take three buses to get here, traveling across the state, each mile bringing a bit of relief as he distanced himself from his latest of seven foster homes. The lumbering vehicle was, for the most part, full of people with a simpler destination. As he grew nearer to the hub, a couple of people with plans to use the trans-teleporter began filtering in, their eyes panicked, breath short and worried, muttering about packages, business, and the like.

The entire trip, he flipped through his small datapad. Government issued, solar powered, tragically slow. The screen was cracked, bits of the digital device unreadable in the corners where the screen had begun bleeding a variety of colors circling a pool of black, like an oil slick on a puddle of rain.

He could still see the feeds, though, news reports streaming through, right next to his two bookmarked notes. One was a news report from a few days ago, issued the day before he left. The other was an email that hadn't left his home screen the entire month.

An email he was having a difficult time figuring out how to respond to.

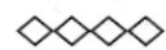

AP, BREAKING [JULY 24, 2187]: After a three-month investigation spawned from leaked internal memos at TELE-CORP, INC., the world's leading manufacturer of trans-teleportation hubs, platforms, and energy conveyors, the United States Department of Transportation has issued a country-wide shutdown of all teleportation devices until further study proves them safe.

Experts in the fields of psychology, sociology, and even parapsychology are convening in the nation's capital next week to discuss findings and next steps, and to analyze the evidence stacked against TELE-CORP, INC., and the practice of trans-teleportation. A reputable source states that several religious leaders have requested a presence at the conference as well, voicing concerns over the state of the soul.

The question of whether or not a person continues to exist in between teleportation, and if the one who arrives is still the same person has provided plenty of fodder for existential discussion amongst the curious. But with the leaked internal memos from TELE-CORP, INC., revealing that the inventors and leaders at the company themselves were not sure, the Department of Transportation issued an immediate shutdown, allowing for only non-organic travel.

What was once referred to as Teleportation Sickness, a seemingly harmless malady that left some travelers with new personality traits and tastes, from the harmless, such as disliking a once-beloved food, to the dangerous, such as violent mood swings. Has this side effect taken on a new, tragic meaning?

Executives at TELE-CORP, INC. were not available for comment. However, USDOT issued a statement regarding the shutdown:

"We're not out to disrupt trade, ruin companies, and have possessions near and dear to our citizens lost in transit," stated the United States Secretary of Transportation. "Trans-teleportation will be available for non-organic materials through Sunday, July 30th, and will be free for all citizens and business owners, until we can determine whether or not it is truly safe for [Click to Continue]"

◇◇◇◇

FWD: RE: RE: RE: So . . . I don't know how to write this subject
July 2, 2187
(22 days ago)
Orzrik Ibaldia orzrik.ibaldia@us.dept.gov
to me

Dearest Arcas,

I understand your apprehension. Your birth mother and I both do. Know this. We are both beyond touched that you found us and reached out the way you did. And I apologize for how long it took to email you back in the first place. This was a big decision, for all of us.

Should you wish it, our doors will always be open to a visit.
[Download Rest of Message]

Arcas shook his head, looking down at his datapad, his mind reeling.

"Hey!" A voice shouted from behind. Arcas turned around to see a woman holding several large packages, an impatient scowl on her face. "Some of us are in a hurry, and you're up." She turned to the man in back of her, shrugging her shoulders with her arms full.

There were so many questions floating through his mind as he stepped up to the panel, his fingers working the keypad, entering the coordinates on his fading tablet. Would it hurt? Would he be the same person?

But if he wasn't the same person, if he was someone new and the old version of himself ceased to exist . . . was it worth it?

He looked around at the other people engaged in getting their mailings together and took a deep breath, finding his resolve. This was it.

He hit send on the panel and leaped over the railing and onto the transportation hub.

"Hey!" shouted a voice behind him as he ran.

"Someone stop that kid!" screamed someone else. "Shut down the hub!"

The protests rang out sharp and fast as his feet slammed against the titanium floor with a sharp bang. Pain shot up his shins from the impact, but he kept running. He was hardly an athlete, and he started to feel winded as he approached the transportation pad. The heat from the pulsing orbs above him began to warm him all over as he moved forward, and he winced as the light from the energy beam illuminated the night.

He stopped, his feet firmly planted on the metal under the

transportation beam. He listened to the sound of the people in the hub retreating away as the beam warmed up.

"Here I come," he said, exhaling and closing his eyes.

As the beam blasted down upon him, he whispered to himself:

"Goodbye."

Eric Smith is an author, book blogger, and literary agent from New Jersey. His books include *The Geek's Guide to Dating* and the *Inked* duology, a YA fantasy series. He's a regular contributor to *Book Riot*, *Paste Magazine*, and Barnes & Noble's blog, and currently lives in Ann Arbor, Michigan with his wife and menagerie of adorable animals.

"I'm lucky. I was adopted as a baby and brought into an incredibly loving home. Growing up, I wrestled a bit with identity, trying to figure out who I was. But I was supported by not just my family, but an absolute wealth of friends who were as understanding as they were kind and uplifting. But not everyone has this experience. My sister struggled a lot. I didn't know what to do. Why was something so easy for me, but hard for her? Because everyone tackles the emotional rollercoaster of adoption differently. And it's important to tell stories like these. It's my hope that these stories will help."

Peace of Paper

by Courtney Stevens

"When you get to a place where you understand that love and belonging, your worthiness, is a birthright and not something you have to earn, anything is possible." —Brene Brown

Denton Calgary asked me to say a few things about my life. Talking in front of people isn't something I do, so I thought I might start with a quote and a story.

I am weary because I belong nowhere and to no one. —Jase.

I'm going to repeat that.

I am weary because I belong nowhere and to no one. —Jase.

I've never met Jase. I don't know his age or his particular circumstances or if he drinks coffee by the gallons or his Mountain Dew in a Big Gulp. I only know he wrote this naked thing on a truck stop shower stall in Cookeville, Tennessee. It was just above a crude poem about beer. About what you would expect from a ten-dollar shower with a rusted-out drain. After I finished rinsing off, I bought a single Sharpie for three dollars and eighty-nine cents from a lady named Denise who called me "Sugar bun," and I defaced my first piece of public property.

Below Jase's quote, in large block letters, I wrote:

Me too. —Kevin.

I don't know what I was hoping. That Jase, whoever he was, might revisit the stall and see my addition? That someone else would see there were two of us and not feel alone? All I knew was loneliness wasn't something I felt; it was something that attacked my chest like a CPR compression, and a shower stall was as good a place as any to admit I felt pretty damn tired to be only eighteen years old.

I've never shared that story.

Back then, I was Kevin Taylor, and I was too full of piss and inertia to believe someone else might need to hear it.

That might sound like a rough description, but people liked me just fine. As a society, we value people who keep their ruckus on the inside and polish their outsides like church pews. I realized this fact on February 12, 2010, two years before I showered in that truck stop.

I was standing on a gym floor like this one. It was maple. Polished. There was a dead spot near the half court mark. There was a dead spot in me too. Completely invisible unless you knew where to look. It was basketball homecoming. I had a crown on my head, an overly tanned girl on my arm. Mr. Carson, our principal, introduced me. "Kevin Taylor is the son of the late SPC Louden Taylor (pause) and the late Jonna Taylor. His guardians are Max and Rita Keller (pause) and the entire town of Barclay, Kentucky."

Mr. Carson said other things about the National Honor Society and Future Farmers of America and basketball, but I heard only those first two lines. The whole gymnasium heard only those first two lines. How do I know? Because they stood up, one by one, and clapped. Like there was something extremely brave about being an orphan. Or maybe they were clapping for themselves since they were the entire town of Barclay, Kentucky. It was so clear in that moment that I had a choice: be made of glass or made of steel.

People clapped for steel.

That's when I started collecting controllable feelings: ambition, gumption, adrenaline. Things no one could take from me when I was napping in Algebra II or shooting a free throw against the Rockham County Rebels.

For those last two years of high school, I'd slept here, there, and everywhere, but primarily in Mr. Keller's basement. Home to his prize collection of *Reader's Digests*, four thousand golf balls stored in egg cartons, a couch (my bed) from his frat house days, and some ceiling mold that looked like an outline of Abraham Lincoln. Abe and I had many conversations about my future. I needed Abe's advice before Mr. Keller, a good-hearted and logical man, could say, "Now, Kevin, have you considered what will happen after graduation?"

Now, Kevin, have you considered . . . was his favorite way to start conversations.

Considered it? I was downright doggish. The Kellers' generosity had boundaries. Known boundaries. They loved helping, but they didn't necessarily *love* me. Didn't hate me either. So it wasn't bad, but it also wasn't permanent.

Finding a cost-effective way out of Barclay Memorial High School wasn't easy. But I was pretty sure I'd heard the undeniable sound of a new controllable feeling in Mr. Keller's living room when I was babysitting his youngest, Nelly—a feat I performed often and actually enjoyed. She had chewed off and then proceeded to swallow the horn of her favorite My Little Pony. Not her first rodeo with swallowing things.

Thank you, Sophomore-Year First-Aid Class, I knew what to do.

Thank you, aptitude.

Calmly, I wrapped my arms around her stomach, making sure they were at her belly button, below her breastbone. I squeezed Nelly until the piece of My Little Pony was out rather than in, and we were both tearstained and shaking. She from the ejection of Hasbro, me from relief and pride. She had forgotten it by the time I made her a grilled cheese; I remember it perfectly even now.

My Little Nightmare.

But for once, someone needed me rather than me needing them. I had control of life itself. I liked the hell out of that idea.

That became the path. Nelly's Heimlich to mower blades. Eight hundred earned dollars to passing my EMT class. A Google search to a job interview. Three days after I wore a cap and gown and pretended to care, I started my motorcycle, waved goodbye to the Kellers, and rode four hours south to Reston, Tennessee, with nothing but a duffle bag, some gasoline, and a thousand bucks I'd gotten for graduation. Ambition, gumption, aptitude, and Kevin Taylor.

I stopped only once. At a truck stop in Cookeville. You know the one.

That trip turned into an interview with Captain Luke Estes and a job with Reston County Rescue. I had held that job for six months when Rachel Goodson knocked on my apartment door and stuck out her hand.

"You're new to town, and I thought you might like a free Christmas tree," she said, hand extended, smile so big it jumped off her face and landed on mine.

Rachel's dad was in charge of one of those pop-up lots around the corner from Luke's. When that night ended, I had a pine tree in the living room and a redhead napping through *Star Wars: Episode V* on my couch.

Fast-forward four months. There's a piece of glossy paper in my front pocket that I'd torn from Luke's Sunday paper without asking. I carried it around, fiddling with it until it rested completely flat against my thigh. The thing was feather-light. The thing was anvil-heavy. Paper can be heavy, people.

It was called the Jewel of the Nile. A square engagement ring that was way above my pay grade, but perfect for Rachel.

She appreciated very square things. "Kevin, can't you see us in one of those salt-box houses?" she'd ask when we drove down Baker Street. "You know what my favorite aisle in the grocery store is?" she'd ask when we were at Market & 5th. "The cereal," I'd answer, because that one long row was uninterrupted by other shapes. She even wallpapered her bathroom with a collection of floppy disks she'd gathered from yard sales and swap meets. Being a mostly square creature myself, I liked that about her. She would love the Jewel of the Nile.

The problem wasn't that I couldn't afford a ring or even the paper it came on. The problem was Luke, my captain, and my closest friend. Who, if you need to picture him, has salt-and-pepper hair, is every bit of five-foot-five, and has a chest made for cage fighting. I trusted him, okay? I trusted him more than I trusted anyone. I'd . . . well . . . I'd cried in front of him. On my mom's birthday. I'm making a big deal of that because I never let myself cry, even though Luke was a tough-ass water faucet around clear blue eyes.

But that barrel chest of his harbored a massive heart that had little cause for jewelry stores. Not anymore. Not after he lost Lucy. I'd overhead him say to one of the other guys on the shift, "Stregg, ask me about hitting a vein, or planting raspberries, or even how to rewire the fan in the kitchen, but keep that engagement junk for someone younger."

Yeah, I heard Luke say that to Stregg, but I figured I wasn't Stregg. Stregg was thirty-one and already had been engaged four times and divorced once. Luke wasn't one for variance. He also liked square, sure things and controllable feelings. Stregg couldn't get control of a hose coming off the truck, much less his love life.

Asking Rachel to marry me was the kind of question that required . . . not a father, as I clearly didn't have one, and not a mother, as I didn't have one of those either, but at least a parental-type conversation. People shouldn't just get engaged without running heart facts by someone with life smarts. Should they? I didn't think so. Even Stregg wanted Luke's approval, and he had perfectly good parents he could ring up or visit.

You have to know that the last time I'd fallen in love was with Molly Jessup. She could pop her shoulder in and out of its socket and didn't mind raising her hand in math class and saying, "I need you to explain that again." That was fifth grade. My parents were still alive, and they'd each employed the useful tactic of saying, "We'll talk about love later, Kevin."

It was later.

And Luke was the closest thing I had to a parent besides Mr. Keller, who had been kind enough to forward my diploma, which I had put in a kitchen drawer next to a whisk. He'd also mailed a twenty-dollar bill and a note that said *Good Luck, Kevin*. I was smart enough to know *Good Luck, Kevin* meant *Goodbye, Kevin*. Smart enough to know this wasn't fifth grade, and Rachel Goodson could do a helluva lot more than wrench her arm out of its socket. She was the sort of girl who'd kill a whole Saturday making flash cards to help me pass my medic test. She studied origami because, "Kev, paper is mostly free and people like tiny gifts." She watched every second of *Apocalypse Now* during my military movie stint knowing it would give her nightmares.

Even if I hadn't thought of Luke parentally, the apartment I rented was over his garage. He would notice if Rachel's Kia stole a permanent place in the driveway.

I put the conversation off as long as I could manage.

It had been Thursday for all of five starlit hours. Which meant I'd had four days of babying the Jewel of the Nile through work and sweat: mostly ambulance runs that week. Two grand dates worth of seeing Rachel laugh and eat Ramen and play knockoff video games on my knockoff system on my knockoff living room rug. Two dates' worth of praying she'd never do that with another guy. Ever. And four days without asking Luke his thoughts.

That paper ring was practically a firework in my pocket.

Luke had given me many things—a chance at this job, low rent, family meals—and I hadn't asked for any of them. So now, when I needed something, really needed something, I wanted him to hear me out.

Luke's smoke-bitten voice would maybe choose an easy rebuttal: you're too young (eighteen, but nearly nineteen). Or a logical one: you haven't been dating her *that* long (four months, fourteen days, seven hours, if you were counting from the Christmas tree, which I was). Or the true one: you can barely afford yourself. I had answers ready on why the diamond ring picture in my pocket was attached to a necessary question. And most of them sounded like, "I love her," and none of them sounded like, "and I know it's a terrible idea."

The sun wasn't nearly as awake as the moon. Our ambulance sat kitty-cornered on the side of I-24, lights blinking, siren quiet. A crew of state troopers finished brushing debris from an overturned semi. We were finally in the truck after being on our feet for most of the night when I decided it was time to pony up and break the news to Luke. I fiddled with the Velcro around my medic scissors, watching miles of headlights crawl by in the emergency lane. Where were all those people going? Were they late? I wondered.

I hated feeling late. Especially when Rachel was the thing I was late to. The picture of the diamond ring traveled from my pocket to Luke's hand.

Luke unfolded it slowly. A torture. He coughed, letting the corners of his mouth settle into a grin he used only for jokes, and that's when I knew I was screwed. His two thumbs tapped the steering wheel as if it were a kick drum. "Aw, thanks, Kip, but you've got too much facial hair to be my type," he told me.

Kip was my station nickname. One step above Kid.

"For Rachel," I said, the scissors now in my hands,

opening, closing, opening again. "And I'm going to fold it into an actual ring. Like her origami gifts."

"You asking for advice or approval?" Luke wanted to know.

When I didn't answer, he returned the ring with some sharp words. "You can't answer that, Kevin, and you're probably not ready for marriage either."

That prompted a tight-lipped, arms-crossed question from me. "That your way of telling me no?"

"I'm not telling you anything yet. Except that's not a ring. That's a picture of a ring. So you'd better be really sure you're doing this for the right reasons."

I wanted to fire off a "You're bitter because your wife died," or "That picture stands for a promise." Or even, "I've got my shit together better than half the people my age," but Landon and Trey hopped inside and closed the back doors.

The remaining forty minutes of our shift was given over to breakfast and ritual tasks. I was tired and ready for a shower when I walked to the parking lot. I was thinking if Luke didn't understand, maybe I'd find somewhere else to live. I'd done it before. I'd do it again.

You guys, that idea lasted a split second. Anger wasn't made of real movement. Anger was only a waterwheel, recycling the same old feelings that went nowhere. I didn't want or need another adult who was good, but disappointing. Kind, but dismissive. So I reminded myself that even if I moved across the country, Luke would stay close. He'd write. He'd call. He wasn't a *Now, Kevin, have you considered* man, and I owed more than my anger to a man like that.

Yes, I wanted this thing with Rachel, but it couldn't be either/or.

My motorcycle sat propped against the station basketball goal. It was the only thing I owned outright. The kickstand was broken when I bought it, and I'd never had extra money to replace the part. Luke's 4Runner was nearby. Luke was nearby too, making the same lonely, eye-squinting march to the parking lot.

"You still good to work at my mom and dad's tomorrow?" he called out of his rolled-down window. He was always inviting me to family meals.

"Leaving at nine?" I asked, as if we hadn't been terse earlier. As if we weren't driving to the same address.

Luke gave me a thumbs-up. "Sleep on it."

I timed my response with revving the motorcycle, letting it roar over my words. "Yeah, you too."

I didn't sleep. Rachel called, and it's shameful, but I picked a fight so she wouldn't come over. I know. I know. Bad idea, but I had to square this with Luke, and I didn't have a clue how to do it.

The next morning I climbed into his 4Runner, and he passed me a pair of gloves from the cargo pocket of his pants. "We're weeding the beds," he said. I'd be lying if I said I noticed that he had an envelope in the same pocket he'd had the gloves in. Anything that might be in that envelope was far from me.

All I could think was:

"She makes me happy, Luke."

"Hear me out, Luke. Be the person who listens."

"Don't make me write messages to someone on shower stalls in effing Cookeville, Tennessee, Luke."

Luke must have been thinking about the late sixties. He asked if I'd ever seen *The Graduate* and cued up the soundtrack. I reminded him I'd been born in 1994. So no, I had not seen *The Graduate*. But I would soon enough. I could feel him mentally downloading the film as we drove. Feel us flopping onto the worn leather couches in his den, eating chili, and splurging on undercooked brownies and big glasses of whole milk. We'd talk about Stregg or my upcoming medic test. Maybe we'd even talk about how my mom always overcooked brownies and bought fat-free milk.

When we reached Luke's parents' house, they had splurges

planned for lunch. Slow-roasted pork. Watermelon. Baked potatoes. Things I would never buy for myself. Things that parents buy and think nothing of.

We worked—planting, digging, weeding, hauling—until there was salt on our skin. We worked—me faster than Luke, him quieter than me. I knew he was thinking about Rachel and me. About Lucy, his wife. How they were once my age. They'd married at nineteen, and I would be nineteen in two months. The only thing he had at my age that I didn't were parents to pay for the groom's cake.

Finally, he asked if he could ask me a question and I agreed.

"Do you think you'd be marrying Rachel if your parents were still alive?"

Again, I couldn't answer his question.

"'Cause it seems to me that you're rushing it," he said in a way that was neither cruel nor hasty. He'd slept on it. He'd thought about it. He was giving me his parental opinion.

"I'm not trying to," I told him.

"That sounds about true," he said, and then we worked until it was time to go to the sun porch for pork shoulder and conversations about the flowerbeds.

I felt the oddness before I took my place across from Luke. Candles on the table. At lunch. Real dishes instead of paper plates. Freshly cut mint in the tea. Add to that the whole Estes family beaming like secondary suns, and something was certainly going on.

Mr. Estes prayed and after his amen he cut his eyes expectantly at Luke and said, "Son?" instead of "Helen, pass me those rolls, please."

Luke drummed his hands on the edge of his plate the way he'd drummed them on the wheel of the ambulance. I wondered if he'd told his parents about the Jewel of the Nile, about how stupid he thought I was.

Luke took a white business envelope out of his pocket and set it on my plate like a meal.

Ten percent—a hopeful, boyish ten percent—thought it was a loan for the Jewel of the Nile. Which would have been crazy kind, but if Luke had come around to the concept, I was good for paying him back. Ninety percent knew there wasn't money in that envelope.

Luke said, "Kevin, we've never talked about this, but I thought . . . well, I thought you might be open to letting us be your family. Not replacing your parents or anything, but . . ." His voice drifted off.

I already thought of Luke as family. His parents too. And I'd heard so many stories about Lucy that I could taste the salt on her famous fried chicken. I knew Luke's couch was still concave with her shape. I never sat in her indentation, so it was like the three of us were watching television together.

"What do you mean?" I asked Luke.

"We'd, well, *I'd* like to adopt you. Officially. If you want it," Luke said. "You wouldn't have to change your name or anything. You'd just always have us as your people."

I was floored.

And I'm ashamed to admit it, but I thought he only asked to stop me from getting engaged. I pushed my chair in and hauled ass out of the sun porch and across the field. Luke's parents lived on thirty acres. In the place where their field became someone else's property grew a massive tree stump and a fledgling willow. I took a seat on the stump and watched the winter wheat ripple like a green ocean. I am not sure how long I sat there. Only that I replayed that conversation more times than I could count. "We'd, well, I'd like to adopt you."

People don't adopt adults.

He thought I was a child, or worse, childish. And I'd been an effing grown-up for longer than most effing grown-ups.

Luke's hand touched my shoulder.

I was not surprised he'd followed me. The balcony off the back of the house faced these trees. "Lucy's African sunset," he told me the first time we'd stood on the balcony. The sun was yellow to orange to red, and I imagined how once this tree had been fifty feet tall, alone in thirty acres, and why this place felt more like a safari than a field. Lightning struck the tree the month after Lucy died, and Luke had planted the willow. "For someone else's Lucy," he'd told me.

Since we met, we've been drawn to the same places.

"You should open that." He pressed an envelope into my hand. "Because I know what you're thinking—"

"What am I thinking?" I asked as I tore the top from the envelope.

"That I'm trying to fix you."

"Are you?" I asked. I could take many things, but I could not take his pity.

"Fixing a situation isn't the same thing as fixing a person," he told me.

"Rachel and I don't need to be fixed," I argued. "Same as you and Lucy didn't need to be fixed."

"Open the envelope," he said.

Inside was a series of emails between him and Judge Gillby discussing the logistics of adopting someone over the age of eighteen. Was it possible? Yes. Was it difficult? Not under these circumstances. What did Luke need to do? Hire a lawyer, get my approval, set it up.

"Look at the date," he whispered.

Now, you guys, here's the part I can't put into words. The date was from three months before. Luke had that conversation with Judge Gillby before I ever considered asking Rachel to marry me. This invitation had nothing to do with her.

It had to do with me.

"I don't know what to say," I said.

"Say you'll think about it," he told me.

I told him I would. But really, by the time we crossed the field and I had a pile of pork on my plate, I knew what I wanted. I wanted to belong not just with someone like Rachel, but to someone like Luke Estes and his parents. With their African sunsets and their uncommonly good pork shoulder. With their conversations and their acceptance. With their love.

One day, when I had my courage up, I asked him, "Why?"

And you know what he said? He said, "Some kids aren't born to you. Some kids just arrive."

That's when I realized it wasn't anything I'd done or hadn't done that made Luke love me. And it might sound silly, but I'm glad for his answer. I'd rather him love me for who I am, because I'll always be me.

And that's why Denton asked me to come speak to you all. Your house parent understands what you need to hear. Some of you think since you're fifteen or sixteen or seventeen you should give up on family. Or maybe you're looking around at each other thinking . . . this group home . . . this is all I've got. Or maybe you're like me and you're thinking you're full of piss and inertia and that'll get you by until you can make your own way in the world.

But I know you. You're writing words on shower stalls. You're weary with not belonging to someone. You're thinking that the girl or guy you love will fix the hole inside your chest. You want a piece of a paper to be a peace, *p-e-a-c-e*, of paper that says you're worthy. Here's the thing: you are worthy already. Every single one of you. Regardless of who does or doesn't love you.

This is the story of Kevin Taylor *Estes*, twenty-five, and I'm telling you that family doesn't happen on a specific timeline. You don't have to be a cute little kid for someone to want you. For someone to love you.

Sometimes you get the girl.

And sometimes you get the dad.

I was lucky enough that I got both.

And I think you can too.

Courtney "Court" Stevens grew up among rivers, cornfields, churches, and gossip in the small-town South. She is a former adjunct professor, youth minister, and Olympic torchbearer. She has a pet whale named Herman, a band saw named Rex, and several novels with her name on the spine: *Faking Normal, The Lies about Truth*, the e-novella *The Blue-Haired Boy*, and *Dress Codes for Small Towns*. As an educator and author, she visits schools, designs retreats, and teaches workshops on marketing, revision, character development, and "Channeling Your Brave." She also likes chips and queso and feels deeply sorry for the lactose intolerant.

"I come from a small, tight-knit family who do holidays and vacations together. I have a brother and three first cousins. One of those cousins was adopted by my aunt after he graduated from high school. He is ours, and this one was for him."

Happy Beginning

by Nic Stone

The End
July 24, 2003

I can't stop crying.

I'm quiet about it because I don't want to wake up my dad, but I dreamed about you last night, and I woke up crying and now I can't stop.

Five days ago, you texted that you'd found her, but when I asked how she was and if you were okay, you didn't respond.

I haven't heard from you since.

Mrs. J said you needed to sort this out on your own, that she and Mr. J were allowing you the space you requested to do so, and that I should do the same.

And I'm trying. But it's killing me that you don't seem to be thinking of me at all.

I grab too many over soft Kleenex and shove my face into them. Partially because you would've hated to see me be so *wasteful.* I blow my nose and squeeze my eyes shut, but your face is there inside my eyelids, looking at your phone, reading my message, shoving it back into your pocket, smiling at the woman you left me—left *us*—for . . . the woman who left *you* to fend for yourself—

My phone buzzes.

When I see the number on the screen, I wipe my eyes and nose and run my fingers through my hair. "Hello?" Only when I hear your voice do I realize you can't see me.

"Hey," you say.

And I can hear it, that edge in your voice that makes it sound like you swallowed a handful of sand: you've been crying too.

The control I've fought to maintain explodes in my head, and a million and one emotions tumble out like the contents of a battered piñata—we had one at our graduation party, remember?

I want to thank you for calling, scream at you for leaving, beg you to come back, tell you she'll only hurt you again, remind you that I *know* what this is like—

"Are you okay?" I say instead.

"She's married," you say. "I have a brother, eight, and two sisters, four and eighteen months. She's totally smitten with them." You sniffle.

It's there, tiptoeing around the back of my throat: the reminder of how I went looking for the mom who abandoned *me* and found her living a life full of dreams I obviously was never a part of. The *I tried to tell you.*

I force out an "I'm sorry" and choke everything else down.

"Yeah," you say. And you sigh.

That's when I know.

"So?" I ask, because I know you need me to. I know what you're about to say is probably the hardest thing you've ever had to say in your life. "What now?"

"I'm, um . . ."

I sit up. Close my eyes, clench my fists, hold my breath.

"I'm . . ." you say, "I'm coming back."

I exhale.

"I'm coming home, Jenna."

Gone

July 20, 2003

Three days you've been gone.

Mrs. J doesn't say a word when she opens the front door to let me in. She's still in her pajamas, and her usually bright blue eyes are shaded with gray and rimmed with red—like a stormy sky at sunset. It's like looking into a mirror.

The moment we make eye contact, we both start crying.

She spreads her arms, and I step into them. We stand there in the open doorway, sobbing together.

After who knows how long, she pulls back and says, "Will you come in and have tea and cookies? I just pulled some out of the oven."

I nod and step inside. The house smells of cinnamon and wood as usual. You used to say walking in always made you feel like it was autumn. Mrs. J points me to the living room, then comes in a few seconds later and sets a tray on the coffee table. Two mugs on saucers, two metal mesh balls filled with loose-leaf tea, a kettle of hot water, a plate piled high with white chocolate macadamia nut cookies.

Watching her pour makes me mad. To think you just *walked away* from this amazing home and these wonderful people? That you refused to call Mrs. J "*Mom*" because her skin was a different color than yours?

"I can't believe she just *left*," I say. "You guys were so good to her, and she just walked away and hasn't looked back."

Mrs. J sits down next to me and rubs little circles in the

space between my shoulder blades. "Do you have any idea what I would give for a mom like you?" I say.

She sighs and looks away.

"My mom walked out on us when I was a baby," I continue. "Just dropped me off at daycare one morning and never came back."

"I'm sorry to hear that, Jenna."

I shake my head. "Ny had all of this. She had *you*," I say. *She had me*, I want to add, but don't. "I just don't get how she could take it all for granted so easily."

Mrs. J shakes her head. "It's not that simple, Sweetheart. She's been through so much, and this place—Mr. J and I—it's all so different from anything she's ever known."

"But it's also the *best* place she's ever known. You and Mr. J are the kindest people she's ever lived with. She told me."

Mrs. J looks at the picture above the mantel. It's you, leaned up against a tree with your arms crossed. I have a matching one of me—they were our senior portraits. I think about the day we took them and smile a little. "For the first time in her life, she never wanted for *anything*. Why would someone walk away from the best thing that ever happened to them?"

You said that to me once. Do you remember? *"You're the best thing that's ever happened to me, Jenna."*

Hearing you say that was the best thing to ever happen to *me*.

"Seems strange, doesn't it?" I say. "That a person who knows the pain of abandonment would be so quick to put someone else through it?"

I look down at my hands. I polished my nails orange the morning Mrs. J called to let me know you'd left. It's your favorite color.

Mrs. J passes me a box of tissues, and I take one to blow my nose. "She hated those," she says.

"Huh?"

"Those tissues. The first time she touched one, she asked why it was so soft."

I look at the box. Kleenex with lotion and aloe. "Really?"

"Mmhmm." She sighs. "Ny was pretty upset. She said, 'There are kids with no parents starving in overcrowded shelters, and people are putting *lotion* in their tissues?'"

I look at the floor.

"We get it so wrong," Mrs. J goes on. "Giving everything to someone who's used to nothing isn't a blessing. It's a burden. We *knew* that. We knew, and yet . . ." Her eyes lock on your picture again.

"This is much bigger than us. You understand that, don't you?"

I shake my head no. Might as well be honest.

"You, me, Mr. J . . . we did our best to make her feel at home, but that only goes so far when you live with people who are so different from you," she says. "Seventeen months with us can't erase the seventeen *years* before. There are just some holes none of *us* could ever fill."

Going
May 17, 2003

We're sitting in opposite ends of the big garden tub in your bathroom. This was strange for me at first—who fills a bathtub with pillows?—but then you told me about that foster home you were in for six months when you were twelve. It had eight other kids, and your one place of solace was the empty bathtub you'd crawl into with a book while everyone else was asleep.

"I'm confused," I say. "Didn't your parents sa—"

"They're not my parents." You turn a page in the magazine you're reading.

"Well, they *would* be if you'd let—"

"No, they wouldn't."

I roll my eyes. "You've been here for over a year, Ny. You have everything you need, they're super good to you, they bought you a freaking *car*, but you still refuse to refer to them as your parents?"

"They're white," you say.

And there it is. Again.

I hold my arm up. "So am I."

"That's different. Black girls can have white best friends. They can't have white parents."

"You keep saying that, but you've yet to say *why*—"

"Parents are supposed to teach you how to navigate the world. Mr. and Mrs. J can't really do that for me. I've got baggage they could never understand."

"Because they're white?"

"Yep." Another page flips.

"What about people who have one white parent and one black?"

"Couldn't tell you. I'm not biracial."

"I seriously don't see how it makes a difference—"

"And you wouldn't," you say. "You *can't*. It does, though. Take my word for it."

That's the phrase that usually means *drop it* . . . but then you shift your legs and your warm skin brushes up against mine. It makes me so delirious that all the stuff I'm not supposed to say comes spilling out like an unclogged pipe. "Is being here really that bad?" I sit up and push your magazine down. "You said yourself you've never lived in a house this nice. That Mr. and Mrs. J are the best fosters you've ever had. I was sitting there when they offered to—"

"I found my birth mom."

I stop talking. Stop breathing, even. Look at your eyes, your nose, your lips, your eyes . . . You're looking at my lips. "Say something," you whisper.

I already told you what happened when I found *my* mom. "What do you want me to say, Ny?"

You sigh and look at our intertwined legs. "Can I tell you something?"

"Of course."

Our eyes meet again. "Most of the time, I feel so connected to you, I don't mind my heart missing beats because I feel like yours catches them for me."

I gulp.

"It makes me forget," you say.

"Forget what?"

"That you have no idea what it's like." And you look away. "I know your mom left you just like mine left me, but when you look at your dad, you see the same blue eyes, sloped nose, pale skin."

I trace circles on your knee. "So I need a tan," I say.

"I'm serious. I was two when my mom gave me up. I know *nothing* about who or where I come from. You say stuff like, *Oh my god, I sound like my dad*, without realizing how *miraculous* that seems to me."

Now you're crying.

"Ny, I didn—"

"This is a really big deal for me. Finding her."

I gulp. "I didn't mean to minimize it. I'm sorry."

When you look away, I know you're about to say something I don't want to hear.

"I'm leaving," you say.

"What?"

"A week after I turn eighteen."

So many questions—*Where? How? Why? Why? WHY?* Exclamations—*NO! PLEASE! DON'T!*

It all rushes up from my gut and jams in my throat, so when I open my mouth to speak, nothing comes out.

"She lives in Biloxi," you say, turning back to me.

"We've talked on the phone a few times. She said she's glad I reached out."

This is going to be a disaster. I know it. No matter what she says over the phone, she won't be what you expect. If she really wanted you in her life, she would've come looking for you . . .

But of course I don't say that.

"Wow," is what I say. "That's great, Ny. I'm happy for you." Except I'm not.

You smile.

I try to smile back, but then I get a lump in my throat and have to turn away.

"Hey." You shift so you're kneeling between my legs, and you bring your face right up to mine. "You know you're the best thing that's ever happened to me, right? I'm only going because I *have* to—"

I kiss you.

The Beginning
August 3, 2002

I'm behind you in line for pictures. Four times now, I've opened my mouth to say something: how nice a day it is outside (*but what if you don't like small talk?*), how ridiculous the fake tree trunk and painted backdrop are, considering how beautiful a day it is and how many trees are outside (*but what if you don't think it's stupid at all?*), how pretty I think you look (*wouldn't want you to take it the wrong way, though that* is *how I mean it*).

I shut my mouth again and go back to staring at your hair. Wondering how long it took to put in all those little braids, and inhaling the scent of your flowery perfume.

Since you moved here in February, we've only talked a handful of times, and I feel bad about that. I've heard a bunch of words whispered around your name—*foster care, passed around, rough life*. My dad is always asking me if I've talked to you, telling me I should invite you over.

After all, you live right across the street.

Last night, Dad and I pulled into our driveway at the same time you were going into your house. He looked at you and said, "Does she ever hang out with anyone?"

I looked down at my nubby fingernails and shrugged. "I mean, it's summer, Dad. Not like I see her every day."

"When I was a kid, your Nana and I got kicked out of our house after your grandpa died," he said. "We wound up moving to a neighborhood where I was the only white kid. This kid, Jamal Crawford, he befriended me. Honestly don't know what I would've done without him."

I stared at your closed front door and sighed.

"Being new in a place where you stand out is hard enough," he said, turning to me. "No one should have to go through it alone."

The photographer calls the next person to take their position against the fake tree.

The flashes begin, and the girl in front of you—she's up next—whips out her compact to check her reflection for the jillionth time. She pulls her long, blonde hair over one shoulder, runs her fingers through it a few times, and then flings it back.

It almost smacks you in the face.

I lean forward so I can whisper in your ear (which I hope isn't creepy). "Geez, are we taking senior portraits or meeting the queen?"

You snort, then lean back to whisper a response. "Pretty sure she bathed in Chanel No. 5 this morning," you say. "You'd think the pictures were gonna be scratch and sniff."

I laugh too loud, and Miss Priss turns around and glares at us.

She gets called to the tree. You look at me and smile.

"I'm Jenna," I say. "I, umm . . . I live across the street from you—"

"I know who you are and where you live, Jenna."

"Oh . . ." I feel my face heat, and I drop my chin. "Nyara, right?"

When you don't respond, I look up.

You smile again. It's beautiful. "Call me 'Ny,'" you say.

Within days, we're "*attached at the hip,*" as my dad puts it, and a couple of weeks later, you invite me to dinner. "Mr. and Mrs. J want to celebrate me being with them for six months," you say as we leave school and walk to the car they bought you last weekend. "Will you please come keep me sane?"

I don't understand why you're all weird about this—from the moment I step into the house, it's obvious Mr. and Mrs. J really love you.

I can tell something's up by the way Mrs. J fusses over little details. Every few minutes, she asks *if the food tastes okay* before tucking her hair behind her ears, and she and Mr. J keep exchanging these looks.

I know you feel it too because you keep kicking me beneath the table.

The only sounds during the meal—delicious pot roast, baked green beans, mashed potatoes, and mac n' cheese—are utensils scraping plates, sweet tea being swallowed, glasses thumping against the table, a grandfather clock ticking in the background, and an occasional throat clearing. No words.

After the empty plates have been taken away, Mrs. J disappears into the kitchen and returns with four dessert saucers. As she sits back down, she looks at Mr. J and nods.

The air in the room is as dense as the cheesecake on the plates.

"So," Mr. J says. He clears his throat. "Guess I'll start by thanking you girls for joining us tonight."

When he clears his throat a second time, I swallow and the tips of my ears go hot. I feel like an intruder. "Maybe I should—"

You kick me under the table.

"Ow!"

"You were saying, sir?" you say.

Mr. and Mrs. J look at each other again. Two tiny nods, then they turn to you. I wonder if you're sweating as much as I am.

"Nyara, you've been with us for six months now," Mr. J continues, "and having you here has brought us a level of fulfillment we didn't think possible."

You hook my ankle with your foot and pull it toward you.

"We know this might seem a little sudden since you'll be eighteen soon," Mrs. J says, "but if you're interested, we'd love for you to become a permanent member of our family."

The clock ticks. The silence stretches. No one moves.

I look at your face for some hint of what you're feeling, but there's nothing there.

Mr. J clears his throat for a third time. "We'd love for you to stay, Ny. To make this your home."

You look at me, and the spot where our ankles touch explodes. The heat creeps up through my stomach, down my arms to my fingertips, and up into my face. I can't see anything beyond how beautiful you are, and the fullness of your lips snatches the air from the room as you inhale.

"Home?" you say, and my heart picks up pace.

"Yes," Mrs. J says. "We want to adopt you."

Nic Stone was born and raised in a suburb on the outskirts of Atlanta, GA. Growing up with people from a wide range of cultures, religions, and backgrounds fueled her love of stories and insatiable wanderlust. After a few years living in Israel, she returned to the US to write YA fiction with diversity in mind. She has a BA in Psychology from Spelman College and currently lives in Atlanta with her husband and sons.

"Adoption highlights the most beautiful thing about humanity: the transformative power of love and acceptance. Growing up, I had two close friends who were cross-culturally adopted, and spending time in their homes with them and their parents and (adopted) siblings taught me almost everything I know about the power human beings have to hurt and/or heal one another, and what it looks like to use that power for the latter."

The Take Back

by Kate Watson

I can't stop seeing her dark gray eyes. They staked their claim on me when we picked her up from the hospital thirteen and a half days ago, and they'll probably never let go. I can't stop remembering her smell, unlike any smell in the world—almost like sweat, but fresh and pure, somehow. I can't stop feeling her tiny hand squeezing my finger, like it made her feel safe, like she knew her big brother would always be there to protect her.

I can't stop thinking about how I don't get to be her big brother anymore.

Her empty car seat sits beside me in the backseat of Mom's Subaru, taunting me like it has for the last six hours. Mom's in the driver's seat because when she's sad or hurt or afraid, she has to do something productive. Right now, she's all those things. Times a million. She won't break down in front of me again, though. Not like she did when we got the call this morning.

Dad is playing deejay in the passenger seat with his "John Hughes" playlist, as Mom called it. I call it his "catastrophic heartbreak" playlist. He'd never admit it, but something tells me he had it ready before we even left for DC two weeks ago. I wonder what the other playlist would have sounded like.

Dad tried to get me to sit up front when we left the hotel this morning, because he knows how my knees knock into the back of Mom's seat. But I need to be back here, staring at the spot where Lucy should be.

Bella, some hateful part of my brain reminds me. *It's Bella to them.*

Is that why Amber took her back? Because we didn't give her some stupid name? None of us liked it, and Amber said she didn't mind if we named her after our Grandma and used Isabella as her middle name. Amber even said she loved our little nickname for her: Lucy Belle. Lucy Belle. Lucy Belle.

Tears burn my eyes, and my throat tightens until I think I'm gonna choke.

"How you doing?" Mom asks, looking at me in the rear-view mirror. Her eyes are ringed with an angry red, eyes that look so much like mine, people stop us in the store to tell us how much we look alike.

Amber said she liked that about us when she saw our profile online. We didn't look like just any other family, she said; we looked like her daughter's family.

Liar.

How could she say that and do what she did? How could she dangle so much happiness in front of us and then rip it all away at the last possible moment? Why couldn't she have changed her mind in the hospital instead of an hour before she was supposed to sign the papers? *An hour?* After two weeks in that stupid hotel, we were so close to being able to take her home.

I hate Amber. I *hate* her.

"Cole?" Mom repeats. Her eyes are welling with tears, and the sight of it makes mine do the same.

My mouth twists, and I put my hand on her shoulder. "Not good, Mom."

"Me neither."

"*If You Leave*" starts playing over the speakers. Dad turns it up.

Ten hours. That's how long it takes for us to drive from DC back to Indianapolis, with stops just to pee and get gas. The snacks we bought along the way lay unopened on the other side of Lucy's car seat.

Bella's car seat. I shake my head. *No one's.* I wonder if we can return the thing.

When we reach our street, I look outside the window. Somehow in the last two weeks, it has gone from winter to spring. While we were holed up in the hotel waiting for word that Amber had signed the papers, too nervous even to run to the store in case someone sneezed near Lucy, the world just moved on. There's so much thriving life, yet we're burning alive in our own personal hell.

The car pulls into the garage, and before Mom can even put it in park, I'm running from my door to the shed out back, where I grab my baseball bat and start beating the shit out of everything in sight. Pots, planters, mason jars, my old bike. Everything. I smash it like it can obliterate every second of the last two weeks. Like it can change Amber's mind and give me back my sister.

After twenty minutes, I'm sweating and panting, and the rusted old shed is groaning in protest. I admire my handiwork by the light of the setting sun. Emotions seethe inside me, but none of them resembles satisfaction or . . . what's that word? Catharsis, maybe? Either way, I don't feel it. Nothing could exist inside me with all the rage and hatred I feel.

Nothing except guilt.

I stare at the bat in my hands. Hands that just this morning held Lucy, fed her, changed her, tickled her face in the way that always calms her when she's fussing. Gave her back to Amber.

I drop the bat and fall to my knees, shaking with a

lifetime's worth of pain and sorrow, both for me and for my parents. I shouldn't have pushed them to adopt again. I should have been content with the three of us, like they said they were. But I just knew they were lying. Knew the house would feel empty when I went to college in a few years. The thought of them feeling so alone without me—the child who completed them—was devastating. What if something happened to me? Or to them? I just didn't want anyone to be alone. Ever.

This is my fault.

If I hadn't pushed them, Amber never would have contacted us. And we never would have known Lucy. And we wouldn't all be breaking apart with grief.

But we never would have known Lucy.

Agony rips through me, and I smash my hand against the hard ground over and over again until I feel something hot and sticky run over my fingers, along with a sharp burning. I look down to see a small piece of ceramic pot sticking out of the side of my hand. My stomach turns.

"Mom?" I yell. And again, louder, "Mom!"

Seconds later, the shed door opens, and Mom is there, her cheeks stained with tears. She must have been waiting just outside the door. Something about that makes everything hurt worse.

I hold up my hand for her to see, and she just nods, puts her arms around me, and helps me into the house.

Dad is waiting in the kitchen with Mom's nurse kit. He pauses, assessing the situation before opening his mouth.

"So? What's the damage?"

Mom groans. "Seriously? Your son is bleeding, and that's the best you could come up with?"

"You just don't get it. See, it's funny, because Cole was breaking everything. Two meanings."

Mom is giving sarcastic nods while she takes care of my hand, like this is normal banter on a normal day. And I know what I should do. I should roll my eyes and tease him, say "Not your best work, Dad," and let him tease me about the shed being *my* best work or something. But I can't. He's trying to lighten the mood, and I hate that he's doing that when it's my fault there's a mood to lighten at all. Well, mine and Amber's.

Just thinking about her pushes my hatred to the surface past so many other emotions. There's another one clawing to get out, something I can't put my finger on with everything else going on inside me.

I don't know how we're just supposed to go on without Lucy.

It's Bella. Her name is Bella.

Mom puts some antiseptic on my hand, and my eyes water.

"I think you should talk to Sammie," she says.

I watch her bandage me up, and my mouth goes dry. "What would I call Sammie for? This has nothing to do with her."

"Cole," Mom says. It's weird how even though I'm looking down at her, I feel like a little kid beneath her gaze. She always knows too much. It's one of the things kids usually hate about their parents. Maybe I should, too. "This may not have anything to do with her, but she is a part of you. I know she'd want to be there for you right now."

"You already talked to her, didn't you?"

Mom nods. Dad hands me my phone—I must have left it in the car when I ran out. The number is already up in my contacts. "You may want to change your password," Dad says with a shrug.

"Or not," Mom says. "But you need to talk to Sammie. And then if you still want to, maybe we can go finish what you started in the shed."

She gives my shoulder a squeeze before she and Dad leave the kitchen. They didn't need to. I go upstairs to my room and sit at my desk, staring at my phone for what feels like an hour.

I don't know why I'm hesitating. My adoption was open—*is* open. Sammie came to my elementary school graduation—despite how embarrassing an elementary school graduation is. My family went to her wedding a few years ago. She sends us videos of her toddler, Xander. She and Mom follow each other on Instagram.

Why can't I just press that little phone icon?

I hesitate so long, my screen goes black. I press the home key, and a picture of me holding Lucy flashes on the screen. Pain stabs my heart. Pain and fury and hatred and guilt and . . . and that *something* I can't put my finger on. Whatever it is, it pushes me over the edge. I swipe my finger across the screen and call Sammie.

She answers on the first ring.

"Hey, buddy," she says in that high, clear voice that always tickles my memory.

"Hey Sammie," I echo, because I don't know what else to say.

"Your mom called last night and told me what happened. I'm so sorry. I can't imagine how you must be feeling right now."

It was a perfectly fine comment. Of course it was. But she's right that she has no idea what I'm going through, and hearing her admit it pisses me off. "Nope. You can't."

My tone doesn't deter her at all. "I just want you to know I'm here if you want to talk or let it out."

"*Let it out?*" I grab a pen and start stabbing at a notebook. "What do you think this is, Sammie? A couch session? You're not my therapist, and you're not my mom. If I want to talk about how I'm feeling, I'll talk to her."

"Of course. If that's what you want to do, you should absolutely do it."

"Don't patronize me."

She sighs. "I'm sorry that's how it feels. I just want to be here for you. You can tell me whatever you want."

I jab the pen down so hard it punctures the notebook. I

feel like it should bleed ink. "What do you want me to tell you? How I talked my parents into trying to adopt again, and now they're crushed? How I hate Amber so bad, I want to physically *hurt* her?"

"This isn't Amber's fault."

I hurl the pen at the wall. "SHE TOOK BACK MY SISTER! How is this not her fault?"

Sammie's voice remains low and steady. "She made the decision that was best for her, Cole. She didn't do it to hurt you guys. How would you have felt with Lucy—"

"Bella," I interrupt, doing air quotes even though she can't see them.

"How would you have felt with her in your home, knowing that Amber regretted it every day for the rest of her life? What would that have done to . . . to *Bella*?"

I grab another pen, this time scribbling fiercely around the notebook's stab wound. "She'd have been better off with us."

"That may be how it feels, but you don't get to make that decision. Amber does. And even though it hurts, I know your parents agree. I think with time, you will, too."

She's so damn calm, it makes me want to scream. To throw a baseball next time instead of a pen. "Good to see you're finally using that social work degree you traded me for," I spit. Even as I say the words, I can't believe they escaped my mouth.

"What?" Sammie's voice sounds like it's splitting in two, warring between outrage and her need for control.

"You heard me," I say, because I've lost the ability to filter any and all thought. Because if I can stay angry and awful, maybe I can keep out all the other emotions that threaten to suffocate me.

Her words are choppy, her breathing erratic. "Is that what you think I did? You think I *traded* you?"

"Your life looks pretty good from where I'm sitting."

I expect her to say something biting back like, "So does

yours." Instead, she pauses before saying, "You're hurting right now. I wish . . . I wish I could take that pain away from you."

"Right, so fifteen years later, you're finally worrying about *my* feelings?" It's such an unbelievably low blow, but I find myself anxious—*desperate*—for her response.

"Cole, I have *never* cared more about someone's feelings than yours. *Ever*." The way she says it, earnest but almost laced with anger, strikes me. She keeps talking, and I can practically see her trembling on the other end of the phone. That's how I sound when I'm pretending not to be upset. "I lost *everything* when I placed you, but it was the only way I knew to give you the life you deserved."

A part of me wants to snap at her again, wants to scream until she screams back. But my anger is cracking, exposing an uncertainty and grief I never realized was there. I open my mouth to say something, but emotion closes my throat. The pain of trying not to cry.

I'm not sure how Sammie interprets the silence, but after a pause, she speaks again. It sounds like she's begging. "Your birth father was a drug dealer, and you know all about my history before I cleaned myself up. Is that the life you wanted? Giving you a family forced me to get back on track. I had to prove to your parents that I was good enough for them to let me stay in your life!"

Tears leak from my eyes. "Don't lie to me, Sammie," I plead, a knot in my stomach. I hunch over, shivering like I'm in the middle of a snowstorm. I close my eyes. "If you'd really wanted to stay in my life, you would have kept me."

"*Don't say that*," she says. I hear sobs coming from her end. "Don't even think it. I wanted you more than I wanted my own life. The day you were born, holding you in my arms and just *smelling* you, I've never wanted something more."

I don't know why, but suddenly I can imagine her in the hospital all those years ago, holding me and staring into my eyes. I can imagine her smelling me, just like I did with Lucy. And then the pain of never seeing or smelling or holding Lucy again crashes into me, and I realize Sammie had that exact same pain once.

The thought breaks me.

I start sobbing—wracking, heaving sobs that burn my lungs. I can barely breathe, I'm crying so hard. And everything hurts. My eyes, my nose, my throat. My stomach aches from how fast and heavy my sobs are coming. "How . . . how could you give me up, Sammie? Why?"

"I wasn't giving you up, Cole. I was trying to give you more."

"Why?"

"Because I felt like a God I didn't even know I believed in led me to your parents."

I hug my legs, rocking and crying. "Sammie. Please."

"Because I wasn't good enough for you."

"Sammie—"

The words rush out of her. "Because I loved you more than I've ever loved anything in the world, and even as messed up as I was, I knew if I did something as selfish as keeping you, that it would ruin both of us. *I* would. So I asked the universe for a sign, and not a minute later, your mom walked into my ob-gyn's office with those cheesy 'hoping to adopt' pass-along cards. She smiled at me across the lobby—a simple smile—but when I looked into her eyes, I just *knew*. I knew what I needed to do to save you. And it broke my heart."

She says everything so fast and fierce, and it's that fierceness that makes me believe her. It makes me realize where I must get my anger from. And for some reason, that comforts me even as it makes me ache.

"I wanted you so much," she says, softly now. "The only thing I wanted more than you was for you to be happy."

I don't know when I dropped to the floor, but the wall

presses against my spine as I cry. My voice cracks. "Then why doesn't Amber love Lucy that much?"

For a long time, it's just the sound of us crying on the phone. Finally, Sammie sniffs. "Amber isn't me, Cole. She's not on drugs. She has a good support system, and you know how much her parents wanted her to keep the baby."

"Lucy," I correct her.

"Bella," she corrects me.

I laugh, thinking how much Dad would like that exchange. Then I inhale, a shaky, hiccupping thing. "This sucks. I just . . . I really wanted a baby sister. I wanted *her.* I told everyone I wanted her for my parents, but the truth is, I wanted her for me."

"You'll always have Xander," she says.

I know it's the truth, but as much as I love the little guy, it's not the same. Xander isn't mine like Lucy would have been. *My* sibling, *our* parents. Such basic things to most people, but the idea of sharing that unique bond, of having inside jokes with someone who couldn't also ground me, it was everything to me.

Maybe the reality of Lucy wouldn't have been all I imagined. I hate that I'll never know.

"Yeah." I clear my throat. "Thanks, Sammie."

"I love you, Cole. Nothing could change that."

"Yeah, you too. I'm, uh, I'm sorry for yelling. I think I was processing some stuff back there."

"You think?" she says, and we both laugh. "I'm here for you, Cole. Always."

"I know," I say, and it hits me that I mean it. "Thanks, Sammie, for everything. For talking to me and wanting to yell at me, even if you didn't do it." I tear up again. "But mostly for my parents."

"You're welcome," she says simply. The words carry so much weight, yet I feel lighter than I have all day. Which is nowhere near light, but still.

We say goodbye, and I set down my phone before breathing into my hands for a while. Ten minutes, maybe more. Then I wipe my face, push myself to a stand, and leave my room.

When I get to the end of the hall, my parents are waiting. They open their arms, and I crash into their embrace. It feels so good, I could almost forget that the last time we all hugged each other, there was one more person here. One perfect, tiny, little person. Her absence brings a painful lump to my throat.

"It's good to be home," Dad whispers. We keep hugging, and Dad takes a big, deep breath. "But kid, you need a shower. You smell like you've been in a car for, I don't know, ten hours."

"I smelled fine when I left the car," I say, pulling back. "It was from the shed. It took a lot of work to break all that stupid sh—"

"Language," Mom says.

I smile as Dad teases Mom about something. It's going to take a long time before we all stop hurting, before this Lucy-shaped hole in our hearts can start to heal. Part of me is afraid it never will. But Dad's right.

It's good to be home.

Kate Watson is a young adult writer, wife, mother of two, and the tenth of thirteen children. Originally from Canada, she attended college in Utah and holds a BA in Philosophy. A lover of travel, speaking in accents, and experiencing new cultures, she has also lived in Israel, Brazil, South Carolina, and now calls Arizona home. Her first novel, *Seeking Mansfield*, debuted in Spring 2017, with the companion to follow in 2018.

"Adoption is the world to me. It is the means by which I grew another heart, and then another still. It created an unbreakable bond between me and the women whose unending love and selfless sacrifice made me a mother. My

family would be nothing without adoption. Through adoption, we are everything."

Jar of Broken Wishes

by Tristina Wright

Daisy collected wishes.

She kept them in a light blue mason jar with a dented copper lid. She imagined at one time the lid had been hard to get off, so someone tapped it all around the edge with a knife, leaving grooves that looked like minutes on a clock. She wasn't sure why someone had tossed it out. Tossed it into the grass by the road like trash. Maybe it'd jumped off a moving truck of its own will, not content to rattle around with the other clear jars anymore. The glass was this shade of blue that reminded her of early morning in spring or the eye shadow her foster mom wore on Sundays.

Everyone else saw an empty jar held tight by a twelve-year-old girl with curly hair that rose in a cloud around her round face. Only Daisy could see the wishes. They were airy and light and different colors. Almost like fireflies all lit up blue and pink and purple and green. She'd shake the jar and the wishes would go fluttering around in a little tornado.

She'd always seen them. As far back as she could remember, those fluttering little wishes danced on the air like tiny fairies, spiraling up and around until they eventually drifted to the ground. She couldn't remember how she'd figured out they were wishes. She just seemed to *know.*

What she didn't know was why she couldn't see her own. She saw everyone else's. Big wishes. Small wishes. Impossible wishes. Emotional wishes. Saw them blossom out of lips and catch the air before plummeting to the ground and splintering into a million pieces.

"Is there such a thing as magic?" she asked her foster mom one day.

"Of course, honey," her foster mom answered as she bent over Daisy's finger with the tweezers. "That splinter is in deep. Hold still."

"Are wishes magic?" Daisy asked, keeping as still as possible.

"I like to think so," she answered. The tweezers pinched the end of the splinter in Daisy's finger.

I wish this wouldn't hurt, Daisy thought desperately.

No fluffy ball of light fell from her lips.

The splinter still hurt coming out.

Maybe she didn't have wishes. Maybe the things she wanted weren't good enough for wishes. Maybe there was some cosmic wish fairy who decided she didn't get wishes of her own.

Fine, then.

She'd collect the pieces scattered across the ground and make her own wishes.

So, she collected and collected and collected, content to pack them in the jar when other kids at the foster home wished for things that they didn't mean.

I wish I was a cat.

I wish you'd never been born.

I wish I had all the chocolate.

I wish I never had to go to school again.

More wishes for the jar. More colors dancing around in the blue glass. More and more and more until they smushed together like layers of colored sand.

One night, she carefully scooped out enough pieces of wishes to make what looked sort of like a whole one and held it close to her lips. She took a deep breath, not sure how to do this or if it would even work. "I wish for a family."

The fractured rainbow wish flickered and winked out, vanishing from her palm.

A time later, the Stevensons came and took her home with them. It was a nice home in a neighborhood where all the houses looked a lot alike but were different because that one was blue instead of yellow. Or that one had a picket fence instead of a stone fence.

The Stevensons had a dog named Rose and three of their own kids. Daisy didn't quite understand why they'd adopted her since they had kids of their own, but she wasn't going to question the wish. She held her jar tight and smiled shyly and sat on the very edge of her very own bed in her very own bedroom decorated with elephants.

She didn't much care for elephants.

But Daisy was the oldest kid there. The other kids were only in elementary school. Resentful of the fact she disrupted the intended birth order of the home, they made it very clear they didn't want a new big sister. She was a live-in babysitter. Someone they could blame for things.

Three months later, after fights and begging and ignoring and being ignored, Daisy and her jar of wishes returned to the little foster home off Market Street. To the same bed with flower-petal sheets and cinnamon air fresheners. To the same breakfast of instant oatmeal made with almond milk and raisins. To the mornings of homeschool and the afternoons of chores.

One night, curled up in bed in the room she shared with two other girls, she scooped out another handful of broken wishes, mashed them together like clay, and touched the stained-glass wish to her tongue. It tasted a little like cotton candy. A fleeting candy for a fleeting wish. "I wish for a family with kids older than me."

After a time, the Blakes took her home, where they had two sons already in high school. She was the new baby of the family and given her own room. Everything was pink.

She didn't much care for pink.

Daisy believed it was an accident the first time the youngest brother walked in on her showering. She even believed it the second time. He blushed too much for it to be on purpose.

She stopped believing it after the sixth time.

That same night, with her hair still dripping wet and the towel growing cold around her shoulders, she scooped out a handful of wish pieces and swallowed them. They prickled as they slid down her throat down like a too-big gulp of soda. It made her eyes water. "I wish to go home."

She didn't even know what that meant.

Two months later, she went back to the home on Market Street, clutching her jar of wishes tight to her chest. She didn't know what to wish for next. Or ever again.

All wrong, all wrong. I don't have wishes after all.

The wishes dimmed and flickered the longer she went without talking to them. She took them on walks instead, intending to throw the jar in the lake.

She never did.

Fall slipped into winter, which gave way to the melting of spring. Daisy left after oatmeal, escaping out the back door and into the first warm day in months. The sun pulled freckles from her starving skin and warmed her to her core as she walked. The breeze kicked off the lake and played with her hair, throwing her curls into a wildness she didn't quite feel anymore.

Daisy found a tree next to the lake and plopped down underneath it. She was thirteen now. Officially a teenager. Officially a woman, according to her foster mom. Mrs. Ainsley had spent the morning explaining pads and tampons and cramps, then gave her ibuprofen for the clawing in her tummy.

She didn't feel any different, though. Other than maybe her hip bones trying to push through her skin. Cramps were the devil.

She peered at her jar of wishes and shook them. They fluttered around the glass, bumping into the walls like errant moths.

"What are those?" A shadow fell across her lap.

Daisy jumped in surprise and squinted through the mid-morning sun, and her tummy did this swoop thing that had nothing to do with cramps. She didn't know the new girl's name yet. Only that she'd lost her parents in a car accident. They'd exchanged quick glances over the past few days before Daisy shied away, nervous and giddy each time. "They're my wishes."

The girl hesitated a minute and then sat next to her, folding her legs up under her dress and patting her head scarf into place.

"I'm Daisy. I like your scarf," Daisy said with an attempt at a smile.

"I'm Farah. I like your wishes," the girl said as her browned cheeks bloomed with a blush. She had three freckles just under her left eye that formed a triangle.

"Do you want one?" Daisy asked. "They don't seem to be working for me."

Farah peered at the jar, tapping on the glass with one polished pink fingernail. "What did you wish for?"

Daisy told her, staring at the jar instead of Farah. She rambled through it all. About the young kids and the older kids. About not being wanted and being wanted for the wrong reasons. About wishing for home and never finding it. About feeling like a boomerang who kept ending up precisely where she started. All the words tumbled out into her lap in a messy heap of failed wishes and splintered emotions.

"Where do the wishes come from?" Farah asked when Daisy was done. She didn't ask about the other families. She didn't ask about the other kids. She didn't ask for details.

Daisy pulled one shoulder closer to her ear and rolled the jar between her hands. "Sometimes people make wishes they don't really mean. And they break into these little tiny pieces when they hit the ground."

Farah tapped the jar again. "And these are the pieces?"

Daisy nodded. "I started putting them in this jar a while back. Only the biggest pieces. The ones I could pick up. Some are too small, and they break up more or fly away."

"Well, there's your problem," Farah said with a smile like she'd solved a puzzle. It made rubber-band balls dance around Daisy's chest. "You're wishing on broken wishes. You need a whole one."

"I've never found a whole one."

"Haven't you ever wished for something without your jar?"

Daisy shook her head. The wind blew her hair over her face and she smacked it away, tucking the biggest curls behind her ear. "I don't have any wishes."

"Everyone has wishes."

"I don't." Daisy pulled her knees to her chest and rested her chin on them. "I've tried and it never works."

"So your wishes break up too?" Farah closed her fingers around the jar and gently pulled it from Daisy's grasp.

"I've tried, and I don't have any. Watch." She licked her lips. "I wish I had an ice cream."

Farah giggled and held her hand out, cupping it in the thin air under Daisy's chin. "Do you see it?"

Daisy shook her head, her skin prickling. "There's nothing there."

"Sure there is. And it's whole."

"Are you making fun of me?" Daisy's face scrunched up and she pulled away from Farah an inch, but it may as well have been a mile.

"I would never," Farah said quickly. She held out the jar. "Here, open it."

Daisy unscrewed the dented lid. She held the open jar out to Farah, who deposited the wish inside. Even though the existing pieces of wishes moved out of the way to accommodate a new wish, Daisy still didn't see anything. She pursed her lips. "Okay, now you do one."

Farah scraped her teeth over her lower lip. "I wish I had a kitten." A feathery blue ball of light slipped out of her lips and fell toward the grass. Daisy snatched it from the air and held it up. Farah glanced at her palm and back at Daisy's face and shook her head. "I don't see it."

"It's blue."

"I like blue."

"You don't like kittens?"

Farah smiled. "I'm allergic. You don't like ice cream?"

"Lactose intolerant." Daisy passed the wish between her palms like a slinky. It felt warm like a tiny candle flame but had no weight of its own, like grasping air itself. She held it closer to her face.

"You can't wish on broken pieces," Farah said softly. She scooted closer, the jar forgotten in the new grass between them as Daisy stared at the whole wish. "What do you wish for?"

"I've always wished for a family," Daisy whispered. "Home."

Farah's shoulder touched Daisy's. "Those are big words. Family. Home."

Daisy rested a bit more of her weight on the warm spot where their shoulders touched. "I don't know if it's real."

Farah was quiet for a moment. "I can't see that wish, but I know it's real because I saw yours. And . . . and even though they're not the same, they both exist, right?"

Daisy nodded. Her eyes stung at the corners. Her vision blurred the wish, smearing the blue across her palm like paint.

Farah's hand covered the wish in Daisy's palm. "Maybe . . . maybe it's something different for you."

"Families or wishes?"

Farah smiled and pressed their palms together. Blue light slipped out of the cracks and warmth rolled up Daisy's arm. "Both?"

Daisy watched the light escape. "I didn't wish for you."

Farah squeezed her hand tighter. "I didn't wish for you either, but it's not all bad, yeah?"

Daisy picked up the open jar and tipped it over, spilling the pieces of wishes across the grass. The wind caught them and spun them up in the air like escaped dandelion seeds. As the girls watched, their whole wish still clasped between their fingers, the pieces spiraled away higher and higher until they disappeared into the sky.

"What did you wish for?" Farah whispered.

Daisy smiled as she stared at the clouds. "Nothing."

Tristina Wright is a blue-haired bisexual with anxiety and opinions. She's also possibly a mermaid, but no one can get confirmation. She writes YA SFF novels and short stories with queer teens who become heroes and monsters. She enjoys stories with monsters and kissing and monsters kissing. She married a nerd who can build her new computers and make the sun shine with his smile. Most days, she can be found drinking coffee from her favorite chipped mug and making up stories for her two wombfruit, who keep her life hectic and unpredictable. *27 Hours* will be her debut novel in October 2017. Meanwhile, you can find her guest posts and short stories scattered around the internet via tristinawright.com. Still trying to figure out the mermaid thing.
